Praise for th

"I love Sara Ackerman's ⟨...⟩
surf won my heart. This luscious love story takes readers from
the lush Maui rainforest to the towering waves of California and
on to Portugal. A captivating novel of opposites attracting, filled
with passion, adventure, and a fight for nature, *The Maui Effect*
will leave you breathless and believing in the power of love and
determination."
— Susan Wiggs, *New York Times* bestselling author
of *Welcome to Beach Town*

"Whip-smart... Vivid, insightful, and as fast-paced as Livy's beloved
plane, Ackerman's narrative is a delight."
— *Shelf Awareness* on *The Uncharted Flight of Olivia West*

"Ackerman's settings blossom with stunning imagery as she brings
to life characters that will stay with you long after you've finished the
book. A fabulous read that makes me want to drop everything and
travel to Hawaii!"
— Madeline Martin, *New York Times* bestselling author
of *The Last Bookshop in London*, on *The Codebreaker's Secret*

"*Radar Girls* is a fresh, delightful romp of a novel... Sara Ackerman
never disappoints!"
— Kate Quinn, *New York Times* bestselling author of *The Rose Code*

"A beautiful and thoughtful novel that pays tribute to the lore of
the islands, their people, and those who stand up for the ones who
cannot."
— Noelle Salazar, bestselling author of *The Flight Girls*,
on *Red Sky Over Hawaii*

Also by Sara Ackerman

SARA ACKERMAN

The Maui Effect

/ll MIRA

/ll MIRA™

ISBN-13: 978-0-7783-6956-1

The Maui Effect

Recycling programs
for this product may
not exist in your area.

Mira
22 Adelaide St. West, 41st Floor
Toronto, Ontario M5H 4E3, Canada
MIRABooks.com

Printed in U.S.A.

For my father, Douglas,
who pushed me into my first wave when I was just a wee thing,
and my mother, Diane,
who showed me the beauty of the forest.

E lei kau, e lei ho'oilo i ke aloha.
Love is worn like a wreath
through the summers and the winters.
Love is everlasting.

—*'Olelo No'eau: Hawaiian Proverbs & Poetical Sayings,*
Mary Kawena Pukui

The Blue Room

Dane

Pe'ahi, Maui, January 2012

The Hawaiian ocean was more blue than he remembered, and it smelled faintly of salt and sea foam. Dane sat on his surfboard watching rays of sun pierce the surface and descend into the depths. Farther out above the trench, the water shone indigo, and inside over the coral shelf, a dappled turquoise. Bathwater warm, smooth as blown glass, deadly. There were sounds—a light splash, the low rumble of whitewater meeting rock on the shoreline—but he didn't hear them.

Someone is going to die.

An old man on the cliff had spoken these words to him just as he was scrambling down the rocks to get in the water, and he was having a hard time shaking it off. The man was thin as a twig and wrinkled, with a shock of white hair against his sun-beaten skin. A complete stranger. He touched Dane's shoulder and looked him straight in the eye, pinning Dane in place for a few seconds, before he pulled himself away. His shoulder still burned.

Now he focused on the horizon and matched his breath to the rise and fall of the swells. Reaching down with both hands, he scooped up water and splashed himself to cool off. The air was thick with a salty haze, windless, hot and lazy. Usually by this time—early afternoon—the waves were blown out and ragged from the wind. But today was perfection. Even the locals were saying the conditions were epic.

All he needed was one wave.

The Maui offshore buoys showed an afternoon pulse, which meant that the swell could get even bigger before it faded away. No doubt it was a gamble to paddle out on his biggest board, a mint green beauty, but risk was his thing, the only constant he knew. While most people moved away from risk, Dane had always sought it out. Not consciously, but looking back, he had been the kid to climb the tallest tree, skateboard down the steepest road or take the highest jump on his bike, and later, often the only one to paddle out on those winter days when the whole horizon was closing out.

He checked his watch. Eighteen minutes since the last set rolled in, but it seemed like days. He could feel the island behind him, a massive volcano with a dollop of white snow on her peak, but he refused to look. *Never turn your back on the sea.* Anyone raised around the ocean knew this.

Four minutes left in the heat and Dane had nothing to show for it. He had missed the only rideable wave on the last set by being too far out. His last hope was the tide. It had just bottomed out, and now began to fill back in, the whole ocean heaving toward the island. All he could do was wait. Mother nature called the shots out here, there was no way around it.

Two minutes left and he was starting to sweat, when he noticed a bump on the horizon. He stood up on his board to get a better look. Definitely a set. Kicking his board out in front of him, he fell back in the water and crossed himself. This was it. Sliding back onto his board, he adjusted his vest, took a deep breath and started paddling toward the horizon.

A live wire ran under his skin, electrifying every cell, every muscle. It was a familiar feeling, and it meant *game on.* The first wave in the set rose up like a liquid mountain and began to feather, but already he could tell it wasn't the one he was waiting for. Too small and a little too west. Let someone else have it. When he reached the top of that one, he got his first look at what was coming—a blue wall of water taller than a small building and farther out than he had thought possible. Lined up perfectly and swinging straight for him.

He scrambled to position himself a little deeper as the wave moved in and lifted him up and up. And fricking up. He turned and went for it. At the top, he hung for a second as he looked down the vertical face of water, half wishing he had wings. Beyond the point of no return, he jumped to his feet and dropped in. The first few seconds were a free fall and he was poised with arms out, as if in flight, while his board miraculously stayed under him. He managed to level out and picked his line. From behind, the lip hurled and thundered and created a bus-sized barrel, spitting out at him.

Still high up on the wave, which felt ready to pitch him at any moment, he felt the burn in his legs, his lungs, his eyes. Spray from the barrel chandeliered down on him and began to blot out the sun and everything else. If this beast closed out, he was done. He'd be held down on the reef for at least a few waves and then washed into a frothy cauldron of whitewater and boulders at the bottom of the cliffs.

Someone is going to die. The words came to him again in a flash, then disappeared. Today was not his day to die.

The avalanche of water behind him was creating its own wind, but he managed to stall for a few seconds in the barrel before getting shot out in the spit. Time slowed, and the outside world slipped away. A feeling of euphoria came over him. Salt water ran in his veins and he looked down on the scene from a bird's-eye view. Albatross or petrel or booby. When he hit the shoulder of the wave still standing, his arms shot up skyward and he fell back, landing with a splash in the very water that could have easily taken him. The horn sounded a few moments later, signifying the end of the heat.

The crowd in the channel went crazy; he heard them even underwater. Jet skis, boats, boards, camera guys swimming—all rushed toward him. People yelling, hooting, clapping, cheering. Shirtless men and bikini-clad women. Not a wetsuit in sight. And there was no need to see the score, or the video. Their reaction told him everything he needed to know.

The Tourists

ʻIwa

What the actual hell? The traffic was backed up again on the Hana Highway, mostly rental cars. Not only that but they were parked on both sides of the road, blocking driveways and making a big mess of things. A lady two cars up decided to pull a U-turn in the middle of it all, and ʻIwa pressed her hand on the horn and didn't let up. Tourists thought that no one actually lived on Maui. That everyone was on vacation and you could walk down the middle of the road staring at your phone for directions to the nearest waterfall, drive five miles an hour in a thirty mile an hour zone and wear hideous aloha print wear made in China. The *No Trespassing* or *Kapu* signs meant nothing to them.

Coming back to Pāʻia after a few days of work in the forest always seemed to magnify the issue. The absolute definition of culture shock was going from time spent alone with trees and rare plants, swimming in mossy rock-filled streams, and listening for vanishing birdsong to the overcrowded roads and beaches and stores. She rarely ever went to Kīhei or Lahaina anymore, it was too disheartening. If she had her way, she'd live in a tree house high on the eastern slopes of Haleakalā. Maybe come down every few weeks or so to see her dad and get provisions. But her dad needed her and she had a life.

A few minutes ago, she'd passed the old cane road down to

Pe'ahi, and seen the mud tracked out onto the main road. A big man in a black shirt had been standing at the entrance of the red dirt road, arms crossed like a human gate, and a bunch of trucks filled with surfboards were backed up on the side of the road to get in. Pe'ahi must have been breaking. She'd caught glimpses of huge surf along the way. Driving past, she thought nothing of it, mind bent on getting to the restaurant on time, but this was worse than usual. The driver's side window was stuck closed and the afternoon sun turned the cab of her old Toyota truck into a steam bath.

Back at the trailhead, she had rinsed off in the stream, knowing she would just make it in time for her shift. Now she'd be at least ten minutes late. When she hit Pā'ia, all of the parking spots were taken, even the one reserved for Uncle's, home of the best food on the island. After searching for five minutes, she hopped the curb and parked up the road under Mr. Kinoshita's mango tree. It was winter, so her truck was safe from falling fruit. She'd bring him a piece of pie after work and he would forgive her, like he always did. Scrambling over the gear shift into the passenger seat, she pulled on her jeans and work shirt and slid out the door as quietly as possible.

Sundays were usually quiet, but when she walked in, half the tables were already full. She dipped into the bathroom, smoothed down her hair and tied it in a low knot, dabbed some lipstick on and poked her head in the kitchen.

"Sorry I'm late, Pe'ahi traffic and there was no parking. Again. What's the special?" she said.

Uncle's was one of those hole-in-the-wall places that didn't look like much from the outside, but pleasantly surprised you when you walked in. Streetside, it might have been any old little plantation house with faded green paint and a rusted tin roof, but step through the door and you entered a warmly lit room with board and batten walls painted a fresh white, a tall ceiling with exposed trusses and an open-air *lānai* out the back shaded by a big milo tree. The tables were handmade and each one had an old bottle with a fern sticking out of it. The menu was written on a chalkboard wall, but most people who came here didn't need a menu. They already knew what they wanted— one of Uncle's famous bowls.

But on a day like today, there was bound to be more tourists than locals, and she was already annoyed at their intrusion into her life and town. She had to remind herself to be nice, that the tourists helped keep the town afloat now that sugar was gone.

Within an hour of her arrival, every table in the place was taken, and she picked up on fragments of the day's events at Pe'ahi, which pretty much everyone in the surf industry just referred to as Jaws. The room was buzzing with surfing tales— the bomber set that broke on the outer reef, Petey Jones's spectacular wipeout, the sheet glass conditions and that final wave. But the thing was, she just wasn't interested. Everyone here was obsessed with the ocean, but give her a mountain any day.

A man across the room waved her over. "Miss, excuse me, miss!"

She was in the middle of taking an order and purposely ignored him. When she finished and headed to the kitchen instead of toward his table, she saw him stand and hold up his glass out of the corner of her eye.

"Hey, pretty waheenee, we need refills over here, pronto."

Mila, the other waitress, a windsurfer from Holland, glanced over at 'Iwa from across the room and gave her an eye roll and a shake of the head. The man in question was sitting with two other guys, all sunburned and beer-bellied.

'Iwa held a finger up, and said, "I'll be with you in a minute."

Built like an aging football player, the man stood there in his too-tight T-shirt with dark circles around the armpits, looking pissed. "Bring us two more rounds, then, will you?"

After serving fish bowls to one of her regulars, she went to the register and wrote up the red guy's check and walked as slowly as she could to their table.

"I think what you meant to say was *wahine*," she said, sounding out the Hawaiian word for *woman* correctly, and setting the check down. "But here's the thing, we just ran out of beer, so I'll take the check when you're ready."

The guy frowned. "You're kidding, right?"

"Nope."

His friend chimed in. "We'll take three margaritas then."

"We're out of tequila, too," she said, glancing at the door as a string of surfers walked in.

Linebacker raised his voice. "I see how it is. Do me a favor, though, and let the cook know that my meal tasted like cat food."

His friends laughed.

"Please see yourselves out," she said, trying to keep her voice level.

By now, she could feel the looks of the other customers. There was rarely any trouble at the restaurant other than the odd whiny customer. *This fish is raw* was the number one complaint, even though it was precisely what they had ordered. Thankfully, the bearded friend threw down some bills, scribbled something on the check and they filed out the door. 'Iwa realized she had been holding her breath and let out a big sigh once they were gone. She counted the money. Eighty dollars on a $79.86 check, and some genius advice: *Grow some tits if you want a tip.*

She shredded the paper and pocketed the money as her eyes filled with tears. She went about clearing and wiping the table so she wouldn't have to look at anyone. On any other day it would have rolled off her back—rude customers came with the territory, but today she was just plain over it. Over everything. Before she could escape to the bathroom to compose herself,

Mila brought over a group of surfers to sit at the table. 'Iwa forced a smile, then ran off without a word.

Fortunately no one was in the tiny bathroom, and she splashed her face and took a few deep breaths, overwhelmed by the mess this world was becoming. For the last few days, she'd been out searching for tiny forest birds only found on Maui that quite possibly were extinct in the wild. The kiwikiu. Someone had reported possibly hearing one on a remote trail, and she'd been so hopeful. But after three days in the area, she'd found nothing. The idea of yet another species disappearing from the planet gutted her. And then she'd had to come back to cover a shift at the restaurant.

When 'Iwa walked back out, the crowd of surfers had doubled and now took up two tables. Strong and wiry, and various shades of tan, most of them were wearing flannel shirts. As soon as the January sun went down, the temp cooled fast. Mila was delivering drinks already, and more people were still spilling in. 'Iwa went to the kitchen to warn Eddie.

"We just got slammed, get ready."

"Mat and Reeny should be here any minute. I had a feeling it would be busy, with the contest and all."

Mat tended bar and helped in the kitchen, and Reeny waited tables like an old pro.

"How come no one told me it was on?"

"I know how you get when you're in the back valleys. One-track mind. There's hardly service anyway, so why bother?"

Bother came out *botha* in his pidgin.

"It would have been nice to know, is all."

The next hour passed in a blur of taking orders, answering random Maui questions and reciting the beer menu, which included a long list of local brews. Big Swell IPA, Bikini Blonde, Aloha Spirit, Overboard IPA. It was making her so tired and thirsty, she did something she hardly ever did: poured herself a beer. Between all the running around and the last few days of hiking, her body felt like it had caught fire. She went into the kitchen, leaned on the cool stainless steel fridge and took a big swig.

Eddie looked up from the grill. "What the heck are you doing?"

"I'm thirsty."

"Put that down and get out there. It's five past six."

She groaned. "I'm fried. Win can play on his own tonight."

"You'll feel better once you get out there, you always do."

He was probably right. She downed the beer, went to the office and changed into a long-sleeved brown *palaka* shirt tied at the waist, and grabbed her old Martin guitar. They had a little spot on the back *lānai* where she and Winston played music on Sunday evenings. 'Iwa on guitar, Winston on ukulele, and taking turns on the vocals. Winston was already out back.

"How were the birds, any sightings?" he asked, as he tuned his ukulele.

She shook her head. "You know I would have told you."

Winston headed Maui Forest Recovery Project, the small organization where she worked, so he knew as well as anyone the predicament they were in. He remained looking down, still tightening his strings, and it felt like he was avoiding eye contact.

"Is everything okay, Win?"

She had known him forever—their moms had taught music together—so she could read him well.

He let out a big exhale and met her gaze. "The eco resort got the green light."

"What are you talking about?"

"On the Hana'iwa'iwa land. The county approved it."

Her body went cold. "No," she whispered.

"I got a call from the deputy this afternoon, as a courtesy."

Using the words *eco resort* had become the new underhanded way to build things you weren't supposed to build. Resorts or condos or cheaply constructed strip malls that branded themselves as environmentally conscious, while consciously ruining the land and wiping out entire ecosystems.

"Some courtesy. Why do we allow this kind of thing?" she said, fingers moving up and down the neck of her guitar.

Winston rubbed his fingers together. "Money."

The Hanaʻiwaʻiwa land covered a huge swath of forest and stream systems near where she'd been the last few days. Her day job sometimes took her there. Home to towering ʻōhiʻa lehua trees and native forest birds, Hawaiian snails and happy-face spiders, and a waterfall that meant the world to ʻIwa for reasons of her own.

The old landowner had recently sold it to a developer, Murphy Jones, in a quiet deal that was done before anyone knew. In effect, selling off some of the most pristine land on the island. ʻIwa knew all about Jones from her mother, Lily, who had been a big part of the Save Hanameli coalition fifteen years earlier, fighting to keep a white sand bay from being built on. The coalition had lost, and now the bay was graced with a big ugly hotel, the beach lined in beach chairs and umbrellas. Island residents had to fight for beach access.

"We can't let him do it," she said, with a hard strum.

"He's already doing it."

It was suddenly hard to breathe. The waterfall would forever be tied to her mom. Going there for the first time had been a rite of passage, a doorway into another world. Before starting off on the hike, Lily had taught her E Hō Mai, a Hawaiian chant asking for permission to enter the forest. To ʻIwa, who was only ten at the time, it felt like being inducted into a secret club. Not many people knew about Waikula.

That moment at the trailhead came back to her vividly. Standing under a canopy of kukui and guava, breathing in overripe fruit and decaying leaves. Her mother tightening the straps on her pack. The morning had been a bright one, and sunlight crisscrossed through the branches. 'Iwa's mom sang the words first, and 'Iwa followed. They repeated the lines several times and when they were finished 'Iwa could have sworn a few birds joined in and the trees were standing taller. Her mother smiled her vibrant smile and they set out on the long hike to the falls.

"We have to figure out something. *I* have to," she told him.

Her mother's memory depended on it.

"Don't worry, we will."

Ten minutes later, the whole group of surfers started spilling out the back door, crowding around the two small empty tables right in front of 'Iwa and Winston. There wasn't enough room for them all, so a few stood off to the side, leaning against the tree limb that was growing across the *lānai*. At that moment, 'Iwa wished they would all just go away. Or maybe *she* should. At the rate things were going, this night was not bound to end well.

One of the problems with surfers was that they were mostly all good-looking and well-built. Wide shoulders and finely carved arms, hair streaked with sunshine, and always a healthy dose of confidence, as if they knew that what they did was the coolest sport on earth, and they were in on some secret with mother nature herself. 'Iwa's only two boyfriends had been surfers. Now she avoided them for the same reason she was attracted to them: with a surfer, you would never be number one. The ocean was always their first love and first priority, and that was nonnegotiable.

Winston nudged her arm. "You ready?"

She nodded.

Winston leaned into the mic, slowly strumming, and spoke in that soft way that he did. "Aloha. I'm Winston and this is 'Iwa," he said, emphasizing the *w* in her name as a *v*, as in so many Hawaiian words. "Our island's best-kept secret. Also, a big shout out to our Pe'ahi surfers in the crowd."

They started with *"Hi'ilawe."* Old-school slack key. The beauty of playing at Uncle's was that they could play whatever

they wanted, which usually turned out to be mostly Hawaiian with a smattering of folk rock that made you feel like you
were sitting on a beach around a bonfire, breaking waves and
crackling flames as a backdrop. His voice was smooth and old-
fashioned, hers deep and husky.

When 'Iwa was onstage—if you could call the little platform
a stage—she did one of two things: disappear completely into
the songs and zone out, or play on autopilot and observe the
guests in great detail. Tonight, as much as she wanted to zone
out, she found herself studying the surf crew. She recognized a
few locals, Billy Rothburn, Lucas Hoapili and Kama Mizuno,
a mainland surfer whose grandparents lived on Maui. With
them was a tallish blond guy wearing a *maile* lei, long strands
of sweet and tangy vine. He looked familiar and was probably
someone, but she couldn't place him. He seemed a little old to
be a pro, maybe thirtyish, but you never knew. Big wave surfing had its own set of rules. It attracted a much wider range of
men—and a handful of women.

After a few songs, a woman who had been sitting at the
other table came over and sat between Kama and the stranger,
her butt on the edge of each of their chairs. She slung an arm
around *maile* lei guy and leaned her blond head against his neck.
He messed up her short blond hair with one hand and squeezed
her knee with his other. Big, strong hands. The two made a
handsome pair, and yet, there was something untouchable about
him, something that said he belonged to no one.

At the end of the song, Reeny came out with a round of tequila shots and a bald man stood up and made a toast. "There
aren't too many men in the world who ride mountains, and
even fewer who slay them the way you did today. Well played,
my friend," he said, lifting his glass. "To a new era of big wave
surfing!"

Cheers.

Aloha.

Roger that.

Everyone on the *lānai* was looking directly at *maile* lei guy, who offered up a one-sided smile, downed his shot, and slammed the glass on the hardwood table with a tan and muscled forearm. "Thanks, brah. Humbled to be here," was all he said.

Interesting. People from the mainland usually said *bro*, not *brah*.

"Speech!" the girl next to him said, waving a fist in the air. A few others chimed in. *Dane-O! Speech! Cheehoo!*

And then it hit her. This was Dane Parsons. A well-known big wave surfer. He had always had long hair, but now it was shorter and tousled, almost as though he had cut it himself. She had encountered him a few times over the years—a party at Kama's grandparents' house, out surfing at Honolua Bay, a barbecue in Spreckelsville. Usually with a hot girl on his arm.

He shook his head. "No speech." Then looked up at Winston and said, "Don't stop on my account."

Winston nodded at 'Iwa and they started up again, 'Iwa singing and working out the cobwebs in her voice. For the first time, Dane turned her way and seemed to notice her. He didn't smile, but his blue-eyed gaze stuck for a few moments. She didn't smile either, then forced herself to look away.

Voices at the table were getting louder as more rounds were consumed, and everyone was talking over everyone. They continued playing on in the background, and then took a water break. The deck was so small that they were almost bumping knees with the closest table, and 'Iwa listened to the guys talk about a surfer put in a coma by a freakish wave off Portugal.

"He was in critical condition for a week," one of them said.

"I thought it was a month," said another guy.

"I heard he was under for ten minutes."

It reminded her of the fishing tales her dad and his friends spun after a long day on the water. Where at five o'clock the fish was forty pounds, four hours and a twelve-pack later, it had morphed into a hundred-pound beast.

Kama's forehead scrunched up. "No one can hold their breath for ten minutes and come out alive."

Dane seemed to disagree. "It's the cold water. Remember *The Perfect Storm*? We need to get over there and ride that thing."

None of them had even noticed the music had stopped, which irked her. 'Iwa picked up her guitar, ready to give it one more go. She smiled at Win and started plucking the chords to "Angel from Montgomery." It had been one of her mom's favorites and the two of them loved to sing it together—always a crowd pleaser.

Winston smiled and said, "Good choice."

They played together often enough that they had their own internal language. He knew this song meant she wanted to get the crowd's attention, maybe even impress someone.

'Iwa leaned into the mic and spoke softly. "This song is for all the waterfalls out there that need saving."

The words poured out, dripping with emotion and sung with as much passion as she could muster. She kept her voice slow and measured, and a little rough around the edges. Where usually this was when the people on the patio went quiet, no one even glanced their way. These guys seemed drunk and full of themselves and clueless. What a waste of her time. Midsong, she just stopped. Winston looked at her, lifting an eyebrow.

She waited a few moments, then spoke into the mic again, louder. "Raise your hand if you know what the word *haole* means."

That seemed to get their attention. Kama and Dane and most of the people at the closest table glanced around at each other, looking uncomfortable. Kama finally raised his hand. As did Dane. Hands shot up here and there, and everyone stopped talking, clearly wondering where this was going. 'Iwa wondered, too, but she felt this simmering anger under her skin that pushed her onward.

"You, guy with the *maile* lei, why don't you tell us," she said, unwilling to acknowledge that she knew who he was.

"A *haole* is a white person," he said, matter-of-factly.

"Is that your final answer?" she asked.

A hint of a smile. "Yup."

Lucas spoke up. "Brah, let me help you out. It means *without breath*, and the Hawaiians used it to mean the missionaries who refused to greet them by sharing a breath, nose to nose." He looked to 'Iwa. "Am I right?"

"That's one school of thought. But more likely, it meant outsider, someone of a foreign kind who doesn't understand your ways," she said.

Like you guys.

"Thanks for the education," she heard a man say to his friend at a nearby table, as he rolled his eyes.

'Iwa's cheeks heated up. "In Hawai'i, when you're out somewhere and people are playing music for you, you usually show them just a tiny bit of respect. My friend Winston here is one of the best musicians on the island and not one of you has so much as acknowledged him."

For the second time that night, tears welled in her eyes. She had been having angry and unexpected emotional outbursts like this more and more lately. And now, knowing her reaction to a bunch of clueless surfers was irrational but unable to help herself, the words of her Uncle Tutu popped into her head.

Grief bites out of the blue.

Kama gave her a sheepish look. "Sorry, 'Iwa, big day on the water and everyone is jacked."

Dane, who was sitting with his side to her, turned. "What makes you think we aren't paying attention?" His voice was deep and full and resonant. 'Iwa noticed voices.

"It's pretty obvious. Every one of you is yelling over the other to be heard. You're like a bunch of mynah birds in a banyan tree at sunset time," she said.

"I heard you. You dedicated that song to all the waterfalls that need saving. One in particular."

Shit.

"Okay, so a point for you, congratulations," she said.

Winston nudged her knee with his. Fighting with guests was not a brilliant business strategy, and Eddie would be pissed, but she could not rein herself in.

"What song were we playing?" she asked.

He didn't miss a beat. "John Prine. 'Angel from Montgomery.'"

The look on his face said he knew he'd won—was probably used to winning. But even if he had been paying attention, no one else seemed to be. Then he whistled through his fingers, loud enough to shut everyone up fast.

"Hey, can we get some quiet? The lady would like your attention for this next song," he said, turning toward her and leaning back with his arms crossed, a look of amusement on his face. "We're all ears."

Now she felt stupid and self-conscious. She glanced over at Winston, who had developed a sheen of sweat on his forehead even in the cool evening air. The smart thing to do would be to just go. Call it a night and leave Win here to finish off the set. But that would mean these people had won, wouldn't it?

"Pick a song, any song," she said.

Dane rubbed his chin and thought for a few seconds. "What about Guns N' Roses. 'Sweet Child O' Mine'? Is that in your repertoire?"

She tried to suppress a smile. "That old eighties band? We'll do our best," she said. "Won't we, Win?"

A quiet stillness filled the night. The leaves on the big milo tree had stopped rustling, traffic noise had all but ceased and the whole side of the mountain was holding its breath. 'Iwa started the opening riff softly and intimately, fingers picking up and down the fretboard, working deftly. Then she took it up a notch. She knew the song inside out and backward. Could have played it in her sleep. As her hands did their thing, she channeled her mother's voice and began singing, eyes on the guitar.

He's got a smile that it seems to me…

After the first verse, in which she changed the words from *she* to *he*, she dared a peek at the audience. All smugness had been wiped from Dane's face, and he was watching her intently as a night heron—an *auku'u*—waiting for a fish. She felt a swoosh on the inside, something warm and dangerous.

He's got eyes of the bluest skies…

She continued on, this time disappearing into the song until the outside world fell away. Her voice caught a few times, but her guitar was flawless and Winston was doing a fine job of matching her on his tenor uke. For good measure, she drew out the ending, and by the time they'd finished, her fingers ached and her throat burned. Around the *lānai*, claps and whistles and cheers arose.

"Well played," Dane said, and she could tell that he meant it. His eyes really were blue. More deep sea than sky. Not that she had been singing about his eyes, but they were hard not to notice.

Breathless, she smiled. For the first time, she noticed Eddie leaning against the door frame. Dane must have followed her gaze, because he swiveled around to see what she was looking at. Eddie was backlit and it was hard to read his expression, but he wasn't clapping. Then he turned and went back inside. Just then, the fairy lights went out. Which meant closing time. She checked her watch and saw that closing time wasn't for another forty-five minutes.

"*Hana hou,*" someone yelled.

"Sorry, the boss says it's closing time. Aloha," she said, turning off the mic, grabbing her guitar, and beelining it across the *lānai* and into the kitchen.

Eddie was wiping down the stainless steel counter and didn't look up when she entered. Obsessive about his kitchen, he made sure the place was sparkly clean every night before leaving. You had to or the bugs moved in and took up residence.

"Hey," she said.

"What was that out there, 'Iwa'iwa?" he said in his angry boss tone.

And using her full name.

"The man requested it, what was I supposed to do?"

She watched his thick arm go round and round with the white rag, polishing one particular spot to death, and felt a rush of fondness for him, even though she was high on his shit list right now.

"You can't keep getting into it with the customers. First those tourist guys and now the surfers. No more beers for you while on the job," he said.

"It wasn't the beer."

"Whatevah. And by the way, *the man* happens to be a legend."

"So, are you going to fire me?" she asked, undoing her bun and shaking her hair out. It was still damp with stream water.

Suddenly, there was movement behind her. She stepped to the side, expecting Reeny or Mat, but it was Dane, looking flush in the bright lights.

"Please don't fire her on our account," he said.

Eddie stopped the polishing and stood upright, dropping the rag. "It wouldn't be on your account, trust me. But even if I wanted to, I couldn't fire her."

"And why is that?"

"She's my daughter. I'm Eddie Young," he said, holding out his hand to Dane.

Dane shook it, studying Eddie for a moment, and then 'Iwa, causing a warming tingle on her skin. He let out a small laugh. "I see the resemblance, clear as day."

Eddie, as usual, had more to say. "'Iwa means well, but when she gets a notion in her head, she's like a pit bull. Sorry about the *haole* lecture. Her mother was full-blooded *haole*, Irish. I'm Hawaiian-Chinese and Norwegian."

'Iwa tried to stick up for herself. "I was just trying to make a point, and technically—"

Her dad held up a hand. "Dane was right, nowadays we use the word *haole* to mean white person, so let's leave it at that."

"I don't mind being put in my place now and then," Dane said.

"Brah, you just won the Pe'ahi Challenge. You did not deserve my daughter acting like a brat."

Dane shoved his hands in his pockets. "Yeah, well—"

Eddie beamed at Dane. "I was born and raised just up the road and been long-boarding my whole life, and tell you what—there's only a handful of guys in the world who could go out there and do what you did today. You earned my respect and then some. Actually, you already had my respect, but now you moved up a rung."

Dane shrugged. "I had some help from the ocean, no doubt about that."

He was close enough now that she could smell a spicy aftershave mixed with salt water and see the true magnitude of his long-lashed cerulean eyes.

"Paddling into a wave like that takes a special kind of nerve," Eddie said.

'Iwa gave Eddie a look that said, *enough, Dad*. At this point, all she wanted to do was take Mr. Kinoshita his *liliko'i* pie slice, head home and curl up under the blankets with Koa.

Dane cleared his throat. "Speaking of nerve, how about I make up for my rude behavior by taking your daughter out to dinner tomorrow night?" he said to Eddie, then shot her a look.

Eddie stood up taller, chest out and chin up. "You're even braver than I thought."

"I...uh...well..."

Eddie laughed. "Just kidding. But you gotta ask her, not me. She's the boss."

Dane turned to 'Iwa. "What do you say?"

'Iwa's heart skipped a beat, but her head quickly took over

and spun out a list of reasons to say no—*mainland* and *surfer* topping the list, with *distraction* and *dangerous* coming in a close third and fourth.

"Thank you but I can't," she said, offering up no further explanation.

Dane wilted a little, then said, "Lunch, maybe?"

"I appreciate you coming back here to apologize, and I'm flattered, but I must decline."

I must decline? Where on earth had that come from? This whole thing was throwing her off. Five seconds later, a big brown moth flew in through the open back door and fluttered erratically around Dane's head.

He ducked and swatted and hopped around, before it found a spot on the beam above him. "You have bats in Hawai'i?" he asked, wide-eyed.

"It's a black witch moth, not a bat," she said.

Eddie was watching the moth, a beautiful lacy pattern on her wings. A knowing look passed between them. 'Iwa willed the moth to fly off and find another place to rest, but she seemed content to remain on the dark beam. *Ascalapha odorata.* This one appeared to be a female, with the telltale white stripe, and blue in her spots, especially iridescent. If the lore was true, the moths were lost loved ones returning for a visit.

'Iwa made her escape. "Excuse me, I have some pie to deliver. Safe travels," she said, leaving them standing there as she went to the bar fridge and took out the last slice of pie. The back of her head burned where she imagined Dane's gaze following her.

Of all things, a black witch moth over his head.

The Attempt

Dane

The rain came down like marbles on the rusted corrugated roof, waking Dane up at least a few times in the night. He was staying in an old sugar shack on Kama's grandparents' property outside of Pā'ia. Five acres of jungle with four million chickens and a couple of donkeys who made it a point to call out to each other every half hour or so. Kama's dad's family had come from Japan to work for the sugar companies until his grandfather broke away and started his own store, Mizuno General Store. Kama's dad had grown up on Maui and moved to California for school and stayed for love, but he brought Kama back home every summer, and winter break.

Dane tagged along for a visit one summer when they were teenagers, helping pick *liliko'i* and bananas, bushwhacking and learning how to surf the heavy Hawaiian waves. Later, he returned when the big swells rolled in. Growing up, Dane effectively had no father and his mom was an enigma, so the Mizunos had become more family than his own. They brought him to Maui whenever they visited, which was why Maui held a special place in his heart.

In the morning, when he finally got up, his head was throbbing from one too many shots of tequila and his whole body felt like it had been through an extra cycle of the wash. He drank a tall glass of water, then, even though the sun was up, he went back to bed.

Only thing was, he couldn't fall back asleep. He lay there, watching raindrops slide down the cracked windowpane and reliving that final wave. Its skyscraper drop. The thrill of the win. He wanted to stay there, in that blue and blissful moment, but his mind stubbornly kept returning to the woman, making him feel like a real dope.

What an ass he had been. First, suggesting G&R—that was just rude, and then being a complete jackass and asking her out in front of her dad in the kitchen. He pulled the pillow over his head and groaned. It was the first time he had been turned down in as long as he could remember, and it stung. Yes, she was pretty, with long brown hair, moss green eyes, and freckles dusting her nose and cheeks, but there was more under the surface, he could tell. The way she called them all out fearlessly. Her hypnotic guitar playing. And that voice.

For all the waterfalls out there that need saving.

There was a sadness in the way she had said it, but also a sureness. As though saving waterfalls was a requirement for living. It made him curious. And it made him wonder—what was he saving, other than maybe himself once in a while? He started drifting off again, but a knock on the door startled him back.

"Go away," he said.

"Get your lazy ass out of bed," Kama said.

"Have you checked the waves yet?"

"Blown out. But we can check the west side."

Kama loved the ocean more than anyone he knew. Swell or no swell, calm or storm, he would find a way to be in the water. Surfing, skin diving, paddleboarding, windsurfing, you name it. They were kindred spirits in this way. Kama lived in Santa Cruz now, just up the road from Dane, but it would only be a matter of time before he moved to Maui where his roots were. Dane could hardly blame him.

"Find me some coffee and then we'll talk," Dane said.

Ten minutes later, under gathering storm clouds, they hopped on bikes and followed a grassy trail and a network of backroads into town. Pāʻia was a little rough around the edges, but had an island charm that you couldn't argue with. Tiny boutiques and art galleries lined up in uneven wooden storefronts. Coconut trees, red dirt and roosters. Even at ten o'clock, the place was hopping. They parked the bikes outside of Maui Bean & Tea Leaf and got in a line that ran nearly out the door, and where clothing was apparently optional. Kama didn't seem fazed by the line at all.

While waiting, Dane stretched out his tight shoulders, and rolled his neck around, trying to loosen the knots from yesterday. He definitely should have stuck to drinking water last night, but what the hell, the win was a big one. Despite this, he only had one thing on his mind.

"What can you tell me about the singer last night?" he said, trying to sound casual.

"Which singer? The guy or the girl?"

He knew Kama was just messing with him, as usual.

"Come on, man."

Kama kept his eye on the menu and acted disinterested. "She's from around here, Dad owns Uncle's, nice family."

"I asked her out last night," Dane said.

"You're shitting me."

"Why do you say that?"

"I should have known what you were up to. Wasn't her dad right there?"

"It's not like she's a kid. She's a grown woman, and a very beautiful one," Dane said, suddenly feeling defensive.

Kama shrugged. "Did she say yes?"

"Turned me down flat. No explanation, nothing. She could be married for all I know, but I couldn't help myself."

Even though she wore no ring. He'd checked.

"I don't think she's married," Kama said.

Dane had avoided asking questions last night on the way home, bruised ego and all. But now that he'd started, he suddenly wanted to know more about her.

"How do you know?"

"My tutu is friends with her dad, Uncle Eddie. And you know Tutu, she's into everyone's business. I'll hear about it if her yard guy's cousin's daughter gets engaged."

"Boyfriend?"

"Not sure. She had one for a while on O'ahu, I think."

"Where'd she learn to play guitar like that?"

"Her mom was a music teacher up at Seabury Hall—everyone loved her. Sad though, she died last year," he said.

"Why haven't I run into her before?"

"Probably because she was younger, and in a different scene. It wasn't until her senior year she suddenly turned gorgeous."

One of the girls turned around, stole a look at them, mumbled something to her friend and they both giggled. Dane didn't care.

"What else does she do? For work, I mean."

"What's it to you? She turned you down so it doesn't matter. And you're leaving tomorrow anyway, so let it go. Every guy that walks out of Uncle's on a Sunday night thinks they're in love with 'Iwa. You'll get over it," Kama said, stepping up to order. "More importantly, what are you going to eat?"

A big breakfast would do him good, maybe clear the cobwebs from his head, so he decided on a breakfast burrito with extra avocado, a banana chocolate chip muffin and a double espresso. They waited off to the side, smashed between a rickety old couple in matching aloha wear and three guys in legit cowboy boots and hats and wearing shirts made from that same Hawaiian checkered print 'Iwa had on last night. *Palaka*, if he remembered it right.

Being in Hawai'i almost felt like being in a foreign country.

There was no place remotely like it on the mainland. He loved how he got a flower lei every time he arrived, how people invited him in like family and how you always left your rubber slippers at the door. Nowhere else did he feel as welcome—or as unwelcome. It was a weird dichotomy. Because along with the friendly people full of aloha, there were also angry locals who were sick to death of tourists infesting their islands like fire ants.

The girl behind the counter called out their number and he followed Kama out back to a screened-in *lānai*. He was so focused on his food at first, that he didn't even notice the woman at the table across the way until he came up for air. Her side was to him, and she was sitting across from the same man she'd been playing music with last night—a strong-looking local dude. 'Iwa's hair was down, and she was twisting it around her hand, focused intently on the conversation.

Dane felt a rush of heat run up his neck. "Don't look now, but three o'clock."

Kama looked. Dane kicked him.

"Are you sure she's not with him?" Dane asked.

"Winston? No idea."

'Iwa must have felt the weight of their eyes, because at that moment, she turned. She saw Kama first and she lit up, then her gaze jumped to Dane, and a different, more complicated expression appeared on her face. Wariness? Surprise? Pleasure? That was probably going too far. She waved, then resumed her conversation.

In the light of day, her hair looked lighter, sun streaked, and her skin a darker brown. She was long limbed and lithe. Serious, intense even. Stunning.

"At least now I know she's with someone. Explains last night," he said, disappointed.

Kama ignored him, fork in one hand, phone in the other, scrolling wind and weather and wave apps. Knowing the elements was an essential part of the surfing life and he probably knew as much as your average meteorologist. "It looks junk on the west side, too," he said.

Fine by Dane. "I'm feeling pretty beat up, anyway."

"Tomorrow should be better, after the storm passes. It's going to be small, though."

Small to Kama still could mean six feet, Hawaiian. Translated, that meant double-overhead.

"I would never hear the end of it if I changed my flight. My client is on the verge of firing my butt as it is," Dane said.

Dane's real job—most big wave surfers had one—was carpentry. Finish carpentry to be exact. He'd been good with his hands since day one, and had honed his skill over the years on moldings and cabinets and custom door and window frames. Though lately, he'd begun making handcrafted furniture because carpentry required him to be in one place, and customers did not understand when he took off midjob in pursuit of waves. He had lost more than one client that way. Surfing came first, but nonsurfers never understood. It was a way of life. A calling. Not just a sport.

"I'm here for another ten days or so, but I have my eye on Portugal. We need to get on that monster wave," Kama said.

"We will," Dane said, somewhat absentmindedly.

His gaze found its way across the *lānai* again, resting on ʻIwa's profile. Her thin wrists. Strong arms.

"Look at me, dude. I'm over here," Kama said, holding a finger up like an ophthalmologist.

Just then, ʻIwa and Winston stood up. He kissed her goodbye on the cheek, nothing fancy. Not on the lips. For a minute, it looked like ʻIwa was going to leave, too, but she sat back down and opened a laptop, never once glancing over.

"You know what they say about second chances," Kama said with a silly grin.

"No, but I know you're going to tell me."

"Never confuse a single failure with a final defeat. F. Scott Fitzgerald."

Not only was Kama a weatherman, he was a walking English textbook. That was one place he and Dane differed—Kama had done well in school. Dane had thought school was a pointless chore, and drove his teachers crazy to no end. *All that wasted potential*, they used to tell his mother. His mom didn't seem to care what he did, so their words were wasted.

"I guess that means you've changed your mind? Now I shouldn't forget about her?" Dane said.

Kama threw down his napkin. "I can see the impossibility of that in your eyes. I'm going to the bathroom. You're going over there."

Dane was left alone. He froze for a few seconds, then 'Iwa looked up and gave him a tiny smile. He went over.

"Morning," he said.

"Morning," she said, as she typed something into her laptop.

His mind went blank. "Beautiful day," he mustered.

"It is."

He heard the whoosh of an email being sent. 'Iwa half closed her computer and turned her face to him, locking eyes. Dane started sweating and bounced from foot to foot.

"Busy saving waterfalls?" he asked.

"Actually, I am."

She wasn't kidding.

"Is that what you do? For a living, I mean?"

"I work for Maui Forest Recovery Project, and one of our forests is in danger of being ruined by a developer. The same forest is home to my favorite waterfall—and birds and plants— and we're going to fight them. So, I guess that's a yes."

"Seems like everyone wants a piece of the island," he said.

"We're already over max capacity and yet we keep building more hotels, more developments, more useless shit. Breaks my heart," she said.

He could feel her sadness, same as last night. Visceral, real. Instead of answering with something smart and witty, he said, "Mine too."

'Iwa studied him for a moment, then opened her laptop again. "Excuse me, but I have work to do."

Her fingers moved swiftly over the keyboard and Dane felt as though he'd grown roots, unable to walk away, unable to think straight.

"I want to help you," he finally said.

She frowned. "I'm not sure how you can help, but thanks for the offer."

"I have a good buddy in California who fights these kinds of things all the time. I've learned a thing or two from him."

"Really?"

"Really."

"You're persistent."

Dane never gave up, which sometimes was a good thing, and other times got him into trouble. "A fatal flaw," he said.

"I guess it depends how you look at it," she said.

"Exactly." He put his hand on the back of the wrought iron chair. "Mind if I sit? Just for a minute." He dropped his butt into the chair lightning fast. Kama could wait.

'Iwa took a sip of her coffee and eyed him over the rim of her mug. "No offense, but you look like hell this morning," she said.

In the mirror earlier his eyes had been bloodshot, face unshaven, lips cracked and hair smashed in eleven directions. He hadn't showered because they'd been planning on jumping in the ocean. A little hair of the dog.

"No offense taken. I took a beating yesterday out in the water," he said, then set his hand over his heart. "And then last night—my heart took one, too."

That earned him an eye roll. "Oh please. I grew up here. I know how you surfers are."

He cocked his head. "How are we?"

"More into yourselves and each other than any girl. The ocean is your one true love, the one you put before all else. I understand how it is, because I'm like that with the mountains," she said with a shrug of her smooth, toned shoulders.

He was intrigued. "Tell me more."

"That about sums it up. Men are predictable creatures."

It was his turn to laugh. "Sounds like a pretty big generalization to me. What do you have against men?"

"Nothing. I love men. My dad and uncles, my guy friends, my boss Winston—the man I was just sitting with. Being predictable is not an insult, Dane, it's just a fact. It makes it easier to deal with your kind," she said, a hint of a smile drawing up one side of her mouth.

Hearing her speak his name did something to his insides, as though there was a fish moving through his chest, tail brushing up against his ribs, swooshing and swimming. That and the fact that her breakfast with Winston might have been a work thing.

He tried to play it cool. "You make us sound like feral animals. Fair enough, we probably are. But I want to hear more about this waterfall."

"It's something you would have to see to believe."

"I'm ready when you are."

She laughed. "Sorry, I can't take you there."

"Why not?"

"I'm busy. Plus, its location is top secret and it's a mission to get there."

"Even better."

Her expression grew more serious. "The falls are tucked away in the fold of a valley on Haleakalā's eastern slopes. The property this guy bought runs along the entire stream, and goes right to the middle of it. He says he's going to build an eco resort but we all know what that means."

"It means he needs to be stopped," Dane said, leaning back and crossing his arms.

"Exactly."

"Do you have a plan?" he asked.

"I just found out last night that he got approval. No one really thought it would go through."

"My friend has fought loggers, drillers, dam builders, you name it. He talks to me about a lot of his projects. Maybe I can help you brainstorm?" She looked as though she were actually considering it and he quickly added, "No strings attached. I just might be able to offer another perspective, which is sometimes what you need in these cases."

"When do you leave?"

"Tomorrow. But I'm free tonight. What do you say?"

She watched a butterfly flitter past and he was sure she was going to turn him down again, but instead she said, "Okay."

Not full of enthusiasm, but it was something.

"I'll pick you up at five, just tell me where."

She gave him her address, looked at her watch and slipped her computer into her bag, "I have to be somewhere—I've got to run." When she'd gone two steps, she turned back and said, "And just so we're clear, this isn't a date."

Dane gave her a small salute. "Ten four."

He had exactly one night to change her mind.

The Non-Date

'Iwa

Most people on Maui had studios or cottages or rooms they rented out. You had to in order to make ends meet. The price of gas was consistently over five dollars, the average home was over a million and everything from food to shoes to toilet paper had to be shipped thousands of miles across the Pacific. The cost of living added up fast.

'Iwa lived in a small one-bedroom apartment off to the side of the main house that she'd grown up in—a classic 1930s plantation house with painted plywood floors, rattly windowpanes and lauhala mats in every room. Her place had once been the garage, but Eddie had turned it into a living area so 'Iwa could be close and yet have her own space during her mother's illness. She'd taken the first plane out of Honolulu the day after she heard the news, and never gone back. Two months shy of graduating, her professors had been understanding, and she finished online.

It had been a fast-moving cancer that started in the right ovary and within a month had spread throughout her whole body. She'd died last spring, nearly a year now, and even still, 'Iwa half expected Lily to walk in the door, red hair corkscrewing to her waist, guitar in hand, saying, "Let's play!"

Losing her mother had knocked her world off its axis, and

'Iwa had responded by going to their favorite places, playing their favorite songs, singing to the sky in the hopes that somewhere up there, Lily was listening. She baked mac nut banana bread and made mango chutney with an extra spoonful of fresh ginger. Watched the stars on clear nights and made up new constellations. Everything she did was to try and get closer, to hold on to a thin residue of her mother's life. It had been even harder for Eddie.

Now part of her wanted to return to O'ahu for her master's degree, but the other part wanted to stay with her dad forever. He thought he was watching over her, when really, she was the one watching over him.

There was also the matter of Koa, who officially belonged to 'Iwa. But he and Eddie had developed a special bond, and she couldn't bear to take Koa away. In all honesty, Koa had saved them both. Right now, he was lying on one of his many dog beds, spread-eagle on his back, all four paws in the air.

"Life's rough, isn't it?" 'Iwa said.

Koa looked up at her with an upside-down side-eye. His gray tail wagged. She sat on the chair next to him and rubbed his belly with a foot, while picking up the newspaper her dad had left on her table. "Dane Parsons Wins at Pe'ahi" was the headline. There were three photographs. One of him as a tiny speck on a massive blue wave, another of him and Kama having champagne sprayed on them on the makeshift podium, and a third candid of Dane standing at the edge of a cliff. He wasn't smiling and was holding his hand up, not quite a wave. A circle of light surrounded him, a play on the lens. She smiled at the photo, then caught herself and dropped the paper on the floor as if it was on fire.

The north winds had died down, turning the day a crisp and sunshiny blue. Her favorite winter weather. She took an extra-hot shower, rubbed coconut oil over her body and opened her tiny closet. She pulled out a strapless orange maxi dress, then decided it was too fancy. Maybe jeans and a gauzy top, tied at the waist? Nope, too casual. Why did it even matter? Annoyed at her indecision, she applied mascara and a touch of lipstick, then dabbed most of it off with a tissue.

She felt twitchy and nervous. But there was also something simmering just under her skin that felt remarkably like excitement. Meeting up with Dane was probably a bad idea, but she was running out of time now that the eco resort was approved, and if he could provide her with any good ideas, it would be worth every minute. Plus, he was leaving tomorrow, what could possibly go wrong?

In the end, she decided on a mint green minidress that had once been a *mu'umu'u*, but had been stylishly reconfigured. From the driveway, she heard the sound of a motor. A very loud, sputtery motor. Koa heard it too and tore out the back door before 'Iwa could stop him.

"Koa, come here!"

Dane was in a fire-engine red truck that looked fifty years old. Koa had both paws up on the driver's side window and was barking and slobbering madly. Dane was leaning clear across the cab to get away from him.

"Koa, down," 'Iwa said in her most authoritative voice. With Koa, it was hard to tell if he wanted to lick someone to death, or to eat them. Most people assumed the latter, just because he was an oversized mastiff mix. She could tell he recognized Kama's truck and just wanted to say hello. She pointed to the house. "Inside, you stay here."

She hopped in before he could climb in with her, which he'd been known to do. Dane was dressed in beige corduroy pants and a blue aloha shirt with waves on it. His thick hair had been tamed with some kind of gel or cream that smelled like waffles, and he looked like a new man since his disheveled morning.

"Hey, sorry, not very gentlemanly of me to not get your door, but your dog wants to eat me," Dane said.

"It's fine. He can be intimidating."

Dane stared at her for a moment, looked like he was about to say something, then stopped, mouth half open. He stayed like that a few beats too long, then grabbed a bunch of gardenias on the seat and handed them to her.

"I picked these outside of my shack," he said. "The world's finest flower."

Gardenias were her favorite, too, especially the *nāʻu*—the native ones, but the non-date was beginning to feel very date-like, and ʻIwa had the sudden urge to climb back out and say, *Thank you, I had a nice time. Have a wonderful life.* Instead, she said, "Did you know they belong to the coffee family? *Gardenia jasminoides.*"

Kill him with nerdiness. It was a tactic she'd used with some success to ward men off when she wasn't interested.

"No. Have you ever brewed one?"

"Never."

"Maybe we ought to try it some time."

She laughed. "No thanks. So, where are we headed?"

"Top secret."

In his low bass voice, he had this way of sounding like he was smiling when he spoke, even though he wasn't.

"Remember, I live here. I've been everywhere," she said.

"That's why I figured I'd take you somewhere you probably don't go very often, if ever. My treat."

They bounced down the road toward Wailuku and she wondered where they were going but didn't ask. Then he took the turn toward the west side. "Really, I'm fine going someplace close and easy," she said.

"I don't mind the drive."

"Are you sure the truck will make it?" she asked.

"This thing is a tank. She'll go forever."

"Famous last words."

"What's wrong, do you have a curfew or something?" he

asked, looking over at her and almost yelling to be heard over the engine and open windows.

She winced. "No, I don't have a curfew. I'm twenty-four. In Hawai'i, people live at their parents' house because no one can afford their own place. That and family means everything to us, so there's no real rush to leave them behind."

"I was just kidding. I know how it is here. I stay with the Mizunos every time I come. They have a full-on compound over there."

"My dad is friends with Auntie Ivy."

Every older adult here was *Auntie* or *Uncle*. No matter if you were related or if you even knew the person. It made the island seem like one big family. Which it kind of was.

Conversation was hard with the noise, so they stayed mostly quiet as they passed through the middle of Maui, the wide, flat neck of old sugarcane land that spread out between Haleakalā and the West Maui Mountains. Every so often he threw out a question, or she pointed out a landmark. When they hit the other side, they went left toward Wailea. The land of white sand beaches, endless condos and tiger sharks. It was hot, dry and swarming with people. Dane was definitely right about one thing. She never came here.

In her eyes, Wailea had one redeeming quality: its sunsets. Now a giant orange sun hovered over the horizon, sending beams of light in all directions like a disco ball. As they drove along the water, the whole ocean glittered gold. Then they pulled into the Four Seasons and she felt her stomach tighten. He led her to a fancy Italian restaurant right on the water, white tablecloths, Tiki torches, the whole shebang.

The hostess was a tan, leggy blonde in a black dress. Literally, the minute she saw Dane, she started smoothing down her hair and fanning herself with the menus.

"Aloha, welcome."

"Thanks, I have a reservation under—"

"Parsons, right? I know who you are. I'm sure the whole island knows who you are after yesterday. Big congrats!" she gushed.

Dane smiled like a pro. "Ah, thanks. I doubt that's true, though."

The hostess led them to an edge table, where you could hear the wash of the ocean running up the lava rocks, and handed them menus. The hostess did not take her eyes off Dane for one second.

"My boss is going to kill me, but would I be able to get your autograph?" she finally said.

"Sure," Dane said, much more graciously than 'Iwa would have.

The waitress produced a napkin, and he signed it. It was hard not to notice the muscles of his forearm. The dark five o'clock shadow that dipped into a cleft on his chin. Or the hard angle of his cheekbones.

When she left, Dane said, "That was awkward. Sorry about that."

"I guess you better get used to it."

"Nah, to ninety-five percent of the world I'm nobody. Which is all right by me."

She looked around at the surrounding tables to see if anyone else had noticed their arrival. They hadn't. It also seemed they were underdressed. Or maybe everyone else was overdressed. Next to them, two sparkly, shiny couples were discussing the merits of visiting Maui over the Bahamas, and how during the holidays, there was little room to park their private plane. Then the waiter came over and took their drink order.

"I'll have an Overboard IPA," 'Iwa said.

"Same."

They sat there for a moment staring out at the ocean. She willed herself to ignore all the manufactured ambience, because it really was beautiful, but she couldn't stop her foot from tapping. She should never have let him choose the place.

"I've been thinking about your waterfall all day, and I have some ideas, but let's order first," Dane said.

This gave her a small measure of comfort. As long as she got what she came for, she could handle anything. But then she looked at the menu. Maine lobster. Alaskan king crab flown in that very day, cod from Cape Cod. All over fifty bucks. Their beers came in tall frosty glasses and she realized those were probably a good fifteen dollars each.

She set down the menu. "You know, I'm not really hungry."

Dane frowned. "What's wrong?"

"Nothing."

"Obviously something."

"No, really. You go ahead and eat. I had a late lunch."

"If you're worried about the prices, remember I'm paying."

It really was the principle of the matter. "It's not that."

"Then what?"

She knew she was being difficult but couldn't help it. "I just get bummed when restaurants fly all this seafood in from all over the place, when we have the best fresh fish right here in our ocean."

"At least the beer is local," he said, holding up his bottle in front of the candle.

She took a big swig. "That's about the only thing that is."

He downed his in one long gulp and set the glass down. "You know what? Let's get out of here."

"Are you sure?"

"Positive." He leaned forward, close enough so she could see the Tiki torch reflection in his eyes, and said, "I should have let you choose. This is your home, not mine."

He seemed so genuine, her heart softened just a little for him.

On the way out, Dane insisted that she choose the next location. The beer had gone to her head, and she felt strangely giddy as they drove back the way they'd come.

"Do you have any towels in here?" she asked.

He glanced over at her. "Will there be swimming with dinner?"

She laughed. "You're kind of a dork, you know that?"

"It's an honest question."

"You'll see."

She gave him directions, and instead of turning back toward Kahului, they veered toward Lahaina. When they pulled up to Tigershark Tacos, it was late enough to be almost deserted. Despite the cheesy name, they had the best Mexican food on the island. Dane grabbed a towel out of the back of the truck and they went to order.

"I usually get the chile rellenos or the veggie tamale with green sauce," she said, as they ducked under a weepy kiawe tree.

"I'm a carne asada burrito guy, myself."

At the window, before 'Iwa could even say hello, the man working stuck his whole arm and half his body out the window. "Hey, look who the cat dragged in. Nice win, bro! The whole truck was rocking when you made that last wave."

Dane reached out and shook. "Thank you, Alex."

Aurora, the owner, poked her face out, too. "*Mijo*, you da big hero. I make the regular for you, on the house." She glanced over at 'Iwa. "And Señorita 'Iwa, you two are together?"

"No," 'Iwa said.

At the same time, Dane answered, "Yes."

"I mean we are but we aren't. We are here together to eat," she said, for some reason feeling the need to clarify.

Dane seemed amused. "Whatever you say."

After ordering, they sat at a tiny table with a rooster perched on the umbrella post overhead. The temperature had dropped some, and she rubbed her bare arms for warmth.

"Why didn't you tell me you'd been here before?" she asked.

"You didn't tell me where we were going until we pulled in, and then I figured you'd know soon enough. Kama brings me here every time we surf on this side."

"I've never seen Aurora give anyone a free meal."

The woman was as shrewd as they came, running her taco truck like a drill sergeant.

"I think she has a crush on me," he said.

"Oh please, she could be your grandmother."

His gaze swept slowly across her face. "Age isn't a big deal for some people. But it doesn't matter anyway because I have my eye on someone else."

A line of heat ran up her neck, but she ignored the last part of his comment. "Auntie is seventy. How old are you?"

Dane laughed. "Maybe that's a little beyond my range. But I'm getting up there, pushing thirty."

"Amazing you can still stand up on a surfboard."

"Easy there."

When their order was ready, they walked down a short path to the beach following the leftover twilight. No one else was around and he spread out the towel, which was more bath towel than beach towel, for them to sit on. He popped open two more beers and they sat. 'Iwa on the far edge of the towel.

"So, tell me about this waterfall. I want to know what we're fighting for," Dane said, after taking a huge bite out of his burrito.

"We?"

"I'm at least trying to help, so yeah, *we*."

He had a point. "Most people don't even know it's there. It's not the biggest or the tallest, and it's way off the beaten path, but it's special for many reasons." She stopped, unsure if he deserved to know the full story.

"What makes it so special?" he asked.

"Does it need a reason, other than just being a waterfall?"

"I get the sense this is personal."

When 'Iwa closed her eyes, she could feel the cool mist lightly touching her skin, and hear the roar of the falls. She had been trailing behind her mother, keeping close and hopping on the same rocks to avoid slipping. Moss lived on all surfaces this deep in the forest. She could still see her mother's mud-spattered legs as they scaled a cluster of truck-sized boulders. When they finally reached the pool, 'Iwa was eager to jump in, but Lily grabbed her small hand and said, "This is said to be the hideaway house of the sun, where he comes to rest and recuperate. We must tread lightly."

"It is," 'Iwa said to Dane.

She blinked the memory away, took a bite and washed it down with beer. Dane inhaled his entire burrito before she was halfway done.

"Have you always been a forest nymph?" he said, changing course.

"Have you always been a sea creature?"

"I asked you first."

Opening up to Dane felt risky, and she wanted to keep things on the surface, but she found herself needing to answer. "Always. Don't get me wrong, I love the beach and I grew up as a barefoot sandy kid, but my best friend had a ranch upcountry and we used to ride horses and hike Haleakalā and do mountain things. I even got lost in the forest once and had to spend the night under a giant 'ōhi'a tree. I was cold but never scared. It was foggy and eerie and I loved it."

"How old were you?"

"Ten."

Dane inched closer to her on the towel, as though now that it was growing dark, he couldn't hear as well. "Sounds like a rite of passage to me. Did you have any big epiphanies or meet your guardian spirit?" he asked.

She looked at him to make sure he was serious. He appeared to be. "Actually I did. But I didn't realize it until later. The fog was so thick I could barely see my hand when I stuck out my arm all the way. I was inching along, watching the ground to make sure I didn't fall off any cliffs when I almost bumped into a *pueo* sitting on an old fencepost. The weird thing was, she didn't fly away when she saw me, just stared at me with the most beautiful owl eyes. There was so much intelligence in them, it floored me. It was like I suddenly saw beneath the surface to the living, breathing beings that were all around me. Every tree, every bird, every spider." She paused, remembering one of her favorite moments. "I have no idea how long I stood there, staring at this profound little creature, but it changed me."

They sat there for a moment, looking out to sea. 'Iwa sipped her beer, noticed Cassiopeia and the Pleiades amidst a now star-spotted sky.

"How did it happen for you, with the ocean?" she asked.

"That's a hard act to follow. You sure you want to hear?" he asked.

She really did.

"I do."

"When I was eight, a storm had washed all kinds of stuff onto the beach and I was down there one morning—we lived close enough to walk—and I found an intact rowboat on the beach. It was small, nothing fancy, but the oars were still in it. The water was sheet glass and I pushed that boat through the shore break and rowed around for hours. I went pretty far out, through the kelp beds and way past where I'd ever been. There were pelicans and cormorants swooping around me, a sea lion followed me for a bit, and then a white shark. I swear the fin was three feet high, and it came right up to the boat, looked up at me with a big dark orb of an eye and swam on past. I knew in my gut that it was only curious and meant me no harm. I felt no fear, only this huge sense of freedom. I was hooked after that," he said, looking at her with a wide smile.

"Did you know we have great white sharks here?" she said.

He nodded. "*Carcharodon carcharias*. No one is exactly sure why they come, but they do come. More so in winter."

"I've wondered. Maybe for a warm water vacation? My dad has seen one out fishing, a big one."

"Did you know they can grow to be over twenty feet?" he asked.

'Iwa nodded. "Did you know they have over three hundred teeth?"

"Yeah, I've seen them. When that shark swam past me, she turned to the side and I could see rows of them, prickly like cactus."

She laughed. "Okay, you win. I've never seen a shark in the water. Not even a reef shark."

Being with Dane was more fun than she wanted it to be. She had hoped to keep it purely business, but she found herself following his tangents too easily.

"I've seen more than I can count. They don't scare me."

"What does?"

He mulled it over for a while, then said with a sly grin, "You?"

She wasn't really sure what she expected him to say, but that was not it. "Are you always this dramatic?" she said, trying to keep it light.

"I'm being serious."

"You just met me."

"Fair enough," he said, looking out at the water. "Maybe the worst thing I can imagine is not being able to surf anymore. That terrifies the shit out of me."

"What about the giant waves? They don't scare you?"

"In a way, but I'm not sure scare is the right word. They energize me and excite me and give me a reason to be here. Fear is part of the equation for sure, but you learn to live with it so it becomes more of a background thing."

"How long have you been surfing?"

"I caught my first wave before I was even born. My mom surfed."

A pale shadow crossed over his face at the mention of his mom, and 'Iwa sensed something beneath the surface there.

"That explains it then," she said.

"Enough about me." He shook his head. "I came here to help you. Do you know if there are any old archaeologic sites on the property? Or anything of historic importance? That can get a project halted these days," he said, snapping his fingers.

This wasn't new information, but she appreciated it nonetheless. And liked that he was following through on his promise. That said something about him.

"Not that I know of. But what about water rights? Anything he does to that stream will affect the whole watershed below," she said.

"But if he agrees to leave the stream intact, that leaves you without a leg to stand on."

A large raindrop landed on 'Iwa's shoulder. Then another on her thigh. The metallic smell of rain hung in the air. She looked up and saw a black silhouette moving over them from the land. "We should probably go, it's going to pour pretty soon."

"I don't mind a little rain," he said.

Thunder rumbled in the distance.

"This is *pakakū* rain, the drenching kind. Trust me, we don't want to be caught in it."

As if on cue, the skies opened up. 'Iwa stuffed everything in a bag and Dane jumped to his feet, shaking out the towel. He held a hand out and she let him pull her up, light as a feather. His grip was warm, hands calloused. She stumbled in a dip in the sand, pressing a palm into his already wet chest to steady herself. He felt taut and warm and smooth, like eucalyptus in the sun, and her hand lingered. Then a flash of lightning sent them both scrambling and they booked it to the truck.

The drive back was a wet and steamy affair. Dane had to keep wiping the windshield with the damp towel, which wasn't much help. Huge mud puddles had formed in the road, and between the hard rain on the metal roof, the occasional bang of thunder and the old motor, they exchanged few words along the way. Every so often, she sensed him glancing her way.

Dane had been surprisingly nice to be around and 'Iwa found herself both wishing he'd be on Maui a little longer, and relieved he was leaving. He was not the kind of distraction she needed right now. Nor was she ready to let anyone in again, not so soon.

When they arrived at her house, 'Iwa was ready to say a fast goodbye and make a dash for it, but he turned off the engine. For a few heartbeats, they sat unmoving.

"That was bad timing with the rain," he said.

"Yeah, but rain is always a blessing."

"What did you call it? *Palaka?*"

"*Pakakū.*"

"Is it true Hawaiians have like a hundred words for rain?" he asked, shifting his body so he was facing her.

"Closer to two hundred. My mom and I used to love to make up our own names, too. Her favorite was cobweb rain, for when it was fine and misty and covered the branches in tiny droplets. Mine was tadpole rain, kind of like this."

He looked outside. "I don't know, this feels more like jelly-fish rain to me."

She laughed. "That's a new one. I like it."

They were silent a moment. 'Iwa admired the intricate patterns of water on the windshield. The cab of the truck felt like a warm cocoon and she suddenly didn't want to leave.

"I wish I wasn't flying out tomorrow," Dane finally said.

Me too, she wanted to say. There was an electricity filling up the truck, humming across her skin. If she felt it, he surely did, too.

"You'll be back before you know it," she offered.

"Are you free to get coffee in the morning? I'm buying."

Her mind raced for an answer. It felt strangely like she was walking a line between life veering one way or another. He was a perfectly good male specimen, and one who seemed to have some depth. But still, she had her own impermeable rules to live by, and a heart to be protected.

It seemed pointless to prolong the inevitable. "I wish I could, but I have to work."

"So I guess this is goodbye then."

The rain turned on even harder. An insistent roar.

"I guess so," she said.

Dane leaned over so that their faces were inches apart. There was that beachy smell again, mixed with coconut and spice. His breath was hot against her cheek. She wondered if he was going to kiss her, really kiss her, but instead he placed a hand lightly on her thigh, sending goose bumps all the way to her toes. He reached for the door and opened it for her, letting in a whoosh of cold air. His mouth was at her ear.

"This isn't the end," he whispered, before sitting back in his seat almost as if he hadn't said anything.

The words sent her heart racing. Unsure of how to respond, and not sure she trusted herself another second in his presence, she stepped out into the night.

How To Stay On Maui

Dane

Outdoor showers were one of Dane's favorite things. There was pretty much nothing a shower under the sky couldn't improve. Scalding water poured down on his shoulders and he didn't want to get out. The shower at Kama's farm was famous, surrounded in lava rock with ferns and ginger growing out of the cracks, and a wheel-sized showerhead that pulsed down fresh well water. Cool raindrops mixed in with the hot, turning the experience into one of pure Hawaiian bliss.

Kama had already taken off with a few friends to surf. Dane would leave the truck at the airport before catching his flight. Leaving Maui was always rough, but this time, he had spent the whole morning trying to come up with valid reasons to stay without losing his gig at the Manning house. *Tropical storm, food poisoning, torn muscle, canceled flight.* He was already on thin ice with Mr. Manning, and he knew none of those would fly.

He dragged himself out of the shower, and down the rock path to his shack. The old clock on the wall was permanently stuck on twelve, so he checked his phone to see if he had time to grab a coffee and maybe run into 'Iwa before he left. There was a message from Manning and his stomach twisted. **Dane, I have a quick trip to Arizona for business. Need to push back the work a bit. I'm back the 20th so see you then. Nice wave, by the way!**

Dane stared at the words and could not believe his luck. A minute later, he was on the phone with Hawaiian Airlines changing his flight.

Maui Bean was jam-packed with every girl in Pā'ia but 'Iwa. Dane found a table for one outside and waited for an hour, trying to look casual as he scrolled through his phone, reading everything he could about a place in Portugal called Nazaré. *Big Mama*. A foggy coastal town once frequented by pirates, named for a statue of Mary brought straight from Nazareth, the holy land, in the fourth century. Just about every photo he could find online was a different angle of the Forte de São Miguel Arcanjo, hovering at the edge of the tall craggy cliffs overlooking the North Atlantic. The lighthouse lantern on the roof of the fort was painted red and sat fifty meters above sea level. Which blew his mind, because in one of the photos, a wave out front seemed to be squaring off, face-to-face with the lighthouse. It must have been the angle, but damn.

Warm summers gave way to wet winters. The time to go was February and March, when massive storms hit, kicking up deadly waves and turning the ocean into a frothy cauldron. According to the fishermen who knew the coast, there was a long and deep underwater canyon, a direct pipeline from the open ocean to the sandy shallows fronting the cliffs, responsible for the monster waves. None of the locals went anywhere near it in the winter. But last year, a couple guys from O'ahu showed up and rode the wave, and now every big wave surfer in the world was chomping to get there, Dane included. He felt an upwelling deep inside. This was the one to watch.

A small bell on the Maui Bean door announced new customers, and whenever someone entered, Dane looked up, hopefully. Lots of visitors and foreigners, some locals, no 'Iwa. After an hour or so he gave up, drove to the west side, paddled out into some playful six footers and met up with the boys. Kama was on the inside getting tumbled when Dane caught his first wave.

"Brah, it really is you. I thought I was seeing things on the way out, or else someone had stolen your board," Kama said, when he finally made it back out into the lineup.

Dane rode mint green boards with brown stringers. His signature. He had a whole quiver of them.

"Me in the flesh. The job got pushed back."

"By you or Manning?"

"Manning."

Kama splashed him. "From the look on your face, I'd say you're not too worried about it." He then nodded at the set coming in and paddled off.

Dane didn't catch any waves in the set. He was too busy staring into the water, thinking about 'Iwa and wondering if he should let her know he was still here. He wavered, because it was obvious she had her guard up. She seemed like a woman on a mission, one who could take him or leave him. But on the beach last night, she had softened some, so maybe he still had a sliver of a chance.

They surfed for a few hours, until Dane was waterlogged and sun roasted. By the time they got out, the waves had dropped and the crowd had thickened. On the inside, a whole contingent of girls sidestepped their way to the front of their longboards, hanging five and ten. Hawai'i had more talent in the water per square inch than anywhere he'd been. The warm water helped.

He waited until five o'clock to pull up to 'Iwa's house. A truck was in the driveway, dripping wet. He stopped behind it and turned off the engine, checking himself in the mirror and trying to tamp down the section of hair that always stood straight up.

"Hey, what are you doing here?"

The voice startled him. 'Iwa had come around to his side

and was standing next to the truck, hose in hand, woven hat on her head, wearing rubber slippers.

"Oh, there you are," he said. He looked around for the dog. "Where's the man-eater?"

'Iwa turned to him and sprayed his windshield. "Koa is not a man-eater, he's a big puppy."

Dane instinctively ducked. "Sorry. Where's Koa?"

"Dad took him to the beach," she said, making no move toward him and getting back to rubbing down the truck. "I thought you left."

"I was supposed to, but my job got pushed back."

Dane hopped out and picked up a brush from the ground. The rusted rims on her truck were stained brown from the red dirt, and there was so much grime in them it was pointless to even try. But he began scrubbing nonetheless. She kept working in silence for a while.

"Is there something you need, or did you come to help me wash my car?" she said, almost smiling.

"It looks like I'll be staying another week, so I was thinking maybe you could use more help with your waterfall," he said.

"Won't you be surfing the whole time?"

"Not the whole time, no." He paused. "And I had a nice time with you last night."

He wanted to say more, but was worried about scaring her off. The words settled between them as 'Iwa rinsed out the truck bed, hosing out leaves and twigs and branches, rocks and shell fragments. She seemed intent on avoiding eye contact.

"Don't you have family to go back to?" she asked.

He shook his head. "My dad's out of the picture and my mom does her own thing, so I'm pretty much on my own."

No need to mention he hadn't spoken to his mom in ages.

Her brow pinched up and she finally stopped working. "I'm sorry to hear that."

Dane was used to it by now, but there was still a sliver of

sadness attached to it all. In that way that you thought you had removed the splinter but months later, it would emerge unexpectedly, poking a hole in your skin and hurting all over again. That was pretty much his life.

"It is what it is. I was lucky in that regard. My second time to Hawai'i, at Christmastime, I stayed at the Mizuno farm picking berries for pies, digging an *imu* to cook the pig, scouring the rocks along the shore for *'opihi*, and wrapping *laulau*. It was the first time I experienced how it felt to be part of a big family. A dream come true for a kid from Ventura with an absentee mom and no other family to speak of," he said.

"The Mizunos are good people."

She smiled at him then, a quick flash of perfect teeth.

"What are you doing tomorrow morning?" he asked.

Her hand was on her hip now. "This feels like a loaded question."

Dane stood up and faced her, so there would be no mistaking his intentions. "Okay, let me rephrase it then. Would you like to do something with me later? Or tomorrow?"

"I work later, and tomorrow. I have a meeting in the morning and I have to cover a shift at Uncle's after that," she said.

"How about the next day?"

"I work all week."

He felt his chances slipping away, so he changed tactics. "I'll just help you wash your truck then, and be on my way."

'Iwa raised an eyebrow. "Sure, thanks."

"Dish soap and baking soda do wonders on hubcaps. Do you have any?" he said.

"Nah, don't worry about that. I'm heading out in the field again day after tomorrow so there's no point."

"Where are you headed?"

"East side, up *mauka*."

"Alone or with a group?"

"Alone."

She wasn't making this easy, so he threw out one last-ditch attempt. "Maybe you'd like company?" he asked, then quickly added, "If I were to tag along, I could gain a better understanding of what you're trying to save, and we could brainstorm tactics. Theoretically, of course."

'Iwa walked over and turned off the hose. Her wet shorts clung to her legs and her face glistened, making her freckles stand out. She turned to him. "Theoretically, if you were to come, would you promise not to tell anyone?"

"Theoretically, I don't even know anyone named 'Iwa."

She surprised him by saying, "Sure, why not? Be here at six thirty the day after tomorrow. I'll text you what to bring."

The Oli

'Iwa

'Iwa had no idea why she'd agreed to let Dane come with her to the valley. Maybe it was because of his sheer doggedness, or how he'd sounded so grateful for the Mizunos for taking him in, and she felt a tenderness for him. But more realistically, it was probably because having someone with her in the forest meant two sets of eyes, and two sets of eyes were always better than one when you were in the field. Not to mention her burning need to halt Jones and his project. At least that's what she told herself. She texted him the list.

Wear: long pants, sun shirt, hiking shoes, hat
Bring: backpack with two bottles of water, bug juice, energy bars, small binoculars, rubber slippers, raincoat, extra socks.
Be ready for anything.

Taking Dane into the back valleys alone was probably not the wisest thing to do, but it was too late now. She had plants to count, water levels to note and birds to find. Dane could be put to good use.

In the soft morning quiet, she heard his truck coming a mile away. He was early, good. She stuffed the two sandwiches her dad made into her pack, along with a big bag of trail mix and two underripe bananas, kissed Koa all over his face and went out to greet the day. Dane was standing by his truck like a kindergartener waiting on his carpool ride. His jeans looked brand new, creases and all.

"Morning," he said.

"Good morning. Is that your hiking outfit?"

He looked down at himself, then up at her. "You said pants."

She held back a laugh. "I didn't say jeans. You'll be hot and miserable in those, and give yourself a rash."

There was nothing worse than the inexperienced hiker getting a rash when there were still ten miles to go. It had happened before and 'Iwa did not want to be responsible.

"It was either jeans or cords. I don't own any other pants, except for my khakis, which are in my closet on the mainland," he said.

"Hang on."

She ran back inside and found an old pair of her dad's camouflage hunting pants. His waist had outgrown them, but 'Iwa was working on changing that. Dane was pure lean muscle, but he was also tall. They could work.

"Here, try these."

He took the pants and looked around. "You want me to drop my pants here?"

"I'll close my eyes."

She turned around and put her hands over her face. A minute went by.

"Okay, safe to open." He held his thumb between the pants and his waist. "A little big but better than me being that kook you took hiking who had to be helicoptered out because he couldn't walk anymore."

She couldn't help noticing his oblique muscles, which looked to be made of stone yet were extremely touchable, fading from mocha to whale bone white. 'Iwa tore her eyes away and dropped her backpack in the back of the truck. "Good, because helicopters can't land where we're going."

Driving the road to Hāna early in the morning always felt like a spiritual experience. Rays of sun shot through a mostly cloudy sky, lighting up blue circles in the ocean. In places, you felt suspended between green jungle and the deep blue sea. Or shallow black sand bays. There were more bushes and trees crammed per square mile than anywhere on earth, or so it seemed. Shaggy cliffs lined up and down the coast, and 'Iwa and Dane were out before the rental cars descended.

"So, what's our plan today? Do I get to see this waterfall of yours?" Dane asked.

"Not today. Today I'm collecting data and checking on an area we've been reforesting halfway up the mountain. You'll see waterfalls, but not Waikula."

"I'm guessing this isn't in the Maui trails guidebook," he said.

"Nope. Most of those trails are short. That's one thing about so many tourists—they want it easy. Most of them won't stray a hundred yards from their cars. So, if you're willing to sweat, you can avoid them."

"*Tourist* is a dirty word around here, huh?"

"Sometimes."

"Do you think of me as a tourist?" Dane asked.

"Not really. You stay with a local family, and you've gotten to know the ocean in a way that most people never would. That elevates you."

He laughed. "Ah, so there are tourist tiers."

"Most definitely."

"If it helps my case, I'm a card-carrying member of the Surfrider Foundation. I do beach cleanups on the regular," he offered.

She couldn't help but smile. "That moves you one more tier up."

As they snaked along, she told him the names of the *ahupua'a*—the land divisions. Mokupapa, Waipi'oiki, Waipi'onui, Hanehoi. Dane stayed quiet, and she glanced over at him to see if he was even listening. His head was cocked and he was staring at her, the corner of his mouth flicked up. She looked back at the road, fast.

"What?" she said, flipping down the visor so she wasn't blinded by the sun, which was now shooting out from behind the clouds.

"Nothing. Just admiring how much you know about this place and how much it obviously means to you. There's something magical about this island that gets under your skin. I have a feeling it'll be even more so after today with you."

She shrugged. "Maybe. Maybe not."

"What is that supposed to mean?" he asked.

Most people came to Hawai'i for the beaches, not the mountains, Dane included.

"Just that these rainforests aren't for everyone. You might change your mind and that's fine."

"Is this a test? To see if I can hack it?"

She hadn't planned it that way, but it *would* be a good gauge. Between the miles of mud and mosquitos, the slippery rocks and dizzying cliffs, you could tell a lot about a person.

"Don't forget, you invited yourself along," she said.

The trailhead was up a long dirt road, through four gates, across two streams. It was at this point in the journey, stretching deeper into the forest, where she always began to feel like she was leaving everything else behind. Increasing crowds, suffocating grief over her mother, concern about her father and his health—or whatever the flavor was that day.

Dane rode in the back of the truck and swung off the pipe racks to open each gate. She was glad he was in the back, because this transition was important to her, and she wasn't sure he would understand. He seemed to be enjoying himself, but she still hadn't told him about the last gate.

As they approached, she saw a figure emerge from the bushes like a ghost. Dressed in fatigues head to toe, he moved to the middle of the gate and stood with arms crossed. A long machete hung from his belt. 'Iwa slowed to a stop and waved. He walked up to her window, unsmiling.

"Morning, Kala," she said.

The air was ripe with the tangy smell of *pakalōlō* buds.

All she got in return was a chin nod. "Who's the passenger?"

"Dane is helping me with the Hana'iwa'iwa land."

"Did you clear him with the boss?"

She gave him her best smile. "No, this was a last-minute invite. You know I wouldn't bring just anyone up here, though. You don't need to worry about him."

Kala looked back at Dane, and 'Iwa willed Dane not to say anything stupid, like *hey, bro.* Dane was now sitting on the side of the truck bed, visible in her rearview mirror. Their eyes met, and he nodded to Kala.

"Howzit," Dane said.

At that moment, she saw recognition dawning on Kala's face, and he did something she'd never see him do before. He reached out and shook Dane's hand.

"Dane Parsons, nice to meet you. I'm Kala," he said.

Dane kept cool. "Likewise. Looks like God's country up here."

"Yep, and we like to keep it that way."

Kala opened the gate, gun bulging out from under his shirt, and let them on through. At the trailhead, a small mud-packed clearing, Dane swung out lightning fast and opened her squeaky door for her.

"You could get high just driving through his land. Who is that guy?" he said.

"Someone you don't want to mess with."

"You two seem like you're on good terms," Dane said.

"He tolerates our team and we turn a blind eye to their weed operation. He calls his brother the boss, but I think Kala is really behind the whole thing. My dad went to school with his brother, Sonny, which might be the only reason we got permission to go through their land."

Dane leaned down and tied his shoelace. "Hawai'i, the land of who you know," he mumbled.

He wasn't wrong. Connections here were worth more than gold. And being able to come through this property allowed them access to a section of Haleakalā that would be impossible to reach otherwise.

When they had gathered their gear and put their packs on, they walked to where two tall koa trees arched over the trail, moon sliver–shaped leaves covering the ground. 'Iwa inhaled their woodsy scent, then stopped Dane.

"This is where we ask for permission," she said.

"Is there yet another gatekeeper?"

"The forest. We ask the forest."

Dane adjusted his strap and nodded. "Right."

'Iwa explained. "When we enter the forest here, we ask the trees and the plants and the streams and even the rocks for entry into their world. And also for protection. It's like a two-way street, we take care of them, and they take care of us."

"You do this every time?"

'Iwa nodded. "It's like how surfers touch the water and bless themselves before they go in the ocean. Do you do that every time?"

"Every time I paddle out."

"Just follow my lead. We chant the *oli* three times. I'll say it once first, and then the next two times, feel free to join in, call and answer style."

Dane got a nervous look, but covered it up with a smile. She reached out for his hand and they faced the forest. Despite the sunshine on their shoulders, the air was cool and smelled faintly of rain and clouds. Even though 'Iwa had done this hundreds of times, the words never lost their power. And as always, they took her back to that very first day with her mother. She took a deep breath and began.

E hō mai
ka 'ike mai luna mai ē
O nā mea huna no'eau
O nā mele ē
E hō mai
E hō mai
E hō mai ē

'Iwa always chanted with her whole heart, but this time, she added a little extra. A new guest to the forest should have a proper initiation. At the end of the first round, she squeezed his hand and glanced over at him. He was staring at the ground. She chanted the next round, voice lifting up into the branches and mingling with the rustle of the leaves and the whoosh of the wind. The birds joined in. Dane didn't.

When this round ended, she felt him shift his weight and exhale. His palm was sweating. She sang the first few lines alone, and then on the second *e hō mai*, Dane jumped in. His voice was surprisingly strong, calling out like he really meant it. Enough so that 'Iwa swore the trees bent down and motioned them in with their branches. The birds quieted, and a misty rain fell from the blue sky.

When it was over, Dane held on to her hand for an extra beat, and 'Iwa felt like she had to pry her fingers away from his.

She stepped away. "I think you've been approved."

Dane was shaking his head. "Wow. Just, wow."

"These chants are powerful."

"I have chicken skin all over my body. See, look," he said, holding up his arm so she could see the still-raised bumps.

"That's a good sign. Getting chicken skin means you're tuned in."

"Doing my best."

They hiked for an hour without stopping, 'Iwa leading at a good clip. Dane kept up and didn't complain, asking questions here and there. She noted a lot of rooting areas—evidence of wild pig, and made a few notes, but they still weren't in native forest yet, which was where most of her work took place. At nine on the nose, they reached the first pond.

She set down her pack and took a long drink of water. "Make sure you hydrate."

Dane kept his pack on. "I'm good."

"With this humidity, you can lose a lot of fluid, trust me."

He took out his bottle and drank.

"We cross here," she said, pointing to the pond.

They were in a narrow gorge with steep walls on both sides—too steep to scale. She could see him searching for a way around the pond.

"We go through it. Put our packs on our heads," she said.

The pond was twenty feet across and deep in the middle, with a small waterfall on the other side. Having a heavy pack on your head made it tough swimming, but it was the only way. And it was also why 'Iwa used a dry bag–style backpack in these mountains. You always came out wet. Even with no rain. Dane took off his pack and set it to the side, bending down to roll up his pants.

"No, silly. Take your pants off," she said.

He gave her a look.

She quickly added, "I mean, you can't swim in those. Don't you have your surf shorts?"

He was trying to suppress a smile. "Yeah, I brought everything you said to."

"Meet me on the other side, then," she said, not bothering to wait for him to change.

'Iwa stripped down to her bikini, stuffed everything in her pack and was swimming across in the icy green water without looking back. She took note of the high water level, and had to kick hard to make headway against the strong flow. When she reached the other side, she stood on a submerged rock, tossed her pack onto a small ledge, and hoisted herself up with help from a guava branch. She turned, expecting Dane to still be on the other side, but he was right behind her.

He did exactly as she had, without the branch. Instead, he placed both hands on the ledge and lifted himself up with ease. The rock ledge was only a foot wide and they were crammed up against each other. Warmth emanated off his skin, and she was tempted to lean into him and absorb some of his heat.

"Feels like snow water," he said, teeth chattering.

"Sometimes it is snow water. The watershed here is from the top of Haleakalā, ten thousand twenty-three feet. But not today."

Clothes back on, they scaled the side of a six-foot cliff and followed a narrow trail that crisscrossed the stream for the next mile or so. Over the years, she had become adept at rock hopping, and knowing which path to take across the water. Now Dane was having trouble keeping up with her. She stopped every so often to let him catch up.

"Part forest nymph, part goat," he said, after teetering on a small, mossy rock in the middle and making a four-foot leap to reach her side.

"It's just practice, like anything else. Pretend you're surfing. When you're on a wave, you pick your line before you've even moved down the face, don't you?" she said.

"Second nature."

"Same thing here. I look for the dry rocks that look most stable, and connect the dots in my mind before I even cross. Try it."

"The theory of river crossing, I like it," he said, obviously amused.

'Iwa felt her cheeks flush. "When you do something often enough, theories arise, what can I say?"

"Do you have a theory for everything?" he said.

She crossed her arms over her still-wet chest. "I'm a scientist, so yeah, I guess I do."

Dane stared at her for a moment, gaze accidentally—or not—falling down her body, then back up to meet her eyes. 'Iwa turned and continued on without another word. Ten minutes later, she could feel him breathing down her neck. Most men she knew did not excel at taking advice from a woman. Dane actually listened.

When the valley came to a dead end, they took a switchback up the steep side, through thick uluhe ferns clawing at their pants. In some areas, the trail disappeared. Sun pelted down on them now that they were out of the lowland canopy and into the Montane. At the top, they were rewarded with a wide view of forest sinking into the sea. They took in the sight and enjoyed a cooling breeze for a few moments.

Dane whistled. "I can see why you love your job."

"None of this feels like work to me. I'd probably be doing it even if they didn't pay me, which is a good thing, because I hardly make anything anyway," she said.

"Nature and music, they seem like good bedfellows, especially with your talent. Have you ever recorded anything?" he asked.

Songs written, yes. Recordings, no.

"Once, and I hated it," she said.

He moved a little closer, turning his hat around backward and looking into her eyes. "Why is that?"

His proximity made her fidgety. "I just want to play in the moment."

He nodded. "I get that."

She steered him back to why they were here. "Now that we're in native territory, this is where our work starts. We are trying to get a few partnerships together to fence off several areas in this watershed to protect from ungulates. See that ridge and the valley below? That's one section that has been identified, and you and I are going to count species and maybe collect seeds."

Seeds were really at the heart of it all. The keepers of life itself.

"Ungulates?" Dane asked.

"Pigs, goats—anything with hooves. They are forest destroyers."

On the ridge, she showed him the gnarled 'ōhi'a lehua trees with their twisted branches and scarlet flowers. "Most often you'll see them red up here, but lehua blossoms come in yellow and orange, too. Even white, though only one person I know claims to have actually seen a white one—the ghost lehua."

Once in the zone, which had been marked by red tape on branches, she explained which species they were counting. "And keep an eye out for honeycreepers—forest birds—too, we are now in their habitat," she told him.

The counting went well, and Dane followed her instructions. The only problem was, he couldn't keep the ferns straight. Hapu'u, 'ama'u, palapalai, 'iwa'iwa.

"Wait a minute. Are you named after this fern?" he asked as he ran his hand over the deep green lacy leaves of an 'iwa'iwa growing beneath a rocky ledge.

"I am."

"All this time I was thinking 'Iwa bird," he said.

"That's because most girls named 'Iwa are named after the bird. But not me. My mom was a plant nerd."

There were so many varieties that he kept mixing up their names. Finally, she told him to stick to the trees. He also kept slipping and falling because he was wearing skater shoes with no traction. It was her fault, since she'd failed to notice until they were already at the trailhead. She should have brought an extra pair of tabis like she and all the crew wore.

"You didn't tell me there was black ice up here," he said, after the fourth time down, caked in mud.

"We call it brown ice."

Dane had mud slathered on his entire backside and forearms, with smears across his face and neck. He was being a good sport, but 'Iwa felt bad for him, so before they stopped to rest and eat, decided to take a side trip down to the stream. Keeping one eye on the mist inching down the mountain, she led him down yet another steep trail.

"Sounds like a lot of water," Dane said, close on her heels.

"It must be pouring higher up the mountain, even though you can't see it. See that mist? The clouds hide all kinds of things," she said.

At the bottom, the stream was running high and fast. Dane immediately started peeling off his shirt. On the rocks where they stood, there were sticks and debris from a recent flood.

'Iwa stopped him. "It's not safe. This is flash flood weather."

"But all this mud on me, I stink."

"Better stinky and alive, than swept downstream so your body turns up in the ocean. Come on."

In The Clouds

Dane

On a windswept bluff, they sat under a tree with flapping waxy leaves, eating mac nut butter, banana and honey sandwiches on fresh sourdough 'Iwa's dad had baked the night before. 'Iwa produced several *liliko'i* she'd picked at the start of the trail, cut them open with a Leatherman, and squeezed their juice into the sandwich.

Dane was still mostly covered in mud and sticky with sweat. "So where is your waterfall from here?" he asked.

She pointed. "Two valleys over, at the edge of that high plateau. See the gulch?"

"Is it as hard to get to as where we are now?"

"Harder. Hana'iwa'iwa is the most difficult to reach watershed in the area," she said.

Not only had they swum across ponds and crossed the stream seventy times, they'd had to scale a hillside and then travel along a one-foot-wide trail with a several-hundred-foot drop on both sides.

"Define watershed. You keep using that word, and I'm embarrassed to say I don't know exactly what it means," he said.

"It's an area of land where all the rainwater collects into a common outlet. Here, it starts in springs and streams and then flows to the ocean. The beauty of a forested watershed is it works like a sponge. Roots, moss and an underground network of fungi form an invisible reservoir that holds the rain for future use," she said, brushing her hair away from her mouth so she could take another bite of her sandwich.

'Iwa seemed to be tolerating him—just barely. Dane had apparently asked too many questions while they were supposed to be counting plants, but he couldn't help himself. There was just so much to take in here.

"And the eco resort would be on one side of the valley?" he asked.

"Yeah, it runs from the stream all the way over to that next ridge. We found out yesterday that he's hired a notoriously questionable firm to do his Environmental Impact Statement, so chances are they'll find no issues with his project," she told him, with a faraway look in her eye.

"It's about more than just Hana'iwa'iwa, isn't it," he said gently.

She gave him a sad smile. "The land is our grandmother, and as such, she deserves to be treated with respect. All of it."

Just then 'Iwa grew very still. Dane followed suit, though he wasn't sure why. Then, a flock of tiny yellow birds descended on them, filling the tree overhead like feathered ornaments. The birds chirped and warbled to each other for a minute or so, then took off for another tree. Their miniature wings made a distinct whirring sound.

"What were those?" he asked, when it was safe to talk again.

"Maui 'Alauahio. They're endangered, like almost everything else up here."

He let her words sink in, then said, "Thank you for bringing me with you today. I know I'm probably more of a bother than a help, but I feel like I'm sitting here in an enchanted forest."

"You are."

"Tell me more about Jones. How much you know about him?" Dane said, struggling to keep up.

"I'm not sure when he came here, maybe twenty years ago?

On the outside, he's a very dapper and charming guy, and talks a good talk, but I would never trust him."

"What else has he done here?"

"Are you familiar with Hanameli Bay?"

"The hotel?"

She flinched. "It wasn't always a hotel, obviously. It used to be the most beautiful and peaceful cove on this whole side of the island. It was Jones who put up the hotel. My mom and her friends fought it, as did so many people, but he got it pushed through. He's smart and slick, and puts on a good face, makes like he cares about Maui but he doesn't. That hotel made him rich and yet he still wants more. He did a few projects on the Big Island, and now he's back."

"So you're following in your mom's footsteps." Her fight now made even more sense.

"I guess you could say that."

"She must have been an incredible woman."

He envied her. Two parents who she clearly thought the world of.

"She was." 'Iwa sat quietly for a moment, then added, "Not only was she talented and smart, but she was really good at seeing the big picture. Jones had a lot of people convinced he was going to do so much good here. Give people jobs and support the community and offer beach club memberships. He was going to *make nature better*, or something dumb like that. My mom and her friends could see through him."

"Did he make good on any promises?" Dane asked.

"Of course not. A few people got jobs, but he imported a lot of his workers and paid them poorly, and his beach club memberships were too expensive for anyone to afford. Then we also had to fight for beach access."

"Sounds like a real winner."

"He's stream slime." She looked past him, then hopped up and held out a hand. "We should get going, the clouds are moving in fast."

Dane took her hand and let her pull him up. They gathered all their gear and started off down the mountain at a good pace. A few minutes later, they were running. They made it partway down the narrow ridge—and still had a few more to traverse—when the clouds caught up, a cool blast of white silently smudging them out. Dane could barely see his own feet. A good thing 'Iwa was wearing a red hat, or else she'd have vanished, too.

"Reminds me of being in the redwoods back home when the fog rolls in," he said.

"I should have seen it coming."

"What's the worst that could happen?" he said.

"Getting lost."

He could think of worse things than being lost up here with 'Iwa.

"We won't get lost, then."

"It's easier than you think in this kind of fog, and trust me, if we get lost up here, we are screwed. I know people who have disappeared and others who've spent days going in circles. So, stay close."

Her voice was muted and faraway. Fog distorted sound, as anyone born and bred on the California coast knew. It reminded him of his mom. *You have to rely on your animal senses, and feel the waves coming before you see them. The ability is in here already,* she would say, tapping on his salty head as they stood on the beach, pulling on their stiff, secondhand wetsuits and getting ready to paddle into a white void.

She had been right, and he credited her for his sixth sense in the ocean. She may not have been a good mom in many ways, but she forged in him an inner strength—the kind of scrappiness a boy can only learn when he has to depend mainly on himself, and the idea that above all else, the ocean was a sanctuary.

Memories like these burned in the hole Belinda had left in him. Moms were meant to be counted on, and if you couldn't count on your own mother, who could you count on?

"Dane?"

He could hear 'Iwa's voice, but couldn't see her.

"Be careful, we turn down the switchback here…oh wait, this isn't it," she said, as the fog swallowed her words.

"Wait up, I'm losing you," he called.

A minute later, he almost walked into her. She was holding something and she reached out to him. "Hold out your hand. I know this seems weird, but it's our fog protocol." She tied a narrow rope around his wrist, her palms cool and clammy. "There, now we can't get separated."

He started to imagine finding a dry cave and having to keep her warm overnight. But his little daydream was sorely interrupted when he slipped and fell on his butt again. When he got back on his feet, 'Iwa turned them around. This time he led, and they followed the narrow pig trail back the way they'd come.

"Look carefully for the main trail. We can't have gone far," she said, tension in her voice.

He stopped. "Maybe we can do your chant again. Ask the forest for help?"

'Iwa almost bumped up against him, and this time, he reached out for her hand. Right now, this felt like the most natural thing to do.

"I like it," she said, close enough to kiss.

E hō mai…

In the clouds, her voice came from all directions. Dane joined in where he could, remembering a few lines from earlier, and following her lead. As they stood on this remote ridge in a blinding whiteout, chanting words as old as the wind, he swore he felt a shift in her. She leaned in closer. He gripped her hand tighter. She gripped back.

Gone Surfing

'Iwa

On the weekend, Dane and Kama had persuaded 'Iwa to go surfing with them, and she found herself riding shotgun across the island, heading to Honolua Bay. Being with both of them felt safer than being alone with Dane. After their day in the forest, and being literally tied to him, she'd been thinking about him way more than she ought to. And while she knew she shouldn't keep hanging out with him—what was the point, really?—she couldn't quite put a stop to it.

Kama was driving, and as they passed through old Lahaina town, 'Iwa admired the sprawling canopy of the banyan tree—an old friend whose lofty branches she hadn't visited in a long time. Kama and Dane were in a debate about which wave you would pick if you could only surf one wave the rest of your life. Men sounding like boys. Surfing kept people young.

"Cloudbreak," Dane said, confidently.

"What about Honolua?"

"Too crowded."

"We're talking purely about the wave itself, forget crowds," Kama said.

"Still, Cloudbreak."

Fiji's most famous wave.

"What about Sunset?" Kama asked.

"A close second. I'd take Sunset over Honolua, sorry, I know she's your fave."

"When you're eighty will you be surfing Cloudbreak?" Kama asked.

'Iwa turned around and looked at Dane, who was looking out the window at the windmills.

"Unless I'm dead," he said, matter-of-factly, meeting her gaze and winking.

'Iwa had seen pictures of Cloudbreak, hollow, with a shallow, jagged reef on the inside, and couldn't imagine any eighty-year-old men out there.

Kama was practically bouncing off the seat as he drove. "What about Pe'ahi? You think we'll be surfing Pe'ahi when we're eighty?"

"Why not?" Dane reached up and squeezed 'Iwa's shoulder, letting his hand rest there and sending spirals of heat running down her arm. "But I want to know about 'Iwa. What would be your wave?"

"I'm going with Kama. Honolua. *Especially* with no one else out."

Crowds nowadays were part of the reason she rarely surfed. Not only were they a nuisance, they were dangerous. Half the people out there were clueless as dead fish and would either sit right in front of you or run you over if you weren't watchful.

When they arrived, the waves were shoulder high and glassy, with a crowd to go along with it. 'Iwa took one look and was tempted to stay on the beach, but the boys were so excited, it rubbed off. And she had to admit, she wanted to get in the water with Dane and see what all the fuss was about.

When Dane unloaded the boards from the racks, he sagged under the weight of her longboard. "This thing is a beast. What does it weigh, forty pounds?"

Full of dents and dings, the board had seen better days. "Go easy there, I love this board."

"I'm down to trade if you want," he offered.

"No, thank you," she said.

There was something comforting about riding her old, yel-
lowed surfboard. It made surfing easy when you knew a board
so well, even as infrequently as she surfed. It had been her father's
board, and he passed it on to her as he did all of his old boards.

"Roger. I get it."

Out in the lineup, Kama and Dane worked their way into
position, while 'Iwa hung on the inside. She saw Dane looking for her, then motion her out when he caught her eye. She
stayed put. She had surfed here a hundred times and did not
need his help. Then a wave came and she caught it. Not the best
wave, but it felt good to clear the cobwebs off. On the way back
out, a set rolled in and Kama caught the first wave, Dane the
second. 'Iwa stopped paddling and sat up to watch.

He was on his feet almost before he was on the wave, and he
cruised down the face in no hurry, easing forward and back,
making a few loose carves. His movements were so fluid, it
appeared he and the board and the wave were all one, with a
trail of whitewater snaking behind him. And then, as the wave
got more pitchy, he picked up speed and—wham—smacked
the lip with such force it was like he was pulling Gs. Again,
wham. 'Iwa was close enough to see every muscle in his back
and torso tense under the force.

Big wave surfing and small wave surfing were two different
worlds, and these waves were small, but she could tell why Dane
was worshipped by so many. Good surfers were commonplace.
Above them you had the more elite professionals who trained
like maniacs, and on top of that, you had the rare few natural-
born watermen—or women. Some well-known, others not so
much. It became apparent to 'Iwa, from just this one ride, that
Dane was a member of that last ineffable category of wave rider.

The three of them spent the next three hours talking story and
sharing waves. Sometimes one on a wave, sometimes three—

party-wave style. Dane and Kama were both generous, and let 'Iwa drop in on them, for which she was grateful. She could hold her own on the wave, but she was rusty at jockeying for position and being in the right spot. There was always a hierarchy, and it helped to have friends out. Especially friends who ripped.

When they let her off at her house late that afternoon, sunburned and salty, Dane invited her to join them later at Kama's farm for dinner and a bonfire with a few friends.

"I should hang out with my dad, he has the day off, but thank you for a fun time," she said, feeling torn.

Her dad only had one day off a week, and this was it.

"Bring your dad," he said, the side of his mouth ticking up. "You won't regret it, I promise."

If he was trying to undo her, it worked, and 'Iwa made the mistake of looking away from his face. Her eyes landed on his chest, which his baby blue T-shirt clung to all too well.

"Maybe," she said. "It's up to him."

After saying goodbye, and giving Koa a peanut butter biscuit, she poked her head in the living room. "Hey, Dad."

"How was it?" he said, keeping his eye on a reporter standing in a snowstorm on the East Coast.

"The surf was fun, you would have loved it."

A half-empty bag of boiled peanuts and a can of Budweiser sat on the side table next to him.

"I bet you got some looks, surfing with Dane Parsons," he said.

"He's almost as good as you."

That got a laugh. "In my dreams."

Her father was actually a really good surfer with a laid-back style and a talent for getting the best waves. He also was friends with everyone in the water, and was out there to talk story as much as surf. Surfing had always been his social hour. But ever since they'd lost Lily, Eddie's life had consisted of three things: work, fish and watch TV. He rarely hung out with his friends anymore, even after fishing. And he never surfed. 'Iwa understood, but also worried about his world getting smaller and smaller.

"If we go again, come with us," she said, hoping it could be a way to get him back in the water.

A thick pause, and he turned to look at her. "So what's going on with you two?"

"Nothing."

"Don't nothing me, 'Iwa'iwa. I wasn't born yesterday."

"Just friends. He's a nice guy and he wants to help, that's it," she said, as much for herself as for her father.

"You gonna see him again?"

"Actually, he and Kama invited us to a BBQ at the farm tonight. Will you come?"

"Thanks, but I'm sure you don't want your old man cramping your style."

She crossed her arms and settled into the sagging couch. "I'm not going unless you go with me." And she meant it.

"Come on, 'Iwa, go and have a good time. Lord knows you need it."

"What's that supposed to mean?"

"Just that you spend all your time working, and part of that's my fault, I know, but you should be out there enjoying yourself more," he said, his voice trailing off. "Ever since Mom died."

Those words were a punch to her gut.

"I could say the same for you. You *never* do anything fun."

He sat up and put his hand on her knee. "Okay, okay. I'll go because I want you to go. What time do we leave?"

She suspected it had a little bit to do with Dane being there, but she'd take it.

"Six o'clock."

It was a big win, and 'Iwa felt more like the parent than the kid, but you adapted. Everything in the natural world did in one way or another.

★ ★ ★

Once at the farm, 'Iwa flitted about, catching up with friends she hadn't seen in a while, and every time she glanced around to find her father, he was talking with Dane or Kama or both. He had a beer in his hand, and a few times, she even caught him laughing. Kama's grandparents were old-school Hawai'i, while Kama was a bit of a foodie. So they ate BBQ ribs and mac salad along with arugula pesto pizza with fire-roasted tomatoes.

Dane sat next to her, a mountain of food on his plate. "Your dad said he'd hire me at Uncle's."

'Iwa almost spit out her food. "Doing what?"

"We were talking about the restaurant business, and how hard it is to find good help. I told him I often think about moving here, and he said if I did, I had a job waiting tables."

It was dark, but his face was lit up by string lights in a way that accented his cheekbones.

"Trust me, you don't want to work for my dad," she said, then caught herself. "Not that you actually would."

"Why not?"

She took a big drink of water, thirsty from being in the ocean. "Dane, be real, you're not going to move here and get a job at Uncle's, so it doesn't even matter."

He winked. "You never know, but now I'm curious."

"Because Dad can be a bit of a drill sergeant. And just because he lives and breathes Uncle's, he expects his employees to, too. Never mind half of them are under twenty-five and here to windsurf and make just enough cash for a tin roof over their heads and a few smoothies a day."

Dane smiled. "The Hawaiian dream, alive and well."

"It's a fake dream for many, but whatever."

He ignored her comment.

"Your dad reminds me of a Duke Kahanamoku type, Mr. Aloha. How did he and your mom meet?"

'Iwa kept her answer brief. "My mom used to sing in Waikiki at a restaurant on the beach."

When she didn't go on, Dane asked, "Did he work there too?"

"No. Dad and some friends came in after surfing and had some drinks, and he waited until she was done and went up and talked to her. The next day, he took her surfing and the rest is history."

He didn't say a word to that. Just sat there for a few blinks. The parallels of their story—if you could even call it a story—and her parents' were not lost on her.

'Iwa tried to fill the silence. "My mom had a beautiful voice. She was a much better singer than me."

"Sounds kind of familiar," Dane said, his turned face half lit.

"Yes, it's a common one here in Hawai'i. The romantic notion of a beach in Waikiki with Tiki torches and hula girls. But my mom was singing bluegrass."

She was babbling now, and she knew it.

"Were they happy together?" Dane asked.

"Very."

"I'm so sorry, 'Iwa. Your mom must have been a real powerhouse of a woman."

"She was."

'Iwa bit into her pizza because she wasn't in the mood to talk about her mom right now. The idea of Dane moving to Hawai'i was far-fetched, and there was no point in even thinking about it.

"When do you leave?" she asked.

"Day after tomorrow. I wish—"

Kama's tutu appeared at his side. "Sorry to interrupt. Can I borrow you to help move tables?" she asked Dane.

'Iwa watched him move away, noticing that he walked on the balls of his feet slightly. His hands were shoved in his pockets and his jeans hung a little too low. He reached back and tugged one side up, then turned and caught her watching. 'Iwa startled, then had to smile when he blew her a kiss.

As the night progressed, she could feel Dane's eyes keeping track of her moves. It almost felt as though the rope that had held them together in the forest was still attached.

At some point, a blonde woman appeared next to Dane and slid her arm around his waist. She set her huge owl eyes on him, and smiled. 'Iwa's whole body tensed. Small as a pixie, with a haircut to match, this was the woman from the first night at Uncle's. The one who had nuzzled his neck. 'Iwa slid back and into a tree shadow and watched.

By the way they spoke to each other, she could tell they knew each other well. But just how well, it was hard to tell. Not that it was any of her business. Then, from across the lawn, the sound of ukulele strumming caught her attention and she headed that way, happy for a reason to tear herself away.

"'Iwa!" Dane called.

She turned to see him waving her over.

"Yeah?"

"Come for a sec," he said.

'Iwa reluctantly went.

"I'd like you to meet Hope, one of my tow-in partners," he said.

This miniature person was a tow-in partner?

Hope gave her a once-over and said, "You're the singer."

"It's nice to meet you, Hope," 'Iwa said flatly, even though to be perfectly honest, it wasn't.

"Hope and I go way back, we met on the north shore when we were both helping out with the Keiki contest," Dane said. "She's like my little sister."

Of course. Hope Ballentine, well-known surfer in her own right, from Kaua'i. 'Iwa knew of her. She was compact and strong, bordering on masculine, but with pretty almond eyes and high cheekbones. She wrapped her arm around his waist. "One of my favorite people in the world. Dane Parsons is the real deal."

Something about seeing Hope's arm around Dane made 'Iwa want to swat it away, and wipe that cute little smile off her face. Instead, she said, "Please excuse me, I'm needed elsewhere."

As she walked away, she could feel Dane's eyes on her. Let the two of then fawn over each other, her guitar was calling her name. Kama and his gramps sat by the fire pit strumming ukulele with a few uncles. *Kanikapila*, one of her favorite things— a spontaneous jam session that produced the most pure music known to man.

'Iwa grabbed her guitar from the truck and joined the group. As soon as she started strumming, Dane and the rest of the world began to fade. The last thing she wanted was to feel jealousy, but there it was, like hot stone in her stomach. Hope and Dane were ocean, she was mountain.

She and the boys played Hawaiian music, the usual stuff, and 'Iwa loved the blend of different-sized ukulele, and melding of on-key and off-key voices, some drunk, some sober, all happy. One guy had a voice as deep as Elvis, another sang in a beautiful falsetto. She kept to the background because she didn't want to overshadow the lively harmony being made, but several songs later, the other voices fell away and she noticed that she was the only one singing "Moonlight Lady." The entire crew of friends and family had circled around the musicians.

Dane stood with her father on one side, Hope on the other. Hope looked bored, Dane was holding a beer bottle, unbuttoned flannel shirt over his T-shirt. The way he was looking at her sent a line of heat down her spine. She offered up the smallest of smiles. He smiled back.

Later, when her fingers were raw and voice hoarse, 'Iwa went to the house to use the bathroom. On the way back, in an unlit stretch of field, she passed a tree with a dark form underneath it.

"Hey," said a voice.

She jumped.

Dane was suddenly standing close. "I'm glad you came," he said.

'Iwa caught a whiff of alcohol and mint.

"Me too. These old guys really know how to play, it was an honor to *kanikapila* with them," she said.

Another step toward her. "They all worship you."

"No. It's just that I'm the only girl playing with them, so they give me more attention. They're all big flirts at heart," she said, feeling herself drawn into his orbit, as though he were a dark star.

"Beautiful night," Dane said.

They were standing under cool moonlight, only a foot or two apart, close enough to feel the warmth of his breath.

"Lovely and windless. My favorite kind," she said, looking up at the sky.

She was unaware she was shaking until he reached out for her hand.

"I have a request," Dane said, hand warming hers with his rough skin.

Being this close weakened her resolve. "Okay, shoot, but no guarantees."

"Will you spend the day with me tomorrow? I leave on the red-eye. We can do anything you want, go anywhere you want. Do nothing, do everything, I don't really care," he said, all in one breath.

'Iwa was torn, but really, what was one more day? "I do have tomorrow off."

"Is that a yes?"

"It is."

Without warning, he leaned in and kissed her. Just a light brush on her cheek, but his lips then remained an inch or two away, waiting. 'Iwa reached out and braced herself on his chest, then turned so he could easily close the distance, knowing full well what she was doing. This time, his lips pressed against her own. They were soft and hot and impossible to pull away from.

'Iwa was acutely aware of how he tasted like coconut Chap-Stick and lime, and how badly she wanted more of him. Dane traced a finger along the side of her face, then stepped back, slowly letting go of her hand.

"Tomorrow?" he said, gaze holding hers.

She took a step back, too, to get out of his force field. "Tomorrow."

He raised a brow. "I have a good feeling about it...about *us*."

The *us* was spoken so softly she couldn't be sure he'd actually said it. 'Iwa moved another foot or so back, smiled, then turned and made off into the night.

The Enchanted Forest

'Iwa

As 'Iwa waited outside Dane's cottage door at the Mizunos', she suddenly remembered her dreams from last night. They had been fragmented, one out surfing with Dane and Kama, and her mom had swum up to them and said she'd been living in Portugal all this time but now she was back. Another with Dane surrounded by black witch moths so thick, they blotted out the sky. She hardly ever remembered her dreams, so these seemed relevant in a vague way.

The door opened and he popped his head out. "Come in, I made coffee."

She was in no hurry, with a rare day off stretching out before her. Nor had she decided where to take him, so she turned off the motor and went in. He was wearing sweatpants with a thin gray T-shirt, UGG boots and an orange beanie, looking cozy and straight out of a Patagonia catalog. She couldn't blame him, the north winds had turned the air icy.

Busy in the kitchen, he motioned to the couch, which was covered in a fuzzy fleece blanket. "Have a seat. How do you take your coffee?"

It was almost as though the kiss last night never happened, and she was fine with that. *Almost.* Her lips had still been smoldering when she woke.

"Soy mocha latte, extra hot with cardamom, please." His eyes went wide, and she laughed. "Just kidding. Whatever you have is fine. Even black."

"Perfect. I'll make you my Maui Special, then."

The whole cottage smelled of roasted coffee and beyond that, something sweet and fruity. "What's that smell?" she asked.

"It's a surprise, just sit back and get comfortable."

'Iwa sunk back in the fleece and watched him move around the kitchen, measuring and scooping powders, slicing papaya and strawberries, then whipping the milk with a hand-frothing wand. His brow creased in concentration, he reminded her of a mad scientist in the lab.

"This little cottage is pretty well equipped," she said.

Dane held up the wand. "This is mine. I take this thing wherever I go, like a toothbrush. I can't live without foam on my coffee."

"Ah, so you're an addict," she said.

He poured a brown powder into two mugs. "I do have addictive tendencies, surf being the primary one, coffee with a thick head of foam a close second."

"Is it surf itself or the adrenaline rush you get while surfing?"

"Can the two be separated?"

"Hmmm, good question." She thought for a moment. "I don't know."

"I do know that chasing waves around the world is its own kind of magic, and even though scientists will say we do it because our brains are seeking high-sensation experiences, I say we do it for the sublime connection with mother nature. The ocean meditates me."

"A close encounter."

"Exactly. *That* is addictive. You would know, spending all your time on the slopes of an active volcano," he said, pointing his knife at Haleakalā.

She corrected him. "Dormant. Last erupted five hundred or

so years ago and is now in the post-shield stage with two rift zones, the southwest and the east."

"I read that it's a matter of *when*, not *if*."

The news hyped up even the smallest seismic activity these days. "We're talking geologic time, so I wouldn't be too concerned," she said.

"I'm not concerned, I just think it's cool. And what you do is cool, too—"

The bell rang on the toaster oven and he pulled out two huge chunks of bread and slathered them in butter. No man had ever made her breakfast so enthusiastically, except maybe her father. It made her feel special.

By her feet, she noticed a few magazines on the ottoman, and she picked one up. But it wasn't a magazine, it was a catalog. A Patagonia catalog, and there on the cover was Dane, wearing the same shirt he had on now, and he was standing on a rock, overlooking a red rock canyon. 'Iwa held it up so she could see him alongside the photo.

"Life imitates art," she said, somehow unsurprised.

He turned around and saw what she was holding. "I think you have it backward."

Dane was leaning against the counter, his sweats hanging low with part of his T-shirt tucked in. Flat stomach, smooth arms—the kind of body made for long mornings in bed. His eyes locked onto hers as though he knew just what she was thinking.

"Come and get it," he said.

'Iwa jumped up, a little flustered, and Dane shook his head slowly, as if clearing it of his own indecent thoughts. He set the two steaming mugs, plates of bread, and papaya boats full of yogurt, granola and strawberries on the table. 'Iwa tore herself from the cozy couch and joined him.

"Cheers," he said, holding up a handmade ceramic mug. "To a beautiful last day in Hawai'i *nei*."

"To a perfect last day," she said, before biting into the soft, warm bread. "Let me guess, banana and *lilikoʻi* and...?"

The ground-up seeds and tartness were a dead giveaway, but there was another flavor in there. Something she couldn't put a finger on.

"Top secret."

"Where did you get it?"

"Again, top secret," he said, then shoved a whole piece in his mouth and chewed with his eyes closed.

"The woman who used to make our baked goods just retired and Dad could use some new recipes."

"Well there you go. Maybe he'll hire me as his baker. I made the bread myself."

She laughed, then quickly stopped when she saw his face. "You're serious."

"I am. Tiny as it is, this place has a full kitchen, so I stock up on fruit when I come and then get my Martha Stewart on. I guess I never mentioned I like to bake. Especially on Maui where everything grows like weeds." He pointed to a hook on the wall where a turquoise flowered apron hung. "See, I even have an apron."

"Don't tell me that's yours," she said.

Dane chuckled. "Tutu Mizuno leaves it for me every time I come, and makes sure the kitchen is stocked."

The idea of Dane in an apron, arms covered in flour, brought a smile to her face. "You really love it here, don't you?"

"My second home."

"So, how about a deal. You give me your banana *lilikoʻi* bread recipe, and I'll take you somewhere special today," ʻIwa said.

His foot brushed against hers accidentally. Or maybe not. "Where?"

"You'll see soon enough."

"Your waterfall?"

"No, but somewhere beautiful."

He wilted a little, but didn't argue. "If I refuse to give you the recipe, are we stuck here all day?" he asked.

"If you don't share it, I'll take you swimming with the tiger sharks."

Dane popped a blueberry in his mouth, then said, "I already told you, I have an affinity for sharks, so bring it on. But I'll share it, just because I like your dad so much."

"Thank you, I'll tell him you said that."

"I mean it, too. I'm not just saying it to get in your…" he drew out the pause "…good graces."

An hour later, as they were about to leave, a burst of heavy rain started up. They stood in the doorway, mashed together, waiting for a break. Dane gave off so much heat, she swore she saw steam coming off his shoulders.

"Maybe we *should* just stay here, wait for the rain to stop," he said, so close she could see a small patch of stubble he missed while shaving.

An image of the two of them tangled in the fuzzy blankets came to mind, and she pushed it away. She glanced up to avoid looking him in the eye, and that's when she saw it. The black witch moth on the beam above.

The rain stopped almost as soon as it had come, and they set off under a screaming blue sky. Dane had learned from past mistakes and was wearing rugged hiking shoes and cargo pants, presumably borrowed. His hair stuck out in fifteen directions, as though it was permanently salty, even when dry. And now that they were in close proximity, she thought she detected sandalwood on his skin. Her favorite smell.

At the fork in the road, 'Iwa stopped. She had planned to take Dane to the West Maui Mountains, but the moth gave her pause. Would it be so bad if she took him to Waikula? The thought of his lips on hers caused a spark to shoot up her spine. They might not have a future, but maybe they had a present.

A brand-new red Jeep rental car behind them honked. 'Iwa turned right.

"Back the same way we went the other day? Are we going to Hāna?" Dane asked.

"Patience."

"Never one of my good qualities."

"Did you get enough forest the other day?" 'Iwa asked.

"Hell no."

"Good."

He smiled.

As they drove Dane remained oddly quiet. 'Iwa was good at quiet. Quiet was her thing. Playing music and singing didn't count, but in her mind, talking was overrated. Especially out in the wild, in places where, if you listened, the plants and the wind spoke to you. The rain and fog whispered stories, and the birds chirped old secrets.

Eventually, she turned up a road several valleys before where they had gone the other day, driving along the edge of an almost dried-up *lo'i*—a taro patch—that smelled of thick mud, and finally turned up a stream. The depth of the water varied depending on the season, and today was only about six inches. Oftentimes, this road was impassable.

Dane held his hands out as though bracing himself against the glove box. "Ho, wait a minute. What are you doing?"

"This is the way."

"Up a stream?"

"Trust me, it's fine."

"Where I live, we drive on roads not streams."

"Well, where I live, we have some of the highest precipitation levels on the planet, and sometimes streams happen when you least expect them," she said.

He leaned back, relaxing a little. "You're the boss."

They bounced along, the sound of water slushing under the Toyota's oversized tires. It took another ten minutes of maneuvering around rocks, through deeper water and around stumps, but they arrived at the trailhead without incident. She had never brought anyone here. Even her father had never been, his idea of a hike a fifteen-minute walk down to the ocean so he could set up his fishing pole. Somehow, it had never bothered Lily.

"He'd never admit it, but he's scared of the *mo'o*, that's why he won't come with us," she used to say with a wink.

It had been a while since 'Iwa had come here, since visiting soon after her mom had died, as if being at Waikula might bring her back. It didn't. A stormy day, stream overflowing from weeping skies. She had taken a big risk going there that day, and could have easily been swept away. Today, there was enough water to keep the stream clean and clear, but not enough to wash out the trails. Blue sky and a lemony sun, air cool and dry.

She still hadn't told him where they were going.

They climbed out and 'Iwa grabbed the ti leaf from the back of the truck.

"What's that for?" Dane asked.

"For the *mo'o*, the guardian of the pond."

His eyebrows arched. "I see."

"*Mo'o* are shapeshifting lizard goddesses. They protect the fresh water sources in the islands and have been around since the beginning of time."

Dane nodded as though her words made perfect sense. "Sounds good. So we feed her some leaves before we go in?"

There was no sarcasm in his tone; he really seemed like he wanted to know.

"Actually, we set the leaf in the water. If it floats, it's safe to swim. If it sinks, we can't go in. The *mo'o* will drown us. Or you, more likely," she said, turning and heading for the arch of trees that curved over the trailhead.

Dane grabbed her arm. "Wait, what do you mean *me*? Why not you?"

"Because you're a man and they eat men."

"So you're saying I can't go in the water if that leaf sinks?" he asked.

She shrugged. "That's up to you."

"Blinding fog and man-eating lizard goddesses. These mountains are more dangerous than Pe'ahi on a big day."

"Depends who you ask, I suppose," 'Iwa said.

He looked her in the eye. "The more beautiful, the more dangerous, is how it usually works."

This hike was more vertical than the last, because they had to cross a tall ridge before they entered the valley. The only other way in on this side was through a narrow chasm full of water that as far as 'Iwa knew, no one had ever passed through. She'd always thought of Hana'iwa'iwa as its own Hawaiian Shangri-la. But according to a plan submitted to the county, Jones wanted to build a zip line straight to the falls. That way, he maintained, there would be far less impact on the surrounding flora and fauna. That way, she and Winston knew, he would turn Waikula into a shit show, accessible to anyone with enough money.

By the time they reached the rope section of the trail, it was late morning. They had been walking on an exposed hogback, covered mainly in *uluhe*—false staghorn fern. The sun melted down onto them. 'Iwa stripped down to a tank top, and Dane took off his shirt and stuffed it in his backpack. She really wished he hadn't because it was impossible not to notice the curves and indents of his pecs and abs, and the rock-hard lines that disappeared below the waistline of his pants. Dane brought a new meaning to the word *chiseled*, and she had to force herself to look away.

Standing at the base of the incline, Dane grabbed onto one of the old and frayed ropes and tugged, craning his neck to see what was in store. "You trust this rope? It looks like it's been here since World War II."

"Your tendency to exaggerate, have you always had it?" she said.

He let the rope go and stepped back. "Nah, just an active imagination. How long has it been here, really?"

"As long as I can remember."

"No one has ever changed it?" he asked.

"Someone may have at some point, I'm not sure."

"You go first then, that way I can catch you if anything breaks."

The way up wasn't technical rock climbing, and coming down was actually easier, but scaling this section definitely took a fair amount of physical strength and concentration. 'Iwa started up and moved quickly, having done this enough times to know the best hand and footholds. The dry weather helped.

Once at the top, she peered down and called out, "All good, come on up."

Two minutes later, Dane was standing next to her, dusting off his hands and smiling.

"I should have known. You're a rock climber, too," she said.

He shrugged. "I climb some."

For the most part, the rocks in Hawai'i were too porous for climbing.

"Where do you go?"

"Yosemite mostly. My buddy is the real deal—I just dabble. When there's no surf, we climb," Dane said, pouring water from his bottle into his mouth.

Big waves, big cliffs, big thrills.

"I would imagine the adrenaline rush is similar?"

"Climbing takes it to another level. The stakes get *much* higher. At least in the ocean, you have lulls between the sets. Twenty-five hundred feet up a wall of granite, you can't turn off the fear button, not even for one second," he said.

"Give me a shield volcano any day."

"Understandable, coming from a *wahine* from Hawai'i." He

held up his water bottle, the squirt kind, and said, "Open up, a little bird told me we need to hydrate out here and I haven't seen you take one sip yet."

She closed her eyes and opened wide. Dane had perfect aim, and filled her mouth with water.

"Want a little more? Cool you off?" he asked.

She could feel a line of sweat forming between her breasts, dripping down her stomach and causing her shirt to stick to her skin. "Yes, please."

She offered him her back and he sprinkled some on, then doused his head and face, and they were off again, toward an 'ōhi'a forest with some of the tallest 'ōhi'a trees on the island, and known for its dense population of honeycreepers. As soon as they reached the forest, the temperature cooled. Birdcalls echoed around them, and they could hear the sound of tiny wings whirring amongst the trees.

"The ones that sound like a squeaky door hinge are i'iwi. They're red with a splash of black and a curved beak," she told him, keeping her voice to a whisper.

"How many species are there?" he asked.

"Not as many as there should be. Hawai'i is known as the extinct bird capital of the world, which is the worst possible thing to be known for. But not all hope is lost. The remaining species now have an army of people on their side, doing whatever we can to keep them from disappearing," she said.

"So, there's a chance."

"Always."

This was one of her favorite sections of the hike. Gray and twisty trunks with branches that reminded her of Dr. Seuss trees, scarlet red puffy blossoms, ferns taller than a house. Dane followed close on her heels, and she imagined seeing all of this with fresh eyes. Would he think everything was as ethereal and magical as she did?

Then, she heard a birdcall, a not-too-distant series of paired bird notes. 'Iwa stopped suddenly, causing Dane to run smack into her. In an attempt to keep her from flying forward, he grabbed her hips firmly.

"What is it?" he whispered, mouth inches away from her cheek, and sending vibrations to her core.

She held up two fingers, tapped her ear. Dane didn't move, nor did she. All around them, the understory dripped with moisture stolen from wandering clouds. Trees were masters at their jobs. A minute later, she heard the notes again, farther away.

She turned her head slightly and whispered, "It almost sounded like a kiwikiu, the one I've been looking for. The newest ghosts of the forest."

Unsure, she fumbled for her phone to record what they were hearing. In her world, unless you had proof, you had nothing. But instead of more singing, she heard a flurry of wings. After five minutes of staying still as lichen-covered stones on the ground, 'Iwa stepped away from Dane. Even after detaching, she felt his red-hot palm imprints on her skin.

"It's been over a year since the last pair released into the wild were spotted. Most believe they're another casualty of habitat loss and disease, but this mountain is huge and I refuse to give up hope."

"I'm in no hurry, why don't we stop and eat? Maybe the birds will do another flyby," he said.

They posted up around the next bend. Her excitement seemed to be rubbing off on Dane, because he kept shushing her and pulling out the binocs at every little chirp. 'Iwa didn't have to see the birds to know that they weren't the kiwikiu. She had every trill and call and song imprinted in her mind. *I'iwi*, Maui Creeper, *'ākohekohe*.

"Those are the Maui Creepers, the ones we saw the other day," she told him.

Dane's face crumpled.

"Don't look so disappointed," she told him. "These little guys are endangered, too."

"I want to see the ghosts of the forest."

"Trust me, so do I."

They ate curried tofu sandwiches on sourdough, with vinegar chips and crunchy bread and butter pickles. Dane had brought two slices of his *liliko'i* bread for dessert. They ate and listened for birds, sitting close together. His knee touched hers, and she did nothing to move away.

When they'd finished, Dane said, "Don't take this the wrong way, but I never thought it possible I would be so into bird-watching."

"I didn't think you would either."

He feigned offense. "You underestimate me."

"No I don't. I can tell there's a lot going on beneath the surface with you."

"Is that a compliment?"

"No, just an observation."

It was true, though, and a big part of his draw.

"I think everyone has a lot going on beneath the surface, if you take the time to look," he said.

"I'm not so sure about that. Some people—even ones that I've known pretty well—skate along in life and are happy just getting by. They do what they're told, or what they think they're supposed to do, and are content. I don't get that from you."

She realized then that maybe it was his passion that was pulling her in.

"Yeah, I guess I'm lucky in that department. As a kid, I had to figure out stuff on my own, and so everything I did was purely based on stoke. Surfing being my top stoke inducer."

She had been wondering about his mom, and now had to ask. "How come you had to figure out stuff on your own? Where was your mom?"

"Away a lot. She was a flight attendant and when she wasn't working, she traveled the world surfing."

"And she never took you with her?"

"Nope. I stayed with neighbors and friends—mostly the Mizunos. She was essentially a kid with a kid and I was extra baggage. But she taught me to surf, and took me up and down the coast when she was around. In our house, waves were God and the ability to ride them brought you closer to heaven."

He started feeling a nearby fern, running his fingers up and down the frond. He looked to be remembering, and 'Iwa felt for him.

"I'm sorry. That must have been hard on you," she said, more gently.

"It wasn't all bad. She gave me surfing and a love for the ocean."

It was hard to fathom growing up alone like that with no father and a globe-trotting mother.

"Do you see her much now that you're older?"

"No."

"At all?"

"I used to see her more, but when I made the pro circuit, she called me a sellout and told me if I went through with it, I wasn't a real surfer. I did it anyway and stayed on the tour for two years. But in the end, I realized she was right. At least for me. I hated surfing all those contests just for points, even when the waves were crap. And the judging and the competitiveness. It wasn't my thing."

"I guess your mom knew you better than you thought."

He nodded. "I hated to admit that she was right. And then when I left the tour, I drifted around for a while, trying to find my own path. I knew I loved big waves, but there was a day at Himalayas that was pure perfection. It was uncrowded, just a few of us out riding hollow blue giants, and when some of the photos circulated and were entered in the XXL Big Wave

Awards, I sat up and took notice. That seemed more my deal. Traveling the world looking to ride the biggest waves out there, without the whole circus, no schedule, just follow the waves and document it on film."

"And the rest is history," she said.

"I still haven't won, though."

"Pe'ahi is a pretty big coup."

"A dream for sure. But not the top prize."

"So that's your Everest? Biggest wave award?"

Their eyes met and he didn't answer for a few heartbeats. "One of them."

'Iwa dared not ask what the others were. She jumped to her feet. "Come on, we have a lot of ground to cover."

They made their way deeper into the valley. Hana'iwa'iwa was as beautiful as the next valley, but the waterfall itself—Waikula—was something otherworldly. Tucked away toward the back, in a fold in the cliffs, you would never even know it's there. Even tour helicopters couldn't get to it. At so many other falls up and down the coast, you spent hours of blood, sweat and tears to get into the wild, only to be dropped in on by a giant metal mosquito. But not at Waikula.

They rock hopped and stream crossed, and as they neared the falls, rocks turned into truck-sized boulders. Dampness coated everything. 'Iwa led the way, turning around every so often to see if Dane was keeping up. He was. About a half mile below the falls, she began to notice little cleared areas with trails leading off from them on the far side of the wide stream. At first she told herself they were pig trails, but in some places, tree branches had been cut cleanly.

Jones.

Sick to her stomach, but not wanting to ruin the day, she kept moving from rock to rock. She could come back in a couple days and follow the trails. Trespassing or not, she needed to know. Leading up to the waterfall was a forest of ferns, and the trail bored through in a tunnel of green. 'Iwa stopped at the entrance.

"This feels like Middle Earth. Is this some kind of portal?" Dane said with a dorky smile. "Because if it is, I have a right to know."

'Iwa laughed. "Oh, it's a portal all right, but not to Middle Earth."

Dane closed the gap between them in a heartbeat and took hold of her wrist. "For real, 'Iwa, where are we?"

His touch made her slightly dizzy. "Soon, we're almost there," she said.

"This is your waterfall, isn't it?" he said, gaze snagging on hers and not letting go.

They were close enough for her to see the gold flecks in his deep water eyes. The tension between them had been building all day, thick as freshly pounded poi. She pulled away and ducked into the ferns, letting his question hang.

Tread Lightly

'Iwa

'Iwa had had exactly two real boyfriends in her life. One Hawaiian and one Californian, both surfers. Her first, Kaiwi, she'd been friends with since fifteen, until one night on the beach he'd kissed her and that was that. They'd been inseparable until the summer after graduation, when he went on a two-month surf trip to Tahiti and decided he was going to move there, alone. Kaiwi was responsible for the first layer of protection built up on her cardiac rift zones.

And then there was Zach. Magnetic, vagabond, going nowhere Zach. They'd met at the start of her junior year at UH Mānoa. 'Iwa and a small group of students had gone out to eat after planting koa trees above Waimea Valley, and he'd been their waiter at Cholos. Before 'Iwa left, he managed to get her phone number and a date lined up. His smooth-talking demeanor should have set off warning bells, but she had been taken in by his aqua eyes and his easy charm.

On weekends, she would drive out to stay with him in a termite-infested A-frame steps away from Rocky Point. 'Iwa would comb the beach for shells, which she would then catalog as part of her marine biology class at the University of Hawai'i. In the afternoons, she was happy strumming her guitar under an old kamani tree while Zach surfed for the third or fourth time. When the waves were small enough for 'Iwa, they would paddle out together.

She loved him in that all-consuming way of young love. Never mind that their futures looked drastically different on paper. Two years later, after a month or so of a nagging feeling tapping her on the shoulder, she found another girl's number on a Cholos napkin in the pocket of his shorts.

When confronted, Zach admitted he'd met someone else. He loved 'Iwa, he swore, but he was young and not ready for something so serious. She cried so hard her nose bled. That was when she swore off surfers. Swore off men entirely for a while and focused on school and figuring out what she wanted to do with her life. And then Lily got sick and everything else faded into oblivion. If losing Zach had scorched her and gutted her, losing her mother had burned her to the ground.

Back on Maui, Lily held her hand and told her, "Sweet pea, the right one will come along when he's meant to. And when he does, you will know it in your bones. Until then, get busy doing everything in this world that you love."

'Iwa retreated to the wilds of Maui, and came to see that the moon never lied and the trees could be trusted, and that the ocean and the wind were her friends—men were never so steady or loyal.

Now, as they moved through the woods, the first inkling she got of the waterfall was a fine mist filling the air and a coolness on her skin. 'Iwa opened and closed her mouth to take in the particles. As a kid, when they'd drive up to the top of Haleakalā, she believed that if you inhaled enough clouds, you could float away. Turned out her thinking wasn't entirely off base.

"Are you familiar with negative ions?" she asked.

He had to crouch a little to avoid brushing his head on the ferns. "What about them?"

"Their effect on the human body."

"You really have to ask? They're little euphoria generators, and are probably partly to blame for my big wave riding affliction. A big wave is a factory for fractured molecules and negative ions. They're probably why you love your waterfall so much, too."

Affliction was probably a good way to put it. As was euphoria. "If you have a wave affliction, I definitely have a waterfall affliction," she said.

"There are worse afflictions to have."

A moment later, they came out of the trees onto a flat, grassy area. A wide wall of water cascaded into the pool below it. Dane went stone still. Even 'Iwa was taken aback. Waikula was at her finest, with liquid sunlight coming down the face of the cliff and exploding in a pool of gold. She stole a look at his face, his cheeks sun-blotched, eyes wide.

"This can't be real." He stepped closer and set his pack down on a rock. "Why is it that color?"

"There is a rare kind of algae, native not just to Hawai'i, but to this valley, this stream, this waterfall," she said.

Found nowhere else in the world. By some miracle, only some of the older Hawaiians, a handful of outdoorsy kamaʻāina, and a small community of science nerds knew of its existence. Depending on the time of year, precipitation levels and humidity, the water color ranged from ochre to straight-up gold. Mix in a few sunbeams, and you would swear the banks were lined in precious metal.

"Is it safe to swim in?" he asked.

She pulled the ti leaf out. "Perfectly safe, as long as the ti leaf floats."

Even though they were at elevation, the sun bore down. Dane, slick with perspiration, literally glistened. 'Iwa had never seen a person glisten before, and thought it only happened in those romance books her mother used to fly through.

He caught her staring, and his mouth turned up on one side.

"Anything else I should know? Like, will you save me if the *mo'o* drags me under?"

"I would never interfere with the *mo'o*."

"Not even for me?"

Firmly she said, "Not even for you."

'Iwa stepped out of her pants and slid her top over her head, so she was just in her bikini. That shut him up fast. She felt his eyes take a slow tour of her body, and he made no move to hide that he liked what he saw. She handed him the leaf, which was as long as her arm and lime green.

"Tell me," he said, taking hold of the stem. "Do you think humans give off negative ions?"

Her fingers were still gripping one end of the leaf, and he held the other end, pulling it slowly closer.

"Probably?"

Being this close to him made it hard to think. Somewhere tucked away in her brain, she knew the answer. Human beings ran on electric currents. Negatively charged cells allowed ions to flow through their membranes. Dane was a human, thus the answer was a resounding *yes*.

"Theoretically, we could be exchanging negative ions as we speak, couldn't we?" Dane said, his voice slightly changed— deeper.

A drop of sweat trickled down her spine, snapping her back to the falls.

"Theoretically, yes."

She let go of the leaf and walked to the edge of the pond, to a smooth, flat stone, warm from the sun. Dane followed and held the leaf over the water.

"So I just drop it in?" he asked.

She nodded. A lot of people thought these Hawaiian legends were just superstitions, but the way 'Iwa saw it, they were about being humble and understanding your place. The forces of nature were vast and many, and little prayers to God or the universe or the plants themselves, depending on your system of beliefs, never hurt. Dane dropped the ti leaf into the water and they watched it slowly make its way to the center of the pond, where it promptly sank.

"Great." He held up his hands. "Now what?"

'Iwa shivered, unsure how to proceed. The ti leaves always floated.

"To be honest, this has never happened to me before."

"That waterfall has my name carved into the rocks above it, can't you see? It would be torture not to get in," he said.

'Iwa eyed the pond, looking for any signs of unusual currents. There were none, just the usual rush below the falls, and where the water flowed through the rocks on its way downstream.

"Ask permission and be extra careful. You should be fine," she said, wanting him to swim probably as much as he did. "And no jumping from the rocks for you today."

Dane bent down, touched the water and crossed himself, then said, "Please go easy on me, Waikula. I will tread lightly, always."

Tread lightly. Her mother's favorite words.

'Iwa jumped in. The cold water stole the air from her lungs and numbed her skin. She swam hard toward the falls to warm up, imagining Dane would probably try to beat her there. But when she turned around, he was nowhere to be seen.

'Iwa rolled onto her back and kicked, scanning the outlying trees. "Dane?" she called.

No answer. When she made it to the falls, she slid onto a submerged rock and let the water pound down on her shoulders and back. She waited and waited, while thoughts of the sinking ti leaf left her slightly uneasy.

"Dane!" she yelled, louder this time.

Another minute passed, and she decided to go back and look for him. He had been right there on the rock behind her, about to get in. She even thought she'd heard a light splash. About ten feet into her swim back, something wrapped around her ankles and pulled her under. She spun around in a moment of panic, reaching to free herself. Then beside her, an explosion erupted out of the water, as Dane sucked in a long breath of air.

'Iwa swatted at him, annoyed. "Not funny. At all."

He smiled ear to ear. "Sorry, I couldn't resist. Did you think the lizard got me?"

"I thought maybe you dove and hit a rock. Or went around and planned on jumping from above, which I told you is off-limits for you today."

"I would never disobey you—haven't you figured that out by now?"

She rolled her eyes. "But really, how do you hold your breath so long?"

"Practice. Every single day."

'Iwa swam back. Dane followed close and they sat under the falling water for a while, then it was 'Iwa's turn to disappear behind the falls. It didn't take Dane long to find her. She was covered in goose bumps but hardly noticed. They stood side by side, leaning against the cool rocks, looking out through watery ropes of gold. Shoulders and hips touching, his hand resting soft as a fern on the front of her thigh.

Outside of the falls, they swam to the far side of the pond, where long, table-like rocks beckoned their warmth. 'Iwa walked through the decaying plant mush of the shallows and climbed out onto one. Dane continued on to the edge, where she'd pointed out a bush of ʻākala berries. With heat from the river rock beneath her, and the winter afternoon sun above, 'Iwa lost her chill within minutes. She lay there, head to the side, watching Dane pick berries.

He turned, saw her watching him, and slid a bloodred berry into his mouth. He chewed slowly, as though savoring the sweet tartness, all the while not taking his eyes off 'Iwa. Between her legs, a thick burning started up. This was not supposed to be happening, but she couldn't do anything to stop it. Once he'd gathered a handful of berries, he slid into the water, shattering its glassy surface. She watched him wade toward her, as if watching a movie, and her skin warmed another eleven degrees.

Without a word, he came back out of the water and lifted himself onto the rock, sitting next to her where she lay, and put a berry into her mouth. 'Ākala were her favorite—Hawaiian raspberry. The water that dripped from his arm onto her chest sizzled, or at least it felt like it did.

She no longer trusted her senses.

As soon as she swallowed, he gave her another. Dane was backlit by the sun, and she squinted to see his eyes, his slightly pointed nose, full mouth. He shook his head, raining down pond water and cooling her off, then undid her completely with another lopsided smile.

"Best thing ever," he said, all hoarse and whispery.

He placed a finger in the notch between her collarbones, and ran it down her sternum, leaving a trail of sparks. Slow as molasses, his finger hopped over her bikini top string and continued on down her abdomen, where he then set an 'ākala berry just below her belly button. Still, he watched her, and she watched him. On some level, 'Iwa knew this had been coming, that the attraction between them made it inevitable, and yet she hadn't expected it. Not like this. Her body was on fire, and he hadn't even kissed her yet.

She took the berry from her belly and held it up to his lips. He bit down just enough to keep it in his teeth, then lowered his face to hers and offered it. She took it gently, with her lips, having forgotten where they were. The outside world reduced to a pinprick. Dane waited patiently, an inch or two away, then kissed her, light as a cloud. So light, she wasn't sure their lips actually touched. His whole hand went to the spot where the berry had been moments ago, and sent a current of electricity through her, pinning her to the rock.

His mouth scraped against her cheek. "Are you sure you're okay with this?" he whispered in her ear.

She managed to say something that sounded like a strangled "Yes."

Please.

This time he kissed her with the force of a hurricane. A massive wave. A waterfall. She took it all, breathless. Her hand slid over his and pressed it hard into her skin. It was weird, they were skin against skin, and yet she couldn't seem to get him close enough.

The kiss tasted of mountain water and sweet *'ākala*, with notes of chocolate, and she did not want it to end.

Ever.

"Tell me something," he said, pulling away for a moment and winding a lock of her wet hair around his finger.

"What?"

"How did you get to be so beautiful?"

'Iwa laughed. "Oh, I don't know—"

Before she could continue, he covered her mouth with his. Soft lips, lazy tongue, in no rush whatsoever. The rock was hard beneath her back, but she could have been lying on a bed of urchins and she wouldn't have cared. With his finger still twined in her hair, he moved from her mouth to the angle of her jaw, dusting her with kisses and hot breath.

She was acutely aware of his tongue as it reached the edge of her bikini top, and she shivered—not from the cold. Dane stayed within bounds, though, and then made his way along her collarbone and back up to her lips. After what felt like an hour, but may have been just minutes, he rolled away and onto his back.

"Ahhh, I can't feel my elbow," he groaned, sitting up and pulling her with him with one hand as he shook out the other.

She gave him a sly smile. "That's what you get for tormenting me."

"You call that tormenting? Just wait."

From the looks of it, he would have preferred to rip her suit off then.

She was dizzy with longing.

Smooth as an eel, Dane slid back into the water so he was standing thigh deep. Now they were eye level. She moved to the edge and he leaned into her, parting her legs naturally. They wrapped around him. He was as warm as the rock, and just as hard.

He pressed his forehead against hers. "You're killing me," he said.

"I'm already dead," she said.

Not a peep from that voice of reason that usually lived in the back of her mind. No *slow down* or *maybe it's time to put the brakes on.* Or *this is all wrong.*

They started kissing again. With one hand on her hip, he slipped a finger beneath the upper edge of her bikini bottoms and slid it one millimeter at a time across her skin, lighting her up like lava. 'Iwa melded into the rock. Maybe this was how those women in the legends were turned to stone. Misbehaving with the gods. At that moment, she would have gladly been immortalized in this position.

Dane's hands moved up her back now, fingers untying her top and pulling it over her head. It fell into her lap and she felt the wet strings on her thigh, searing into her skin. Neither could be bothered to tuck it someplace safely. Somewhere nearby a bird called, as a gust of wind blew down the valley, clattering branches and bending shadows.

A finger made broad circles on her white skin, slowly closing in on her nipples. Then his face moved down her neck and his tongue flicked flames as he took one in his mouth. There was a gentleness to his touch, but also a hard-edged need. 'Iwa felt it, too. Like if they weren't both completely naked soon, she would spontaneously combust.

He laid her back and searched deep into her eyes. "This is the part where you tell me to stop."

She just looked at him, mute.

"Because if you don't..."

His voice trailed off. 'Iwa had waited too long to be with a man, she realized, and now her body was making decisions for her. The only words she could think of were *ravage me*, but they remained unspoken, so she placed a finger over his lips.

Off to the side, a strange buzzing started up. Faint at first, but growing louder. It sounded like a motor and 'Iwa thought it might be a helicopter with exceptionally bad timing. But the sound was all wrong, and closer. She turned her head in time to see an off-road vehicle pull right to the edge of the pond. Dane was faster than she was and threw her top back over her head, stepping between her and the Polaris to block her from view.

"This can't be happening," she said, bolting upright.

Two men climbed out. They could have been military, beefy with short-cropped hair and pale skin, wearing camouflage pants and tight black T-shirts.

Stone-faced, one called, "How'd you two get up here?"

"We walked," 'Iwa said simply.

"This is private property."

Anger flashed white-hot through her veins. "We came up the other side, on the public trail. The waterfall is not private property," she said.

He was partly right, though. In Hawai'i, landowners often owned to the middle of a stream and according to county records, this was the case here, too. An absurd notion. Streams, as oceans, should belong only to the land, the fish, the birds, the sky.

The taller one, wearing a holster, walked closer to where Dane had been picking berries. "We're going to have to ask you to leave."

'Iwa took Dane's hand and swam him back to the middle of

the pond. "Who do you even think you are?" she said, order-ing herself to keep calm.

"We work for the landowner. And I'll repeat, you're tres-passing."

"Tell your boss to go screw himself. He may own to the middle, but this side is public. You have no right to tell us to leave. In fact I should be telling you to leave. You don't belong here," she said.

Her entire body filled with venom.

He folded his dense arms and stood with his legs apart. She recognized it as some kind of bully stance. "Don't make us es-cort you out of here," he said.

Dane jumped in. "We don't want any trouble. And you may want to check your facts, because she knows what she's talk-ing about."

"These guys have no clue," 'Iwa murmured.

"They have guns."

She would die before getting escorted out of the valley by these two kooks. "Why don't you just shoot us? For swimming in the place I've been swimming in since I was a kid."

Dane flinched.

The guy lurking in the back stepped up and said something to Stone Face. There was a short exchange, then he told them, "You two get dressed and go back the way you came, and we won't press it. But you need to leave now."

'Iwa and Dane were now on the far side of the stream, and she turned her back to the men and climbed out. "They can't make us go."

Dane's lips on her skin felt like a distant memory.

"Are you sure about the property line?" Dane asked.

"One hundred and ten percent. It's public record."

'Iwa lifted her water bottle and took a long drink, then sat down with her legs dangling in the water, startling several small fish. Dane sat, too. She started humming "Sweet Child O' Mine" and saw a smile forming in his eyes.

The guys glared at them from across the pool, but made no move to enter the water. They probably didn't know how to swim, she thought. The spell had been broken, though, and being here with these two idiots made her heart bleed. One started talking into a radio, and then they got back in the Polaris.

"Oh good, they're leaving," she said.

But they didn't.

She and Dane sat there for a while longer, as a rainbow formed in the waterfall spray. He made no move to go anywhere, and she got the feeling he would sit here with her all night if he had to. It was lovely and magical and painful. But Dane had a plane to catch, she knew, and there was no point in outlasting these two dingdongs, nothing to gain. They were just enforcers, paid thugs.

"This isn't over," she said, as she stood up and got dressed. "Not by a long shot."

It was a quiet hike back to the truck. 'Iwa could think of nothing but the encounter. Not Dane leaving. Not whether she would ever see him again. The only thought occupying her mind was that these outsiders had violated one of her most sacred places. And the worst part was, they probably couldn't even pronounce its name.

Waikula.

When she pulled up at the Mizunos' to drop him off, he did not open the door, just sat there for a few breaths, then said, "When can I see you again?"

'Iwa looked out at the billowing shower tree, lit by the setting sun. "You and I can never happen, Dane."

The words seared her throat and tasted bitter on her tongue. But they needed to be said.

"Seems to me like we're already happening," Dane said, voice weirdly high.

"I like you, and we had a good time while you were here—

and definitely got a little carried away, but you're a surfer and you're from the mainland. Both of those are deal breakers for me."

"Can you at least look me in the eye and say that?"

Her gaze danced around, to the gear shift, the floor, anywhere but his face. "I have too much going on right now, and long-distance relationships don't work. There are a million reasons why you should just go and forget about me."

"That would never happen."

"When that next big swell rolls in, I'll be a distant memory. That's how it works," she said.

"You're making a big generalization, 'Iwa. I am not the men in your past."

Her foot started tapping on the floorboard. "You're used to getting your way, aren't you?"

"Is it so wrong to want to see you again?" he asked.

She finally turned to him, a dangerous move, she knew—because sitting there, with his golden skin and windblown hair—replete with token twig fragments—he looked more handsome than any man had a right to.

"How about this. If in two weeks you still want to see me, you can send me *one* text message," she offered.

"Just one?"

"Just one."

Dane had to laugh. "So you're saying there's a chance."

A tiny smile broke. "Not really. I'm just trying to get you out of my truck."

He leaned over and kissed her cheek, dusting her with a leafy, spring water scent, then was gone before she could change her mind.

The Message

Dane

Santa Cruz, California

All signs pointed to a massive swell. Dane had arrived home fourteen days ago, finished the Manning job, and since then he'd been spending his evenings tracking a huge storm brewing off Japan. By all accounts, it would be the biggest swell of the winter so far, and coupled with light winds, a west-northwesterly direction, everything was lining up for epic conditions. A Code Red in big wave surfing jargon.

But there was a problem. Since the day at Waikula with 'Iwa, he'd developed a peculiar kind of delirium. Every night, she prowled his dreams in Technicolor, and during the day, he kept wandering off into daydreams of her on that rock, only to snap out of it and remember where he was. It was messing with his head. *She* was messing with his head.

Everything had been going so well until those two assholes showed up. On the hike out and the ride back to the Mizunos', 'Iwa had given him one-word answers, withdrawn back into that turtle shell he'd been trying to coax her out of. Then, gutting him with the final blow. All he could think was that someone had done a real number on her heart, and he wanted to know everything about the man or men who had left her so jaded. Unfortunately, his own track record with women was not something to be proud of. He always started off with good intentions, but he usually grew bored before too long. Except for with Sunny—but that hadn't ended well either.

Now he met Kama, Hope and Yeti at their usual spot, Firefly, for coffee. Yeti had shown up on the scene eight years ago, looking like he had just emerged from a five-year stint in the redwoods. Paul Bunyan beard, thin as a potato chip, clothes worn thin. But he was a nimble surfer with natural grace, and a closet genius who could fix anything—especially jet skis. Dane liked him because they spoke the same language: ocean. Within months, they'd absorbed him into their crew. The older, wise one.

Yeti had his laptop open and they all crowded around, drenched in the smell of coffee and fresh-baked cinnamon rolls. Outside, a cold light rain sifted down.

"Look at all this red and purple," Yeti said, pointing to the NPAC eighteen-hour forecast.

"I'm more interested in that gray and black," Dane said.

The forecast was a color-coded rainbow of surf heights in the North Pacific, much like a topographic map. Gray and black corresponded with forty-six and forty-eight feet—giant towers of water brought to life by a winter polar jet stream creating low pressure that whipped up wind speeds, which then transferred the kinetic energy to the ocean below.

"Do you think it's going to swing too far north?" Hope asked.

Yeti shook his bushy head, hair now long enough that in the water he pulled it back with a rubber band. "I think we need to tune up the skis and head north on Wednesday."

Today was Sunday.

"Why so early?" Kama wanted to know.

"Because we don't want to be late to the party. Remember last time?" Yeti said.

Last time they'd gone to Mavericks, the swell had hit before they arrived, and they missed the biggest and the best waves in years. The whole world had been talking about the six-story, silky faces. And all they'd ridden were black, choppy waves, twelve to fifteen feet, max. Dane had been kicking himself ever since.

"I'm in," Hope said.

Kama grinned ear to ear. "We go!"

Dane only half heard them as the door opened and a cold burst of air rushed in, along with a brown-haired girl. She was looking down, fumbling around in her purse. That hair looked so familiar, the lanky limbs. He froze.

Could it be?

Hope snapped her fingers in front of his face. "Earth to Dane."

"Right, yeah, I'm good to go," he said, sipping his coffee and stealing another look at the girl who was definitely not 'Iwa.

Tomorrow would be two weeks. Fourteen nights, so maybe technically fifteen days? All he knew was that he'd been obsessing over what he was going to say in his one and only text message.

"'An infatuated man is not only foolish, but wild.' You ever heard that?" Kama said.

Kama knew him well enough to know that this was unusual behavior on his part.

Dane sat up straight and gave him a nod. "You don't have to worry about me. I'm all in."

"All in California or Hawai'i?" Hope asked.

Dane leaned back and stretched. "This one is different, I swear it."

"You said that about Melinda. And Sunny. And—"

Hope pushed his buttons like a kid in an elevator. For about one second, after her divorce, he considered hooking up with her, but she was too much like a sister.

"You want to drive the ski at Mavericks?" he said.

"Yes."

"Then not another word out of that pretty little trap."

Yeti was all business. "My house, tonight. Six on the nose of the board."

Despite his scraggly appearance, Yeti had no shortage of funds and lived in a modern farmhouse surrounded by Monterey pines and oak trees. On the property was a barn full of toys—jet skis, surfboards, many of them collectables, snowboards, climbing gear, a vintage Land Cruiser and a Harley worth more than Dane made in a year. Yeti never said where his money came from, and Dane never asked.

"I'll bring the tequila," Hope said.

They all looked to Dane. "You bring the bread."

Dane was famous among his friends for his habanero and cheese sourdough, baked in his toaster oven. Go figure.

The early morning rain came down quietly, reminding him of Hawai'i. Only this wasn't jellyfish rain, it felt more like snow rain. So faint and light, the tiny droplets evaporated before hitting the ground. Maybe he should text 'Iwa something smart about the rain. Or tell her he'd gotten her name tattooed across his wrist, so there was no chance of forgetting. Or maybe asking a question was a better way to go—that way she'd have to answer.

All lame ideas.

Annoyed at his inability to think of something brilliant, he got up and made coffee. He had Mavericks to prepare for, and he needed to be in the right headspace. Mavericks commanded full respect. Cold water, and a reef with grooves that funneled open ocean energy into mammoth waves. If you weren't careful— and even if you were—Mavericks could swallow you whole.

Last year one of Hawai'i's best watermen and all-around solid humans, Sion Milosky, had taken a bad wipeout on a big out-side set, been held down, and never surfaced. Dane knew Sion, and if Sion had died out there, anyone could.

After coffee, he went for a run on the beach, dodging kelp, mollusks and dirty seagulls. Running was part of his training, which was probably why he'd been able to keep up with 'Iwa in the forest. At the base of a cliff, beneath a leaning cypress tree, he did push-ups and crunches, followed by pull-ups on a branch. In the zone, arms burning and abs on fire, he finally forgot about 'Iwa for a moment. But when he finished his mini workout, he heard the sea whisper.

Send her a ticket.

She would never come.

You won't know unless you try.

It would be pointless.

Giving your best is never pointless.

He ran the beach back in record time, went online before he could chicken out, and used his Hawaiian miles to buy a round trip flight from Maui to San Francisco. Then he sat down to compose his text, going through twenty-nine variations be-fore he settled on one.

You showed me yours, let me show you mine. I'll pick you up at the airport. Dane

He pasted in the Hawaiian link, took a deep breath then hit Send.

Shared Static

'Iwa

Wanting something you know is a bad idea is a strange paradox of the human psyche. Which was why 'Iwa kept very busy that first week after Dane left, surveying plants and collecting seeds, playing guitar until her fingers stung, scouring the house top to bottom and researching land use laws in Hawai'i. But for every ounce of energy she spent trying not to think about Dane, it seemed his presence would be twice as intense the minute she lay down to sleep.

Despite all her best attempts, 'Iwa must have relived the waterfall scene two thousand times in her mind. His lips. Hands. Hard body. Hot breath pricking her skin.

The second week wasn't much better. Day fourteen came and went. 'Iwa pretended she wasn't counting, but that was a big fat lie. She'd left her phone at home all day on purpose, and when she got back, there were no messages. Her mood soured and she felt like climbing into bed and pulling the covers over her head. It was her own fault.

On day fifteen 'Iwa popped in for lunch at Uncle's. The place was empty, post-holiday crowds had thinned, and she persuaded Eddie to sit with her as she wolfed down a grilled sweet bread and cheddar sandwich. She'd had a quick surf session at Ho'okipa that had left her ravenous.

"Since when do you go surfing by yourself anymore?" her father asked.

"I don't know. It was small and glassy and I figured I should get out there."

He gave her a knowing look. The one with his head dropped, dark eyes boring into her, that said, *You can't fool me, I'm your dad.*

She shrugged. "I had fun surfing while Dane was here. It made me want to get back into it a little. I mean, we live so close to the beach."

This was the first time Dane's name had come up between them since his departure. She'd purposefully avoided talking about him, as if that might make him less real, and her father never asked.

"I like da guy," Eddie said, picking up the other half of her sandwich and taking a bite.

He never liked the guys she dated. 'Iwa was too good for every single one.

She gave him a love swat. "Hey, no cheese for you."

He took another bite, a bigger one. Eddie would do what Eddie wanted to do, heart trouble be damned. On the table, her phone began to vibrate. They both looked at it. She made no move to grab it, but craned her neck so she could see who the message was from.

"No mind me," her dad said.

She slid the phone over, as though not that interested, but then her heart did a somersault. She saw that it was from Dane. Without reading it, she flipped the phone over.

"*Auwe*, girl. Read the damn thing."

Unable to say no to her father, she read it.

You showed me yours, let me show you mine. I'll pick you up at the airport. Dane

She read it a few times, trying to make sense of the words. Then she noticed that the link was to Hawaiian Airlines. She

opened the link, which showed a round trip ticket to San Francisco, leaving in two days. The tips of her ears began to burn,
and a warm sensation coiled up and around her chest.

Eddie lost patience. "You can't just leave me hanging. What
does it say?"

"He bought me a ticket to San Francisco—on Wednesday."

He raised his eyebrows and whistled. "I better get your shifts
covered."

She held a hand up. "Stop. I'm not going."

"Why not?"

"I can't drop everything and fly to California because some
dude sent me a ticket. That would be absurd." And reckless and
weird and impossible. "Wouldn't it?"

"Sometimes love makes you do absurd things."

"Love? I just met the guy, Dad, come on."

So why did the thought of being with Dane again, in his ele-
ment, make her all morning-sunshine and honey-sweet feeling?

His face turned serious and he reached out for her hands and
held them in his cracked leather palms. "I know more than
anyone how you've been burned, 'Iwa. But you can't just shut
down like an old sugar mill and make up a million and one
excuses why you nevah goin' date again."

"Dane is all wrong—"

"Hang on. Is that how you really feel? Because if it is, I'll
stop right now. Hell, give me the phone, I'll even text him
back myself."

He reached for the phone, but she held on tight.

A plum pit formed in her throat. "What if I go and I hate it?"

"What if you go and you don't?"

"The waterfall—"

"Will still be here when you get back. Think about what your
mom would have said if it was her sitting here instead of me."

'Iwa closed her eyes, imagining Lily across the table from
her, smelling like lavender and chocolate, quoting lyrics from

obscure love songs, and then she would have said, *Your choice, sweet pea, but choose well and choose love.* As a kid, this phrase annoyed her to no end. It felt like she was being given a choice, and in the same breath, that choice was being taken away. Now she was coming to see the wisdom in it. Lily had left her fingerprint on everything, which made her humungous absence almost bearable.

"Choose well and choose love," 'Iwa said.

His eyes turned watery and he gave her a sad smile. "I miss her."

"Me too."

Who knew what the future held with Dane, but what did she have to lose?

"Three days?" she said.

"Piece of cake."

She picked up the phone and tapped away, butterflies swarming in her stomach.

Be careful what you wish for. See you soon x.

Then hit Send before she could chicken out.

Dane stuck to his word. Only that one message was sent. 'Iwa had packed light, bringing her only winter gear, which wasn't much. She pressed her forehead to the cold window as the plane descended, looking out at dark water and gloom. Nerves began to creep in the closer she got to landing, and then once on the ground, she found it hard to breathe. Sure, they'd spent some time together, but her introvert self wasn't used to spending three full days with a person, especially one she didn't know all that well. In the bathroom, she splashed water on her face, smoothed out her hair—which had gone limp in the dry plane air, and dabbed on some lipstick. Then she made her way to the curb, petrified.

When the doors opened, she was struck by a stiff blast of cold wind. The air smelled foreign here, of cable car brakes and fog and fish. 'Iwa had no idea what she was looking for, and began searching all the cars for a familiar face. People were all business here, zooming in and picking up their passengers in winter coats and stylish boots. Wearing her old cowboy boots, ripped jeans and an old wool sweater of her mom's, 'Iwa was most certainly the least stylish person in the whole airport. When you came from a land of rubber slippers and summer dresses, fashion was easy.

After standing on the curb for ten minutes, teeth chattering, she checked her phone again. It was still on airplane mode. When she turned it on, there were three messages from Dane. **Running behind, five minutes late. Sorry, make that ten.** And finally, **We didn't factor in traffic, hang tight.**

We?

Moments later, a black Ford truck piled high with board bags and towing a jet ski pulled up right in front of her. The passenger door opened and Dane hopped out. 'Iwa stood still, unsure of how to approach. But Dane held his arms in the air, as he would coming off a perfect wave, and made a beeline for her. He wore a rust-orange jacket and a beanie that accentuated the angles of his cheekbones.

When he reached her, he pulled her in for a hug and whispered into her hair, "You came."

His arms felt strangely like home.

She thought of the moment she saw his message. "You left me no option."

"I was thinking my chances were fifty-fifty at best, then when you weren't answering my texts, I started to wonder," he said, taller than she remembered.

Dane pulled away and smiled, grabbing her hand and leading her to the truck. Kama, who had been waiting in the driver's seat, came around.

"Welcome to Cali, where the water's cold and the sharks hungry," he said, hugging her tight.

Having Kama there with Dane was like a pressure release valve, and 'Iwa immediately loosened a little.

Dane knocked Kama in the arm. "Don't listen to him."

They refused to tell her where they were going, and 'Iwa had no idea if they were headed north, south, east or west, but they climbed over some scrubby hills dotted with conifers filled with squirrels. On the other side, the ocean appeared, slate gray under a monochromatic sky. A sign said *Half Moon Bay*. She should have known. They were headed to Mavericks, California's best known big wave.

As daylight dimmed into night, they met up with Hope and a light-eyed, bushy-bearded man named Yeti with the demeanor of a monk. His voice carried hints of an Australian accent and he seemed to float around the house they were staying in—a modern wood and glass structure that belonged to a friend. Everyone had their own bedroom, which made 'Iwa breathe easier. And yet, every time she looked at Dane, a line of heat shot up her spine.

There was a heightened energy in the air, a shared static between the four surfers, that rubbed off on her. From growing up on Maui, she recognized it well. Yeti and Kama were welcoming, if not all business, but Hope barely acknowledged her presence. It made 'Iwa wonder how many girls Hope had seen Dane cycle through.

Over deep-dish chunky tomato and pineapple pizza—Yeti was a vegetarian—and sparkling water, they plotted the morning's approach. By first light, the swell should be already pumping, so they'd be ready to launch the skis at dawn.

"Intervals are seventeen seconds. Looks like the waves are still tracking to move under the Farallones, and winds should be nonexistent, at least for the first part of the day," Yeti said, after reading the latest update.

"When's low tide?" Dane asked.

"Ten forty-five."

Hope surfed big waves, but she had a limit. She was also an experienced ski operator. On days like tomorrow, Dane, Kama and Yeti would each switch off with her as partner, allowing more time for catching waves as she drove the ski. 'Iwa, it turned out, would ride in a motor boat with Jeff and Hilton, two Patagonia photographers, so she could see the waves up close.

"Only if you want to, though. There's always the beach on the north side, but you can't really see much from there," Dane was quick to say.

Apparently, Mavericks broke a half mile offshore, and Vandenburg Air Force Base owned the bluff, so cliff viewing was not the same as Pe'ahi, where you could get a bird's-eye view if you knew where to be.

"Put me in the boat," she said.

She was here, might as well get the full experience.

After everyone had drifted off to their rooms, Dane and 'Iwa sat on the patio wrapped in blankets and sipping hot cocoa, talking about everything and nothing. It felt like being at a sleepover, except in this case her friend was a very hot man. But she also felt a shyness she hadn't felt on Maui. Maybe it had something to do with being on his turf. Or feeling guilty for all of the thoughts she'd been having about his mouth working its way down her abdomen.

After a time, he dragged his heavy wooden chair closer, and said, "So what was it that changed your mind?"

"Changed my mind about what?"

"About seeing me again. Coming here. In the truck that last afternoon on Maui, you seemed pretty skeptical about the whole thing."

She had hoped she wouldn't have to explain herself. Even she didn't know quite what she was doing here. "My dad talked me into it."

The corner of his mouth curled up. "That's not what I expected to hear, but I'll have to thank him."

"Yeah, well, he thinks I'm too serious and I work too much and I need to have fun. Your invitation sounded fun and a little bit like a dare, so here I am," she said, realizing she probably sounded more standoffish than she meant to. On one hand she wanted to be here badly, and was so happy she came. On the other, she was scared at how much Dane made her feel.

"You like a good challenge, huh?"

"In the right circumstances," she said, then tried to soften her response. "But really, he asked me what I thought my mom would say, and I know she would have told me to come, to take a chance."

"Don't feel you have to explain any more—I'm just happy you took me up on my offer," he said, standing up and holding a hand out to her without another word.

'Iwa took it and he pulled her up and into a warm hug. She inhaled deeply, breathing in the smell of citrus soap and California on his skin. She let her cheek rest against the rise and fall of his chest as he ran his fingers through her hair. They stood there for a while, not saying anything, and he felt so solid— more mountain than wave.

She, on the other hand, had a chest full of moth wings. The desire to properly kiss him had been building all day, and when she could no longer take it, she stood on her tippy-toes and lightly pressed her lips to his. He seemed caught off guard, but immediately recovered, and kissed her deep and slow, and a little rough. One of his hands ran up her shirt, brushing up against the bottom of her breast, while the other tugged at her hair. Before she knew it, she was practically straddling his thigh.

God, he felt good.

Then sanity struck like ice water. What happened to her plan to take it slow? See how things went? This was more a reconnaissance mission than anything, she told herself.

Behave.

Dane seemed to register her change, and he stepped back and said, "Let's get you inside and to sleep. We have a big day tomorrow."

Steep And Deep
Dane

The morning started with the usual rituals, while 'Iwa still slept. Dane woke up at 3:00 a.m. and couldn't fall back asleep, so he climbed out of bed at quarter to four, brewed an over-sized pot of coffee and stretched his body. Yeti rose a half hour later, meditated, then drank a mushroom tea that tasted like dirt. No one else ever touched it. Kama rolled out of bed late, on Hawaiian time, chipper and ready to take on the world. Hope buzzed around with her checklist, organizing and ordering everyone around in a loving way.

Dane had been nervous to bring 'Iwa into the mix for this trip, and he hadn't even told anyone until they were already on the way. Too big a risk. He dropped the news when they were about to pull out of Yeti's garage.

"By the way, I have to make a stop at SFO," he'd said.

No questions asked, they all knew exactly what was going on. Kama grinned, Yeti nodded once, Hope rolled her eyes, and that was that. Having 'Iwa in California had given him the same kind of high as pulling into a stand-up barrel on a sheet glass day.

Fog pooled under the street lamps as they made their way to Pillar Point Harbor, turning the morning an eerie yellow. The boat ramp buzzed with trucks and boats and skis, and hordes of amped-up surfers in wetsuits and beanies, coffee flasks in every hand. Each vehicle that rolled in had board bags or boards stacked high on its racks. Rainbows of expensive fiberglass. Dane had brought a 10′2″, his trusty big wave gun, with a 9′8″ as backup, in case the waves were smaller than anticipated. Both mint green, his signature color.

Until they made it out in the water, there was no way to tell what the waves were doing. A consistent roar came off the ocean, stirring up sea spray, adrenaline and stoke. It coated everything—boards, jet skis, cars. Jeff and Hilton showed up soon after they arrived, and Dane introduced them to 'Iwa, who was wrapped head to toe in Patagonia he had handpicked at their headquarters in Ventura. Jacket, beanie, fleece, even a wetsuit—but that was for later. One of the perks of being an ambassador.

"Take good care of her and keep her dry. She has tropical blood," he told them.

'Iwa laughed. "You forget I swim in ice water streams high on a volcano."

"Not the same."

Hilton and Jeff were two top surf photographers, and Dane felt lucky to have them on his team. Nowadays, in the remote places they were riding waves, you brought your own. The XXL was a different beast than the pro circuit with its staff photographers and hundreds of freelancers. And the XXL judges took their job seriously, with help from researchers at Scripps Institute for Oceanography. They weren't just looking at the photograph or video; they took into account tides and sunlight, something called wave setup phenomenon, the height of the surfer, and a whole slew of other fine details. Last year, the analysis explaining the winning wave had been fourteen pages long.

Dane gave 'Iwa a hug, leaning in and pressing his forehead against hers. "Wish us luck."

No matter how many times he did this, the fear remained.

"*E hoʻoikaika nō,*" she said.

A puff of steam came from her mouth when she spoke, and he felt doubly blessed by her words and her warm breath.

"Be ready," he said.

A crease formed between her eyes. "Ready for what?"

"To ride on the ski with me later."

She nodded him off. "I'm fine in the boat, Dane, really I am."

"I didn't bring you here to leave you on a boat with two other guys all day. I promise, you'll love it."

The look on her face said otherwise, but she smiled and said, "We'll see."

In the world of big wave surfing, there were heavies among the heavies, and Mavericks was the West Coast's saltwater bad boy. A monstrous green slab of heavy water. Some waves were in a league of their own, a surfer's paradise or worst nightmare, depending on a number of variables. Swell direction, wave height, wind speed, water temperature, marine life (aka sharks, especially great whites), coastline topography (aka deadly rocks), which all conspired to enlighten you or rip you to shreds.

As far as Dane was concerned Teahupoʻo in Tahiti took top honors in the heavy department. In a weird twist of bathymetry, the water sucked out so you were actually below sea level when on the wave. But the wave's hollow barrel and crystalline water somehow made it doable. If any wave was a freak of nature, Chopes—as everyone called it—was *it*.

Then you had Cloudbreak in Fiji, which would be the world's most perfect wave if it weren't so shifty, with a razor-sharp living reef waiting for you, jaws wide open. He had the scars on his back to prove it. Dungeons in South Africa, with its double ups, unpredictability and shark-infested water, was Dane's least favorite. Hold-downs there were legendary—long and dark and vicious. One of his favorites was Waimea, big wave surfing's original darling, but now Waimea had become so crowded it was almost pointless to go—unless you were in the Eddie Aikau Big Wave Invitational, which only ran every few years.

There were also a few outliers. Cortes Banks was in a realm all its own—one hundred miles off Southern California, waves seemingly formed out of nowhere. An ancient island called Kinkipar had left behind shoals surrounded by deep, deep water, and those shoals caught giant swells that were sometimes ride-able. If anyone dared. Dane dared once, and watched another surfer nearly drown under the mountain of whitewater. The boat ride back to shore took hours. Knowing CPR was a given; they were all certified.

As Mark Foo once said, "If you want the ultimate thrill, you have to be willing to pay the ultimate price." In 1994, Foo had paid the price—at Mavericks.

Nazaré was another outlier. The newest initiate. The one now looming large in Dane's psyche. The next frontier, waiting to be ridden. But right now, he was at Mavericks, and Maver-icks demanded his full attention.

There was always a moment of boiling anticipation as they approached, before the wave came into view. Thunder rever-berated through his teeth, letting him know the ocean meant business. The sun was still trapped in the fog and sea spray. It was hard to see anything through the veil, and they gave the boneyard—rocks on the point—a very wide berth. Several boats and skis had beat them out and were circling like vultures, but with visibility so low, it would be suicide to attempt to ride.

"What do you want to do?" Kama asked.

"Wait."

Yeti and Hope were close behind, but the boat broke away, and went farther outside and into the safety of the channel. The last thing anyone wanted was to be caught inside when a freak set swung in. But it happened. Dane had seen it more than once. Yard sale in the impact zone. Dangerous for everyone.

Nineteen minutes later, the sun burned through the clouds, thinning the fog and dropping pools of light on the ocean's surface. At the same time, a set moved toward the break. Dane and Kama both stood up on the ski to gain a better view.

Then Kama said, "Ho-ly shiiiiit!"

A mountain range on the move.

Dane felt a squeeze in his chest. "Damn, looks like she's awake." He glanced toward the boat and waved them farther into the channel. Not that he needed to, because Captain Lenny had already seen what was coming. "Easy, biggest swell of the season."

They watched wave after perfect wave hit the reef and jack up into A-frames and barrels big enough to drive a school bus through. The only two guys in the lineup had scratched for the horizon when they'd seen the set, and were now sitting in the channel, no doubt shitting their pants. Explosions of whitewater turned the whole inside into a white and frothy cauldron. That was actually the name—The Cauldron, just inside the Corner, where boils and whirlpools and riptides would readily drag you across the bottom or pull you into the abyss given the chance.

"Ready?" Kama asked.

"Roger."

Dane threw his board in the water, jumped on, crossed himself and grabbed the rope. Slow and even breaths through his nose dropped him into the space where he noticed everything and nothing all at once. Water droplets on his board, a pelican skimming the glass in front of him, the pungent smell of broken-up kelp.

Mavericks was a right-hand break, but the occasional hellman would go left, if the opportunity arose. Lefts were out of the question today. Within minutes, the two guys from the channel, legends Jeff Clark and Peter Mel, came over, as did Yeti and a couple north shore O'ahu guys. The big wave brotherhood was small enough that most of them knew each other or at least *of* each other.

"Any Outer Bowl action?" Dane asked Peter.

"Not yet."

Whenever they were paddling in, Yeti had a penchant for sitting outside and deeper than everyone else. He usually caught fewer waves, but was more discerning and only took off when all things aligned, which meant he rarely wiped out. The difference in danger levels between Mavericks and Waimea or Pe'ahi was all in the cold water, and if you weren't used to wearing a wetsuit, it could feel suffocating and restrictive.

But none of these things were going through Dane's mind. A set was coming in, and all his senses heightened. Not as big as the last, but still big. Jeff took the first wave, a steep one with a spooky face, Peter took the next, and Dane got thirds. Dusty and Mark were screaming *"Go, go, go"* as Kama pulled him up to the high point, then dropped him into a near free fall, several stories down. Thank God for the oil slick conditions, or his nose would have caught a bump and sent him. He made a sweeping bottom turn, then came back up, picked a line, just trying to stay ahead of the cracking lip. Next thing he knew, he was on the shoulder, wave over, legs burning, his whole body smiling. A series of calls, whistles and yells came from the channel and the lineup.

That's how it was there—every wave, every guy. Either cheers or groans, depending on how things went.

And so it went for the next few hours. As the tide dropped, the waves hollowed out and became more consistent. Dane and Kama switched places a few times, then Hope and Yeti switched. There were now about twenty-five guys out. Most knew what they were doing, but a cocky kid from Brazil who kept taking off way too deep got slammed by the lip, broke his leash and was dragged inside. Dane could see him stuck in the froth and getting pulled toward the rocks.

"He's in trouble," Kama yelled.

Dane waved down Yeti and hopped on, leaving his board

with Kama. Dane climbed in front with no objection from Yeti. They all knew Dane was the guy you wanted driving the ski when things got really hairy. The kid's head was bobbing around like a coconut. Dane drove in as far as he could safely, keeping one eye on the kid and one eye on the surf. Then the kid's head went under, and stayed under. If Dane and Yeti went in, they risked getting slammed into the rocks themselves, but if they didn't, there was a good chance the kid would die.

Full throttle, they beelined just inside of where he had gone under. *Come on, come up!* But the kid didn't come up.

"Outside," Yeti said calmly, as if announcing Dane's tea was ready.

Dane turned to see the first wave of the set about to break. That meant they only had seconds to get out of there. Whitewater thundered on rock. Spray shot fifty feet in the air. Fragments of light fell around them. Everything went quiet, and he heard his mother's voice. *You are never more alone than in the ocean, and yet the ocean is always with you. Best friend, worst enemy. Murderer. Savior.*

He arced a quick turn, and as he did, he saw something red just beneath the surface up ahead. The kid's wetsuit. Then a head popped up.

He slowed. "Grab him!"

You could tell by the dazed look on his face, the kid didn't know which way was up. But Yeti knew the drill, leaned down and scooped the guy onto the sled behind the ski. All in one fluid motion. Dane punched it as a wall of whitewater came at them.

"Hold on!" he called back to Yeti.

There was no way through it, so he turned in and headed toward the cliffs, then skirted along toward a narrow gap of calm between the chaos. They were feet away from the skull-crushing boulders of the boneyard. Yeti remained silent and stoic in the back, lying on top of the other guy to keep him on the sled. The next line of foam was bigger than the last. This time, punching through it was the only option.

He thought he heard Yeti say "Fuck."

Yeti never swore.

For a moment, Dane felt a sickening inertia, as though the ski might go over backward, but they made it over. A hard landing, then they were in the deep green water of the channel. Dane slowed to a crawl.

"Is he okay?" he asked.

"Seems to be, but I don't think he speaks English."

Yeti slid off the Brazilian, who rolled over and lay on his back, arms out. He was shaking. Whether from nerves or cold or injury, it was hard to tell.

"That red wetsuit probably saved your life," Dane said, resisting the urge to tell him how reckless he'd been.

At the boat, 'Iwa and Jeff stood on the side waiting and helped Yeti transfer the guy aboard. Jeff wrapped a blanket over the trembling kid, who nodded his appreciation. These were the kinds of experiences that stayed with a person and shaped the way you approached surfing and life. Hopefully, it would be a valuable learning experience. School of long hold-downs.

Dane shook his head and smiled at 'Iwa. "Another day at the office."

"You guys are a little bit crazy," she said, cheeks pink from the cold.

"So I'm told."

"I will admit, I'm a little bit in awe."

Yeti turned off the ski and they floated alongside the boat. "Big waves are spiritual. We're hardwired to be drawn to them."

Dane was with him on that. It was the only explanation for why he kept throwing himself into life-ending situations time and time again. Kama and Hope came by with Dane's board, then took off back to the lineup. Dane and Yeti joined them after downing an energy bar and one of Yeti's power dirt mixes. Coffee, cacao, coconut butter, cinnamon, oat milk and a few secret ingredients he swore turned you into a Ninja. This one tasted miles better than the mushroom one, and had a kick.

Back in the crowded lineup, a new pulse had arrived, bumping up the size considerably. Dane had had plenty of good rides, but none big enough to be a contender for the XXL Big Wave Awards. Yeti turned around and gave him a glance, and Dane nodded. Without a word, Yeti drove them to the Outer Bowl, prepared to wait however long it took. One other team joined them, but kept their distance. Above, the sun crawled east to west. Dane took in every nuance in current, checking his place between the big satellite disc on the hill and Mushroom Rock.

Then, a mammoth appeared on the horizon. When it approached, the wave was much farther out and bigger than anything else that day. Yeti towed him out toward the wall of water, which was now standing up like a mutant.

"This one!" Dane yelled.

Yeti turned. "You sure?"

There was probably something ungodly behind it, ready to clean them all out. "Now or never." Yeti whipped him in and Dane took the high line, speeding ahead to avoid the lip. The rail of his board carved into an olive green face, high as a cliff. Immaculate, deadly. Every pore in his body was firing.

This was not the kind of wave you fell on if you wanted to live. But if he did fall, he knew Yeti was there for him. A brotherhood of trust. The board hummed beneath his feet. Somehow, he managed to make that section and continue into the Corner, where all the other skis had scattered like sea lions from a shark. In pure survival mode, Dane crouched as low as he could, feet turned into gnarled old pines, rooted to the board.

And then he was out.

In the channel.

He threw his arms up, not claiming, but in prayer.

Wanting more.

The law of the ocean.

Incoming

'Iwa

Why someone would want to surf in gloves, booties and a hood, 'Iwa would never know. But apparently a whole slew of them did. She was happily swaddled in fleece on the boat. It was strange to think that this was the same ocean as hers, with its ice water, kelp and abundance of seagulls. The cliffs were sand colored rather than black lava, and everything seemed bigger, even the waves.

Dane was easy to spot, with his mint green board. Her eyes seemed to automatically find him in the crowd of black wetsuits. He looked so comfortable, so completely at home, as if it were all so easy. *Another day at the office.* He hadn't been kidding.

Now Yeti pulled him back out, after riding the wave of the day. She pointed her camera toward him and he gave a shaka and a high-octane smile. They came to the boat.

"Unbelievable. How big do you think that was?" he said, as he sat up a few feet from the boat, pulled off his hood and hooted.

"Easy forty-foot face," Jeff said.

Hilton leaned off the rail. "Glad you came out of that thing alive, mate, is all I have to say."

"For a second I thought I was going down."

"No one on the boat was breathing for a good minute," Jeff said.

"Any good shots?" Dane asked.

"Good shots for sure, but I don't think it'll be an XXL contender."

Dane and Yeti switched places, and Yeti hopped onto the boat.

Hilton tossed Dane a sandwich. "Eat."

Dane unwrapped it, took a few bites, then turned his bloodshot eyes on 'Iwa. He gave her a playful smile. "Time to put on that wetsuit, you're up."

After witnessing that last set almost take out a few jet skis, she wasn't so sure she wanted to be anywhere near where the wave broke. On the other hand, she'd be with Dane, who looked to be the most competent person in the water. She slipped into the thick wetsuit, pulled on the booties and climbed onto the jet ski behind Dane.

"Hang on tight, and don't forget to breathe," Dane said.

They circled around and putted toward the break, where a few other skis hovered. Everyone out there was spaced out evenly, as though according to some unspoken law. She clung like an *'opihi* to Dane's waist, which was hard as a plank, and rested her head on his shoulder. His body heat passed through her, warming her up from the inside.

"Shouldn't we be outside further?" she had to ask, nervous about another cleanup set.

He put a hand on her knee and squeezed. "I got you."

There was a lull, placid water belying the real state of the ocean. But eventually, on schedule, another set appeared. All eyes were on the horizon, including 'Iwa's. The skis all began the rush out.

"Here we go," Dane said.

She waited for him to drive them farther out, but they remained floating where they were. Her heart feather dusted the inside of her rib cage where Dane could probably feel it against his back. When the peak of the wave hurled up and steepened, a bald man dropped in. A second later he was screaming down the face, straight toward where 'Iwa and Dane sat. The roar was constant. From sea level, the wave took on a distorted mass as it hurled up over them. 'Iwa closed her eyes for a moment, too afraid to look. But space and time had warped, she realized, because when the wave finally spit him out onto its shoulder, he was still a good twenty feet away.

"Yeah!" Dane yelled.

'Iwa wiped the spray from her face, unsure whether she was laughing or crying. Either way, she was glad for the salt water on her skin. Being in the thick of it made her feel *of* the ocean. It also gave her a peek into Dane's world. She hugged him closer and readied for more.

They sat and watched, moving a little farther in or out depending on the size of the sets, until she could no longer feel her toes, even in the booties. The wind had kicked in, too, roughing up the waves. From there, conditions deteriorated fast.

"A Hawai'i girl, through and through," Dane said, when she finally asked to go back to the boat.

That evening, the wind had cleared away any leftover clouds, and twilight went on forever. They gathered at a joint called Half Moon Bay Brewing Co., which had a sweet open-air deck. A man in a cowboy hat was playing guitar—a vintage Martin that had 'Iwa swooning—and singing covers. They sat next to heat lamps, gulping down freshly brewed beer. The atmosphere was reminiscent of the night she'd met Dane at Uncle's, with surfers of all shapes and sizes milling about. But this time, 'Iwa understood what the fuss was all about. That powerful wave energy had transferred into her, and she still felt lightheaded.

She sat with Dane on one side, and Yeti on the other. Dane kept at least one body part touching her at all times. Shoulder to arm, thigh to thigh, hand to knee. Electricity was building between them, causing little sparks in their field. 'Iwa wondered if Dane felt it, too.

Yeti intrigued her. Beneath all that hair, he was handsome, with a strong nose, and yellow-gold eyes that seemed to notice everything, even the unseeable. It was impossible to tell how old he was, but she guessed at least forty. He was the only one drinking water.

Word was going round that soon after they had gone in, a great white shark had cleared the few remaining guys in the lineup. A ski operator had spotted the shark—which was longer than his ski and sled combined—cruising by one of the two paddle surfers out there, then swinging around for another pass. The man blasted in and plucked them out of the water.

Now, at the table, the group shared shark stories.

"I got the shark vibe a couple times today, but then I always get it at Mavericks, so what am I supposed to do?" Kama said.

Dane shrugged. "They're always out there."

"I always thank the sharks before I get in the water, for watching out for me," Yeti said, without a hint of sarcasm.

It was a very Hawaiian thing to say, and it made her like him even more.

Hope had just shown up and squeezed in across the table. "The first time I ever came out here, I saw a two-foot fin in the channel. It's mostly why I stay on the ski."

"And here we all thought it was because of the waves," Dane said.

Hope gave him the finger.

"What about your story, Yeti?" Hope asked, then said to 'Iwa, "Yeti has the best one of all."

Yeti took off his jacket, pulled up his sleeve and revealed a jagged scar running almost the length of his forearm. The skin around it was puckered and purple. Smaller scars branched off from the main one. "This was my fault, I reckon, I don't blame the shark. I was surfing a river mouth in Mexico, and there had been bloody weeks of heavy rain. The water was murky and I knew I shouldn't go out. River mouths are notorious for sharks, but the waves were firing, as good as I'd seen it. So I went out," he said, pausing, looking down at his arm.

He then continued in the most nonchalant way. "I was with Doc Randall, a surfer friend from San Francisco who rips, but likes to keep his surfing on the down-low. We'd only been out about twenty minutes, when something slammed my board from the side and knocked me into the water. I knew right away what was happening, but it was so murky I couldn't see anything. I rolled into a ball and then felt this tremendous pressure on my arm. I kicked and punched as hard as I could with my other arm. It was just Doc and me out, and a Mexican kid. '*Tiburón!*' he started screaming.

"It was the wildest thing. I was outside my body, looking down at this shark holding my bloody arm in its mouth. It had a round nose. A bull shark with fishy breath. I wasn't so much afraid as I was intrigued. In awe even, to be witnessing my own death, you know? The fear of dying is so elemental, so ingrained, but this was so different from how I had imagined it to be.

"Then I snapped back to the thrashing shark, somehow shoved the nose of my board into its nose, and it disappeared back into the murk. Doc had ridden a wave in and wasn't around, and I could hear people screaming on the beach—the break isn't that far out. I was in this bloom of red water, and I lay on my board and tried to limp in, but instead, I passed out.

"Lucky for me, a bloke on the beach had a paddleboard, and Doc snagged it and came out to get me. If it had been anyone else there that day other than him, I wouldn't be here telling this story. He knew exactly what to do, made a tourniquet with his leash and got me to shore."

Dane rubbed his own forearm in the place where Yeti's scar was. "Doc is a legend," he said.

"He's my guardian angel, is what he is," Yeti said.

Maui took top honors in Hawai'i for shark attacks, and yet

'Iwa had never met anyone who had lived to tell. Plenty of near misses and sharks stealing fish, but no actual bites.

"Did the shark come back around?" she asked.

"I was lights out, but Doc said it bumped the paddleboard a couple times, and he kicked it in the snout. He was certain his foot was going straight into its mouth, but it must have had enough, because we made it in without further incident."

"You're lucky," 'Iwa said.

Yeti put his jacket back on, then flexed his left hand. "I have some nerve damage, but the fact that it works at all is a miracle. I came back from that trip a changed man and never take any day for granted."

His gaze then went to three women walking toward their table. Two brunettes and a knockout blonde. To 'Iwa, they all looked like supermodels—long hair, middle part, tight jeans, leather boots.

"Incoming," Hope said under her breath.

Dane turned to see what she was talking about, then quickly looked down into his beer, jaw tensing. The two brunettes sat at a nearby table, but not the blonde.

She came over to the table, stopped behind Dane and put a hand on his shoulder. "Hey, guys. Hey, Dane."

Everyone at the table said a lukewarm hello.

"Big day out at Mavs, huh?" she said with a forced smile.

Yeti nodded.

Kama said, "Yep."

She pushed back her hair. "Congratulations on your win in Maui, Dane. We were all rooting for you back here."

On Maui. 'Iwa wanted to correct her. You were *on* an island, not *in* one.

"Thanks, Sunny," Dane said, unenthusiastically.

Sunny smelled like clean sheets, sun-dried and dusted with lemon balm scented oil. She wore silver bracelets all the way up her delicate arms, and a long chain with a sunrise shell pendant nestled between full breasts.

"I didn't realize you were back. Are you home for a while? Wingnut would love to see you. You should stop by and say hi one of these days. He misses you," she said.

'Iwa couldn't help but wonder how many Sunnys there were out there in the world. Women who Dane had hooked up with, dated or even loved. The thought made her throat constrict.

"I won't be around long, but give him a hug for me," Dane said.

"Another big surf trip?"

An awkward pause.

Dane looked over at Kama. "Secret mission. Sorry, I can't talk about it."

This was news to 'Iwa and she glanced at Dane. His face gave away nothing.

Sunny took a step back. "Well, you know where to find us. Key's still in the same spot. Take care of each other on your mission wherever it is."

'Iwa watched her walk away, a sticky feeling in her mouth.

Dane turned. "Sorry about that. Sunny is my ex-girlfriend and Wingnut is our dog—was. He's hers now. We split last year."

Some of the color had drained from his face.

"I guessed that. It's fine," 'Iwa said.

"Cool dog, too. He surfs," Hope said, seemingly to lighten the atmosphere.

Of course he did.

"Speaking of dogs, did you know Mavericks was named after a dog?" Dane said.

'Iwa was still trying to take in the prior interaction, but welcomed the change in subject. "I did not."

"It's true. Sometime in the sixties, this white German shepherd used to try and follow three surfers out when they paddled out. The dog belonged to one of the guy's roommates, but he knew a good thing when he saw it, I guess."

Kama nodded. "Dogs are way smarter than people."

"You got that right," Yeti said.

'Iwa laughed. She liked these guys. Her mother always said that you could tell a lot about a man from two things: the company he keeps and how he treats animals. Dane was winning in those two departments. And as much as she hated to admit it, her mom would have liked him. A lot.

Later that night at the house, Dane walked 'Iwa to her room, stopped at the door and put his hands on her shoulders. Tentatively, he leaned down and kissed her lightly. She had been waiting all day for this moment and now that it was here, she wanted to savor it.

But Dane broke away, but stayed close enough so their noses were almost touching. "I hope you enjoyed it out there today. Not everyone has the guts to do what you did. It can be intimidating, I know."

Being in such close proximity caused a flurry of leaves to fall across her skin, or so it felt.

"Do you know, really?" she asked, looking up into his eyes.

"Even now, the waves intimidate me. How could they not?" His hand still cupped the back of her head. "Look, I know today was all about the waves, but I promise, tomorrow will be all about you. We can do whatever you want," he said, voice scraping across her skin.

"This is your town, Dane, I have no idea where to go and what to do. You pick something you think I would like."

He thought for a few moments, then said with a straight face, "How about we go to the mall?"

'Iwa was dumbstruck, then noticed the smile in his eyes, the tease in his voice. She laughed. "What's a mall?"

"Oh right, I forgot you're a forest nymph. Would you rather see some wildlife, then? The California kind?"

"I would love to."

"It's settled then. These guys will probably dawn patrol Mavericks again, so we'll have the place to ourselves in the morning."

'Iwa felt like she should take a step back, relieve the tension between them, but she was unable to. It seemed like Dane was having trouble doing the same, because he moved in again and his stubble rubbed rough on her cheek as he spoke softly in her ear. "We can take it slow."

Her mind flashed to a long, slow morning under the covers with him, those strong hands slowly making their way over her entire body.

"I would love to come in and tuck you in, but if I do, I worry I'd never leave," he said, eyelids at half mast, but a hunger in them nevertheless.

A few times on the way back from dinner, Dane's head had fallen to the side, and he'd jerked awake. 'Iwa was exhausted, too.

Against her body's wishes, she said, "It was a huge day for you. Get some rest and I'll see you in the morning."

He remained rooted in place, hair askew, bloodshot eyes— sexy as hell. 'Iwa willed him to kiss her, just as he leaned in, mouth catching hers. His hand moved to her sacrum, where it made smooth circles.

"Unless…you want to sleep in my room? I have a king-size bed and promise I would be a perfect gentleman. In fact, I can guarantee I'll be out the minute my head hits the pillow. But it would be nice to have you near me."

'Iwa felt her heart go thump. It was such a sweet and honest thing to say, and it took her less than a heartbeat to answer. "How can I say no to that?"

He rested his forehead against hers. "You can't."

Anything's Possible

'Iwa

The following morning, 'Iwa woke up in semi darkness. She was on her side, facing the window, Dane's hand resting on her hip. His breaths were deep and even and peaceful. The cawing of crows echoed through the valley, reminding her where she was. No blustery trade winds or cooing doves or roosters. Dane had been true to his word, and fallen asleep spooning her with his cheek in the curve of her neck. It was tender and innocent and made 'Iwa feel warmly cared for.

She lay there watching the sky lighten, and a few minutes later, Dane stirred. He pulled himself closer and nuzzled his face in her hair, making little contented noises.

"Morning," he said, all rough and muffled sounding.

"Morning."

"How'd you sleep?"

"Amazingly well."

It was true. Being with him in bed for the first time had felt strangely comfortable. *Dane* felt strangely comfortable, like a favorite blanket or a faded pair of jeans. But his touch made her toes tingle, and heat gathered at every point of contact.

He traced a finger down her arm. "I can't believe I'm waking up with you."

"Strange, isn't it."

A laugh. "Not strange. Amazing."

"You kept your end of the deal, so I figured I ought to honor that. Plus—" she paused, unsure how to voice what she was thinking "—the waterfall."

Dane kissed her neck lightly, breath hot on her skin. "What about the waterfall?" he asked.

"You know," she said, flushing at the memory of his mouth on her breast.

"I want to hear you say it."

She rolled over, looking into his eyes. "It felt like we had unfinished business there."

He drew a breath. "You're so right about that."

'Iwa's mouth opened and she was about to say something else—what, she had no idea—but Dane kissed her. Small, delicate kisses that made her thighs press together. She was wearing a tiny nightie, and his hand lifted it up, just a little to rest on her upper thigh. The roughness of his palms on her skin dialed up the heat.

Then, on the other side of the bed, a phone began to vibrate loudly on the wooden table. 'Iwa felt his jaw tighten, but he ignored it. It buzzed again just as his hand had moved its way to the hollow of her hip. 'Iwa willed it to stop. For a moment it did, but a minute later started up again.

Dane rolled away, groaning and looking at his phone. "Sorry, it's Kama, I should probably see what's up."

"Yo," he answered, shook his head a few times, then said, "You owe me. I'll be right there."

To 'Iwa. "The ski isn't starting and Kama forgot that I had the new spark plugs in my truck. I need to run down there. Bad timing—I'm sorry."

"It's fine. I'm happy just relaxing in bed, since I rarely get to do it back home."

He leaned over and smoothed down her hair, kissing her again, long and slow. "I'll make you breakfast and a special latte when I get back. Should be less than an hour. Wait for me, okay?"

She laughed. "Where am I going to go?"
He shrugged. "Just sayin'."

After a leisurely breakfast of cinnamon oatmeal and fresh berries, Dane took 'Iwa on a coastal trail that ran along cliffs and down onto endless beaches, where beach breaks pounded and seals lounged high up on the rocks. It was cold, gray and breathtaking. Thankfully there was no rain and no fog and they could see for miles. It was crazy to think you could just keep following this coastline up and down two whole continents, and the expansiveness made her dizzy. The entire Maui coastline would only be about 180 miles. So *manini*. So small.

"Those are harbor seals, but we also have elephant seals, northern fur seals and sea lions," Dane explained, when asked one of a thousand questions.

"What's the difference between a seal and a sea lion?"
He looked surprised. "You don't know?"
"We have no sea lions where I'm from."
"Their ears and flippers. Seals have no ear flaps, and sea lions' flippers can rotate under them, letting them sort of walk on land."

With only monk seals in Hawai'i, which you maybe saw once or twice a year, 'Iwa was thrilled by all the pinnipeds.

Most of the area they were hiking in was a marine preserve, and 'Iwa was impressed at how well maintained it was. Clearly marked trails and plaques and vistas with benches went on and on, seemingly forever. They hiked through gnarled old trees that held plenty of secrets, fields of succulents and rocky outcrops. She kept an eye out for bird nests and feathers. In the monochromatic lighting, it all reminded her of something you'd see in an old photograph, haunting and forlorn.

'Iwa was bundled for an Antarctic voyage, and still, the chill bit into her. The temps had dropped significantly since yesterday.

"How do you live in this cold?" she asked him as they stopped on a bluff to overlook the sea.

"This? This is nothing."

Dane was only wearing a long-sleeved shirt, jacket stuffed in his small pack, and seemed immune. Blood ran thicker here on the mainland. She tried to imagine herself living here, walking this coast and studying these plants or animals. Going home to Dane in the evenings. It had its own charm, but she wasn't sure it could ever feel like home.

"You must be part polar bear," she said.

"I prefer to think elephant seal."

She raised an eyebrow. "Oh, really?"

He laughed. "Get your mind out of the gutter, girl."

"I see you more sea otter than elephant seal," she said. *They're cute and everyone loves them.*

They arrived back at the house in the midafternoon and went straight to the hot tub. 'Iwa had been dreaming of sitting in the steaming waters since the moment the ocean tugged at her feet on the beach.

Dane had warned her. "I know it's a hard concept to grasp, but here we wear shoes on the beach."

"That's sacrilegious."

"If you go barefoot, those little toes of yours might freeze and crack off."

She had ignored him and took off her shoes, dodging cracked mollusks and huge clumps of tangled kelp and seaweed, covered in little flying bugs that Dane had told her were kelp flies.

Now she was facing the opposite problem. Sitting on the edge of the hot tub, unable to get in because the water was scalding hot. Dane watched her. He looked harmless enough, until he took off his shirt. The others were still away, and it was just the two of them. All day long, there had been this big unspoken agreement between them, that they weren't going to talk about anything serious, just enjoy the day. They both stuck to that, fiercely. But now, alone and half clothed, a new tension arose between them.

The setting was outrageous, really. Straight from the pages of a magazine, hanging over a gulch full of conifers, spacious and decorated sparsely with teak furniture and willowy plants. Everything revolved around a giant stone bowl—a gas fire pit, with chairs spread out around it. Whoever owned this house had boatloads of money.

"So what exactly does Yeti do?" she asked, with just her feet soaking in the water.

"He's a writer."

"What does he write?"

"Articles for *Outside, Inertia*, esoteric stuff usually."

"You two seem close."

"As close as anyone can get with Yeti. He's kind of like a friend and a dad and a teacher all wrapped into one. I owe him, big-time."

Dane had only spoken of his dad once—*he was out of the picture*, and that was that. It was hard to imagine not growing up with two loving parents by your side every step of the way, and his tight-knit group of friends now made more sense.

"Why is that?" she asked.

"For one, he saved my life. Literally. But he also changed my perspective. Yeti's this inner warrior kind of guy, and when you spend time with him, it rubs off on you. Before I met him, I thought I was so in tune, so in the groove with mother nature, that nothing could touch me. Yeti was the one who taught me discipline, and how discipline is a kind of worship in and of itself. Up until then, everything came easy to me, you know?

"One day, Yeti dropped off all these books at my house and told me not to call him until I'd read every last one of them. At the time I thought he was crazy. *Zen and the Art of Motorcycle Maintenance, Starlight and Storm*—a climbing book, *The Old Man*

and the Sea, *Light on Pranayama*, a pretty eclectic collection. He
left town for a few weeks and when he came back, he asked if
I'd read any of them."

"Had you?"

He wiped his forehead, which was now beading from the
heat. "Not a one. I remember the silence on the line, and how
loud it was. I've never heard anything like it. That night, I
started reading. It took me a while to get through them, but
I did and now I've read each a few times. And every time, I
learn some new truth."

"None to do with surfing?" she said.

"And yet all to do with surfing."

"Books are magic that way, aren't they?"

He nodded. "Pure alchemy."

"So, how did Yeti save your life literally?"

Dane, who was now sitting in the water with steam lifting
off his back, floated over to her side. "Sorry, ma'am, but you've
reached your question quota for the day. Now it's my turn."

She laughed. "I know, I know. My dad used to do the same
thing. Cut me off when he'd had enough."

"Curiosity is a beautiful thing," he said, standing up and
placing both hands on her knees, sending a swish below her
navel. "You...are a beautiful thing."

All dripping and steamy and flushed in the face, he leaned
in and kissed her. As his hands slid up her thighs, she moved
toward him slightly, a flower to the sun. His grip was firm,
and he massaged her taut muscles, which had been shivering
much of the day, kneading and slowly parting her legs as he
made room for his hips.

"I've been wanting to kiss you all day," he said.

It felt like they were resuming where they'd left off at Waikula, dripping wet and drawn together through the invisible
pull of water. 'Iwa stood to meet him, pressing hard against his
abs, wanting every square inch of her skin to be touching his.

Dane kissed her harder, and she stood on her tippy-toes, fever building. He tasted like pine forest and clouds, salt and a little bit of chai spiced latte. The kiss made her feel that everything was right in the world. Maybe he'd spend a couple years kissing her, then move on down to her breasts for another few years, and after that, several decades exploring below her waist.

Dane brushed his lips over her ear. "Any chance you could stay a little longer?"

She wished she could. "I have to work on Monday. Next time, give me more warning."

He set his hands on her shoulders and faced her, so close she could see water droplets on each individual eyelash. "So, there will be a next time?"

She was in up to her teeth and realized in that moment there was nothing she could do but surrender.

"Anything's possible," she said.

"Can I get that in writing?" he asked.

In response, she kissed him and gave him a playful bite on the lip. A few minutes later, when 'Iwa was beginning to feel lightheaded from the heat or maybe from his proximity, the rest of the crew arrived home. Car doors slammed, Dane straightened her bikini top and they sat back up on the side to cool off. A hawk blew in on an air current above, circling, and nearby, a crow screeched.

That night, after a take-out dinner of Indian curry with coconut rice cakes, samosas and spicy mango chutney, Yeti brought two guitars out from the bedroom. He handed one to 'Iwa.

"I hear you play," he said. He sat down on the edge of the fireplace, which was crackling and popping and filling the house with the smell of burnt cedar, and began to strum. "Do you know much Crosby, Stills & Nash?"

"Some," 'Iwa said.

Actually all, but she wasn't going to tell him that. When playing with new people, she liked to start off modestly, and let them take the lead. She stayed on the couch, next to Dane, tuned the guitar and joined him. Yeti kept a nice even rhythm, and his elegant fingers moved effortlessly up and down the neck.

"You, who are on the road..." he sang, in a voice that brought to mind whisky and crowded speakeasies.

She sang the next line. *"Must have a code that you can live by."*

It took them a few verses to sync up. 'Iwa used to sing this with her mom. Yeti's voice had notes of Eddie Vedder and Chris Cornell, but a style all his own.

Dane clapped when they were done. "I told you," he said to Yeti.

'Iwa set down her guitar. "But you didn't tell me. Yeti, thanks for taking me back to a song my mom and I used to play together. You're amazing."

"Nah, just playing around."

"Take the compliment, mate," Dane said, then to 'Iwa, "He used to play in a band in the outback when he was in high school."

"A band in the outback?" 'Iwa asked.

He winked. "Yeah, me and the dingoes."

They played on, 'Iwa enjoying the release after two full days of pent-up feeling. The more time she spent with Dane, the more time she wanted to spend with him. Which made her even more conflicted. Living for the moment had never worked out well for her, and those cracks in her heart still bled sometimes. So what was she really doing here?

Later, 'Iwa was lying on her stomach on the bed leafing through a book called *Ten Poems to Change Your Life*. She was so absorbed by one of the poems, that she hadn't realized Dane had come in, closing the door behind him. He slid in next to her, and she slammed the book shut, but kept a finger in place. The poem was sensual and arousing, and strangely reflected their experience at the waterfall. She felt as though someone had used her entire body to strike a match on.

"Have you read this?" she asked.

"No. Should I?"

"This poem could have been written about us at Waikula."

"Sounds like my kind of poem," he said.

"It's uncanny."

"I have to admit, most of the poems I've read were in school, about fifty years ago. They were about dead people or socks and I had no idea what any of them were really saying."

"You must have had a shitty English teacher," she said.

"Either that or I was a shitty student. Will you read it to me?" he asked, drawing circles on her low back with one finger.

She felt too shy to read it. "Here, you read it."

He studied the page for a few seconds, while 'Iwa studied the architecture of his face and his chapped lips. This close, she noticed an ever so slight dimple in his chin. His eyes grew wide, and then he set down the book and whistled. "I see what you mean."

"I wasn't imagining it, then?"

He leaned in and kissed her, feather light. "If you had been imagining it, I wouldn't fault you." Then, in a deep blue voice, he read from the beginning, whipping up her insides like the ocean bottom.

"She sits naked on a rock." He spoke each word slowly, intimately, giving 'Iwa plenty of time to conjure up images in her mind. A naked woman on a rock. A naked man picking blueberries. Swallows flying above. By the time he reached the part where the man kneels and the woman opens to him, she was nailed to the bed, unable to move or think. Dane took a breather for a moment, then continued.

"A great maternal pine whose branches
Open out in all directions
Explaining everything."

The second he finished the poem, Dane tossed the book on the floor. His fingers wove into her hair, pulling her head onto the pillow. Hard, soft, she didn't know which way was up. His mouth all over hers, her hands all over him. She slid them up his stomach, drawing out goose bumps on his marble-smooth skin, then down to his waist, tracing beneath the carved edges of his obliques.

A sound rose out of her. Somewhere between a cry and a whimper and a moan.

"You," he said, breathlessly.

His hand began to unbutton her shirt, and when he was done, she wiggled out of it. She held her breath as a heat ran through her. Next, he undid her jeans, moving as though he couldn't do it fast enough. And he couldn't. 'Iwa needed them off. Needed to feel his skin on hers. When she was down to just panties, he pulled back and took off his own jeans, but kept his briefs on.

They stared at each other for a moment, desire blazing, then Dane knelt over her and began to work his way down her body with kisses and love bites. Neck, nipples, ribs, waist, hips, then skipping down to the inside of her thighs. 'Iwa felt her seams begin to rip. A hot fullness building, ready to spill over.

"I want to taste you," he said, breath hot on her tender skin.

He ran his finger along the edge of her thong, dangerously close. Her breathing had become shallow and ragged, and the room, it seemed, had lost all its air. Dane was watching her, which for some reason, lit her up even more, and she nodded. Then he pulled the lace to the side and flicked her with his tongue, paused, flicked again, then drew a long, very slow line of fire up her middle. Her knees fell open and she moaned.

"I hope you know that I'm all yours, 'Iwa," he said.

She would have told him anything to keep him going at that moment. "I do."

Replacing his tongue with a finger, he moved back up so he was on top of her, hard as stone.

"You're killing me—again," he said.

"I'm already dead."

Her hips tilted up and she roped a leg around him, pulling him even closer. Their bodies began to move in tandem, ocean surging onto shore, then receding. Every surface of her skin hummed with anticipation, and she grazed his neck with her teeth. Goose bumps formed on his ivory ass.

He panted. "Should we talk about this?"

Talk?

"Definitely not," she said.

She opened herself wider to him, felt him pressing against her edges, and nothing else in the world mattered.

Por Qué

ʻIwa

Six weeks later

Kama slammed his fist against the steering wheel. "Brah, this happens every single effing time. I swear, I'm *pau* driving anywhere near Tijuana."

The outburst was so unlike him, it shocked ʻIwa, until she heard the siren whoop, and noticed the flashing lights behind them in the dusky sky.

"Federales. Let me do the talking," Yeti said.

"I don't think I was speeding, was I?" Kama asked.

"It doesn't matter. You were if they say you were."

It was ʻIwa's first time in Mexico, and she had no idea what to expect. They were already two hours behind schedule, thanks to a backlog at the border. Two men took their time getting out of the patrol car, then came to their windows, one on each side. Both holding scary-looking guns.

"Passaportes, por favor."

Everyone handed over their passports.

"Where you headed?" the guy asked in halting English.

"Ensenada," Kama said.

"Por qué?" said the other.

Yeti rattled something off that could have only been spoken by someone who'd lived in a Spanish-speaking country at some point in his life. He and the portly one with a handlebar mustache went back and forth for a while, then Yeti handed him a hundred-dollar bill, he handed back their passports and they were off.

"The price of doing business this side of the border. Pro tip: always bring a couple crisp Ben Franklins," he said, as they continued down the desert road.

If anything, the arid landscape had flavors of the south side of Maui. Dry and scrubby with its own kind of beauty. Somehow, that contrast with the ocean always made the water seem even more blue, more inviting.

According to Dane they were a little late in the season for perfect conditions, but a massive swell was approaching Isla Todos Santos, and this could be one of his last shots at winning an XXL award this year. After seeing Mavericks up close, the thought of free-falling down the face of one of those beasts made 'Iwa queasy. But boys would be boys and apparently, so would a few girls. Hope was already in Ensenada waiting for them, and from there they would take a boat to Isla Todos Santos.

This was 'Iwa's third trip to California. In February, she'd come to Santa Cruz for five days to see Dane's hand-built house, hike among the redwoods—she'd wept at their remarkable beauty—and meet his friend who'd had a hand in saving a particular grove of them. Dane made her laugh and tremble and sing. He seemed unable to get enough of her voice, and she seemed to be unable to get enough of his kisses. But it was his mind that really drew her in, and how he could talk for hours about the intricacies of the tides or the mechanics of bird wings and flight, then put on an apron and bake a mean sourdough. She loved his contradictions, and how beneath that sexy exterior, he was almost as big of a nerd as she was.

He had also made two weekend trips to Maui, timing them with back-to-back swells. Whether she wanted to admit it or not, Dane had become a part of her carefully constructed life.

Letting herself fall like this had been scary, but love wasn't always convenient, her father reminded her. It showed up on its own time and demanded attention.

With work and the Waikula fight in full swing, 'Iwa had been reluctant to come this time and felt a little guilty about leaving Winston and the small team at Maui Forest Recovery Project, who were trying to line up a good attorney. Even worse, Jones had begun a slick marketing campaign for his resort, which irked her to no end. But Dane had bribed her with another free ticket and the news that they'd be visiting a marine preserve full of migrating gray whales, whale sharks, manta rays, sea lions and white sharks. She promised herself that after this trip, she was going to focus her attention on Maui, and told Dane as much.

"I need to be there for our fight, for our organization," she said.

"As you should be. Can I help?"

She wasn't sure she was ready for him to get involved beyond giving her ideas. Not that there was much he could do, but opening this fight up to Dane somehow felt too intimate, too close to her heart.

"I'll let you know."

The name of the break in Ensenada was most appropriately called Killers. Their quarters were a rambling Spanish-style house on the outskirts of town—a whitewashed, red-roofed bed-and-breakfast run by a surfer couple from San Diego.

Crystal and Holmes were the groovy kind of folks who kept their own hens, cultivated herbs and vegetables growing out every nook and cranny, collected honey from their own hives, built their own furniture and sewed their own clothing— beautiful and summery and, yes, sustainable. Crystal, it turned out, had a successful line of dresses, and the oversized black-and-white photos of empty waves and windswept coastlines adorning the walls were all taken by Holmes, a cinematographer who everyone wanted on their team.

Their industriousness, though admirable, gave 'Iwa a major inferiority complex, because from the looks of things, they weren't much older than she was. She had to remind herself that things were different in Hawai'i, where a place like this would easily run a cool five million—or more.

It was just the two of them, her and Crystal, sitting on the patio sipping organic red wine that Crystal had probably mashed under her own two pretty feet. The guys and Hope were planning their morning assault on Todos Santos and placing bets on the exact swell angle and what time the wind would kick up.

"You two sure have created something special here. How long have you been in Mexico?" 'Iwa asked Crystal.

"Five years. We used to drive down and camp on the beach when we were in high school, sleeping under the stars and amongst armies of scorpions. Roughing it in the best way," she said, laughing. "When this house came up for sale, we jumped at the chance to buy it. You should have seen it back then, it was almost a teardown, which was the only reason we could afford it."

Impossible to picture now.

"Do you surf big waves, too?" 'Iwa asked.

"Depends on your idea of big. Holmes and I have always measured the face of a wave by the height of our old Land Cruiser. So, my limit is two Land Cruisers, no more."

"That's still pretty big. How about Holmes?"

Crystal coiled her long blond hair around her hand and sighed. "Holmes is fearless. He'll go out in anything. Rain or shine, *grande o pequeño*—sorry, do you speak Spanish?"

"*Poquito.*"

"*Bueno*, I don't even realize I'm doing it. What about you? You're from Hawai'i, you *must* surf."

"My dad surfs, so I learned young. I longboard, mostly head

high or smaller." Then she asked the question that had been plaguing her recently. "How do you handle Holmes going out in the huge stuff? Does it worry you?"

"He's safer out there than on the roads," Crystal said, swirling her wine in the oversized glass and pondering for a moment. "And, we have an agreement—he never goes out alone. Part of the beauty of the big wave culture is this intense brotherhood they've formed. These guys have each other's backs."

In the massive farm-style kitchen the group ate a quick breakfast of goat cheese and herbed potato frittata, crusty sourdough dripping in honey, tangerines and bananas, and barrels of coffee. The spread was waiting for them when they got up in the dark, and 'Iwa helped pack hummus and veggie sandwiches into the cooler, along with sparkling water and a twelve-pack of Pacifico bottles and limes.

Even this far south, the early morning air carried a surprising chill. Skies were clear and shining with stars, and in the east, turning a pale blue. They met Manuel, their local boat captain, down at the pier, and he helped load all their boards, dry bags, coolers and camera equipment onto a larger and more luxurious boat than they'd been in at Mavericks, with a wide covered bridge section. Its name—*La Ballena*. The Whale.

"You have your wetsuit?" Dane asked her for the twentieth time.

"Got it."

"What about an extra jacket?"

"It's in the bag."

"Gloves?"

'Iwa held up her hands to show him. "Dane. I have it under control."

He pulled her in with one arm and kissed her hard on the cheek. "I just want you to be comfortable. And have a good time. And want to keep doing this with me because…well, you know why."

Smiling, she said, "Do I? Please tell me."

"Because I surf better when you're around."

She poked him in the ribs. "Give me a break."

"Really, though," he said, scraping his lips over hers and lowering his voice so only 'Iwa could hear. "I can't get enough of you. Selfish, but true."

They traveled fast on the water, the approaching sun at their backs, the island a dim outline surrounded by a silver veil. The plan was to get out there before anyone else, and hit the surf at first light. With a middle tide, conditions were lining up to be all-time. Holmes was with them, checking his camera water housing.

"I'm only shooting for an hour if it's epic. Last time I waited too long and the wind got on it and I missed out," he said.

"Do what you need to," Dane told him.

"The grapevine says you guys have plans on going to Portugal this spring, am I right? Garrett says maybe end of March early April. It'll be warmer and maybe less de—"

He stopped himself when 'Iwa turned, a guilty look on his face.

"Deadly?" she said, finishing his sentence for him.

Dane pulled 'Iwa in close. "Nah, he meant delirious."

Right.

"Delirious? No one in the history of the world has used *delirious* to describe waves," she said, shaking her head.

"No, I was going to say decrepit," Holmes said.

'Iwa laughed out loud. "You guys are funny. It's okay, Holmes, they talk about this Nazaré wave all the time. I know it's huge. I know it's dangerous. I know it's cold, and I know it could be deadly. But then, being alive is deadly, isn't it?"

One side of Holmes's mouth went up. "I like your thinking, woman."

"She knows what she's talking about. On the Portugal front, we've been waiting for the right conditions. When we go, we want her to be just right," Dane told him.

Like most Hawaiian streams' *mo'o*, waves seemed to be female.

"You going to tow or paddle?"

"Tow. I think. Why, can you paddle in there when it's huge?"

"I haven't seen it myself. But Kama said he wants to paddle in."

Dane looked surprised. "We'll see then, I guess? You want in?"

"Hell, yeah."

From the look on Dane's face, 'Iwa could tell it was just a matter of time before he was on a plane to Portugal. Until they all were.

As they drew nearer to the island, 'Iwa noticed it wasn't one, but two. Manuel, who reminded her of her father with his quiet focus and bearlike build, gave her a little history, and she was glad he spoke English far better than she spoke Spanish.

"My father used to fish these waters. Said you could smell the islands from a mile away, so much bird poop."

"What kind of birds?"

"Ah...*cormoranes, gaviotas, pelicanos y ostreros*. Nowadays not so many, but they're coming back. I drive scientists here for years now, and they tell me bird numbers are improving. I came here as a *niño* with *mi papa*, but for fish, not birds."

"Are people allowed on the island?"

"Yes but not today. Too dangerous to land."

"Sounds like your islands and our islands have much in common," 'Iwa said.

He flicked his hand. "Same ocean, same planet."

Barrels, Tubes & Shacks
Dane

As they rounded the point, everyone on the boat was holding their breath, waiting to see what Todos Santos had in store. The wave broke on the western tip of the north island, off a rocky outcrop outside of two lighthouses, and was hidden from view from the mainland. Dane trusted Manuel—he knew these waters better than anyone—to keep them outside the surf, but close enough to get a good look. Now they were in between sets, the water silver smooth with patches of foam floating here and there.

Kama was already zipping up his wetsuit. "Evidence."

"The calm before the storm," Holmes said, eyes on the horizon.

They were the first ones out, but it wouldn't be long before others showed up. Initially ridden in the sixties, the break had managed to remain off the radar for another twenty years or so until *Surfing Magazine* ran an article that reverberated around the world. Suddenly, a world-class wave right off the coast of Baja California. Every big wave surfer wanted in.

Yeti, who had been sitting alone in the back, meditating on the ocean like he always did, came up to Dane holding his phone, his bushy eyebrows arched.

"Mate, the buoys have jumped up. Looks like the swell is going to be bigger than expected."

Last they checked, it was already going to be huge.

"What's the interval?"

"Harvest Buoy 24 feet, 17 seconds. Tanner Bank Buoy 26 feet, 17 seconds."

Dane almost spit out his coffee. "You're shitting me."

"I don't shit."

They had now slowed and were motoring outside the red and white lighthouse and brown cliffs splattered with white bird poop. Slick current lines flowed out to sea, and sucking boils appeared near the rocks. Manuel cut the engine and they waited. A few minutes later, two jet skis showed up. Water safety, care of Holmes, since a good portion of surfers who came out here stayed at his *casa*.

'Iwa came over and rubbed Dane's shoulders, saying nothing. One of the things he like about her. No wasted words. On the way out, he'd been watching her watch the ocean, observe the islands and birds, sniffing the air and looking stunning even under five layers of clothing.

"A penny for your thoughts," he said.

"It kind of feels like we've stepped back in time."

"Mexico has that effect. It's why I love it."

"What was Yeti saying to you a minute ago?"

For a split second, he thought of skirting the truth, but with 'Iwa it felt like he'd taken some kind of truth serum. In the past, when it came to women and surfing, he sometimes told white lies to make life easier. *Nah, it's not that big.* Or when he'd paddle out alone. *Going out with the boys.* But now, nothing untrue could come out of his mouth.

"That the waves are going to be bigger than we thought."

"It seems so peaceful now."

On the other side of the boat, Yeti said, "Incoming."

Dane leaned down and kissed her, inhaling the scent of coconut lotion coming off her skin. "What's your Hawaiian word for wishing me luck again?"

She held on to him a little longer than usual, her thin arms surprisingly strong. "*E hoʻoikaika nō.* It's not luck you want, but strength."

The waves seemed machine generated. Big—but not too big—peaks that stood up on the rocky point and peeled down the line. Wave faces glimmered in the morning sun with pieces of kelp glowing gold. For a blissful half hour, it was just the four of them in the lineup, with Holmes shooting. The waves were supposed to build throughout the day, so this was just the beginning.

Dane kept an eye on Hope, who sat closer to the shoulder, taking the smaller waves. She could charge with the best of them, but after a double-wave hold-down in Fiji last summer, she'd become more cautious. In big surf, the double-wave hold-down was every surfer's looming nightmare. A one-wave hold-down was bad enough in waves this big, lungs ready to burst, darkness and disorientation already critical. And then to get held down in that state as another wave passed over you, well, the experience would bring you to the brink. Dane hoped to never have the honor, but knew it was probably a matter of time.

The ocean will humble you.

When the next boat showed up, letting loose a posse of Hawaiʻi guys—Saville, Barels, Middleton, Christensen—Dane was stoked to share the lineup with such solid surfers, legit watermen. Guys who did it for the stoke, like him. Mother ocean kept the waves coming, providing enough for all. Then, as promised, Holmes went in and exchanged his camera for a long red gun. Hope also went in, setting up her giant telephoto lens on the front of the boat. ʻIwa sat with Manuel on the bridge, probably picking his brain and memorizing the names of every plant and creature around. Gulls skimmed across the face of unridden waves.

Could life get any better than this?

Slowly more boats began arriving, with more surfers. Every wave that broke peeled fast and clean. Todos Santos was delivering in the best possible way. But a little after ten o'clock, the sets started breaking farther out, and Dane got a prickly feeling on the back of his neck. The ocean gave off a briny scent, as though new levels of bottom were being stirred up. Wind came on, not too much, but enough to hold up the waves even more and making them harder to paddle into.

In order to catch a wave, you had to be moving faster than the wave. And the bigger the wave, the faster the water moved. Waves formed when the water traveling underneath the surface hit a reef or a sandbar or something solid, and then slowed. But the water on the surface kept moving at a higher speed. Once the water underneath could no longer support the water above, the wave broke, crashing down on itself. Barrels or tubes or shacks—whatever you wanted to call them—were formed.

As a kid, Dane knew this intuitively, but it was Yeti that made them all study the physics of waves and surfing. *Know your opponent*. Now the waves were getting harder to paddle into. His arms burned as he scratched to get into the last one, a fast, hurling right that almost took him down. A boil appeared and nearly threw him off the wave. At the last minute, he managed to come up high and fly off his board, over the feathering lip. The water tried to suck him over the falls backward, but he kicked with all his might and pushed through.

Dane paddled back out to where Yeti sat, noticing a strengthening current along the way. "I don't know how much more it can hold."

This was as big as he had seen Killers while still being able to paddle into it.

"I guess we'll find out," Yeti said, not taking his eyes from the ocean.

"Have you seen Kama?"

"He's on the boat. He lost a fin."

A small bump rolled in, lifting Dane and Yeti. He turned to look at the smattering of surfers in the lineup. The crowd seemed to have thinned and those remaining were not talking amongst themselves. They were all quiet in the way that surfers were when the situation became critical.

Yeti lay down and started paddling. "I'll see you back in the boat."

"You're leaving?"

Yeti didn't answer.

"One more and I'll be there," Dane said, wanting that wave that would at least put him in the running for the XXL.

Seven minutes later, the wave he had been waiting for came right to him, an enormous, burly thing that flung him down the face at Mach 5. This one threw a thundering barrel behind him, but he was too far ahead to pull inside. The remaining surfers scrambled to get out of his way. He barely made it past the pitching boil, when the wave walled up even steeper. He had no choice but to keep riding, on and on and on, closer to the cliffs.

When he kicked out on the inside, he understood why everyone had been paddling wildly toward the horizon. The next wave was bigger than anything they'd seen yet and cleaning out everything in its path. An absolute closeout. Dane watched Saville and Barels get sucked over the falls backward and detonated, and the rest of the guys were bobbing around in the whitewater trying to collect their boards.

He started paddling out, but got mowed over by froth as he tried to duck dive. The water ripped his board out of his hands, but his leash held. *Breathe, Parsons, you got this.* Once he slid back on the board, though, he took a few strokes and was hit by another explosion of whitewater. Another unsuccessful duck dive. Then another. His ears ached and his lungs felt the squeeze. And the waves just kept coming. His board felt wobbly, and it took him a moment to understand it had buckled in the middle.

Fuck.

He turned to see how much room he had before he hit the shoreline and saw half of a yellow surfboard high up on the rocks.

There were only two options: keep trying to paddle out and risk getting taken by the rip and smashed to pieces where the yellow board had landed, or paddle toward a less formidable area beyond the lighthouses. He chose the latter. Or rather, the latter chose him. With the force of the waves and the sheer amount of moving water, he had little say in the matter. The rocks were getting closer. Boulders the size of televisions, then farther along, basketballs.

Still, the whitewater kept coming. All around him the ocean was just being ocean, doing its thing. The boom of rocks smashing together, water sucking. Sharp tang of seaweed and bird shit. Murky water, brown cliffs. Then his leash snapped and his board disappeared. This was close to worst-case scenario, but at least he hadn't hit bottom. Or had he? He felt a little loopy. Up ahead, he saw a bunch of rocks sticking out of the water like spires. Those would tear him apart, no question.

With every ounce of remaining energy, he swam straight in, ready to cut his losses and wash up on the smaller rocks. What happened after that, who cared. There was no timing it, no control at all, really. All he knew was that he wanted out. Just before impact, he lay as flat as he could to lessen the brunt of an inevitable hard landing. His knees bumped rock, but he washed up without major consequence. Slippery moss on the sea-smoothed rocks made it impossible to get any kind of grip. Another wave came behind him and washed him farther up, then retreated.

Dane lay face down, arms and legs spread out like Spider-Man. Ragged breaths, heart jackhammering in his chest. Slowly, he half crawled, half dragged himself to a patch of dry rocks at the bottom of the embankment. There, he sat and took inventory. Sore left knee, bleeding right hand, just a small gash. Everything else seemed intact. Except there was a metallic taste in his mouth. He wiped his upper lip and his hand came away bloody. He rubbed his forehead, and a chunk of skin came off in his hand.

Then, either he was hallucinating, or he heard a dog bark.

Mountains Of Water

'Iwa

As 'Iwa knew all too well, you might have all the latest equipment and all the best forecasts, all the knowledge in the world, but you were still one hundred and ten percent at the mercy of the elements. Manuel had slowly been motoring out and away from the point. He seemed nervous, which made her nervous. She watched Yeti and Dane sitting near each other, speaking, then Yeti paddled back to the boat.

"This is where it goes downhill," he said, as he climbed up.

Kama grabbed Yeti's board, a long white gun with a red lightning bolt on it. "Man, you can feel it brewing."

"What about Dane?" 'Iwa asked, trying to keep her voice casual.

"He'll be in soon enough. He wants that XXL, maybe a little too much."

Now it wasn't so much the size of the waves, but a certain ferocity to them that sent shivers down to the bone. And their angle seemed to be shifting slightly, creating more closeouts. Even 'Iwa could tell. Building swell always made her uneasy. She thought back to a time when she was younger—she and two friends had been out surfing, the waves playful and shoulder high. Next thing they knew, they were out past the point and a friend of her dad's nodded to them and said, "You girls are pretty far out, better head in."

None of them had even realized how far out they had drifted, but instead of paddling in, they got sucked in the rip farther down the coast and out. A huge set broke outside, double the size of what they were used to, washing them apart from each other. 'Iwa's leash stretched to the point where her leg felt ready to rip off, then the leash snapped.

By now she was out in deep water—sharky water—with no board and a throbbing ankle. Trying not to panic, she let the water carry her. *Never fight it*, her dad used to tell her. At the next cove over, she managed to ride the whitewater to shore where it coughed her up on the sandy beach, exhausted. Wendy had already washed in down the way, but Caroline was missing. All 'Iwa could think was, *How am I going to tell her parents?* But a little while later, the lifeguards told them that a fishing boat had picked up Caroline and was taking her in to the Kahului boat ramp. It was a big wake-up call for all of them.

Out here, at Killers, the waves were of another magnitude. Broken body parts, blackouts and reef scrapes were part of the program. The guys seemed not to mind the risk, so she was trying not to mind it herself. But that was easier said than done.

"Holy mother," Hope said, behind them, taking her camera from the tripod.

Just then, Manuel gunned the motor, heading for deeper water. The waves coming in looked like something from one of those apocalyptic movies, a computer-generated wall of blue migrating in from far across the ocean.

Kama stood at the stern, jaw slack. "Watch—Dane's gonna go."

Dane paddled for the first wave of the set, which dwarfed him as it pulled him up.

"He has no idea what's coming," Hope said, clicking away.

Yeti, with his hair wild, and wetsuit peeled down to his waist, said, "He knows. He just doesn't care."

His words chilled 'Iwa. What did that even mean? How could he not care? It looked like he made the wave, but everyone else got annihilated by the second and subsequent waves of the set. They were way beyond the break now, and it was hard to tell what was happening beyond the mountains of water. The two jet skis zoomed in, their engines barely audible above the ocean's roar.

"Two broken boards on the rocks in there," Kama said, holding up the binocs and scanning.

"Dane's?" 'Iwa asked.

"Nope."

The skis ferried guys to other boats and deposited them, but none brought Dane. He had all but disappeared. The feeling aboard went from mild concern to outright alarm. 'Iwa tried to appear calm, but felt anything but.

Holmes flagged down the jet skis, and a young Mexican guy came right over. "Parsons is still somewhere in there, did you see him?"

"*Negativo.* I go now."

They watched him disappear in the gap between sets, the whole inside still a white swirling cauldron. A minute later the other ski followed.

"Damn, here comes another one," Yeti said.

More swells moved in, just as big, if not bigger. No one had returned to the lineup, and the waves broke unridden. It went without saying that anyone on the inside was in trouble.

Kama came over and put his arm around 'Iwa. "How you doing?"

"Worried."

"He'll be fine. He always is."

Holmes chimed in. "Ramon and Z are top-notch. They'll get him."

"At least his board isn't tombstoning," Hope said.

'Iwa shivered. "I don't even want to know what that is."

"When a surfer is down, way down, and the leash is still at-tached, it pulls the board partly under so it's vertical with only the tip showing. Never—"

Yeti spoke calmly but firmly. "Let's stick to what *is* hap-pening."

One of the skis came flying back out, catching air before splashing down. 'Iwa got her hopes up, and then dashed when she saw an empty sled. When the set subsided, the other ski came back out with half a mint green board tucked in behind the driver's leg. Her stomach twisted in on itself.

"Ah, hell. Come on, buddy," Kama said.

"Let's head down the coast a ways, on the off chance he went down there," Holmes said to Manuel.

They picked up speed, heading into the wind and slamming hard against the chop. It was hard to see beyond the spray, but 'Iwa kept her eyes on the shoreline, searching for any sign of Dane or his board. She had no idea how much time had elapsed, but knew it had been longer than anyone could hold their breath—much longer.

Then Kama yelled, "Hold up."

Manuel cut the throttle.

"There's someone on the cliff."

'Iwa was tempted to rip the binoculars out of his hands, when Manuel pulled out another pair and handed them to her. Heavy, clunky things with one side blurry, she aimed them at the shore. They were surprisingly strong, showing her rocks, rocks and more rocks. A patch of seagulls sunning themselves. A turf of grass. A man in a wetsuit standing on the top of an embankment. He was waving.

"Oh my God, it's Dane!" she said.

At the same time, Kama said, "Is that a dog?"

Covering up a sob, she adjusted the binocs, focusing them on a small sand-colored dog standing next to Dane, then back up to his face, which was partly covered by one hand. It looked

red. On the rocks below, there was no sign of the other half
of his board.

"He's holding his head, like maybe something's happened,"
she said.

"At least he's standing, and he somehow got up the cliff, that's
a good sign," Hope said.

"How the hell did he get up there?" Kama asked.

It appeared to be a sheer drop to the rocks below.

Holmes ran to the stern and pointed toward Dane, sending the two jet ski drivers closer to shore. There looked to be
a shelf inside of them, where waves were breaking in a disor-
ganized manner. Pillars of rock jutted up as though part of an
ancient dinosaur spine.

"I've never seen anyone wash in this far down the coast,"
he said.

"Do you think the skis can make it in there?" Kama asked.

"Doubtful. He's going to need to swim out past the reef."

Yeti, who had been consulting with Manuel, turned and
said, "Either we wait till the swell drops or he has to swim out."

Kama didn't miss a beat. "I'm going in to help him. Get
Ramon back out here and he can drop me."

No one tried to dissuade him, and Holmes whistled for
Ramon. It was impossible to imagine swimming in amongst
the whitewater and rocks, but 'Iwa was thankful. Ramon came
by, picked up Kama, who brought a body board with him, and
they were off.

Ashore, Dane followed the edge a short ways, weaving
through a patch of green succulents, and then slipped down
a chute of rocks that looked like it had a rope tied to it. The
little dog followed him. When he reached the bottom, he disappeared behind rocks and whitewater, then appeared again,
dog still by his side, barking at the water, or maybe at Dane,
she couldn't be sure.

Ten minutes later, Kama was onshore standing with Dane,

who 'Iwa could now see had a gash on his forehead. After a lot of hand gesturing, in a lull, they both jumped in and swam for clear water. Kama pushed the dog on the body board.

Hope dropped her binoculars. "They're bringing the dog."

Yeti shook his head. "It's always something with those two."

After a few tense minutes of watching Kama plow through the whitewater, with Dane helping hold the dog on the board, they made it into deeper water and were immediately scooped up by Ramon and Z. The mood in the boat flipped around, and relief swam through 'Iwa like a long fish. But there was a voice in the back of her mind whispering, *to love someone is to lose them, remember that.*

Dane came aboard holding the scrawny little dog close to his chest. Blood trickled down the side of his face, but he was smiling with those sea-colored eyes that had turned an even deeper blue. The first thing he did was come over and kiss 'Iwa, dog between them. She tasted blood on his lips, as Hope threw a towel over his shoulders.

"Sorry to put you through that," he said.

'Iwa held on to his arm. "I'm just glad you're okay."

He sat on a cooler, shivering slightly and setting the dog in his lap. "This little girl showed me the way up the rocks. Someone tied a rope there and dug in notches to climb. Otherwise, I couldn't see much beyond the surf. She climbed down and started licking my face and dancing all around me, barking. Then she led me up the hill."

"We need to take care of your head," Hope said, eyeing the two-inch gash above his left eye.

Holmes came over and opened a first-aid box that looked like something you might find in a hospital, not on a fishing boat. "We're prepared for open heart surgery if need be. Can someone take the dog?"

'Iwa reached out, but the dog bared her teeth and snarled.

"Try this," Manuel said, handing her a hunk of ahi jerky.

She tried again, speaking softly and waving the fish. The dog narrowed its crusty eyes, but hunger won, and within a few minutes she was nestled against 'Iwa. Poor thing was all spine and bones beneath a coat of wiry fur full of burrs.

"Are you sure that's a dog? It looks more like a cross between a capybara and a porcupine," Kama said.

"Be nice, that thing saved my life—ouch!" Dane yelled, as Holmes wiped his gash with alcohol.

"Sorry, bro, I need to clean it. Good news is, I think this butterfly tape will do the job, and no sign of concussion. Your pupils look normal."

"Thanks, doc. So you think I'll live?" Dane said.

"I'm afraid so."

Yeti handed him water. "Drink up, soldier."

"Where's the coffee?"

"Water first."

Dane took the stainless steel water bottle, downed the whole thing, then leaned over to pet the dog, his arm resting heavy on 'Iwa's leg.

"I've already named her," he said.

Hope stood with her hands on her hips. "How do you know it doesn't belong to the lighthouse, or someone else on the island?"

Manuel said, "There's no one there permanently. Either someone dumped it, or it swam here somehow."

Hope frowned. "Swam here? From where?"

"Maybe it fell off a boat, who knows? Stranger things have ended up on islands," Yeti said, filling a small cup with water and offering it to the dog, who lapped it up with a small pink tongue.

"*It* is a girl, and her name is Isla," Dane said with finality.

"Stay still," Holmes ordered.

He wiped the gash, while Dane closed his eyes and clenched his jaw, then taped it shut with hands that looked like they'd done this before. They had slowly motored out to sea, away from the surf break, and were in much calmer water. All the other boats had left, and the ocean still kept pumping in swells.

"Where are we going?" Dane asked.

"Back to Ensenada."

"Doesn't anyone want to surf again? All I need is a board." For a moment, 'Iwa thought he was serious, then he winked. "Nah, but seriously, thank you, guys. It wasn't a two-wave hold-down, but it was close. It's nice to know you have my back."

"Always," Kama said.

Hope too. "Always."

Yeti nodded. "Always."

It was only then that 'Iwa realized she was shaking, and not from the cold. The possibility of losing Dane to the ocean had rocked her more deeply than she had imagined possible. Fear for yourself was one thing, but fear for another, something more slippery and more terrifying. It was a familiar place where helplessness reigned. A place 'Iwa was not sure she was ready to return.

Isla

Dane

Isla seemed to know her good fortune at having been rescued from Todos Santos with only seagulls and a lighthouse for companions, little food, and even less water. Dane wondered how long she had been there, and how much longer she would have lasted. If only dogs could talk. In the two weeks since he'd been home, her ribs had slowly disappeared and patches of fur he'd had to cut out with the burrs began filling in. She wasn't the best-looking dog in the world, but she made up for it with an oversized personality.

He had always heard that rescue dogs knew exactly who they owed their life to, which is why they made such loyal pets. The truth in those words had become evident from the minute he brought her onto the boat back in Mexico. She mainly had eyes for him, but could easily be swayed by food offerings, especially sardines, and loved to curl up on anything soft—after pawing it for a good minute or two. And those button eyes and fox ears followed his every move.

He hadn't meant to keep her. With his solo lifestyle, a dog had been out of the question, but Isla had become so attached to him, he was determined to figure out a way to make it work. On his street, there were plenty of neighbors with big yards and kids who were happy to watch her. Kama, Hope and Yeti, too.

THE MAUI EFFECT   183

Dane brought her everywhere, and she quickly became part of the team. Still, they razzed him.

"Never thought I'd see the day a twenty-pound mutt ruled your life," Kama said.

"Isla needs me. She was abandoned on a deserted island for Chrissake."

"You have it backward, brah."

Somehow, Dane had gone from no woman in his life to two. Usually, by this time in a relationship, he was starting to feel the walls closing in. No matter how gorgeous or intelligent or talented the woman was, there always came a point where he started making excuses, not being available. He'd crave time alone and his beach runs and surf sessions grew longer and longer. He knew plenty of guys who balanced surfing with wives and kids. Not always easily, but they managed. So why couldn't he?

With Sunny, he had come close. She was light and fun and breezy, and he had loved her, but when things turned more serious, he'd bolted. He'd had this grating feeling that Sunny wasn't *the one*. Hope always said it was a mother wound, and he needed therapy. Which was probably true, on some level. Yeti's advice, as for everything, was to meditate on it. Dane tried, but the problem persisted.

Recently, the situation had begun to haunt him, plaguing his dreams. Because everything with 'Iwa was different. *He* was different with her in his life. He only hoped he could sustain these feelings and that the damaged part of him wouldn't fuck things up.

Every time Dane picked up 'Iwa from the airport, his entire world brightened. She always had her nose in a book, usually nature or science related, and was wholly absorbed. Someone could walk by naked and she wouldn't even notice. She was always wearing colorful clothes and a lei around her neck, which she'd then give to him. Now, when he pulled up, she was sitting on a bench, absorbed in a book as always. He watched her for a few moments before getting out, but Isla poked her head out the window and started yapping. 'Iwa looked up and waved, laughing.

Dane jumped out and met her at the curb. "I missed you," he said, hugging her tight.

This time, 'Iwa had taken more convincing to come, and he had a moment of panic that she wouldn't. But he'd found a friend of Yeti's, a conservation guy, who'd agreed to meet with her.

"It's only been two weeks." 'Iwa kissed him, long and lingering, then pressed her face into his neck. "But I know, I missed you, too."

He could have stood there all night, inhaling Hawai'i and rainwater off her skin, but Isla started whining and dancing around at the window.

'Iwa pulled away and rushed over. "Oh my goodness, look at you! All clean and pretty and…round."

Isla wiggled and grunted and hopped all over 'Iwa, trying to get to her face with that fast tongue of hers.

"I've been spoiling her, a little too much. And I guess there's no question whether she remembers you," Dane said.

"I forgot how small she is, like the size of one of Koa's paws."

"Don't let her size fool you, she runs the show here now. So be ready."

They took the scenic route to Carmel, stopping at his place in Santa Cruz to pick up his boards and a dog bed for Isla, and then headed out. Isla rode in 'Iwa's lap and moved between snoring peacefully to head out the window, wind in her fur, barking furiously. Seeing her so happy made Dane happy. Lately, it felt like his heart was stretching to new dimensions. Woman. Dog. Who knew what was next.

"How did it go yesterday?" he asked.

"We had a pretty good turnout, but only got a thousand signatures, which doesn't go very far when you're up against deep pockets and backroom deals."

"At least you guys are making some noise. Backroom deals don't work as well when people are watching," he said.

"We're making noise all right, and this was just the beginning. Next weekend we're doing a big fundraiser. We were going to wait until summer, but we have to move fast on this so we can afford an attorney. Winston and I will be singing, want to come?"

He turned to see her face, wrapped in so much hope, there was no way he could say no.

"Hell, yeah. I'm there."

He prayed he could deliver.

"It'll be fun, we're doing it up at my friend's ranch in Kula. Silent auction, live music, food catered by Uncle's. I'm excited!"

"I can donate one of my surfboards. If I had more time I could make something, but this should at least get you a few thousand dollars, maybe even more."

"That would be wonderful, and generous."

"It's the least I can do."

That waterfall had given him a memory he would never forget. He had been reading that poem every night before drifting off. It was a way to keep 'Iwa close, even though she was an ocean away. He found her hand and wrapped his around it. They rode for a time in silence, Dane feeling his chest swelling with a new fullness, as though someone had blown up a balloon inside of him and filled it with salt water and rays of sun.

Endangered Creatures

ʻIwa

Their first stop was a surf check disguised as a walk, but ʻIwa didn't mind. They stood side by side, looking out on the rock-strewn coastline and the sleepy ocean beyond. It was hard to tell that come tomorrow, enormous waves would be breaking right in front of where they stood. A dead and twisted cypress tree jutted out from between two boulders.

"This is the *tree* in Ghost Tree. But the locals call the break Pescadero Point. It's not for the faint of heart," Dane said.

"Where do you actually surf?"

"See that rock at the point? That's where the peak usually is, but when it's bigger, it breaks farther out."

ʻIwa squinted to see better against the glare. "That rock?"

"Yep."

If you caught a wave where he was pointing, there was no-where to go but into a field of grayish white pinnacles, smooth like marble. It looked far more precarious than even Mavericks or Todos Santos.

"It looks unmakeable," she said.

He nodded. "It can be critical, but the wave is one of the best in Cali when it hits right. You can skirt the rocks if you're careful and if you know the break."

"Same as you did in Mexico?" she couldn't help but say.

He gave her a look. "Every now and then you have to pay to play. For all the times I've been out there, I seem to manage pretty well."

'Iwa saw movement in the water. Something small and brown, with fur. Isla seemed to notice it, too, because she had stopped and was eyeing the water and sniffing.

"What is that?" 'Iwa asked, nodding to the creature.

"Sea otters. This whole area is a marine sanctuary. We pass through six protected areas to get here from where we launch in Monterrey Harbor. Word on the street is that NOAA is threatening to shut us down."

A whole family of little heads kept popping up in the kelp, and two otters looked to be playing chase with each other. Nearby, another came up and floated on its back.

"Good," she said.

"Um. Yeah," he said, hands fumbling in his pockets. "I guess it depends who you ask."

"Why wait for NOAA to tell you to stop? I bet if you asked the sea otters, they'd probably have an opinion."

"It's only a handful of times a year that we do it."

"Aren't sea otters endangered?"

A long pause. "Yeah. They are."

"Then maybe you should reconsider. Or just paddle surf. You guys keep talking about wanting to get back to the roots of surfing. Why not now? Set an example."

Dane kicked a pebble off the trail in front of them. "When it's bigger than twelve feet or so, you need a ski to pull you in. The water is moving too fast."

The scenario sounded familiar: Endangered critters. Man moving in on their territory for personal gain or glory. At least here in California, someone was actually doing something about it.

'Iwa shrugged. "It's your conscience."

"My sponsors are here, and everyone's counting on me. I can't just *not* surf tomorrow."

"You'd be making a statement. And anyway, aren't your sponsors supposed to be environmentally forward-thinking?"

"They are."

"Then they should understand."

He watched the otters for a moment, then said, "Let me think about it."

It was a lot to ask, and she felt bad for putting him on the spot. But not that bad when she thought about the otters.

She put an arm around him and drew closer for warmth. "They're bigger than I thought they'd be, and even more adorable in real life, aren't they?"

"Cutest little creatures on the planet—aside from this one," he said, nodding down at the scruffy little creature sitting by their feet.

Later, Dane surprised her with a room at a cozy inn overlooking a stand of cypress trees that filled the air with a woody, evergreen smell. They snuck Isla in by putting her in a surfboard bag, though no one was even around to notice, and she tore around the room when they released her. Someone had lit candles for their arrival, and the room carried a rustic charm. Bottles full of daisies and wildflowers lined the shelves on the walls, giving it a whimsical and romantic vibe that made 'Iwa want to step out of her clothing and into Dane's arms.

Which, it turned out, was exactly what she did. Dane tore off his own shirt and laid her onto the bed, pinning her arms above her head. Skin on skin. Heat coiled around her body, sending pulses to every point he touched. His mouth hovered just over her throat as he moved down the length of her neck to the midpoint between her breasts. A light kiss. She whimpered. 'Iwa was high on his musky scent, drunk on the feel of his hand now trailing up her inner thigh, creating a sizzle wherever it passed.

Dane kept her panties on, but moved his hand across her

rhythmically, with growing pressure, all the while kissing her hotly. Her breaths became more uneven, and she felt her hips rising to meet him.

He pulled his mouth away, up to her ear and whispered, "I think about doing this with you all the fucking time. Way more than I should."

Oh. My. God.

"Me too."

Her answer seemed to stoke his want, because he pressed himself hard against her, and slid her black lace to the side. She arched, gasping. The whole world had shrunk to one small spot in her center, burning brightly. 'Iwa wrapped her legs around him and he eased himself in, just barely, then pulled back. Her thighs gripped tighter, trying to get closer and take in more of him.

"Are you in some kind of hurry?" he said, a sensual smile spreading over his face.

She laughed. "Yes."

"We have all night, 'Iwa. And I want to savor you. Savor *this.*"

He slid in again, a little further this time. 'Iwa thought she might lose her mind. She bit down lightly on his neck to keep herself from crying out. But he was right. There was no rush. They had all night.

Though in the end, it didn't take that long.

Not even close.

After the lovemaking, they took a long Jacuzzi bath, ordered veggie burgers made from scratch with a side of thick-cut French fries from local potatoes, and shared a bottle of red wine, which 'Iwa ended up drinking most of because Dane wanted to be *on* tomorrow. He caught her watching him and that sensual smile appeared on his face again. His shadowed jaw, sunstreaked hair and double-wide shoulders made her stomach flip.

Her mother once told her, "There is no such thing as a perfect man, but there is a perfect man for *you*, designed by God and built to specs. He will be even better than you could have imagined, and also different than you might expect, so just be open. And here's the best part, it will feel so right, there will be no question at all."

Those words had been showing up a lot lately, running across her mind in bold teleprompter letters. The thought that Dane could be that man felt like a real possibility, but it also made her want to turn and run. On paper, he was so many things she hadn't wanted in a man. But, her heart said otherwise.

"I have a confession to make," Dane said as they sat on the floor cross-legged in their underwear.

A lump formed in her throat. "Okay."

"After you showed me that poem, I started reading more poetry. Not in a thousand years would I ever think poems could get under my skin so much, but there's something about those words and how so few of them can do the job better than a whole bookful. Truth be told, I'm kind of hooked," he said.

'Iwa threw her napkin at him. "And here I thought you were going to tell me some dark secret that I didn't want to know."

"What if I had? Would you stick around?"

"Depends on what the secret was, obviously. But loving poetry? Probably not going to chase me away. Whose poems are you enjoying?" she said.

"Neruda, Rilke. I need to at least be able to grasp the meaning. Too obscure and they lose me. I'm not that sophisticated."

But 'Iwa had seen his bookshelves. Philosophy, nature, physics. All the books that Yeti had given him and more. The kinds of books that made you think, deeply.

A knock came on the door. 'Iwa threw on a bathrobe and peered through the peephole. Dane climbed into the bed with Isla and held her under the covers, trying to dampen her growl.

"It's a man with an ice bucket. Did you order champagne?" she said.

"Open it."

The man bowed when the door cracked. "Mrs. Parsons? The hotel would like to extend our warmest congratulations on your nuptials."

Her cheeks flushed. "Oh, I'm not Mrs. Parsons."

The man tried to look inside, but 'Iwa kept the door open just a slit. "Is she in here, then?" he asked.

Isla barked. Dane coughed.

"Mr. Parsons is, but there is no Mrs. Parsons," she said, then added, "Not that I know of anyway."

The man seemed perplexed. "This is the honeymoon suite, and—"

Suddenly, Dane was beside her. "Thank you, Sergio. My lovely wife here keeps forgetting she married me. I try not to take it personally, but sometimes it stings."

He took the bucket of ice, slipped Sergio some cash and shut the door before 'Iwa even had a chance to blink. When she turned around, she realized Dane was stark naked.

She laughed. "What just happened?"

"I should have warned you. This was the only room left and they reserve it for honeymooners, but I really wanted to stay here with you. So I told a little white lie."

The flowers and candles now made sense, and the thought of Dane going through all this trouble for her made her chest thrum.

Dane held up the bottle. "We'll save it for tomorrow, after we surf."

"So you're going to go out tomorrow? It's decided?" she said.

Dane cupped her chin and looked her in the eye. "I have to, 'Iwa. It's too late to back out. But I promise, this will be the last time we do this here. No more jet skiing through marine sanctuaries."

"Promise?"

"I promise."

★ ★ ★

In the morning, rain floated down like fish scales, light and iridescent. Dane and crew had left early, while 'Iwa and Isla took their time waking up and eating a honeymooners breakfast in bed.

"You can be Mrs. Parsons this morning," 'Iwa said to the dog, as she handed her a chunk of cheesy egg.

Isla inhaled every morsel of food with fervor, sauce on her muzzle to prove it. 'Iwa could hardly blame her. After breakfast, they walked to the coffee shop to meet Paul Gladwell, one of the California spotted owl's greatest defenders. Yeti knew him and at Dane's request, had set up the meeting for 'Iwa. This trip, she was actually on the clock.

As with so many birds in Hawai'i, the California spotted owl was a casualty of habitat loss, mostly at the hands of man. And though their populations were in serious decline, they still weren't recognized as endangered. Paul headed up a group that was getting close to changing that, and Yeti believed Paul would be a good resource for 'Iwa and Maui Forest Recovery Project in their fight for Waikula. The middle of an endangered forest was no place for a resort, and the sooner they could prove that the forest surrounding Waikula contained endangered flora and fauna, the better their chances of stopping it.

In the shop, she spotted Paul right away. He looked like an older, grayer version of Yeti. Lumberjack attire, John Lennon glasses and a beard that could be housing several owls. He zeroed in on 'Iwa and Isla, and welcomed them warmly to his table.

"Sorry to meet under these circumstances, but we're fighting the same fight. All of us," he said.

"Yeti's told me so much about you, I feel like I'm meeting a superstar," she said, and it was true.

She spent the next half hour filling him in on Waikula and Jones and his plan. He let his tea go untouched as she spoke.

"How far along are they, exactly?" he asked.

"I expect the Environmental Impact Statement to come out any day now, but he's already clearing trails and bullying people out of the stream, which is not technically his. He claims the project is low density, but we want no density. This is pristine native forest we're talking about."

In development terms, low density meant fewer homes or dwellings per acre. But *low* was often a matter of opinion.

"Endangered species?"

"Honeycreepers, mainly."

"Any critical?"

"One. But I'm not even sure there are any left in the wild."

"There's your ticket. You need to create buzz around that one bird. Even if they're gone. Get people to care. And get a good attorney. Do you have one?"

"Money's been an issue, but we're working on it."

"With the owls, we kept hammering away at the US Department of Interior, filing notice after notice of violation of the Endangered Species Act. You have to go big or go home."

He pulled out his phone and showed 'Iwa photos of spotted owls with round eyes and white spots. They were beautiful creatures. Intense gaze. Elaborately painted feathers. Blending in perfectly with the forest behind them. 'Iwa thought of the kiwikiu. Olive green and yellow, like leaves and koa flowers, they were so tiny compared to the owls, but just as beautiful. Just as essential.

Paul began scribbling notes as he spoke. "Look, every creature in our ecosystems evolved for a reason. Losing just one can have a devastating effect. Birds are major pollinators and seed dispersers. Without them, the forest can't continue. That's your angle."

"The thing that worries me the most is that Jones will say whatever he needs to get the green light, and do whatever he pleases in the meantime. He knows people, too," 'Iwa said.

"Do you have a public land trust?"

"A small one."

"That's another way to go. Make him an offer he can't refuse."

'Iwa let out a sad laugh. "We're talking Maui here. Land prices are some of the highest in the nation."

"I bet there are people on Maui with more money than this guy. Can you tap into any of them?"

"We can try. And we're having a fundraiser next week, grassroots style."

"Fundraisers are great, but unless you can get a big benefactor, they're mostly just for show."

Discouraging news. Their organization felt *he mea 'ole*. So powerless.

He took off his glasses and wiped them on his shirt. "What are the chances of you finding any of those lost honeycreepers?"

"Slim at best. And if we did, it could be years. The forest unveils her secrets only when she's ready, you know that."

"Still, focus on it. Get out there, make it a campaign. You need to be loud."

"One thing about people from Maui—we can be loud."

"Good. I can make some calls, too. I know a few people. So does Yeti."

His voice trailed off and he seemed to retreat into his mind for a moment.

"How do you two know each other?" she asked.

"He's my brother-in-law."

"So you're married to his sister?"

Paul sighed. "Actually he married my sister, Grace. But she passed about ten years ago. A small plane crash over the mountains."

'Iwa was shocked. "I'm so sorry, I had no idea."

"Grace was one of the good ones. She was studying to be a veterinarian and wanted to work with wolves and wild animals. Beautiful and young and with so much promise. They say the good die young, and I never really believed it until we lost Grace."

She sounded like 'Iwa's kind of girl. "Yeti's never said a word to me, but I don't know him that well."

"That's Yeti for you. He took it harder than anyone, naturally. He went off alone to the mountains for years. No one even knew where he went, but he'd send postcards every few months letting us know he was alive. When he emerged, he had this new inner power. Seems like grief can flay you, shatter you to pieces, and then slowly reconstruct you with new facets and fortifications."

'Iwa could relate, and liked the idea of a reconstruction stage. Maybe she was in its foothills, ready to keep climbing.

"Does Dane know about Grace?"

"I honestly don't know. I've met Dane a few times, but don't know him well."

"I'm just surprised he never mentioned it."

"He may have his reasons. Yeti is a tough nut to crack," he said.

"I like him a lot."

"I love the guy, too. As real as they come."

They talked more about the fundraiser and plans for Hawai'i, and then said goodbye. Having an expert in her back pocket gave her a nice confidence boost.

'Iwa could hear the hiss of the surf before she could see it. It was midmorning now, and she and Isla walked on a well-manicured path, with signs pointing out the fragile beauty of the Carmel Bay Ecological Preserve. Wind-sculpted Monterrey cypress stood watch, some mere ghosts of what they used to be, thanks to an invasive bark beetle. Isla noticed not. All she was concerned with was sniffing out every nook and cranny, hunting for rodents. 'Iwa kept her on a short leash. The clear blue sky was deceptively cold, and she kept her jacket on even in the sun.

Dane had given her explicit instructions for the best viewing point, which was actually at the edge of a golf course. When she arrived, she could see why. The surfers and jet skis were only a stone's throw away. There were at least fifteen skis and it looked like mayhem. A crowd had already gathered on the grass in front of the 18th hole. Tripods everywhere. 'Iwa found a spot off to the side and Isla sat down on a towel and watched. A set brewed on the horizon, and several of the skis towed their surfers into position.

Through her telephoto lens, she could see Yeti driving Kama into the first wave. A tall, pitchy kelp-speckled wall of green. As soon as he let go of the rope, Kama pumped the board a few times and then was screaming down the face. The next wave was even bigger. A guy on a yellow gun made the drop only to be mowed down by the whitewater. Everyone in the crowd groaned. He was precariously close to the rocks, but his ski buzzed in and seamlessly swept him onto the sled.

It took her a while to finally locate Dane. He was driving the ski and towing Hope. They missed the first set, but Dane pulled her into a nice open wave. Their timing was perfect and Hope peeled down the line effortlessly, or so it appeared. 'Iwa was impressed.

Wave after critical wave poured in, and the jet skis buzzed around, towing surfers and rescuing them from wipeouts. More kept coming out. 'Iwa wondered about the seals and sea lions and otters they'd seen here the day before. Where did they go in swells this big? Hopefully out to sea, far from the slamming waves and jet skis. It seemed like anyone and everyone who owned a ski was out here now. Chaos reigned. One ski even went vertical at the top of a wave, and for a moment everyone on shore watched with mouths hanging open.

He's not gonna make it, someone screamed.

Holy fuck.

Yard sale.

But the ski landed just beyond the crest, tail end down, leveled off and sped down the back of the wave. Disaster averted. The crowd cheered.

Enormous camera lenses lined the entire bluff. 'Iwa snapped a few hours' worth of photos, mostly of Dane and crew when they could snag one, but also of unridden waves dappled in sunlight. Of people in warm clothes on the beach. Of seagulls. Of Isla. Isla was smart as a whip and seemed to know when to ham it up and cock her head, showing her little underbite for the camera. Dane kept saying he was going to find her a proper home, but 'Iwa knew better. Isla wasn't going anywhere. Except maybe Hawai'i.

That night, the entire lineup of surfers and their entourages all packed into a pub called Bluewater Tavern, everyone buzzing off adrenaline and ocean. Beer and booze were flowing, and so was testosterone. Two Patagonia guys had joined them, as well as a few bigwigs from other surf companies. They had the largest table in the place, and 'Iwa was squished in between Dane and a tatted-up man that Hope introduced as Vance.

As usual post surf, the talk was centered around the biggest waves and the best wipeouts, but there was also a debate going on about the threat of shutting down Ghost Tree to jet skis. Dane kept his arm around 'Iwa the whole time, and made a point to try and include her in the conversation. But Vance kept pissing her off.

"Screw the little furry bastards, Ghost Tree is our holy grail. A bunch of nerds can't shut us down for riding waves out here a few times a year. They have no fucking idea how much money we bring into the state," he said.

Vance was a chief something or other for Kelp, an up-and-coming surf brand that sponsored a whole army of groms—kids who surfed. He had a buzzed head, a flattened nose and one of those voices that rose above all others in the room. If 'Iwa had been closer, she might have slapped him. Instead, she squeezed Dane's leg, expecting him to say something. But he didn't.

So she did. "Those furry little bastards are in danger of being wiped off the face of the earth pretty soon here. Do you want their extinction on you?"

She had read up on them last night, doing her homework as any good scientist would. During big surf, otters joined together to form rafts, often wrapping themselves in kelp to stay together, out beyond the breakers or in protected coves. The photos she had seen of these otter communities made her fall for them even harder.

He studied 'Iwa for a moment before answering. "I guarantee you the sea otters were nowhere to be seen today."

"How would you know?" she asked.

"I didn't see any out there. Did you?"

"I wasn't out there."

"Exactly," he said, smugly.

The word KELP was screened on the front of his shirt in gold letters, and it made 'Iwa want to puke just looking at him. He of all people should know about the wildlife here, and that kelp was not just some fancy seaweed. They were a foundational species. A mother of the sea.

"Did you know that sea otters eat urchins, which eat kelp, balancing the ecosystem to save the kelp forests, which I'd think would be important for your brand?" she said.

Dane piped up. "Anything that eats urchins is a friend of mine."

"Look, little lady, I'm not against the sea otters. I know they're cute and all, I just think we need to keep things in perspective," Vance said.

He was the kind of guy who made her want to retreat to the forest and never leave.

'Iwa wasn't done. "They're not just cute, they're intelligent—they use tools. Also, otters are nonmigratory, so they stay in one place, which makes it even more important to keep their home free of boats and jet skis. Tell me, whose perspective are we talking about?"

Vance took a swig of his beer and looked to the guy on his right. "Help me out here?"

"You're on your own, bro," 'Iwa heard him say.

A few others chimed in, and 'Iwa was relieved that everyone else was in favor of the otters. Surfers, after all, relied on a clean and healthy ocean and tended to be good stewards. They weren't happy about being kicked off a legendary wave, but they understood.

Dinner came, in the form of burgers oozing with cheese and mushrooms, and truffle fries. 'Iwa had ordered a burrata salad on fresh-picked arugula with a peppery kick. Conversation all but ceased as the group devoured the food and replenished their spent energy from a long day on the water.

Then Yeti brought up Portugal and the mythic wave of Nazaré. "Models are hinting that late next week could be our window," he said, truffle oil glinting on his beard.

"I think it's going to be too big. But it's your call," Kama said.

Was there such thing as *too* big? 'Iwa wondered.

"We could fly into Lisbon, make the hour-and-a-half drive north, and be standing at the Forte de São Miguel Arcanjo in less than a day. So we have a little time before we pull the trigger. Let me know by the fourteenth, if we want to be there by the sixteenth," said Hope, who acted as their travel agent.

March 16. 'Iwa's gut twisted.

Rusty from Patagonia said, "Keep me in the loop, because I'd love to send Jeff to shoot you. Sounds like this is the new frontier. Just what we're looking for."

"Just when we thought there were no new frontiers," Kama said.

Yeti rested his hand on Kama's back. "There will always be new frontiers, mate."

Dane got a nervous look on his face and remained uncharacteristically quiet. 'Iwa knew exactly why. The dates that Nazaré might wake up fell on the same weekend as the fundraiser on Maui. She felt her face heating up. You couldn't plan for good swells. They came when they came, and a surfer would always choose the sea. It was part of the deal—but it was up to 'Iwa if she accepted the deal.

"I'm down," Hope said.

"Me too," Kama said.

Yeti nodded, and they all looked to Dane.

He glanced at 'Iwa as if he might find an answer to his dilemma in her eyes. No way; she wasn't giving this to him. Let him figure it out on his own.

"I'm supposed to be on Maui next weekend for a fundraiser," he said, placing his hand on 'Iwa's knee.

Supposed to be. Not *I will be.*

"Fundraiser for what?" Hope asked.

Just then, Vance, who had been at the bar, slid back into his seat.

Dane said, "For a waterfall and the land around it. A developer plans on building an eco resort in the middle of a virgin forest. 'Iwa and her group are trying to protect it."

"Aren't waterfalls a dime a dozen on Maui?" Vance asked.

By now, his words were slurred and you could tell he was flat-out drunk.

"This one is special," 'Iwa said, then added, "Actually, they're all special."

A dark smile slid over Vance's face. "Book me a room with a view then. I'd love to roll out of bed and into that ice-cold spring water. Maui *Nō Ka Oi.*"

The whole table went quiet and 'Iwa bit down on her tongue hard enough to draw blood.

Then Hope, bless her heart, said, "Why do you always have to play devil's advocate, Vance? You're just saying all this to get a reaction. It's not cool."

He held up his hands. "Freedom of speech, man. An eco resort at a Hawaiian waterfall sounds killer, tell me you wouldn't be all over that."

Dane leveled him with a hard look. "Time to go home, bro. One too many drinks. I'll call you a cab."

Vance stood up and waved them off. "Nah, I'll walk. You guys are no fun," he said as he headed toward the door, steadying himself against chairs and people's backs.

Once he was out, everyone started talking at once.

"Bruddah needs to lay off the sauce," Kama said.

Dane shook his head. "I didn't realize he was drinking again."

"Don't mind him. He has issues," Hope said to 'Iwa.

'Iwa tried to unruffle her feathers, but there was still the unanswered question hanging in the room. Something told her she already knew the answer.

She forced a smile and said, "No worries. I'm used to people like him."

Back at the room, Isla greeted them as though they'd been gone for months, whimpering and running laps around the room. Dane dropped to the floor and Isla rolled over between his legs, belly up. 'Iwa went and lay on the bed. She was so bone-tired she just wanted to go to sleep. They could talk tomorrow. Or not.

But Dane had other ideas. "Hey," he said.

"Hey."

"Are you okay?"

"I'm tired."

He came over and sat on the side of the bed, resting his palm lightly over her breastbone. He leaned down and kissed her lightly on both cheeks. "I know what you're thinking," he said.

"Do you?"

"You're wondering if I'm still coming to your fundraiser like I said I would or if I'm going to bail and go to Portugal."

"No, I'm not. You're going to Nazaré, it's already written in the stars," she said, unable to meet his gaze.

"Can you at least look at me? I know I promised you, and I want to go, believe me, I do, but the timing could not be worse."

"I know."

"This wave has a weird siren call for me—"

She turned her face up to him. "You don't need to explain yourself. I get it. I'm not going to be the reason you miss out on your dream. But it doesn't mean I can't be bummed. This fundraiser is a big deal to me."

Dane wrapped a strand of her hair around his finger. "What if we plan another fundraiser? Like a surf off. I could probably round up a bunch of pros who would do it in a heartbeat."

'Iwa shook her head. "You focus on you and I'll focus on me."

"Aren't you and me an *us* now?" he said, a frown forming.

She wasn't in the mood for this talk now. Dane had made it clear how much he wanted to be a part of her life and how he couldn't get enough of her, but he had yet to say he loved her, which made her wonder.

"In order to be an *us*, we have to do *us* things," she said.

"We do *us* things all the time."

"I just feel like I've been in your world so much lately, it would be nice for you to come to mine again."

Spend time with her dad and Koa, explore more of Maui, drink coffee and bake banana bread, meet more of her friends and just *be*.

His voice took on an edge. "Hang on, you came here to meet Paul, and I just offered to come to Maui and put on a contest for your waterfall. And earlier you told me you understood about Portugal, so now you don't? Say what you mean, 'Iwa."

"What I mean is, I want you to go to Portugal and do your thing, and I'll go to Maui and do mine, and then after that we'll see."

"We'll see? About what?" he asked.

"About everything."

The muscles in his jaw tightened. "We only have a small window left of big surf in the northern hemisphere. After that,

I can come hang out for as long as you like, and I'm looking forward to it."

"But isn't that when you do more woodworking?"

"I'll carve out time for you, as much as you want. I'll come for a month," Dane said.

"And what if Fiji starts breaking? Or Tahiti."

"Well, then it'll be faster to fly out from Hawai'i than California. I would only be gone a few days. We can make this work, 'Iwa, but only if we want it to."

She didn't respond.

"Do you want it to?" he said, finally.

Yes.

No.

"I'm not sure," she whispered.

'Iwa felt sick to her stomach and rolled over, away from him. What *did* she mean? There was a part of her that wanted to not care. Not caring was easier. But she did care. Dane had promised to come to Maui, and then promptly broken that promise. In her experience, one broken promise meant more down the road. Her own words from that first morning at Maui Bean came back to her. *The ocean is your one true love, the one you put before all else.*

Dane got up and went into the bathroom, and 'Iwa drifted off, suddenly not sure of anything.

'A'ole

'Iwa

'Iwa stood in the pasture in Kula looking out across the flat expanse between the West Maui Mountains and Haleakalā, a view of rolling green hills, white-capped ocean, Kīhei condos and small puffy clouds. The weather had cooperated, blessing them with light trade winds and a generous sky. The whole conservation crew as well as volunteers from around the island had been sweating all day preparing for the fundraiser, and she needed a moment to herself.

This entire week had been a study in second-guessing how she had handled the Dane dilemma. Either way, she was on Maui and Dane was in Portugal paddling out into some of the biggest waves on the planet. His text this morning—nighttime for him—should have reassured her, but it left her with a heaviness deep inside. **Good luck over there, I'm rooting for you. Going to dawn patrol. Swell hasn't hit yet but will send pics. Call you tomorrow, after we surf. Miss you, my beautiful mo'o.**

While she was sleeping, he'd be facing off with the North Atlantic.

The floor of the giant barn and riding arena had been covered in hay, and glass jar lanterns hung from the chunky trusses. Big round tables were set up on one side and smaller standing tables dotted the other. People had paid a premium for those in front of the stage. Along the back wall, silent auction items begged to be purchased. Local art and books and jewelry, a trip for two to Tavarua Resort, handcrafted birdhouses, a three-night stay at the Hāna Hotel, a boat trip to Lānai. But, the most exciting thing up for grabs was the brand-new mint green surfboard that had shown up on her doorstep two days ago. Opening bid, $1500. Not that it replaced Dane, but it helped.

It warmed her heart to see how many people had jumped in without expecting a dime in return. Not only that, but tickets had sold out within a week of going on sale. None of this meant a thing, though, unless they could find a legal reason to stop the eco resort, which now had a name. Zen Mountain Retreat.

"Really, that's the best they could come up with?" Dane had said when she'd told him.

"I know, right?"

"What about a Hawaiian name, or something related to the place? Did they ever think of that?"

"Who knows what these people think."

At five o'clock, 'Iwa and Winston took to the stage, and people who had been standing out on the grassy lawn began to trickle into the barn. Winston had come early to set up, and she was grateful for his calming presence. They started off with slack key, no singing, just background music, and 'Iwa tried not to think about her little speech coming up. Singing was one thing, but public speaking gave her sweaty palms and a dry mouth. Then, just before dinner, the time came to address the crowd. She had been rehearsing for days, but her mind was still blanking out on whole sections.

Winston gave her a subtle thumbs-up and she pulled the mic close with sweaty palms. "A big, warm aloha to you all, thank you for being here. When we pulled this event together, I had no idea what to expect, but I was blown away by your generosity and support. We are about as grassroots as they come, and our organization is tiny, so having the backing of the Maui community—actually, the whole Hawai'i community, means everything. On this island alone, we already have over seven thousand hotel rooms, over two hundred condo complexes, and close to nine thousand vacation rentals—most illegal.

"We reached max capacity a long time ago. So, raise your hand if you think it's a good idea to build another resort in the middle of some of our most pristine rainforest with plants and birds found nowhere else on earth."

A hush fell. No hands. Someone in the back started clapping. Then another person. Someone else whistled. A woman in the back caught 'Iwa's eye, a redhead. For a split second, she thought it was her mother, but of course it couldn't be.

When the crowd quieted, she went on. "'Any fool can destroy trees. Trees cannot defend themselves or run away.' John Muir said that in 1920, and the same could be said for our lands and waterfalls and creatures today. Any fool can destroy these things that cannot save themselves. Saving them is up to us." A fire started up in her heart, and her voice grew louder. "*Auwe.* Enough is enough. And while Murphy Jones wants us to believe he has our best interests at heart, I assure you, he does not."

"Beat it, Jones!" someone yelled.

"'*A'ole* Zen Mountain Retreat."

'A'ole. No. A Hawaiian word she had been hearing more and more frequently. More people were questioning, fighting, sick to death of being lied to and walked on.

And then she spotted another face in the crowd that shouldn't be there. She blinked, looked again. The man stood staring at her with a flat smile. He wore a cowboy hat and boots, and an orange and brown aloha shirt, blending right in. A shark swimming through a bait ball.

Murphy Jones.

Her heart started thundering. Why was he here? To see what he was up against? To rattle his opposers? But aside from a few people, no one would even recognize him. 'Iwa debated saying something, but did not want to let him see her sweat. Calling attention to him would ruin the night.

Instead, she smiled right back at him and said, "Now, please enjoy the food, make sure you bid in the silent auction and dance your hearts away. This one is for Waikula. And if you recognize the tune, it's a nod to Joni Mitchell, and my mom."

Amid the applause, she glanced over at Winston, whose beaming face said it all. They had spent the last month writing the lyrics and rehearsing the song they were about to sing. She hadn't told anyone about it. Not even Dane.

There's a girl who's been out searching
In a decade full of green
And she takes it to the mountain
And she speaks it from the stream
Bearing truths from her mother
With golden eyes so clear
In the draining and the drying
Of the watersheds

There's a time we all remember
Before the birds have flown
Before the forest is gone
We can taste what we will lose
Waikula, lifeblood
yellow feathers, sunshine

There's a land who's sent a message
And she's waiting for a reply
She has asked for a reprieve
Between the ocean and the sky

She sings in broken branches
And soil and things alive
You will find it hard to shake her
From your memory...

When they finished, a man at the front table stood and clapped, and little by little, people popped up until the whole place was standing and cheering. Above, the skies opened up, raining down hard as river rocks on the metal roof. Goose bumps formed along 'Iwa's arms, and tears welled in her eyes. If only Lily could be here now. And Dane. But those thoughts passed quickly, as she soaked in the love filling up the barn. Winston reached over and grabbed her hand and lifted it up. She held on tight.

They continued on with a mix of Hawaiian songs, Dylan's "A Hard Rain's A-Gonna Fall," Joni Mitchell's "Big Yellow Taxi," Cat Stevens's "Where Do the Children Play," and finished up with John Denver's "Sunshine on My Shoulders"—something hopeful. She and Winston had picked the songs carefully.

When they finally left the stage, 'Iwa beelined to a cocktail table in the back where she'd spotted Keala and Parker—other members of their team. Winston was at her heels.

"That was perfect," Keala told them.

Still shaken up and breathless, 'Iwa asked, "Did you see Jones?"

"What do you mean? Where?"

"Jones was here. I saw him in the crowd, he made sure of it."

Parker frowned. "That man, no class. I see him, I'll show him to the pasture out back with my boot."

"We must have really rattled him, or else he wouldn't bother. But still, it freaked me out," 'Iwa said.

Straight-faced, Winston pushed an envelope toward her on the table. "This might make you feel better."

'Iwa opened the envelope and pulled out a white piece of

paper that said "A little something for a big cause." There was no signature. Then she slipped out a cashier's check made out to Maui Forest Recovery Project that she had to read twice, all thoughts of Jones temporarily forgotten.

"Fifty thousand dollars! Who is this from?"

Winston shrugged. "I don't know. Some guy handed it to me before we went onstage, then disappeared."

"Weird."

It could have been any number of wealthy people on Maui, but she sure wished she could know. Fifty thousand dollars would go a long way.

"It feels clandestine, doesn't it?" Maya said.

"No matter, our legal fees are beginning to stack up, but this will more than cover Kawika's retainer," Winston said.

Kawika Wong was the new attorney from Honolulu who had an impressive list of wins. At long last, things were starting to swing their way. But time was running out, because 'Iwa knew that guys like Jones did not wait for permits. He was bound to be clearing forest already.

In the morning, 'Iwa woke to a shattered windshield, and a message from Kama that drained her body of all oxygen. The call had come from Dane's phone. "'Iwa, this is Kama. Call me back as soon as you can."

Tolos

Dane

Nazaré was like California, only fifty years or so ago. With Mediterranean flavors of fishing village meets farmland meets Mavericks, and seagulls soaring across the wide expanse of beach, the town was pure enchantment. Men herding goats up the cobblestone road. The smell of ocean permeating everything. White houses with red tile roofs reminded Dane of Mexico, with a European flair.

Hope had booked them a house a block away from the ocean, and they'd hit the sack early. But between the jet lag and the anticipation, Dane flopped around on the saggy mattress like a fish on the beach. He found himself listening for the sound of rising surf, timing the period between waves. One one thousand, two one thousand. At sunset, they'd sat on the cliff watching the waves, which were still in the double-overhead range. Nothing close to how they'd be by morning if the predictions held.

When he finally drifted off, he dreamed he was riding a dappled horse up and down the beach, galloping through the shallows. The ocean was pancake flat. No waves had come. He saw a person in the distance, an old man in a straw hat waving him down. When he reached the man, his horse stopped. The man slowly took his hat off and raised his gaze.

"Someone is going to die today," he said.

Dane bolted upright in bed. His cheeks were wet as though he had been crying. He went to the bathroom and splashed water on his face, then downed a glass of water and went back to bed. Something about this trip was spooking him in a way that never happened.

He thought of his mom and how when he was young and she'd be off on one of her "extended work trips," he would lie in bed and stare at the ceiling—sometimes all night long— listening for the rattle of the old Wagoneer's motor and its squeaky suspension. It never came.

Even when Belinda would come home sunburned with chapped lips and smelling like weed, she never said where she was on those long layovers. If she had wanted, he knew she could have changed her flight route. By then she'd racked up enough seniority. But she never did.

Dane would skip school those days and head to the beach, surfing until he could no longer feel his toes, then passing out on his threadbare rust-colored towel. Then surfing. Then sleeping. Then doing it all over again. The ocean filled up his emptiness and became his best friend.

His mother had chosen waves over him. Ironic, because choosing waves over women was the story of his life.

Fog prowled the hilltops quietly as they readied the skis, and Jeff and Rusty loaded their camera gear into a wooden fishing boat that looked like it had been around longer than any of them. The air was crisp, wind absent. Yeti had led them in a short meditation and stretching routine back at the house, helping Dane regain his equilibrium. On their way, they grabbed high-octane espresso and *pastel de nata*—a Portuguese custard pie.

A small crowd had gathered on the dock, speaking amongst themselves. Some shook their heads, others chuckled.

Tolos.

Idiotas.

Americanos burros.

A younger fisherman stepped forward. "Man, today is not the day to go to sea. The waves, they will swallow you," he said, in heavily accented English.

Yeti spoke for Dane and the group. "Thank you for your concern, my friend. We understand the risk. Riding big waves is our religion, we do it all the time."

The man translated back to the others, who still wore skeptical looks on their sea-worn faces. With likely centuries of collective fishing between them, they would know the ocean here intimately. Know how deadly she could be.

It had been hard to scrounge up a boat driver, but they had thrown enough money at him he couldn't refuse. Another American, a waterman from Hawai'i named Garrett, had helped set up the whole trip. Garrett had come last year, at the invitation of one of the locals who had recognized the potential of these waves, and had ridden a wave taller than the cliffs. With the fort and lighthouse for perspective, you could tell the magnitude. A photo of it had spread through the surfing world like wildfire, and that wave was singlehandedly responsible for Dane being here.

Last night at Garrett's place, they'd studied maps of the underwater topography more closely. The Nazaré canyon beneath them went down five thousand meters, with steep cliffs that funneled water in from the depths. It was the deepest undersea canyon in Europe, and those cliffs were responsible for amplifying the waves up to three times what they'd normally be.

"Check this out. There's even a German U-boat down there," Garrett said, pointing to a spot not far off the point. "The tip of that canyon is right under you when you're out there on big days. You can sense it when you're over it."

Now they followed Garrett and his partner, Andrew, out through the harbor and beyond. These Yamahas had more juice than what Dane was used to. "Trust me, you're gonna need it," Garrett had told them.

Not only that, but Andrew had explained that at Nazaré, they didn't use the "kill switch." That was news to the group. In every big wave scenario they'd been in, jet ski drivers always wore the lanyard around their wrist, so that when disconnected from the switch, the engine would automatically shut off.

"Why?" asked Hope.

"Because here you want that ski to keep moving away from you. Anywhere nearby and it becomes a twelve-hundred-pound projectile. It's just not worth the risk."

Dane wasn't sure of the logic behind that, but he went with it. All around, the water was lit up red thanks to the fog-filtered sun. Dane and Kama rode together, Kama driving. Once they made it out into the deep, visibility improved.

"Brah," Kama said, when the point came into view.

Dane was rendered mute by the sight. He knew the cliff was over three hundred feet high, and from this angle, the waves seemed to be clawing for the top. White plumes lifted off tall green walls that created their own wind. The group approached from the south side, outside of Praia do Nazaré, a long ribbon of white sand. He glanced across the water at Yeti, who gave him a nod, as if to say *we're doing this*.

A shiver ran across his skin and that same full body rush that he craved. This was what he lived for. But even as he thought it, an image of 'Iwa played through his mind, alone at her fundraiser. His jaw clenched down, and he tasted blood on his tongue. What kind of selfish asshole was he? Choosing waves over a woman that meant everything to him.

Is this more important than love?

The question had been swimming just beneath the surface, poking up its head more and more lately. It threw him. Knocked him off balance. He knew what the answer *should* be, and yet, here he was.

Up ahead, Garrett slowed, then circled back around. Yesterday from the cliffs, he'd pointed out where they would line up, emphasizing that the waves moved around a lot and were largely unpredictable.

"It's looking a little more north than ideal, but let's see what comes."

Garrett handed the wheel over to Andrew and pulled his wetsuit hood up over his head. Dane did the same, and so did Yeti. They floated for a few minutes, and were close enough to the fort and the cliffs that you could hear the voices of the small crowd that had gathered. Dane swore he smelled coffee. What he would give for another hot mug right now. He was freezing his nuts off. Even in his five mm wetsuit. When the first set marched in, Andrew pulled Garrett into a bomb—a vertical mountain that peeled north of the point. As with all point breaks, one slipup and a graveyard of rocks awaited. These rocks were school bus–sized, as though someone had driven them off the edge of the cliff and they'd landed nose down.

"Brah, this one's all you!" Kama said, as the second one approached.

Dane was already in the water, and Kama gunned the engine, gaining enough speed to sling him onto a wave. Dane let go of the rope and sped along the feathering top, then dropped down the face. He sensed something off, and when he looked up, he saw a second peak forming. He crouched and straightened out to avoid getting slammed. The cliff loomed, but he barely noticed. He cut out before he hit the inside foamy beach break section, and Kama sped in to get him. Outside, they regrouped.

The next set was bigger and cleaner, and Dane had a screaming ride, glad he had brought his thickest board. But so far, nothing like the larger-than-life waves he'd been hoping for. His last few big wave sessions in California and Todos Santos had been better than this. Between the three jet skis, they picked off the best waves of the sets, letting many waves go unridden. Some were too north, almost sideways. Garrett played conductor, telling everyone which ones to ride. It was nice to have someone out here who had even a little experience with the break.

By lunchtime, the day warmed enough to remove their hoods, and the sun shone deep into the water. Everyone got at least one good ride—nothing epic, and everyone had at least one wipeout. Proper beatings, but nothing out of the ordinary. The sun had traversed from land to sea, and Dane was feeling the burn in his legs. Soon, a texture appeared out the back.

"One more set and we go back to the harbor," Garrett yelled.

Kama said he was done, so Dane—still waiting for that mythic Nazaré wave he had traveled all this way for—said he'd take it. He needed something to clear his conscience, because every time he thought of the look on 'Iwa's face when she realized he wouldn't be coming to her fundraiser, a cold wind blew through him.

"You going?" Kama said.

Dane found himself staring down a big one. Taller than anything else today, thick as a house. It was too late to catch it, but the next wave was even bigger. He gave Kama the thumbs-up.

At the top, looking down, time slowed. White strings of foam ran up the green face of the wave. A gull swooped in, wing skimming the water just below the top. Dane heard nothing but the thudding of his own heart. And then he was unceremoniously pitched into an eight-story elevator drop. For a moment he was weightless, arms wide, gracefully falling. He knew if he went down now, nothing good would come of it, but at the bottom, his board reconnected with the water.

Yes!

Making the drop gave him a sense of immortality, and he carved a deep bottom turn and headed higher up the line. Far ahead, the lip began to throw, and he pumped his board to get beyond it. The wave slingshot him along with an unusual violence. He barely made it through the first section and could feel a cavern forming behind him. An invisible echo of water. But he couldn't look, he just wanted to get off this thing.

The wave, however, had other ideas. Spray from the closing barrel exploded out and flattened him. The side of his head hit the water as though hitting concrete, filling his vision with fuzz. The wave carried so much force, he felt himself being sucked back up the face. There was nothing he could do but try to relax and go with it. Then he went over the falls and his whole world went dark.

On Drowning

Dane

They say drowning is peaceful. Dane felt anything but. He was somewhere dark underwater, choking and looking up toward the light. There was no surface, only lighter shades of white overhead. He went to kick and nothing happened. Desperate for air, he gulped reflexively to keep from sucking in the water. He used his arms to pull himself to the surface, summoning every bit of strength he could muster.

What scared him most was not the dreaded two-wave hold-down, or that his body might be coughed up on the rocks at any moment. What had him freaked was that his legs didn't seem to be functioning. There was no sense of peace, only panic. People are wrong about that, he thought.

The surface seemed to be getting farther and farther away, and he was about to give up the fight when he broke through to the air. His mouth opened and he heaved and coughed and sucked in more water. Instinct had him searching for his board, but it was nowhere in sight. Then he felt around to see if his leash was still attached to his leg, but he could not find his legs.

Breathe, motherfucker!

Dazed and half blind from the sand-stirred water, he managed to make out that the current had pulled him up the coast and he was drifting toward the inside beach break. He wondered where Kama was. There should have been the sound of a jet ski engine. When a wave broke just outside of him, he tried to dive under but had no leverage. Instead, the wave plunged him beneath the surface. Lightning shot out from the middle of his back.

He went limp and descended into darkness again, thinking of 'Iwa the whole way down. Her hard-won smile. Sitting on the rock at Waikula. How she always tasted like rainwater. How he hadn't told her he loved her, even though he did, because for him those three little words were more frightening than a hundred-foot wave.

Dig deep, brah.

Unwilling to fade into seawater, Dane began to claw toward the surface again. He broke through, keeping just his face above water. Another one of these and he would be fish food. Then he heard an engine. He weakly held up an arm, but realized he needed both to stay afloat. A few seconds later, Hope and Yeti sped in. Hope came in fast, slowed as Yeti leaned down and reached out his hand. Dane grabbed on.

"I can't feel my legs," he yelled as Hope punched it.

With the momentum, his body swung onto the sled, proving his legs were still there, even though he couldn't feel them, Yeti holding tight to his wrist. They went over a wave and came down hard. Dane screamed and as he put his face down, everything went black again. When he folded back into consciousness, Yeti was lying next to him, holding him to the sled with one arm. "We got you, bro. Hang in there."

On the beach, Dane lay on the sled fading in and out as pain radiated from a point in his back. A crowd had gathered, some speaking in English, some in Portuguese. Someone placed a towel over him. *Call 112! Can you feel your fingers? How about your toes?* At some point an ATV drove up. Yeti shooed everyone back, and with help from a young fisherman, slid Dane onto a rescue board. Dane wondered where Kama was but was too exhausted to speak.

Yeti squeezed his shoulder and looked him in the eye. "You're going to be good, mate. Hold that thought and don't let it go."

Dane could only nod.

Time had become as fluid as water, and at some point, Kama appeared and refused to leave his side, even though he was shivering so hard his teeth clattered. Two women brought them blankets and hot tea. He lay on the beach staring up at the sky. Clouds, seagulls, an airplane way overhead. And was that 'Iwa singing? He tried to sit up to see where she was.

"Where is she?" he said to no one in particular.

Yeti gently held him down. "Who?"

"'Iwa."

"'Iwa is on Maui, mate."

That couldn't be. "No, I just heard her voice."

Yeti shook his head and Dane closed his eyes and faded out again, coming to as he and Kama were loaded onto a helicopter headed to Lisbon. Rotors whirred, and they lifted off.

Kama sat by his head. "I'm sorry."

"Not your fault."

Rule one. No blame.

"The whitewater took over the ski and I lost power. I had to bail and swim in."

"I'm just glad you're okay."

"I'm sorry," Kama said again.

This time his voice caught.

Dane opened his eyes and looked up at his friend. "Can you call 'Iwa?"

"As soon as we get there."

"Will you tell her I love her? Please."

"Brah, tell her yourself, you're going to be fine."

The hospital was full of shiny floors, white coats and bright lights. The paramedics transferred Dane into the emergency room, where he was poked and prodded and hooked up to an IV, then sent for an MRI. They had him doped up just enough to not feel much without losing his awareness of what was happening.

A fracture at T11/T12. Neurologic involvement. Pinched spinal cord. Emergency surgery. Kama, Yeti and Hope were all in his room when the news was delivered. No one said a peep. Dane stared down at his legs under the sheet, willing them to move. They didn't.

"Can I get an interpreter? I have questions," he asked.

Yeti stepped forward. "I speak Portuguese. What do you want me to ask?"

Of course he did.

"Ask him when the fuck I'm going to be able to move my legs again."

Yeti and Dr. Monteiro broke into a discussion, with the doctor repeatedly shaking his head. The balance of Dane's life hung somewhere in that unintelligible conversation and he was scared. After years of good fortune, his luck had run out. The medication made him sleepy and he went down a rabbit hole. What if, in this lifetime, you were doled out a finite amount of luck? You could use it all at once, or you could spread it out to last until you died. Maybe Dane had been going about life all wrong.

"I fucked up. I've been overspending my luck," he mumbled.

Hope came over and stood by his side, resting a hand on his shoulder. "Nonsense. Luck is something we generate ourselves. And the more you make, the more you'll have. At least that's what my grandpops used to say. So you actually are not out of luck, you are in luck. You survived."

Dane felt a sting in his eyes. "You call this luck?"

Yeti held up a hand. "Hang on."

Dr. Monteiro was pointing to the large image of Dane's spine on the light box on the wall and rattling on about something.

Yeti went in for closer inspection, then turned to Dane and said, "The good news is your spinal cord isn't severed, it's most likely just badly bruised. But they need to stabilize this fracture to prevent the bones from moving, and that means surgery. He believes your situation will improve once the steroids kick in and the inflammation goes down."

Kama jumped up. "Yes!"

"When will I walk again? Or surf?" Dane wanted to know.

The word *surgery* slinked around the edges of his consciousness and he shuddered at the idea of someone cutting into his spine.

"He says that nerves heal slowly, so it could be weeks or even months."

"Months?"

Dane turned to the window, where murky shafts of light shone in. He wanted to close his eyes and drift off, change the dream.

Yeti loomed over him. "You sustained a hard blow to your back, mate. It's going to take some time. But you will heal, we'll make sure of that. Your biggest battle is going to be in your mind."

Dane looked around at his salty-haired friends wrapped in blankets, a ragged, bloodshot crew, and felt a deep affinity for them. Still, he wanted nothing more than to tear this hospital gown off and run out the door. To rewind time back to the moment when he chose Nazaré over Maui. Over 'Iwa.

Regret was something he had usually steered clear of. He had never seen the point. You might regret the thing you did or regret the thing you didn't do, but you couldn't go back and change any of it. In his mind, regret had always seemed like a way of not owning up to your choices, a sentiment for weaker-minded people than himself. Now he was assaulted by the force of it as he lay here in this sterile bed, and it was far worse than any two-wave hold-down.

The worst part was, at the time, a voice inside had told him he was making the wrong choice when he had bailed on 'Iwa. But he'd made it anyway. Maybe he wasn't cut out for love after all. Or maybe he was too messed up in the head to even know what love was.

Room Two Twenty-Two

'Iwa

Dane got hit in the back by his board. He's okay, but right now, he can't feel his legs, 'Iwa. He can't move them. Is there any chance you can come to Portugal?

Kama's words haunted her the whole way across the Pacific, in the skies above the continental United States, and freezing her butt off over the Atlantic. She called to check in on his condition on both her layovers. Kama said the surgery went well, but still no feeling, no movement. She couldn't understand how *went well* equated to still being paralyzed, but dared not ask.

Before her illness, 'Iwa's mother had cooked up a plan of hiking the Alps, cruising the fjords in Norway and drinking wine in Galicia for a month after 'Iwa finished grad school. Just the two of them. That trip had never happened, and now, 'Iwa was headed to Europe for a reason she never would have imagined.

This will all blow over. Dane is going to be fine. He has to be.

Walking down the halls of the hospital threw 'Iwa back into memories of watching her mother fade away. The sound of her slippers on cold tile, those bright photographs of flowers on the walls in stark contrast with patients in hospital gowns being helped down the hallways with their IV poles trailing behind, doing their best to stay alive while the outside world kept forging on without them. Hospitals were places of death, but she reminded herself now that they were also places of new life and healing.

At room two twenty-two she stood to the side of the open door and peered in, half her face showing. Kama sat in a chair next to Dane reading. 'Iwa steeled herself. He must have sensed her there because after a few moments, he looked up. 'Iwa waved. He stood, holding a finger to his lips and walking to her. They hugged, long and hard.

"He's asleep now, but he's going to be so happy to see you. He's kind of in and out," Kama whispered.

Dane was pale and looked as though someone had taken a pin and let all his air out. There was a machine attached to him, displaying his vitals. 'Iwa went to the side of his bed and watched his chest rise and fall. His eyelids moved and fluttered. Feather light, she pressed her lips against his cheek. It was all she could do to stop herself from climbing into his bed and curling her body next to his.

His eyes opened.

'Iwa smiled. "Hey there."

He stared at her. "Where am I?"

"You're still in Portugal, in the hospital. I just flew in."

Dane rubbed a hand through his hair. "That's right. I thought maybe I was on Maui."

She leaned down, took his rough hand in hers and pressed her lips softly to his. Dane pulled her in, and she rested her forehead against his, nose to nose. He inhaled, she exhaled.

"You smell like heaven," he said.

'Iwa had doused herself in Monoï oil in the bathroom downstairs, trying to get the smell of airplane and two days of travel off her skin.

"Nah, just Hawai'i."

"Same thing."

"I guess you could say that."

She had no idea what was to come, and she wanted to stay just where she was for a few moments, breathing him in. When she finally pulled away, she noticed he flinched, and a new look she didn't recognize passed over his face.

"Did they tell you I still can't feel anything in my legs?" Dane asked.

A pause that burned her heart.

"Yes."

Kama, who had been standing in the doorway, said, "The doc keeps saying we have to be patient, that it's not unusual in this kind of injury."

Seeing him now, like this, she realized there was no way she could leave him until he was released. "From what I've read, this isn't terribly rare. And I'm here, Dane, we'll get through this together."

"I can't even give you a proper hug," Dane said, holding tight to her hand.

Her eyes went to his legs, she couldn't help it. They were under several layers of blankets, spread out, lifeless as dead branches.

"I would lie down with you, but I don't want to hurt you," she said.

"You lying next to me would never hurt, I promise you that."

The door swung open and a nurse came in. "How you doing, Senhor Dane?"

"Better, now that she's here. Gabi, this is 'Iwa. The girl I was telling you about."

Gabi gave 'Iwa a glowing smile. "He's been waiting for you. I am so happy you came."

'Iwa nodded. "I left Maui as soon as I could."

Gabi checked the IV bag, tapped down the length of his legs and asked if he felt anything.

"*Nada.*"

★ ★ ★

'Iwa stayed with him all day and into the evening, giving Kama a break. Dane slept a good portion of the time, but even when he was awake, he didn't say much. Whether from medication or the reality of what he was up against, she had no idea. Hope came and went, bringing food and magazines, and later in the afternoon, Yeti arrived with a ukulele in one hand and a box of steaming coffee cups in the other.

'Iwa perked up at the sight of the familiar instrument. "Where did you find that?"

"It's a braguinha, not a ukulele."

She remembered then that Portuguese immigrants from Madeira had brought their instruments to Hawai'i in the late 1800s. Here they were, nearly eight thousand miles away, and Yeti was holding a forefather of the ukulele.

He held it out. "They're almost the same but tuned differently. I went on a treasure hunt to find this thing, tracking all over Lisbon. I finally found it in a tiny music store downtown. Then when I heard you were coming, I had it tuned for you."

She glanced over at Dane, who suddenly seemed interested. She strummed a few times, getting a feel. "Name your tune."

His eyes cut through to her heart. "You need to ask?"

The opening riff to "Sweet Child O' Mine" was tricky on the ukulele, but no one here would be complaining. She moved close to the bed and sang quietly. *You've got eyes of the bluest skies…* Her throat was dry from airplane air and crying. She slowed the song down, imagining herself back at Uncle's on day one of this crazy journey. Her eyes never left Dane's.

When 'Iwa was done, he patted the bed next to him. "I don't care if they kick us out or arrest us, come lie with me."

Yeti said goodbye and 'Iwa eased herself onto the hospital bed. She went hip first, made herself as narrow as possible and lay on her side facing Dane. Even now, he still smelled of ocean and kelp and sea otters.

"I hurt," he said.

"I hurt for you."

She felt the density of his predicament in her own legs, if that was possible. Maybe it was from all the travel or maybe it was because she felt connected to him in a way she'd never felt before—with anyone. At that moment, looking into his tired and glassy eyes, all uncertainty fell away. Only love was left.

"I'm sorry, 'Iwa, for not coming to Maui for your fundraiser. I wish I had, and not just because this wouldn't have happened. It was a shitty thing to do."

She pressed a finger to his lips. This close, she could see a groove in his brow and the beginnings of sun lines around his eyes. "Apology accepted."

"I promise it won't happen again."

"We don't need to talk about it now."

"I just want you to know," he whispered.

Within seconds, Dane was asleep.

The Prognosis
Dane

Whenever the meds began to wear off, Dane would fixate on his legs, begging, pleading, willing for them to move. They looked the same as always. Same hair, same bony knees and shins, same long and wiry feet. Having 'Iwa there helped in some ways, but in others it just made him more frustrated.

Since the moment she'd arrived, she had barely left his side. There for his bathing, feeding and physical therapy, where he stood between two bars and practiced supporting his weight—he couldn't move but it turned out he could bear weight. She also participated in Yeti's group meditations, where they breathed together to raise the frequency in the room. She sang to him and lay with him and read to him nature essays from a book she'd brought called *A Sand County Almanac*.

Through it all, Dane was half checked out. The thought that he could be this way for the rest of his life was more than he could bear. And the days kept on unspooling out before him with little change, other than a little less pain in his back. He knew that the longer you went without any signs of recovery, the worse your prognosis. No one would tell him this to his face, but he'd read up on his phone.

On the fourth day, Dane woke to the sound of ukulele and soft singing. Waking up was the worst, even with 'Iwa in his room playing music. He would linger in that between time when he hadn't yet remembered where he was and why he was here, before being blindsided by the harsh truth. He looked over and watched her elegant fingers for a few moments, how her mouth made this cute little movement she wasn't even aware of, and how the music absorbed her. He had thought he would be able to tell her he loved her when she arrived, but the words lodged somewhere between his sternum and his throat and remained there, unspoken.

She caught him watching her. "Hey, you. How about a massage?"

The nurses encouraged massage on his legs to keep the blood flow up, and 'Iwa took it upon herself to rub him down every other hour.

"Sure."

She came over, leaned down and kissed him, then got to work. She pulled back the sheet on his left leg, started kneading his thighs and worked her way down around his knee, and then to his calf.

"Did you know the soleus muscle is considered your second heart?" she asked.

He wasn't in the mood to play this game. "Nope."

"It pumps all that blood back up from the periphery, which is why it's so important to..." Her voice trailed off.

"Walk? Yeah, well, not gonna happen anytime soon."

"Dane, don't think like that, it is going to happen, and until then we will pump them manually."

Watching his legs be massaged and feeling nothing was surreal and humbling. He hated it. But it gave 'Iwa something to do. He could tell being here was hard on her, too.

"I know this isn't what you signed up for—"

She wouldn't even let him finish. "Dane, stop."

"I just want you to know I don't expect you to stay with me here. Or back in Santa Cruz if I ever get there."

She moved down to his foot and began jamming her thumbs into his sole. "I'll just pretend you didn't say that. Let's stay positive, okay?"

"I'm serious, 'Iwa. You have a life."

That was when his leg jerked up.

Her eyes went wide. "Did you just see your leg move?"

She did whatever it was she had just done to his foot, and his leg flexed up again toward his hip.

"You moved!" 'Iwa cried.

Staring down, Dane spoke to his toes. "Move, please." They didn't.

"Try again," she whispered.

He concentrated harder this time, and several breaths later his big toe bent down slightly. Their eyes met.

"I need to tell the doctor," she said, leaping up and running out of the room, door swinging behind her.

A few minutes later, she returned with nurse Gabi, who explained in limited English what had happened. Apparently when 'Iwa had dug into his foot and bent his toes back, that stimulated a deep reflex.

"Is a good sign. We use it to join pathways, to strengthen the leg," Gabi said.

It wasn't much—what could a person do with just one big toe?—but it was enough to get him transferred home.

Two days later, Dane and 'Iwa and Kama flew back to California, arriving with a wave of sooty shearwaters traveling up the coast. Spring and all its bounty were in the air, with bourgeoning krill and schools of sardines. Usually, for Dane, this was when he took on more carpentry jobs and built furniture for a shop in town that sold rustic pieces of art and housewares. The furniture building was a newer thing, and had recently begun to gain more traction. He loved the free-form artsiness of it, too. It worked well because he could do it on his own time and there were no clients to upset when he left town midjob. Now there would be none of that. Instead, it would be a time to heal and try to get his head straight.

Arriving back in his own home was a temporary balm. Isla froze when she first saw him, creeping up slowly, sniffing the air and making sure it was really him. When she realized it was, she howled and zoomed around the room. It was good to be back, and yet he still felt a vacancy pressing in from all sides.

A week passed. Then another. There was little change in his condition, other than being able to stand for longer periods of time. He spent large swaths of time watching surf movies, reading old surf magazines and living vicariously through images of blue barrels. The rest was spent going to physical therapy or sleeping. Sleep had become his best friend, along with the little white pills that took the edge off everything.

If he thought being in California would turn things around, he was mistaken. Here there were no experienced nurses and no IV strapped to his arm administering pain medication. In Lisbon, as depressing as it had been, it felt like a bad side trip that would come to an end. Here, he was reminded of all the things he couldn't do. No walking, no working, no swimming until his five-inch incision healed, no surfing, no nothing. 'Iwa was still with him, but to be honest, he was starting to wish she'd go back to Maui. Let him wallow in his worthlessness.

Yeti showed up one evening, around sunset, and handed him a stack of books. "More lifesaving inspiration from the pages. I highly recommend you check these out in your spare time."

It was all spare time. Dane set the books on the bedside table without even looking at them. "I don't need books—I need to get back in the water."

"What, four more days?"

"Not sure, all I know is it's too long." It was hard to keep anything straight.

'Iwa came out carrying two glasses of water with lemon, set

them down and hugged Yeti. She hung on him for what seemed like a really long time.

"Babe, my back is really sore right now, can you get me another pill?" he said quietly to her.

She shot a look at Yeti, then went off to the kitchen without a word. She returned a moment later, handed him a pill and picked up Isla from his lap. "I'm going to take Isla for a walk, be back soon."

Once 'Iwa was out the door, Yeti pulled up the leather chair so he was sitting close, his beard freshly trimmed. He smelled like evergreen trees and mountain air and Dane craved a walk in the hills behind the house.

Yeti looked at Dane with those piercing eyes of his. "Look, I know you're suffering, mate, but this is where I tell you man to man that it's time to wean yourself off those narcotics. You think they're helping, but they're doing more harm than good."

Coming from anyone else, Dane would have asked, *What do you know of suffering?* But Yeti had suffered the kind of loss that breaks a person in half and had come out the other side. Yeti had told him early on of his wife's death, and then never spoken about her again. People always said you needed to talk about your grief, but coping had a thousand faces, as Dane well knew.

"I'll stop taking them when I stop needing them."

"Pain is there for a reason. It's your body talking to you if you're willing to listen."

Dane picked up his lemon water and drank. "I got this, man."

Yeti shook his head. "I don't think you do."

He had no energy to argue. "Yeah, okay, maybe tomorrow I'll stop."

"I'm serious, man. Those things are venom. I talked to Xiao and he said he'll come over here and give you acupuncture every day if you want. Needles are effective for your kind of injury."

"Fine. Send him."

He'd be a pincushion. Anything to get Yeti off his case.

Apparently Yeti wasn't finished. "Also, that woman out there? She's giving up a lot to be here, and I see you pushing her away. You have so much anger, and I get it, but lashing out at the people you love is not the answer. I suggest you read those books. Do a little inner work. It's the only way through."

"Did she tell you I was pushing her away?" Dane asked.

"I see it with my own two eyes every time I come over here. We're all rooting for you, but we need you to trust us, listen to us," Yeti said, eyes pleading.

Yeti was right about the anger. It was writhing inside of him, expanding and contracting and feeding on itself. Sometimes he felt like howling, other times he wanted to whip the remote across the room. And then there were moments when he wanted to bury his head in his pillow and bawl like the child he'd been reduced to.

"You know what? I'm tired. You can see yourself out," Dane said.

Did anyone think he really wanted to be on this shit?

Yeti softened his tone. "I'm on your side."

"Then give me a break."

Once he heard Yeti's engine start up, he reached over and popped a pill in his mouth. Swallowed. Glanced over at the bottle. Oh fuck it. He took another one and was lights out before 'Iwa and Isla came back.

The Longest Plateau
'Iwa

When things got to be too much, 'Iwa began escaping to the loop trail at the end of the road, which was crowded with oaks and conifers. She blamed it on Isla needing another walk, when really it was her who did. Being among the trees and walking on the rich soil soothed her. She began asking her mother for guidance on what to do, and how to handle these muddy waters.

The answers never came immediately, but small signs would appear to make her feel less alone. A blue jay leading her down the path. Two bushy-tailed squirrels scampering through the brush. An old log covered in familiar lime-green moss. And then, deeper in the woods, something large and dark fluttering between two tall trees. At first 'Iwa thought it was a bat, but when she got closer, she saw it more clearly. Some kind of silk moth with spots that resembled eyes. It reminded her of home.

It was a good thing Isla was small, since she was terrible on a leash. She darted this way and that, straining against her harness, trying to smell every blade of grass and every tree and shrub. But if she let her off, there were cougars and poison ivy to be concerned about. Isla also had more pee in her per square inch than seemed possible, and squatted every ten feet. Her cuteness was infectious, though, and she pranced along with her tiny, furry feet. She was a lot more pleasant to be around than

Dane. Not that anyone could blame him for hurting, but the meanness she hadn't seen coming.

In the first couple of days, he had seemed so grateful to have her there, talking about places he wanted to take her—trekking in New Zealand, snowboarding in the Canadian Rockies, sailing in Tahiti, surfing in Bali, hiking in the rainforest of Costa Rica. But those moments had trailed off, and last night when she had rested her head on his chest he said, "When you touch me, it hurts."

No emotion. No touching her back. For the first time she started rethinking being here. The idea made her panicky and she wasn't sure how to handle it. She had met Kama and Yeti for coffee this morning, and finally come out with her concerns.

"Dane is strung out on meds. He's becoming nasty if I suggest holding them back, and I wonder how much is because of pain and how much is wanting to numb reality."

"I'm sure it's both. We need to get him outside more," Kama said.

"It would be nice, but it's hard to get him into the wheelchair by myself, and he refuses to let me call on the neighbors."

Kama or Yeti had been trading off coming by to help get Dane up, but this week Kama had had to travel down the coast for work and Yeti had been nursing a cold.

"I'm feeling better. I'll come by and help more," Yeti said.

"Can you please talk to him about the medicine, too? It's tweaking him, and he won't listen to me."

'Iwa wanted the old Dane back and felt guilty about it. None of this was his fault, and she had promised to stand by his side, but it was growing harder by the day. Maybe a short break would do them good.

"Will do. How much longer are you planning on staying?"

She had already been gone twenty-two days. "I have to go home next week, at least for a little while. The eco resort is still steamrolling ahead, and we are running out of time to stop them."

"I can stay with Dane while you're gone," Kama offered.

"Hope said she would."

Hope had been by a lot, which was a big help. Early that evening, as promised, she came over again, wearing flowy pants and a white crop top. She'd been growing out her hair, and now loose waves layered below her cheekbones, softening her look.

"Dude, you are never going to guess who I ran into," she said, dropping a basketful of *Surfer's Journal*s on the table and then walking over to the couch where Dane lay.

"No clue," he said.

"Makua Rothman, in the flesh."

Makua had won the XXL ten years or so ago when he was only eighteen. A monster wave at Pe'ahi that had made him look like an ant. 'Iwa remembered the photo, and thinking it was the biggest wave she had ever seen at the time.

Dane sat up. "Did you ask him to marry you already?"

Hope smacked him on the head with a magazine. "Not this time. We talked mostly about you and how you're doing, but I'm still holding out hope."

"Hope springs eternal," Dane said.

"Yeah, well, most of the good ones are taken, so maybe not."

"Keep the faith," he said.

She smiled and slid in next to him. "Wise words, my friend. How are you today?"

"Same as I was yesterday and last week and probably next week," he said in a flat voice.

Hope squeezed his leg, hard. "How about we get your butt off the couch and do some standing practice? You'll feel better, I promise."

"Not now, I'm feeling pretty tired."

"I won't leave until you say yes. Remember what Yeti used to tell me when I hurt my shoulder, *motion is lotion*. That means you can't lie around all day and expect to get better, you need to do the work. The same way we train for waves."

Dane groaned but held his hand out. Hope helped him up and talked to him while he stood in place.

"Yes! Give me one more minute, Dane, you got this! I can see those muscles developing one fiber at a time." And on and on.

Hope was a natural-born motivator, cheerleader and preacher all in one. 'Iwa could see why the kids on the surf team worshipped her.

Progress was slow, but there *had* been progress. Dane could hold himself up indefinitely, and move his leg forward at the hip, but the fine muscles of his foot were not working, and he couldn't lift and turn it over to take a step. The top of his foot would just drag across the floor.

Doc had said to expect long plateaus and then a leap. It could go on like this for months or even a year. Physical therapy was the hardest part of the week, and Dane would leave the building spent and red in the face. Once home, he would take more pills and pass out on the bed. He kept saying he was going to stop them *soon* or *next week*.

One day, when 'Iwa was coming back from her walk, she saw an unfamiliar car parked out front of Dane's house. There had been plenty of visitors, so she thought nothing of it. Then, his front door opened and a long-haired woman with an arm full of bangles stepped out. 'Iwa recognized her right away. The black lab at her side darted down the stairs and came right up to Isla, sniffing and snorting. Isla bared her teeth.

"Sorry about that. Wingnut, get over here," Sunny said, coming to where 'Iwa stood in the grass.

"Isla can hold her own, no worries," 'Iwa answered coolly.

Sunny smiled and held up both her hands, a peace offering of sorts. "I was hoping to meet you, so I'm glad you came back before I left. I'm Sunny."

"'Iwa. Nice to meet you." What else could she say? Sunny being here felt wrong, but maybe she was being overly sensitive.

"I hope you don't mind, I brought a little care package and thought seeing Wingnut might cheer Dane up. I didn't realize you have a dog, too."

"Isla is Dane's dog. He found her in Mexico."

Sunny shifted on her heels. "It's hard to see him like that."

"Yes." 'Iwa simply did not have the energy to engage, or pretend that they might somehow commiserate together. "It was nice of you to stop by, but excuse me, I need to get inside."

"Sure, of course."

'Iwa wrangled Isla and headed in. Dane lay on the couch staring at the TV when she walked in. There was a basket on the coffee table in front of him, with a few things scattered around it, and the faint smell of lemon balm in the air.

"Hey," he said, not looking her way.

"I met Sunny."

He groaned. "Yeah, she brought a bunch of random stuff."

From what 'Iwa could see there was a bag of coffee, a tin of dark chocolates and several pouches of herbal tea.

"That was nice of her," she said, trying to sound unbothered.

"Don't worry, 'Iwa, it was an innocent visit."

"I never said anything to the contrary."

"Yeah but you're thinking it. I know how girls are."

'Iwa stood in the middle of the room for a few moments, wishing she had something to hold her up. Something or someone to lean on.

"What is wrong with you, Dane? It's not fair to take your anger out on me," she yelled, throwing the leash on the floor and walking back toward the front door, sick of tiptoeing around his mood swings.

"I'm not angry—you're angry," he said flatly.

'Iwa slammed the door, then realized her phone was in there. Shit. She went back in and grabbed it. He ignored her. Once outside again, she called Eddie. Told him everything. Until now, she had been withholding information because she didn't want him to worry about her. Lord knew he had enough to worry about, but she didn't know who else to turn to.

"Dad, I don't know what to do," she cried softly into her phone as she walked toward the short trail at the end of the road. "I want to just take the bottle away and flush the pills down the toilet, but I know you can't stop them cold turkey," she said.

"It's not your *kuleana*. If you do that, he's going to resent you."

"He already resents me."

"For what?"

"For being alive? I don't know."

"Men aren't good at hurting, 'Iwa girl. It goes against our nature to show weakness. You're going to have to wait this one out. This is his fight, his life, not yours."

A blue jay swooped past, startling her.

"He's getting worse, not better. At least in how he's coping with it all."

"Come home then, take a break. Dane will still be there when you get back. With you gone, he'll remember to appreciate you."

"I need to, anyway. For work. Winston and the others need me there. *I* need to be there."

He had already been more than accommodating, and picking up the slack. Fortunately, he now had Kawika working on the legal end of things.

"There's your answer. Koa misses you, and so do I."

"I miss you too, Dad."

Dane had been checking the surf forecast like a maniac, a form of self-torture in 'Iwa's mind, and announced that he wanted to go see the big, late season northwest swell slated to hit Santa Cruz this weekend. Saturday came and the trees wore their finest greens. Parties of golden poppies and purple hound's-tongue populated the hillsides. Kama and Yeti came to the house early, helped Dane down the steps and into the car, and they were off, picking up coffee and breakfast burritos first, en route to Steamer Lane.

The parking lot was packed with cars, but Kama pulled into a handicapped stall front and center. The wave broke just off the point, and outside the car they could see a paved walkway and railings that led right up to the edge of the cliff. Dane grew quiet as he stared out at it. A weighty kind of quiet that spread out and coated everything around him. Isla was the only one who seemed unaffected by his mood, and was trying to climb out the window to get to a grassy area.

'Iwa did her best to remain upbeat. "What a gorgeous day! Let's get out there and soak up the sun."

They walked and Dane wheeled along the meandering pathway, through spectators and surfers and people walking dogs. Isla stopped to greet everyone, spinning in circles when they came upon a Newfoundland fourteen times her size. Then she rolled over, belly up, right in front of him, rubbing her back in the grass.

"What a flirt," 'Iwa said, laughing.

Dane didn't even notice—he was staring at the surf. "Here comes a bomb. Middle Peak," he announced.

They went to the edge and looked out on the bay, where line after line of swell pumped in. The surf was well overhead, and clusters of surfers filled the water. Red boards, yellow boards, white boards, green boards. Shortboards, guns and even a few longboards.

"And I thought Honolua was crowded," 'Iwa said.

Kama stood by her side. "Welcome to Steamer Lane. Inside here is the Slot. Middle Peak is that A-frame outside, and that long right is Indicators. You can actually go both ways, but the current can get pretty serious over there. Do you know the history here?"

"Should I?"

"Hawaiians were the first to surf this place in the late 1800s. Nephews of Queen Kapiʻolani—Prince Kūhiō and his brothers. They went to school here and made boards out of redwood planks. So this is really the birthplace of surfing on the mainland."

"I had no idea."

"Not many people do."

A peanut gallery of surfers, with wetsuits peeled off their burnished shoulders, were leaning on the railing nearby, with a running commentary on every wave. *Goooooo! Look at this kook, who does he think he is? No way you're gonna make this, bro. How was that right? Sick!* They were in their own world, until at some point, one of them noticed Dane.

"Yo, Parsons. Sorry to hear about your accident. How you doing, man?" he said, coming over.

Dane held up a hand and they did some kind of fancy Santa Cruz handshake.

"Hanging in there," Dane said.

The others all came over, stood around Dane a little awkwardly. They talked surf for a while, asking about Nazaré, and Dane lit up. Then the guys moved on, just like the rest of the world. ʻIwa had seen it with her mom, and she was seeing it now. People were there for a little while, mobilizing and helping and holding your hand, but there came a time when you were on your own. No one else lived in your skin.

Yeti and ʻIwa helped Dane up, and the railing turned out to be perfect for standing practice. Dane braced himself against the cool steel with ʻIwa on one side, hand on his lower back, just in case. Breathing in the salty air had to be good for him. Lord knew it was good for her.

"What's that saying? The cure for anything is salt water," she said. "Think about all those negative ions we're breathing in right now."

"You got that right," Yeti said.

Dane didn't respond. 'Iwa followed his gaze to where a guy on a red board hung at the top of a wave at the Slot, right below them. Though not as big as the waves outside, this one had some heft to it. In a very late takeoff, he dropped onto a pitching face. From the physics of it all, you could tell he wasn't going to make it. Sure enough, at the bottom, he lost his balance and skidded off the board. The wave then pulled him back up and over the falls, slamming him into the shallow water at the base of the cliff. The guy took two strokes toward his board, then went face down in the water, limp as kelp.

Yeti started yelling and waving his hands at the closest surfer in the water. "Help! He needs help."

Kama was already sprinting down the path toward a set of stairs, pulling his shirt off. 'Iwa felt Dane sway, and she guided him back into the wheelchair. His face had gone milk white.

"Are you all right?" she asked.

His breathing picked up and she could tell by the way his chest heaved up and down, and the distant look in his eye, that he was having some kind of flashback. Isla sensed something wrong and stood on her hind legs, paws on Dane's thigh. With her little nose, she nudged his hand.

"Get me out of here," he said.

'Iwa knelt down, eye level. "Dane, you're on dry land. You're with me and Isla. Take some deep breaths." Even though the sun melted down on them, he was shivering. She rubbed his back and took a few deep breaths herself. "This will pass."

All around, the crowd, which had gone silent, began cheering and 'Iwa turned to see another surfer with the downed one, who was now conscious and hanging onto his board.

Yeti appeared back at their side. "Looks like the dude's going to be fine."

"Dane wants to leave," 'Iwa told him.

Dane pulled his beanie down over his eyes, which 'Iwa noticed were watering. "I can't watch this shit. It's making me crazy."

Yeti tensed. "What are you talking about? This shit is your life. This shit is real. You can't just hole up and stare at waves on your computer all day with everyone tiptoeing around you. Healing means joining the living. Going back to what you love."

Dane's eyes blazed. "I can't do what I love. Haven't you noticed that?"

"Maybe not now. But you will. And on the off chance that you can't, you'll find something else to love. It's called being human, mate."

Dane wheeled himself away, leaving 'Iwa and Yeti behind.

Surprises
'Iwa

Life will always, always, always surprise you. You can count on that just as much as you can count on a beautiful Haleakalā sunrise, her mother used to say. 'Iwa was ready for a surprise. Something happy and bright and good. Something to turn things around. And wouldn't you know it, life delivered. But not in the way she was hoping for.

Surprisingly, Dane was up early the next morning. 'Iwa helped him into the wheelchair and they went out onto the porch to watch the sunrise. Spears of yellow light filtered through the trees, spreading onto the dew-covered grass. They were both bundled up in blankets, sipping dark roast coffee and soaking up the stillness. Dane hadn't asked for a pain pill yet, and 'Iwa had her fingers crossed that today would be the day. Maybe seeing the waves up close had shifted something in him.

She closed her eyes. "Did you know that your eyes can absorb all that Vitamin D from the sun even when they're closed?"

"Never heard that one, but I do know Vitamin D is as essential as oxygen. It's sunshine in vitamin form."

"Probably why you surfers are such a healthy bunch."

"And you Hawaiians," he added.

'Iwa shrugged. "You know what they say. *Lucky we live Hawai'i.*"

"Would you ever live anywhere else?"

His question caught her off guard. "Right now, it's my home and I'm happy there. But who knows, down the road. I could feel differently."

Doubtful.

The truth of the matter was, being on the mainland, as nice as Santa Cruz was, was sucking the life out of her. Maybe it would be different if Dane was his old self, but maybe not.

"You're lucky to have roots like that," he said.

"You have roots. They might not go as deep, but look at the life you've created here and all the beautiful souls you've surrounded yourself with. Your branches are broad, and that makes up for shallower roots."

He smiled, and it sent shockwaves through her. He still had it in him.

That night, Yeti invited them over for tapas, along with a random assortment of other Santa Cruz friends. As with the group in Ensenada, they were all hip, all outdoorsy, all salt of the earth. One couple owned a local candle business, another ran a doggie day care, and yet another, an organic winery. Expensive wine flowed freely, as everyone sat around a big fire pit on the *lānai*. The glasses were double oversized, but what the hell, 'Iwa felt like she could use a little too much wine about now.

Dane was drinking, too, even though they both knew he wasn't supposed to. His chipper morning mood had gone south as soon as he'd taken his first pill at ten. Now every time she looked, someone was topping him off. Not her problem. He was a big boy, and she wasn't his mother. 'Iwa stuffed herself with cheese and crackers, olives and nuts, and crusty sourdough bread, and then did what she did best: sat back, warmed her toes by the fire and observed. Yeti busted out his guitar and plucked idly, adding a new layer of folksy ambience. It would have been perfect a month ago.

Then, a dark-haired man with a Kiwi accent arrived with

a woman who from the side looked a lot like Sunny. 'Iwa felt
her face heat up, and tried to get a better look, but the woman
shifted so it was impossible to tell for sure.

Kama went up and simultaneously shook his hand and gave
him a half hug. "Luke, buddy, it's good to see you. I had no
idea you were in town," 'Iwa heard him say.

'Iwa did not have the energy for this, and wished she was
back home in the forest, or playing at Uncle's with Winston,
or hanging with Koa on the living room floor. It all seemed
too much.

Hope suddenly appeared next to 'Iwa and sat down. "Mind
if I sit?"

"Of course not."

"Luke is visiting from New Zealand, Muriwai is his home
break. But why he's here with Sunny is anybody's guess."

"So it is her."

"Yeah but don't give it a second thought. They were over
long before you two were a thing."

"Not that long."

"You don't have anything to worry about, 'Iwa, trust me on
that," Hope said.

'Iwa sighed. "I'm not worried, just tired, I guess? It feels like
Dane is retreating into this dark place in his own mind, and I
don't have the power to stop him."

"It worries me, too, but he'll snap out of it. He's the stron-
gest guy I know."

'Iwa watched Luke move over to Dane and fall into conversation with him—the two obviously knew each other—Hope
left to make her rounds, and 'Iwa drank more wine. More plat-
ters of food appeared and everyone seemed loose and happy.
Even Dane. Voices grew louder, one of the couples started slow
dancing, and 'Iwa somehow found herself sitting with Luke, enjoying the sound of his Kiwi accent as they compared Hawai'i
and Aotearoa. Birds. Trees. Indigenous cultures.

"Aotearoa is like Hawai'i through the looking glass. Every-thing's a little bigger and a little older on the evolutionary scale. You'd love all the flightless birds. And we have penguins on the South Island—Te Waipounamu," he told her.

Aside from being a surfer, Luke made wire sculptures of animals and Maori *atua*, or gods. He was fascinating and well carved, but 'Iwa didn't care. She only had eyes for one man. When she finally pulled her attention away, she caught Dane watching her. She smiled, but he turned and wheeled himself inside the house. She poured herself more wine and didn't go after him.

When he had disappeared inside, Luke said, "He's having a rough go at it, I reckon?"

Tears pooled in her eyes. "Very."

Feeling extra weepy and hanging on by a hair, 'Iwa unloaded on him the whole story. Luke knew how to listen. When she finished, he looked her hard in the eye. "You can't feel guilty for something that's not your fault."

It struck her then that this went deeper than Dane. This went back to her mother and that horrible, dreadful feeling of not being able to save her. The powerlessness had been crushing, and now she was trying to save Dane.

To save *them*.

"Sometimes we can't save people, all we can do is love them. But even that isn't always enough," he said.

Sometime later, buzzed and in need of the bathroom, 'Iwa went inside. No one was in the kitchen or living area, but she thought she heard Dane's voice coming down the hallway. The lights were on low, and she heard the sound of a woman's laughter. She moved in that direction, heat pricking the back of her neck. Yeti had a movie room in the back of the house, and 'Iwa approached cautiously, remaining in the shadows for a few moments before entering. The scene before her took a moment to register, and then there was no air left in her lungs.

Dane and Sunny were the only two there. 'Iwa scanned the room hoping to see someone with them. Another warm body, another woman who might have been laughing. But they were alone. The scene unfolded in slow motion from there. Sunny in Dane's lap. Their heads close together. Were they kissing? No, that couldn't be right. 'Iwa steadied herself against the wall, unable to believe what she was seeing. Sunny stood up, but Dane yanked her back into his lap. She landed hard. Dane pulled her face down and kissed her deeply. *Stop*, 'Iwa wanted to scream, but the words caught in her throat. Sunny kissed him back, then pushed away. She was looking right at 'Iwa in the doorway. Their eyes met. 'Iwa reversed out, then turned and ran.

No Second Chances
Dane

The world looked different when you were lying on the floor. Dane's area rug was covered in dog hair, dust gathered along the baseboards and an empty wine bottle lay under the bed. His hands moved down to his crotch area, and sure enough, he had pissed himself. He had fallen while trying to drag himself from the bed to the wheelchair, and decided that this was as good a place as any to spend the day. Isla came over and licked his face, and then began circling around and pushing on his body parts with her snout.

"You think I want to be down here?" he said.

She growled at him.

"Yeah, I know. I'm an idiot."

'Iwa had left town five days and seven hours ago. No good-bye, just a note that said, *DANE, I HOPE YOU GET BETTER, I HONESTLY DO, BUT PLEASE DON'T CONTACT ME. I DON'T BELIEVE IN SECOND CHANCES.*

Sunny had been the one to see 'Iwa standing there like an apparition in the hallway. 'Iwa didn't say a word, just backed away slowly. Yeti had driven Dane home soon after, and railed into him about how he was throwing everything away. It was time to shake things up, do something about his sorry-ass attitude. By the time they arrived home, 'Iwa and all her stuff were gone.

"She was always too good to be true," Dane slurred.

Her leaving was an inevitability, one that he no longer had to dread. Beneath the numbness, there was something like relief. Relief that he would no longer have to think about 'Iwa twenty-four seven. Relief that what he feared most had already transpired and now he could get on with things. Women were definitely overrated.

"You don't really believe that."

"Oh yeah I do."

"You have no idea what you're even talking about. Keep spewing this bullshit and you won't have anyone left to spew to. You're burning through everyone's patience, mate."

Now, flat-out on the rug, Dane felt like crap on so many levels. Back sore, hip throbbing and a ragged ache in the center of his chest. On the bed, his phone buzzed. He pulled himself up and felt around for it hoping like a dumbass it might be 'Iwa.

It was Kama. **Coming over in 30. Be ready.**

Dane texted back, **Ready for what?**

Kama didn't respond, so Dane stayed where he was and eventually drifted off, hugging Isla close, her dog scent the most comforting thing in his dark life. He awoke to the sound of voices, Kama and a woman. Familiar, but not Hope. It must have been dark outside now, and someone hit the lights.

"Dane?"

"Dane! Oh my God!"

A warm hand gently shook his shoulder. He opened his eyes. Closed them again. Blinked open, sure he was dreaming. Then not so sure.

"Mom?"

"Are you okay?" she asked, brow furrowed as she peered down at him.

"That depends."

Belinda and Kama exchanged looks.

"How long have you been down here?" Kama asked, as his

mother felt his forehead with the back of her hand. Weirdly, her touch caused him to tear up.

"A while. I'm not hurt, just resting, so you don't need to worry."

They could probably smell the piss, but neither said anything. Together, they hoisted him up and sat him on the bed. Kama had obviously called Belinda as a last resort and he could feel their pity rubbing off on him. Dane was ashamed at what this had come to and figured he was probably better off dead than in this sorry state.

"Your mom is taking you home with her," Kama said, matter-of-factly.

"Thanks but no thanks."

"Brah, right now you don't have a choice. None of us can be here full-time and look what just happened. You need help," Kama said.

Dane closed his eyes and flopped back, tired of fighting. Tired of being angry. Tired of everything, really. "Fine, but the dog comes, too."

The next morning, he woke up in a dark place that smelled like clementines and Danish tung oil. He lay for a few moments trying to remember where he was, but there was only one place he knew of that had this combination of scents. His old bedroom in Ventura County. He hadn't slept here in years. The old oak tree outside his window now housed a family of crows, who were all noisily talking to each other. Dane wanted to tell them to shut up, but he was too worn out. Instead, he put the pillow over his head.

"Did you sleep okay?"

The voice startled him. He pulled off the pillow and turned to see his mom sitting on the floor cross-legged in a pool of morning sun. Blond hair gone dark. Isla was in her lap.

"I don't know," he said.

"If you don't know, then you must have."

Dane rolled over, away. "It feels like I have a line of red ants running down my leg, other than that, I'm fine. How long have you been sitting there?"

"A while. I get up early."

"Good for you. Now leave me alone."

"I told you if you came here, we'd do things my way, and I meant it, Dane. You and I have a lot of work to do, and it starts now."

If he had agreed to that, he couldn't remember. The whole previous day had been a blur. He looked toward the bedside table, where back home he had kept the pills.

His voice was gravelly. "Where are my meds?"

"Somewhere safe."

"For fuck sake, Mom, I need them when I need them. Just leave them in here."

She left the room and came back with a glass of water and half of a pill. "It's obvious to everyone around you that these are poisoning you. As of today, you're on ration."

He groaned. "You have no idea."

Those pills were his lifeline. His only means of erasing the deadness in his legs, and more recently, the absence of 'Iwa. But somewhere in the back of his awareness, he also knew they were eroding his soul.

"I do have an idea."

"Just let me do this on my own time. I'm getting better," he said.

"You might be physically, but not mentally. Come on, take the pill and let's get you up."

Dane took the half pill and felt like throwing the rest of the water in her face, which had formed new lines and creases since the last time he'd seen her. All that time in the sun was finally catching up to her, but she was still beautiful with her golden hair and big chocolate eyes. "Just do me a favor and don't act as though you're suddenly an expert on what's best for me. You're no doctor or counselor, hell, you're hardly even a mother."

Belinda paled, and he felt bad for half a second. "That may be true, but there's something you should know, something I should have told you a long time ago." Her gaze went to the window and he saw tears in her eyes. "Your father was an addict, Dane."

A cold wind blew through the room. How would she know this?

He shook his head, unwilling to believe her. "No, my father was a one-night stand on a layover in Australia. You didn't know him."

"I lied, Dane. I thought I was doing the right thing to protect you," she said.

He forgot all about the meds and pushed himself to sitting, hair matted on his forehead. "Holy crap, Mom. Is he still alive?"

"No. For a few years, he was on and off the streets, but then I got a call from one of his friends, who told me Butch had overdosed. You were four then and I figured why bother," she said.

Butch.

"Did he know about me?"

"Yes."

"And?"

"And he was too strung out to know the difference or be able to do anything about it. I told him he could meet you if he could be clean for at least a year. I think he tried, but he couldn't do it. I didn't want to put that onto you, too."

Dane looked down at his hands. They were trembling. "I can't believe you never told me."

"I'll never know if it was the right decision, but it was the one I made and we both have to live with it."

"What kind of drugs are we talking?" he asked.

"In the end, heroin. But when I first met him, we would just get high on weed and sometimes coke."

He looked out the window. Most of the crows had left, but a dark one with equally dark eyes was sitting on a branch staring in at him. He swore the bird nodded, as though it had been in on the secret. He tried to kick the blankets off and wanted nothing more than to get up and leave. But he was trapped.

Dane had not talked to his mother in years, and things had been strained before that—ever since she'd called him a sellout. Being the quintessential soul surfer, she had not been able to accept that Dane would be on the tour and making money off the sport.

"Guys like you are ruining surfing," she'd told him, a week after his first contest on the tour.

"If someone had offered you money when you were my age, doing what you love to do, traveling and riding the best waves in the world, don't tell me you wouldn't have taken it."

"The money will change it for you. As will the glory and girls that go along with doing what you're doing."

That had just pissed him off. "I had glory and girls long before I earned my first dollar surfing," he said, more to spite her than anything.

"That attitude is exactly what I'm talking about."

"You're a hypocrite, Mom. I gotta go."

He'd hung up and spent the next few weeks soul-searching and questioning. What bothered him the most was that her words carried a grain of truth, it just took him a few years to realize that. Not everyone had the good fortune to grow up, like his mom had, in the sixties and seventies when surfing was still pure. Easy for her to judge.

The crow on the branch flapped its iridescent wings and flew off, leaving him alone with Belinda.

"Come on, let me make you some juice and I'll tell you the rest," she said.

Dane groaned but pushed himself up. He positioned his legs so they were hanging off the edge, and braced himself. He'd yet to cross the hurdle of going from seated to standing. He'd almost done it a few times and had been trying like a madman since 'Iwa left, but that was how he'd ended up on the floor yesterday.

On several acres, his mother's house was surrounded by rows of olive trees and a thick oak grove. Inside, it had changed some since he'd last been here. Less clutter and big new sliding doors onto a patio that faced down the valley. His mom had inherited the property from an uncle in the late seventies who'd lived by the theory of *why buy something when you can make it*.

Growing up, the house hadn't seemed like much—a big lot with a tiny hand-built timber cabin—but over time, Dane had come to appreciate how every piece of it had a story. *This section of the wall came from an old barn swept away in a flood. This tabletop comes from an olive mill in Santa Barbara. This bench is made from an oak tree felled in a storm.* It was why he'd ended up a carpenter. Wood was a living, breathing thing with many lives.

He sat by the sliding glass doors, looking out and counting crows. How had he messed things up enough to end up back in the house he had spent his whole life trying to leave?

He could hear his mom's knife on the cutting board behind him. As if reading his mind, she said, "When you were little, you used to go through these periods of only eating one thing, do you remember? Everything else you would turn up your nose at. One month it would be eggs, the next month potatoes and a few weeks later tangerines. There was no swaying you. I worried about malnutrition and being a bad mom without giving you a balanced meal, but nothing I did could change your little mind."

He did remember. At one point, he had lived and breathed grape juice. No water, no milk, no nothing.

"Eventually, you grew out of it with food, but your single-mindedness carried over to other areas of your life, surfing being the most obvious one. I recognized your father in you, the way you focused on something until you were the best. It scared me."

"You should have told me."

She seemed not to hear. "And now it feels to me like you're teetering on the edge of a very dark place and those pills have become your latest addiction. You can't get your natural high, but you've found an alternative."

A twitch started up in his leg and began working its way down the side of his calf. He felt clammy and cold and uncomfortable in his skin. "Stop already. You think lecturing me is going to help anything?"

She threw a bunch of spinach in the blender, along with chopped pineapple. "This isn't a lecture, this is me telling you that you have addictive tendencies."

"Old news," he said.

Her voice wavered. "How about this then? Your father died, Dane, because he could not stop. Are you sure you want to go down that road? Or would you rather spend a few painful weeks here with me and dig yourself out before it's too late?"

"I'm here, aren't I? And enough about me, I want to hear more about my dad."

She looked away as she turned on the blender, blocking out any more conversation. Then she poured two tall green drinks and carried them to the table. "Come over here and I'll tell you."

In January of 1982, Butch Getty had made the drive from St. Augustine, Florida, to California in a yellow VW van full of surfboards. He showed up at Venice Beach one day with an attitude and an enormous alligator airbrushed onto his longboard. Belinda and her friend had laughed, until he paddled out and scored a few perfect waves. Within a few weeks, Butch had made friends with all the local heavies, and ended up with Belinda's phone number in his board shorts pocket.

"He was the kind of guy who could talk anyone into anything. Butch would make friends with a homeless guy and later that day be serving drinks to the mayor and have him ready to build a new boardwalk. It made him a great bartender and he made a lot of money that way, but it also got him into trouble."

Dane realized he was clenching his fists and tried to relax. "What kind of trouble?"

"Hooked up with the wrong guys and pretty soon he was pulling all-nighters, flaking on plans, missing work. Three months after we met, we were living together in a tiny studio on Horizon Ave. We were madly in love but things began to fall apart pretty quick once he started using coke. He was always chasing the next high. And he could never do just one line. Looking back, he had the classic addict behavior.

"When I found out I was pregnant, we had only been together about nine months. I ended up leaving him and coming to live here with Uncle Warren. I was so young and clueless, but I knew if I didn't leave then, I never would. Butch had this irresistible pull. To this day, it was the hardest thing I ever did. But I did it for you."

As Dane drank, the glass shook in his hand. He stared down into the green-flecked liquid trying to make sense of it all. His father was a VW-driving drug addict named Butch from Florida.

"So you weren't already a flight attendant when you had me?" he asked.

As a kid, he had never done the math.

"Not then, no. I was waitressing to make ends meet. I got a break with United when you were almost two, a year before Uncle Warren died."

"A break for you maybe. Would have been nice of you to stick around more," he said, feeling hard and bitter inside, and full of resentment.

She set her palm on his hand, sending heat across his skin. "I made mistakes, Dane. We all do, it's a part of being human."

He downed his smoothie and set it on the table. "This is going to take a while to digest, Mom. I'm going to go back to bed."

"Fair enough, but I want you to do one more thing with me before you do."

"What's that?"

Her eyes were full of determination. "Feed the horses."

Horses?

A Male & A Female

'Iwa

On Maui, 'Iwa returned to find that Jones had threatened Maui Forest Recovery Project with a lawsuit of his own if they kept trying to block the eco resort. He was claiming all kinds of injustices, and still maintained that because he owned the property, he could do what he wanted. The way he saw it, they were spreading false information and dragging his name through the mud. Everything fell into approved uses for the zoning. At least in his mind, where you could bend words, fudge plans and break car windows in the middle of the night to make sure everyone saw things your way.

Not that 'Iwa had ever been able to prove anything, but she knew. Her father had insisted she report it to the police, which she did, but they told her the broken windshield could have just as easily been caused by a falling mango, or kids playing ball. She didn't even bother telling them it wasn't mango season. Waste of time.

"What about 'No one on the island wants you here, dickhead'? Isn't that enough of a reason to admit defeat and hit the road?" Winston said, as they sat on the back *lānai* of Uncle's sipping post-jam-session beers.

'Iwa clinked his bottle with hers. "Right? If a whole island was against me, I'd leave with my tail between my legs and never look back."

"It's all just dollar signs," Win said.

It felt nice to be home. Nice to be around Winston and her dad and Koa, who'd slobbered her half to death when she arrived. Still, she thought about Dane every other minute, and continued to have flashbacks of that horrible night at Yeti's. His betrayal had flayed her and she worried she might never recover.

That, and it dredged up the trauma of reaching her hand into Zach's pocket those years ago and finding a napkin with the name Petra, a phone number, a heart and the word *tomorrow* written on it. Since it already *was* tomorrow, she'd called him at work. He wasn't there. A hot and sticky feeling had come over her, just as it had with Dane and Sunny. Like she needed to somehow get out of her own skin, but was trapped. A sickening revelation that the man you loved was not who you thought he was.

Maybe hurts accumulated, stacking up on each other like big waves on a high tide. And the key to surviving them was to avoid them in the first place.

"Good luck," her mother would have said.

On this particular evening, 'Iwa had played on autopilot until the final song—"Waikula"—which stirred up her insides every time she sang it.

"The whole island is talking about your song. But it's not the same when I sing it. They love you," he said.

"They love Maui, and the song resonates."

"No," he said, looking straight into her eyes. "They love you."

'Iwa looked into her bottle, at the floorboard, then back up at him. She had such a fondness for him, and for a split second, she let her mind wander. Her friend Kirsten swore by the "friends to lovers" thing. *Trust me, friendship to love makes for the best relationships because you already know what you're getting. And that first time you have sex, it blows doors.* On paper, Winston was a perfect match. Handsome, so much in common, long-time friend, born and raised on Maui, dependable. No massive ego to burn the whole thing to the ground once you were hooked.

'Iwa arrived at the trailhead at dawn, threw a little extra love into her *oli* and entered the forest. It had rained in the night and now the trees made their own rain whenever a gust of wind shook their branches. Fifteen minutes in, she was already drenched and her pack felt like a bag of rocks after not carrying it for a month. Her legs burned and her heart was heavy, but the mud on her boots made it all worth it. Today, she was here for no one but herself. A night in solitude with the mountain.

She took her time getting to Waikula, stopping to photograph a new bloom of orange *lehua* blossoms, sitting crosslegged in a koa copse, honeycreeper-watching and absorbing all the healing properties of the forest. She moved slowly along, wary of coming across Jones or his thugs again, and scared of what she might find at the waterfall—aside from those remarkably vivid memories of Dane kissing all parts of her body.

No one was at the waterfall, at least there was that. 'Iwa stripped down to her bikini and warmed up on a smooth boulder. Not thinking about Dane and Sunny was a constant struggle. Her mind would simply not cooperate. Instead, she sat up tall and sang her waterfall song. Quietly at first, and then loud enough for all the *mo'o* on the mountain to hear. Loud enough for Jones, in case he was in the area. Loud enough for her mother up in heaven. When she jumped in and swam to the falls, the ice water burned across her skin. She gave the rock where Dane had fed her berries a wide berth.

Had she followed her own rules, she wouldn't be in this mess. No surfers, no mainland guys, no assholes. This time, she made a pact with herself, with Waikula as witness, that she would not make the same mistake twice. No second chances.

★ ★ ★

Upstream a ways, above the falls, 'Iwa went in search of a place to hang her hammock and rest. The only flat spot was on the far side of the stream, on Jones's property. There was no trail, and she had to bushwhack through ferns and undergrowth to get there, so only the mountain would know. Drained, she tied her hammock up between two trees and dozed off to the rush of running water on rocks, and the fluttering of 'ōlapa leaves in the afternoon breeze.

Sometime later, in the midst of a black and dreamless sleep, something startled her awake. It took a moment to recall where she was, and she listened for any sign of what had woken her. There were no manmade sounds, no pig sounds, nothing but stream and bird chirps. Then she heard the whir of tiny wings. Her favorite sound. A greenish yellow bird with a distinctive stripe over its eye landed on a branch overhead. 'Iwa dared not breathe.

Chew-eee. Chew-eee. Chew-eee.

A kiwikiu. Trying to hold herself together, she slid her hand into her pocket, feeling for her phone. She *had* to capture this on film, but her Canon was on the ground. The first bird began hopping from branch to branch, poking at the mossy bark with his curved parrot-like bill. The second one, a female—she could tell by her smaller bill and muted colors—did the same in the next tree over. They were small and busy and oh so beautiful.

In her green camouflage hammock, 'Iwa blended right in, and slow as growing grass, pulled her phone up, turned off the sound and started shooting. She was able to zoom in on the female, who then took a break from foraging and began singing. A high-pitched, complex string of notes floating light through the forest. Birdsong usually had two main purposes, to defend territory or to attract a mate. The same could be said for most things in life.

The birds stayed for a while, searching for insects and larvae, oblivious to the human in their midst. If there were two breeding kiwikiu, there must be a nest in the area, and there would likely be more birds not too far away. It was too late to hike down now, but first thing in the morning she would race back to Pā'ia and tell Winston. A breeding pair of kiwikiu on Jones's property! Winston would flip.

When the birds disappeared, she replayed the video again and again. The sound was good, the picture clear. The little female's throat warbled as she sang, making her feathers look alive. 'Iwa felt a strong kinship with this tiny bird. Eventually, she set her phone down, jumped up and swung around with her arms wide open, hugging the closest tree. This was just what they needed.

The sun had gone down behind Haleakalā, but there was at least another hour of light. Enough time to go in search of more birds. She grabbed her Canon and was about to head out, when she heard a twig snap behind her. She spun around to see a man ducking under a low-hanging branch.

Same guy from last time. The taller one with the giant arms. Thug number one. "Trespassing is against the law here in Hawai'i, ma'am," he said.

Here in Hawai'i.

'Iwa turned to grab her pack. "Oh, I'm sorry, is this private land? I didn't realize," she said, hoping to make a clean getaway before he recognized her.

"It is."

"I'll be on my way then."

He came close enough that she could smell his citrus after-shave and feel his eyes boring a hole in her back. "Once I can overlook, twice I'm going to have to escort you out."

She swung her pack over her back and turned to face him.

"I'm out here doing a bird count and I did not realize your land went above the falls. My mistake. I'll just cross over to the other side and head to the next valley."

His eyes fell down over her body and he made no move to hide it. "Not today, Miss Young. You'll follow me."

His use of her last name caused a new level of wariness. "This was an honest mistake, sir, and I don't believe you have the authority to force me to do anything."

'Iwa cinched her hip strap, then noticed her phone on the ground, a few feet from where the man was standing. Instinct told her to not draw attention to it, to leave it where it lay.

"Negative. Let's go," he said.

For a beat, she wondered if she could outrun this guy. Maybe on a good day, without a pack. But even with his oversized muscles, he was lean and had at least a foot on her.

Talking fast, she said, "I'm a scientist. I have every right to be up here on this mountain."

"Save it for Jones."

The man took her to a massive warehouse on a clearing that spread out for several acres. There were excavators and bulldozers and backhoes all lined up for battle with the trees, and the thought of all this native forest being mowed down caused a physical ache in her body. Thug number one had radioed in that he was coming back with a trespasser, and he took 'Iwa to a room inside the warehouse and opened the door.

"Leave your pack out here," he said.

"I'd rather keep it with me."

Jones came out, dressed in jeans and a khaki T-shirt and looking two shades too tan. "Miss Young, this is my land, so I'm not asking. Leave the pack and empty your pockets."

"It's just camping gear and food."

"Then it shouldn't be a problem."

'Iwa felt her face heating up. She wanted to object, but there was an edge to Jones and these men that felt dangerous. Like it would be easy for her to conveniently fall off a cliff and break her neck, or wash out to sea with the stream waters. But her car was at the trailhead. They would never be so stupid, would they? 'Iwa dropped the heavy pack and followed him into the office. One whole wall was security camera screens. All blank at the moment.

He caught her looking. "We aren't online yet, but we will be soon."

"How did you know I was up there?" she asked.

"Clancy heard you singing at the waterfall. Sound travels up here."

Her anger had made her reckless, and now she was paying the price. "Yeah, I know."

Clancy closed the door and left the two of them alone. "So, you come all the way up here just to sing, or were you looking for trouble?" he said, motioning for her to sit.

She remained standing. "Mr. Jones, I have been coming up here since long before you bought this property. I came to Waikula as a girl with my mother, and now my work brings me up here. Being on your property was purely accidental."

She wondered if he knew who her mother was, but he answered her question straightaway. "I remember your mom well from the old days. A real firecracker. I admired her, even offered her a job, but she turned me down."

This was news to 'Iwa, but talking about her mom with Jones felt sacrilegious, so she just stood there.

"Your organization is costing me a lot of money, you know that?" he said.

She shrugged. "We have a vested interest in this land."

He blew out of his nostrils, like a horse. "*My* land."

"*The* land."

"What you fail to see is that we have already jumped through the hoops. We are moving ahead. The sooner you accept that, the better things will be for all of us."

"The court will decide."

"It won't get that far," he said.

Talking was pointless, and 'Iwa just wanted out. "I guess that remains to be seen."

Jones leaned back and rested his head in his hands, studying her for a moment, as though he was considering whether to throw her to the pigs. "Everyone has a price, Miss Young. What about you?"

'Iwa wished to God she had been recording this, thinking of her phone still back on the forest floor and praying she would be able to find it when she went back. "I have nothing more to say to you, and I can show myself out."

A spot under his eye twitched. "Imagine your father, no mortgage on the house. Owning that greasy little restaurant outright. Wouldn't that be nice?"

"Not everything can be bought," she said.

He laughed. "Yeah, I didn't think so." Then he stood up and his expression turned stormy. "Get out of here and don't let me find you on my property again. Next time, I won't be so friendly."

Outside, her pack was leaning against the wall. 'Iwa could tell by the bulges in it that things had been taken out and put back haphazardly. Clancy was standing next to it with his back to her. When he turned, she saw her camera in his hands.

She reached for it. "Hey, what are you doing?"

"No photos allowed up here."

"Those pictures belong to me."

"Not anymore."

He handed her the camera, which she knew would be wiped clean of all her photographs from the day.

Jones came out. "Take her to the road."

As she was walking down the Hāna Highway in the dark, all 'Iwa could think about was her cell phone lying in the clearing in one of the wettest places on earth.

Out To Pasture

Dane

Sometime during the past year, unbeknownst to Dane, his mother had retired from the airlines and opened up her land to a small herd of horses, all rescues. Beyond the olive trees, they followed a hard-packed path that used to lead to dusty earth, pepper trees and rattlesnakes. Now there were five horses in a fenced pasture all beelining toward Dane, Belinda and Isla. Hooves thundered on the ground as they snorted and whinnied and kicked.

"They don't like it when I'm late," Belinda said.

Isla stopped and sat, eyes bugging out, and Dane was having a hard time imagining his mom owning horses. The only animal they'd ever had was a stray one-eared cat named Bob who took care of himself. Belinda went into a small shed and came out with several metal bowls of pellets and set them on the ground.

"These are my gurus. Horses are great teachers to those who are willing to listen. The more time you spend around them, the better," she said.

He pulled up next to the fence, and the animals loomed over him in his wheelchair.

Belinda pointed out who was who. "The black one is Captain, and the dappled gray mare is Peony. This skinny guy over here is Cabernet, he's my newest and I'm still trying to fatten him up. The paint horse is Leo, short for Leonardo, and that pinto, believe it or not, is called Dane. He came to me already named," she was quick to add.

"Do you ride them?" he said, imagining himself on a horse instead of a wheelchair.

"Only two of them, occasionally, Captain and Dane. I prefer just to be around them and absorb their fabulous auras."

It seemed bizarre that his mom had a horse named Dane, but then everything in his life had gone sideways lately, so why not this?

"Do you want to stand up, stretch out a little?" Belinda asked.

He did want to get out of the wheelchair; he hated the thing. "Sure."

She helped him to standing and he leaned against the fence and watched as they finished eating. Tongues slurped, tails swished, then Dane the horse farted.

Belinda laughed. "Come here, you big stinker."

Dane trotted over and opened his lips in a funny horse smile. He began sniffing Dane's arm and tickling him with his chin hairs.

"Does he bite?"

"He nibbles."

The horse then lowered his head to Dane's waist and sniffed around. He moved down Dane's legs, blowing hot air onto his knees, all the way down to his feet. Then he worked his way back up and turned his head so they were eye to eye. Long lashes. Pale blue irises. A deep well of compassion. Dane was suddenly choked up.

"Horses are mirrors," Belinda said, quietly.

Dane would have stepped away if he could have, but instead closed his eyes for a few moments. When he opened them again, Dane was still there, still peering into him. He took a deep breath, unsure he wanted to be here. The day had hardly even started, and his world had already been bent and folded and tucked in a back pocket.

★ ★ ★

Back at the house, in the harsh morning sun, Dane noticed how much the place needed work. Windows needed to be re-hung, gutters sagged and weeds crept through the floorboards of the front steps. It was a big place for one person to keep up, especially a fifty-three-year-old woman. Or was his mom fifty-four? He had lost track somewhere along the way.

He couldn't stop thinking about his father. "Do you have any pictures of Butch?" It felt too weird to say *my dad*.

"Just a few. Hang on."

Belinda left him on the patio, and came back with a small plastic photo album. Butch was thin with dark hair and Dane's smile. In several of the shots, his arm was slung casually around Belinda, who beamed out at the camera, her face half hidden by rivers of thick golden hair. They looked like kids.

"It's been a long time since I've seen these. We were so young and full of life," she said.

Dane glanced at her and felt a stab of sadness. To walk away from someone you loved at that age took a lot of guts. He tried to imagine how his life might have turned out differently if this man—this stranger—had taken a different path. Family out-ings to the beach and picnics in the redwoods. Or more likely drugs and drinking and fights. Maybe Belinda, in her imper-fect way, had saved him from an even uglier life.

He was suddenly tired. Bone-tired.

"I'm going to go back to bed."

This time, she let him.

Heat collected wherever his clothes touched his skin. The next few days were some of the hottest on record, and Dane was restless and itchy and brooding. His mother put him on a regimented schedule and he didn't have the energy to protest.

It went something like this: wake up and take a cold shower, drink a celery pineapple mint ginger smoothie—Yeti would have been proud—feed the horses and let them nuzzle you for a while, meditate on the patio, eat oatmeal with nut butter, berries and maple syrup, read a few pages from *The Book of Secrets*, get poked full of acupuncture needles by Dr. Xiao, fall asleep on the table and wake up feeling like you've been inhabited by a whole hive of honeybees, eat more, watch a documentary on yoga or meditation, perform stretching and strengthening exercises to the sound of crows and Krishna Das, watch the sunset with lime sparkling water, eat a salad, pass out.

The nerve pain in his legs and feet still made appearances, but it was no longer the dominant force in his life. And the pills were loosening their hold.

"When you focus on other things, you forget about the pain," Belinda said.

She had every second planned out, and he was coming to see a certain logic in this. There was no time for fear, no time for anything other than the task at hand. Meditating was the hard part, lying on the hard wood floor alone with his thoughts, usually of 'Iwa. He imagined her hiking through the cloud forest or at Uncle's strumming her guitar, eyes lasered in on him alone. He saw her on the rock at Waikula, dripping wet and waiting for him to kiss her. Had she *really* meant it when she said not to contact her? That question swam at the edge of his consciousness, day and night.

On the first two days, nothing unusual happened, but on the third day, the knot in his chest began to move up to the base of his neck, swelling and sharpening, then slowly make its way into his throat. For a moment it felt like he might choke on this living ball of sadness, but instead tears began streaming from his eyes, until the yoga mat beneath his head was soaked.

"Why are you doing this, Mom?" Dane asked Belinda late one afternoon as they sat on the patio and watched the sun sliding down behind the pepper branches. "Why now?"

She pulled her knees into her chest, and stared at her long, elegant toes, not saying anything for a while. "I was so young and clueless when I had you—not to mention selfish and terrified. I told myself that you were better off spending all your time with the Mizunos because they were a real family, and so solid, you know? The only thing that made me feel better was surfing, so I took off every chance I could. I was just a kid myself with no idea what to do with her own child. How sad is that? I know I can never make up for lost time, but this is me trying."

Nothing would give him back those years, but being with her now gave him an unexpected sense of well-being. An unwavering feeling that he wasn't alone. Maybe that was mother love for you. A bond that couldn't be broken, even after a lifetime of hurt.

On day five, Dane woke up with a tingle of expectation. Not quite hope, but for the first time since the accident, he was looking forward to something. To seeing the horses, especially Dane, who had a fondness for nibbling on his legs—a soft, whiskery sensation that Dane could actually feel. After an ice-cold shower, he and Belinda went to the pasture. Sunlight danced on the grass and the horses trotted around, all muscle and grace. Isla had become friendly with them and dashed off to make her rounds.

It felt good to be around his mom with no real agenda, and for the first time in his life, she was really there with him. Not about to dash off to catch a plane, not searching for surf, not disappearing with one of her boyfriends, who she never brought to the house. Seeing her from this new vantage point thawed the cold edges of hurt that had accumulated over the years.

Belinda stood on the other side of the fence brushing Peony, and Dane sat in the wheelchair as the other Dane hung his head down so Dane could rub his neck. His breath smelled pleasantly like oats and alfalfa and quite similar to the juice his mom had made for him that morning. The big horse was remarkably patient, but eventually he moved back a little. Not wanting to let him go, Dane kept his hand on his neck, purely for balance, and felt his legs pushing him up and up, until he was standing.

He grabbed the railing, glancing down at his legs to be sure he wasn't imagining it. "Whoa."

His mom turned. "Dane! What just happened?"

"I stood up! On my own!"

Belinda hopped up and down, clapping. "I knew it was coming soon!" She rushed over and wrapped herself around him from behind, laying her cheek on his shoulder blade. Her arms were strong, her scent flowery.

Dane had wanted to believe the doctors, but had also been afraid. In his mind, no hope was better than false hope. Horse Dane whinnied and snorted, and Peony and Captain trotted over to see what the fuss was about.

"They know this is a big deal," Belinda said, stepping away and pressing her nose against horse Dane's.

Dane bent his knees slightly, moving up and down, and reveled in this newfound ability that he once took for granted hundreds if not thousands of times a day. The human body was a study in miracles all its own.

"You're going to come back from this even stronger, I promise. If there's one thing I've learned, it's that disasters are blessings in disguise. It may take a while for it to hit, but you'll see," she said.

"Yeah, give me a minute."

"It's not a race. But this is a first step. Literally."

If only he could call 'Iwa and tell her the news.

The Search

'Iwa

'Iwa and Winston reached the trailhead at first light, racing up the mountain along with the sun. At noon, they reached the rocks where she had crossed the stream above Waikula the day before. She gave him detailed instructions on how to find the clearing where she had last seen her phone. They were both dressed in camouflage gear, and after watching Winston quickly dissolve into the foliage, 'Iwa retreated back from the stream and leaned against a koa tree with a wide and weepy canopy. Off Jones's property.

Ten minutes passed. Then ten more. The area shouldn't have been that hard to find. 'Iwa listened for voices, praying Winston had not been met by Clancy, or fallen into a booby trap of some kind. In the old days, on Mauna Kea, the paniolos used to trap wild bulls by digging deep holes and covering them up with branches and brush. Unsuspecting bulls, or bullocks as they were called, would fall into said pits and die there. After yesterday, she wouldn't put it past Jones to do something like that for anyone who got in his way.

Just when she was about to go looking for him, Winston came rock hopping back her way. 'Iwa ran to the edge of the stream, seeing that his hands were empty.

"Did you find it?"

He smiled wide. "Got it, it's in my pack."

"Were you able to see anything?"

"Either the battery's dead, or the phone is."

There was no phone charger in her truck, so they drove straight to her house, plugged it in and waited for it to charge. 'Iwa made a plate of dried *aku* and poi, and they ate in silence, filling their worn bodies with sustenance. Koa circled around them like a tiger shark, drooling for handouts. A few minutes later, a sound came from her phone. Winston stopped chewing and 'Iwa ran to it. A photo of Haleakalā dusted with snow appeared, with the time, 4:40 p.m.

"It still works, thank God," she said.

'Iwa swiped through her photos and pulled up the video of the kiwikiu. Winston hunched over her shoulder, and she swore she could feel the emotion coming off him. They played it a second time, this time zooming in on certain sections. Not only could you tell the birds were kiwikiu, this was some of the best footage of them 'Iwa had seen.

"You done good, girl," Winston said.

Coming from him, this was high praise.

'Iwa sent the video to Winston's phone, backed it up on her computer, geotagged it and then shared it with their attorney the following morning. They crafted letters and called the media, effectively launching an all-out war against Jones's project. A day after that, 'Iwa had four interviews lined up with local newspaper and television stations. One even wanted to put together a documentary on the birds and Maui Forest Recovery Project's work.

Meanwhile, the courts did not move as fast as the media, and their legal paperwork got bogged down in an already crowded system. Jones jumped on the lag, and started his own campaign, using slick advertisements touting his eco resort as *sustainable tourism*. A load of crap if there ever were one. He had the audacity to turn things around and use the kiwikiu as selling points. But he failed to mention that aside from avian malaria, loss of habitat was one of the main reasons for the bird's decline. Birds depend on forests as much as forests depend on birds and he was already primed to tear down their home.

Auwe.

In Water

Dane

During his second week in Ventura, Dane got the go-ahead to get in the water again. His scar had sealed up, though the skin was still raised and tender. Today was day one of only taking a quarter of a pill. Now he couldn't wait to be done with them. He had Butch to thank for that, because hearing his father had struggled with addiction was like a hot slap in the face. The idea that he could lose everything and still not be able to pull himself out spooked him to no end.

Belinda's friend had a swimming pool, and offered for them to use it anytime, day or night. Kama had driven down, and now the two of them sat on the granite pool deck, legs dangling in the cool water.

"Have you heard anything from 'Iwa?" he asked Kama.

Dane had been working up the nerve to ask all morning. He didn't want to put Kama in an awkward position, but the itch became too strong.

"Nah. Have you?" Kama said.

"Radio silence."

"Can't say I really blame her."

"I fucked up. I know it."

"Brah, you were already on shaky ground, treating her like trash when she gave up everything to be there for you, and then you went and made out with Sunny. What were you thinking?"

Dane had thought long and hard about this. He had no idea what had compelled him to come on to Sunny, other than the fact that he'd felt sharp jealousy when he'd seen 'Iwa talking to Luke. It was like getting a glimpse into the future, and how 'Iwa would eventually find someone whole.

"This may be more than you want to hear, but it goes much deeper than 'Iwa."

"You think?" Kama said, sarcastically.

"Cut me some slack here. I've never told you this—I've never told anyone. But I don't think I've ever been fully in love. The way I feel about 'Iwa."

"You think I don't know that?"

"I kept wondering why I was always running away from women when other guys seemed so happy to lock in. I tried with Sunny, but you shouldn't have to *try* to feel it, should you? With 'Iwa it just *was*."

"I think if you get things squared away with your mom, it could help answer some of those questions," Kama said, nodding over at Belinda, who was standing across the pool deck talking to her friend.

Dane nodded. "Working on it."

Isla slid herself between the two of them, staring into the pool as though there might be sharks lurking in the bottom.

Dane lowered himself into the pool, while Isla circled the perimeter, barking at underwater shadows. He had been imagining this moment for over a month now, and had expected his arms would have to do most of the work, but something magical happened. When he began his crawl, his legs started kicking in time with his arms. Not strong like they used to be, but moving nonetheless. The buoyancy felt so damn good.

"Brah, you're doing it!" Kama yelled.

Dane buried his face in the water. He was laughing and crying at the same time, and felt like an idiot. He swam the length of the pool, came up for air, turned and swam back. Then did it again and again. The muscles in his back began to burn, and his legs tired quickly, but he kept going. He could have swum forever. All the way to Hawai'i.

That night at dinner, Kama told him he had a ticket back home to Maui in two weeks to help on the farm. Bananas were ready to be picked and it was that time of year for canning mango chutney and *liliko'i* butter. Surf was small and the entire island bloomed. What Dane would have given to go with him. Usually, he was on southern hemisphere trips during the summer months, so Hawai'i was out of the question.

"Tell 'Iwa *hi* for me."

"Why don't you write her a good old-fashioned letter?"

"She wants nothing to do with me and I really can't blame her. I was an ass and a half," Dane said.

"How do you even know? People change their minds all the time. At least with a letter, you can be honest with your feelings. Tell her what you told me."

Dane had thought about just coming out with it and sending her a message, but saying *I love you* via text for the first time ever felt like cheating.

"Maybe I will."

"Or go to Maui. In person is usually the best way to go. You could come with me?"

"When I go to Maui, I'm going to be walking."

Kama looked out at the mountains, and Dane imagined him wondering when that might be. Dane wondered the same thing, but he had crossed over a threshold and now firmly believed it was a matter of *when* not *if*.

One foggy morning several weeks later, Dane was standing in the kitchen making a smoothie, bleary-eyed from reading late the night before. The coconut water was just out of reach and he took a step to get it. Even with all the practice, his foot still hadn't been turning over. He could move his leg forward, and drag the top of his foot, but it wouldn't quite flex enough and land correctly. This time it did. He went still as a mountain. *Here it was, the moment he'd been waiting for.*

His training picked up from there and soon after, he graduated from the wheelchair to a walker. No matter that he looked like someone's grandfather, it was one of the best things that had ever happened to him. They also took to the ocean.

Belinda suggested they swim around the point to a small sandy cove. The salt water was like a healing accelerator, and he loved to feel his muscles flexing as he kicked. *Did you know the soleus muscle is considered your second heart?* 'Iwa's words came to mind and he missed their nerdy banter and her soulful bursts of wisdom. In the middle of the bay, Belinda pointed down to a cluster of rocks on the sand below the surface. He knew exactly what they were for. She took a big breath, swam down, picked up a rock and began to run with it along the ocean floor.

She came up for a burst of air. "Your turn."

The water was only about eight feet deep, and clear as spring water, but Dane got a prickly feeling when he thought about swimming to the bottom. "No thanks."

Belinda looked at him, but didn't say anything, then dove down and repeated her underwater rock run. Dane watched with a gnawing feeling in his gut. The corners of his vision went dark. No way he could go down there. Instead, he swam for shore, where he dragged himself onto the beach like a sea lion and lay in the warm sand, arms wide open, trying to catch his breath.

Belinda came up a few minutes later. "Are you okay, hon?"

It had been a decade or two since she'd called him that.

"Yeah."

"Your eyes were full of fear back there."

He didn't respond.

She lay down next to him, and found his hand. Soft and cool and now smaller than his, it was a hand he had always wanted more of, whether rubbing his young bony back or tending his banged-up knees. There had been something magic in her touch. Even now, he could feel it seeping into all his wounded places.

"It's perfectly normal after what you went through, but you can't give in to it. Fear is—" she said.

His eyes stung. "I don't need a lecture in fear, Mom. I've spent my life chasing fear."

"This fear is different."

"Fear is fear."

"The kind of fear you deal with is real. This fear, what you experienced just now, is created by your mind. It feels every bit as real, but it's not."

Dane thought about that for a moment. Running rocks in eight feet of water was something he used to do all the time. There was nothing scary about it, except for possibly blacking out, but that's why you never ran rocks alone.

"My body's reaction was real," he said, giving her a sideways glance.

"That's how it gets you. When you let fear stop you, you're feeding it. And the more you feed it, the stronger it gets. You need to show the fear who's boss."

Dane pictured himself diving down and his heart jacked up again. "Not right now."

"If you swim away without going down there, next time will be even harder. Just go down and take one step. I'll be with you."

I'll be with you.

Belinda stood and pulled him up. They looked into each other's eyes and the ground beneath his feet shifted.

"Let's do it," Dane said.

She helped him walk into the water. Out over the rocks, Dane gave himself a pep talk and then took a big breath and went for it. He picked up the smallest rock, took two steps, then kicked up as fast as he could. Belinda came up with him and gave him a high five as they broke the surface.

"Can we come here every day?" he asked, ready to bury this fear in the sand.

"Every day."

The News

'Iwa

September arrived, sticky and swelling with moisture, and Kona winds brought with them still nights and termites. 'Iwa was driving to Uncle's with her back being branded by the creases in her seat when she got a call. Winston's name flashed on her screen, and she hoped he wasn't backing out at the last minute.

"Hey there," she answered, trying to sound casual.

"Judge Mālama's secretary just called me," he said in a flat voice.

Not what she was expecting this late on a Friday.

"And?" she asked, breathlessly.

"And he had a mild heart attack and had to fly to O'ahu for treatment. It sounds like he's going to be okay, but he's taking a medical leave and it's going to prolong things."

'Iwa hit the steering wheel. Sad for Mālama—she liked the man, and sad for what this could mean for the forest. He was the best judge in town, smart and fair and fearless.

"So," he continued, "they're assigning a new judge."

"Do you know who?"

A long pause.

"Steven Atkins."

She hit the steering wheel again, harder. Steven Atkins was

not a friend to environmental causes, though when called on his leanings, he always cited obscure laws that backed him up.

"But he knows nothing!" she said.

"True, but there's no telling when or if Mālama will return."

"Can't we wait and see?"

"No. His whole docket has been cleared."

'Iwa wanted to cry, or maybe she was crying, as salty tears bled into her mouth.

"We'll be starting from ground zero. It's going to take years," she said.

"Not entirely, he'll be briefed. And we have a strong case, don't forget that. Your kiwikiu footage really gives us a boost."

She walked into the restaurant in no mood to sing, and to make things worse, she wasn't even supposed to be there. It was Friday night and her dad had asked if she and Winston would come in as a favor. A news crew from *Maui Time* would be there doing a story on the restaurant. The paper had a new feature, where each week they spotlighted locally owned small businesses in the islands, and tonight it was here.

Eddie had been uncharacteristically nervous the past few days, and 'Iwa had helped him the past two evenings, scrubbing floors, wiping the walls and stringing new fairy lights out back. The old ones had begun to flicker off and on at random times in the evening, making the place feel haunted. He had also asked all his friends to come in, to make sure the place looked bustling. As if they needed help with that.

"Invite the Mizunos," he had told her last night.

"Dad, enough already."

"Just do it, okay?"

Winston was already there. 'Iwa walked up with her guitar, set it down and twirled her hair into a bun on the top of her head. At least with him, there were no pretenses, and she could sulk if she wanted.

"Hey," she said.

Winston set his hand on her knee. "I know losing Judge Mālama was a big blow, but try not to worry too much yet. Things could still go our way."

Her eyes prickled. "I can't help it. Just let me mourn and I'll get over it in my own time."

She grabbed her guitar, tightened her strings and went right into James Taylor. Sad song for a sad mood. Winston strummed along and they watched as people filed in, and suddenly the whole place was full, inside and out. Through the window, 'Iwa could tell who the *Time* team was, a man and a woman, because Eddie and Mila kept hovering around their table. Regardless of whether they needed more business, this was a good thing for her dad, she realized, and that helped turn her mood around. She picked up the pace, played some Van Morrison and Indigo Girls. Tonight was a lost in the music kind of night, when she wanted an escape.

Pretty soon, the news duo came out back and sat at the table right in front of her and Winston that her father had reserved. 'Iwa smiled and nodded, and the woman pulled out a big camera and set it on the table. Mila, bless her heart, came out with a trayful of shot glasses, offering them to all the guests, complimentary. Winston snagged two for them. 'Iwa downed hers in between songs, squeezed a lime in her mouth and continued to play as the warmth spread through her.

When it came time for the next song, Winston did something he rarely did. He started without warning. This time, Eric Clapton. There was nothing to do but go along. Maybe it was time to let down her wall with him and see where it led. So what if they were good friends. So what if she worked with him. Maybe she should give him an honest chance. All things considered, Winston was a far better bet than Dane.

She put everything into the song. The crowd seemed to love it, and the news woman held her camera up and began snapping away. When they ended, the audience clapped and cheered loudly, and someone whistled. Winston turned to give 'Iwa a smile at the very same moment she leaned over and kissed him. She was aiming for his cheek, but planted one right on his lips. Their eyes met and she felt a dull buzzing take up residence in her skull. Winston looked almost as shocked as she was. Reflexively, she wiped her mouth. She held her breath and prayed that no one had captured the kiss, while the audience cheered even louder.

Meditations On Fear

Dane

In early October, Yeti came to bring Dane home to Santa Cruz. They took the Pacific Coast Highway, passing through Big Sur, with steep cliffs to the ocean on the left. Craggy rocks and white-caps and the sharp smell of pine trees. Dane rode with the window down, cool, salty air in his face. Isla rode in his lap, head out.

"Big day, glad I could be a part of it," Yeti said.

"Thanks, man, I'm glad you're here."

"So what comes next? What's your end game?" Yeti asked.

Dane didn't have to think. "Ride Pe'ahi again. And Nazaré. XXL."

"So, the flame hasn't gone out."

"The flame will never go out. You know how it is."

"Did you get the invite?"

There was only one invite that mattered to Dane and that was for the Pe'ahi Challenge. "Not yet, but I'm going to Maui even if they don't invite me."

"You won last year, don't they have to invite you?"

"I haven't been in touch with anyone on the tour. Just focusing on getting myself back together. Kind of a vulnerable place to be, but hey, the alternative is worse."

"Vulnerability is sexy," Yeti told him.

"I don't feel sexy."

"In many eyes, you're even more elevated. Before, it was because you were a surfing legend, now it's because they've seen you fight your way through hell and back."

"You think?"

"I know. The industry has enough egos to fill the whole state of California. You keep being you and vulnerable and you'll move from legend to icon status in no time."

Dane laughed. "Wait, I thought a legend was better than an icon."

"Nope. An icon tops a legend."

When he walked into his house in Santa Cruz for the first time since he'd left for Ventura, it felt damn good to be back. A milestone he wasn't sure he'd ever reach. The strong smell of surfboard wax mingled with dried wildflowers made him feel right at home. Hope and Kama and Jeff were all sitting at his kitchen island with a bottle of bubbly on ice. Isla bounced up to them and began howling. Kama picked her up and swung her around.

"Looks like I'm not the only one happy to be home," Dane said.

Kama poured glasses for everyone, and Dane took only a tiny bit. His balance was still not all the way back and alcohol was not part of his new program, but this called for a toast.

"Cheers to Dane, our fearless leader back with us again, powered by his own two legs, no less," Yeti said.

"To Dane, friends for life," Kama said.

Hope, who was standing next to him, bumped him with her shoulder. "It hasn't been the same without you around. I'm glad you're back, even if you do like to fuck up my hair."

Dane grinned. "The band is back together, watch out, world."

Once dinner wound down, and everyone else had left, Dane and Kama kicked back on the cracked-leather couch making winter plans. Kama seemed uncomfortable, especially when

Maui came up, but Dane figured it was because he was worried for him. They were shooting for late October or early November. Swells weren't usually enormous yet, but there were likely to be waves of substance. He was still haunted by his reaction to the guy wiping out at Steamer Lane, but the underwater rock running had helped rebuild his faith in himself. Hawai'i was also a good place to start because the warm water was less dangerous.

Kama slid down so his legs were way out in front of him on the floor, and finally came out with it. "Did you see the picture in the *Maui Time*?"

At some point in the summer, Dane had picked up the habit of checking the Maui news almost daily. Every now and then there would be a mention of Zen Mountain Retreat, or Jones, or 'Iwa and Winston and their fight. This morning, in all the madness of leaving Ventura, he hadn't had a chance to look.

He frowned. "What picture?"

"The one of 'Iwa and Winston."

"No. Should I have?"

Kama pulled out his phone and held it up to Dane, who grabbed it with a growing sense of dread. The headline said, "Uncle's: A Feast for the Senses." Beneath the story was a carousel of photos, the first one of Eddie standing out front holding up a big fish with both hands. Dane hit the arrow, skimming the next ones, until he came to the one Kama had been talking about. 'Iwa kissing Winston under fairy lights on the back deck of Uncle's. Dane may as well have been coldcocked. Would have preferred it actually.

He handed the phone back, and was afraid to ask, but forced himself to. "Are they together? Like together together?"

"I have no idea, but I thought you'd want to see this, in case."

"It was probably just a matter of time—those two have a lot of history. He seems like a solid guy, too."

"Don't jump to conclusions until we find out the story."

"Looks pretty conclusive to me."

Dane leaned back into the pillows and covered his face. His worst nightmare had come true. 'Iwa with another guy. His fault. He had properly blown it with the one woman who could have actually been *the one*. He should have written her a letter, like Kama suggested. He should have flown to Maui, got down on his knees and told her how he really felt.

Late that month, Dane and Kama both got the official call for the Pe'ahi Challenge. The opening ceremony would be in two weeks, and the holding period for the contest would run from mid-November through the end of March, waiting for clean conditions and a giant northwest swell.

When they stepped off the plane into the brisk trade winds, a near-full moon and croaking bufo toads were there to greet them. Returning to Maui felt like coming back to hallowed ground. Dane had been having this fantasy that 'Iwa would know he was coming and would be waiting by the curb with a lei. But there was only Kama's grandma in the old red truck, two chain-smoking cab drivers and an endless loop of rental car shuttles. They lumped all the board bags and Isla's crate in the back and headed off to the Mizuno compound.

The next morning, Kama dragged him to Maui Bean & Tea Leaf, and Dane felt skittish as a feral cat. He knew his chances were probably fifty-fifty that 'Iwa would be there. The worst part was wondering who she might be there with. Kama had not been able to gather any more intel on her status with Winston. Facing his underwater fears was one thing, seeing 'Iwa hitched up with another guy would ruin him. But his worries were for nothing, because she never showed.

At the opening ceremony that afternoon, a gathering of Hawaiian elders, contest sponsors, twenty-one invitees and fourteen alternates stood on a windswept bluff above Pe'ahi for the blessing. They were each wrapped in a red piece of material—a *kīhei*—that represented a Hawaiian cloak worn for ceremonies, and they each wore a *maile* lei.

A bald man with a deep voice spoke, his words swept up by the salt-infused wind. "We are here because of the ocean, not the other way around. The sea gives us life and we must treat it with the ultimate respect. So as you enter, your *kuleana* is to always do so humbly and to care for it as you would your own. And as you leave, to pass on this awareness to our brothers and sisters around the world."

Each surfer had been told to bring a surfboard, and as they all lined up for the photo, Dane's whole body bumped up in chicken skin. This dinged-up mint green board had been around the world with him, and leaning against it now, with the blue waters of Pe'ahi as a backdrop, hit him hard. A few months ago, this moment had seemed out of reach. Walking had seemed out of reach. At times, even a future had seemed out of reach.

If the right waves never materialized, the contest would have to wait until the next year. Or the next. Or the next. Dane was happy to wait as long as it took. If the contest happened sooner than later, there was no telling whether he would be ready to paddle out. Maybe an alternate would get his spot, but he was here, and that was all that mattered.

Dane had contemplated texting 'Iwa before the ceremony to let her know he was here. He felt like he owed her at least a warning that he was on island. Especially if he showed up at Uncle's, which seemed an inevitability. According to the laws of small-town life, their paths would cross at some point. But in the end, he chickened out. A text message seemed like a wimpy way to contact her after all this time.

In the weeks leading up to this trip, Dane had been practicing breath holds, and yesterday he and Kama had paddled a downwind Maliko run on prone paddleboards in preparation for the sizable north swell arriving tomorrow. But he knew there was no substitute for the real thing. Waves made their own rules, and surfing involved so many variables, faith was often your only choice.

As they made their way down the cliff, the throaty rumble of surf on rock shook the ground they walked on. They had picked up Yeti at the airport last night, and it was suddenly old times. Except for the fact that Dane was having to coax himself to take each step along the narrow, rocky path. Then he thought of the words of that old man last year, *someone is going to die*, and he felt even more shaky.

Yeti moved with the grace of a cat. "After this hike, I imagine the waves will seem tame to you, mate."

"It *all* seems sketchy right now."

At the bottom, they had to traverse a small field of smooth boulders before leaping off into the shore break. He stood and watched for a while, working up the nerve to make the leap.

"You don't have to do this, you know," Kama said.

"Yes. I do."

Yeti came up beside Dane, zipping up his wetsuit. "Let us help you in, at least."

They waited for a lull, then the three of them scrambled across the rocks and shimmied onto their boards. By the time they arrived in the lineup, Dane was vibrating with nervous tension. He sat on the edge and watched the other guys go, set after set. The waves were a solid twelve to fifteen feet, Hawaiian. Conditions were not epic and the crowd was mellow, which suited him just fine. One wave was all he needed.

When one finally came to him, Dane put his head down and paddled. Instinct took over, and he jumped up, made the drop and went straight down the line. No fancy moves, just pure, unadulterated wave riding. When he kicked out, he heard his friends cheering, but their voices were swallowed by a bigger set behind them. Dane paddled wide, so as not to get cleaned up on the inside, and he had to coax himself into paddling back out. *When you let fear stop you, you're feeding it. And the more you feed it, the stronger it gets.* Belinda's voice rang clear in his mind.

There were long intervals between the sets, and he told himself he was just being picky, waiting for an open one. His legs felt strong, his back solid. The fear was there, but had loosened its grip since his last paddle out. Still, something was missing.

He let himself drift out, away from the lineup, to where he had a clear view of Haleakalā. He slid into the water and dove down, following the sun rays, searching for answers at the bottom of the ocean, bubbles and silence surrounding him. When he came back up, he floated with his arms out, weightless.

The ocean was his soul.

He knew that.

But his heart was in a little restaurant in Pāʻia. In the rainforest. At a waterfall full of golden algae.

The Other Uncle

'Iwa

November

It was impossible to live in Pā'ia and not know that all the world's best big wave surfers were in town. 'Iwa had seen the list of invitees in the newspaper. Her father had made sure of that. He dropped the newspaper on the table in front of her as she sipped her coffee Sunday morning.

"Your boy is in town, did you see?"

Her friend Lucy had already texted her. "He's not my boy, and I saw."

"You ever gonna talk to him again? Every person past and present makes mistakes, you know. But oftentimes it's what happens *after* the mistake that's important."

'Iwa avoided talking to her father because she knew he had a soft spot for Dane and she didn't want to be talked out of her decision.

"Shouldn't you side with your daughter?" she asked.

"Not when your daughter has a head like a coconut."

"What am I supposed to do, call him and ask him why he was kissing someone else? No thank you. And he hasn't bothered to get a hold of me."

Even though she had asked him not to. It had been in the heat of a terrible moment, and she had meant it at the time. It just seemed like if he really wanted her, he would have at least tried.

"Things aren't always as they seem. You might be surprised at what you find out."

Koa did not like when they argued, and came up and leaned against 'Iwa with all his hulk. "You're upsetting Koa, please stop," she said.

"I just want you to be happy."

"I am happy."

"You act like you're okay, but I see right through you. You're becoming a hermit at the ripe old age of twenty-five and it's not healthy. You've lost weight and I can practically see through you. At least do yourself a favor and talk to the guy."

He was right about the weight. Her jeans now fell below her hips and she had moved up a notch on her belt. She told herself it was all the hiking and stress over the waterfall, but the truth was, her appetite had evaporated when she had left California.

"I love you, Dad, but you can be annoyingly pushy. I'll think about it," she said, heading for the door.

Late that afternoon, when she arrived at Uncle's, she found an 'ōhi'a lei po'o with her name on it in the kitchen.

"Who is this from?" she asked.

"Uncle Tutu."

Uncle Tutu was Eddie's hānai uncle. He lived upcountry and came down now and then for provisions. As part of his rounds about town, he usually stopped at Uncle's to catch up with Eddie and join 'Iwa out back for a few songs. He was one of those underground musicians, the best ukulele player no one had ever heard of. At least no one outside of central and east Maui. 'Iwa set the lei on her head, tying the two ends together, then walked out back. Tutu sat with Winston, showing him a complex picking sequence.

"How's my favorite uncle?" she said, leaning in and giving him a hug.

"Aloha, girl."

Everyone was either *boy* or *girl*. It had always been that way with him.

"To what do I owe this gorgeous lei?"

His voice grated like sandpaper. "Special day, special *wahine*."

No one knew how old Uncle Tutu was, but he was leathery enough to be two hundred, with a shock of white hair. His appearances were not usually accidental, and mostly coincided with something big occurring in their sphere. Before they even knew Lily was sick, Uncle had come in one day out of the blue, handed Eddie a piece of paper with a phone number on it and walked out the door. Eddie knew enough to call the number. It belonged to an oncologist. Which was why seeing him made 'Iwa's neck itch.

"Not that every day isn't special here, but really, what's the occasion?" she asked.

"I saw dis lei at the farmers market. Made for a queen, and you da queenliest *wahine* I know."

She laughed. "Aw, thank you, Uncle, I love it. Are you going to stay and play with us?"

"Just a couple."

"Stay as long as you want."

Winston was wearing a long-sleeved brown *palaka* shirt, which set off his chocolate eyes. Every now and then, his striking looks caught her off guard, and tonight was one of those nights. The place was mostly empty, so they played and talked and talked and played. Uncle chose the songs, and 'Iwa and Winston played along as best they could. After about an hour or so, 'Iwa noticed the small reserved cards on most of the tables. Uncle Tutu and his lei had distracted her.

"Who are these tables reserved for?" she asked, fearing she already knew the answer.

"Your father didn't tell you?"

'Iwa felt a pressure building in her chest. "No, he didn't."

"The Pe'ahi Challenge people."

She was going to kill Eddie. Blood on coals, she set her guitar down and marched back into the kitchen, where the scent of fresh-out-of-the-oven *liliko'i* pies swallowed her whole. "I'm outta here, Dad. Win and Uncle Tutu can play tonight."

Eddie stopped fanning the pies. "If you leave now, you're fired."

She knew he didn't mean it, especially since she only worked there to help him out. "You would never fire me, I'm your daughter. And that is a direct quote from you yourself."

He folded his arms. "Watch me."

"Come on, Dad. If you had at least given me warning about who was coming, I could have mentally prepared."

"If I had told you, you would have run for the hills."

"No."

Yes.

"They specifically requested you, so you have to stay." He opened his arms and walked toward her. "Please, 'Iwa."

The love she had for this man made it impossible to stay mad at him for longer than a few heartbeats, and she let herself fall into him. "Just be ready for the fallout because I guarantee you there will be some."

"I make a good fallout shelter," he said, with a half-cocked smile.

Seventeen minutes later, several contest organizers arrived, followed by a slow trickle of surfers. 'Iwa was all nerves and refused to look anywhere other than her guitar strings. Uncle Tutu kept plucking away and she strummed along with him. He had this incredible voice that could sound like Gabby Pahinui one minute, Israel Kamakawiwo'ole the next.

Eventually, all the tables filled up. Tutu had been playing longer than he usually did, and 'Iwa forced herself to say hello to the crowd, letting her eyes sweep over the sea of sun-streaked hair. Two men were missing. Dane and Kama. Maybe Dane wasn't coming. Probably didn't want to see her. Her mind would have kept going down that road of maybes, when a tall, familiar, bearded man walked through the door.

Yeti.

If Yeti was here—

Kama followed.

She waited, but there was no sign of Dane.

Better that way, she told herself. Kama blew her a kiss and Yeti nodded, as they squeezed in with a few other guys. 'Iwa smiled and kept playing, trying to appear unfazed. As though having them all here was an everyday occurrence. She had moved on. Dane was old news.

Yeah right.

"Uncle," she said, "let me sing the next one."

Over the past few months, she had been playing Adele's "Someone Like You" at home. By the time she would finish singing, her cheeks would be damp and her heart pounded raw. In some strange way, it gave her permission to grieve. Singing the song in front of a crowd was probably a foolish thing to do, but if Adele had survived a soul-crushing breakup and lived to sing about it to the entire world, 'Iwa surely could manage in a tiny restaurant in Pā'ia.

I heard that you're settled down...

Up until her voice hit the mic, their little trio had been background music, but soon, people stopped talking and looked her way. 'Iwa did Adele well. Same rich, husky voice, same angsty anguish. When she finished, a fine dusting of feather rain came down, and she felt an overwhelming sadness for all that might have been.

It was probably the last song a patio full of testosterone wanted to hear, but what the hell. A few people clapped, if a little unenthusiastically. Uncle Tutu squeezed her hand and nodded toward the back, under the eave. She followed his line of vision to a figure in an orange aloha shirt holding a wire-haired dog. A tremble started up in her abdomen and spread out in waves from there. 'Iwa felt lightheaded. She had no idea what to do. Smile, look away, say something? None seemed adequate for the moment, so she glanced over at Winston.

"Your turn. Maybe something more upbeat," she said.

Win chose Jack Johnson, "Banana Pancakes."

Uncle Tutu slipped away and she watched him weave through the tables and make his way to Dane.

For a moment 'Iwa forgot what she was playing. Isla wiggled in Dane's arms, trying to lick Uncle Tutu in the face. 'Iwa missed a beat. Winston bumped her knee with his. They finished out the song, but she had gone numb. They played a few more songs, then took a break. Eddie had come out back and was now talking to Dane as if they were old buddies. The whole world seemed to be conspiring. Dane caught her looking, smiled and lifted his hand in a half wave. 'Iwa half waved back.

"Some nerve he's got, showing up here," Win said.

He knew how badly 'Iwa hurt, and she knew he was just being protective.

"Doesn't seem to bother my dad."

"Does it bother you? Because I'll tell him to leave if you want me to."

It felt like someone had taken her feelings and thrown them in a blender. She did not want to see Dane. But she did want to see him. She did not want to talk to him. But she was aching to talk to him. She wanted nothing more than to walk over there and fall into his arms. Seeing him actually walking again, looking strong and vital, made her blindingly happy. But she also wished he would leave.

"Nah. I'm fine. It was just a matter of time before I ran into him. Probably good to get it over with," she said.

A moment later, a small whirlwind of fur leaped onto her

lap, set her paws on 'Iwa's shoulder and started making moves to kiss her chin.

"Isla! It's good to see you, too, little friend," 'Iwa said, unable to hold back a laugh.

Dogs would always break through the bullshit, you could count on that. Kama and Yeti must have decided it was now safe to come up and say hi, too. Yeti commented on her guitar, and Kama invited her to a party at the farm the following weekend. They told her about the ceremony, and about the swell coming tomorrow. No one mentioned Dane, and Dane stayed where he was, holding up the wall. Tutu had disappeared inside.

"Is Dane going to make like a tree all night?" she finally said.

"He wasn't sure he should come."

"Am I that scary?"

"You know it's not that. He just wants to respect your space," Kama said.

Winston cleared his throat and strummed his ukulele. "Time to start up again. Guys, would you mind?"

He began to play then, and Uncle Tutu shuffled back over with his ukulele and joined in. "You. Go," he said to 'Iwa, nodding toward Dane.

There was nothing to do but follow his order, and she worked her way around tables, stopping to say hello to a few surfers she had met this past year with Dane, prolonging the inevitable just a little bit longer. When there was no one left between her and Dane, she crossed the empty space slowly until she was standing an arm's length away.

"Hi," he said.

'Iwa watched his lashes touch his cheekbones when he blinked, remembered the feel of them feathering on her neck.

"Hi."

He had grown a beard, not as long as Yeti's but full and darker than his hair. It aged him, but in a good way. The air between them crackled, and she backed away a step to keep herself out of his gravitational field.

"It's good to see you, 'Iwa," Dane said.

Good was not the word she would have chosen for this moment. Complicated maybe. Or conflicted. Actually, tragic might be the best way to put it.

"You're walking again," she said, for lack of any other available words.

"Took a few minutes, but yeah. I'm at about ninety percent. Balance is still not all the way there, but it's coming."

"I'm happy for you."

His eyes were still deep ocean blue and he still smelled like surfboard wax. The effect was intoxicating, and she eased away a few inches further. Dane raked his fingers through his hair, sending it out in all directions, and bounced from one foot to the other.

Then he surprised her. "It was Yeti, you know, the anonymous donor."

"What?"

"He swore me to secrecy, but said I could tell you. I guess you made a big impression on him."

She searched for Yeti in the crowd, and found him sitting with his back to them, deep in conversation with someone. They could certainly use more Yetis in the world.

"Unbelievable. Why didn't he just tell me when he gave it to us?"

Dane shrugged. "You'll have to ask him. He likes to fly under the radar, helping people and causes without making a big deal."

"Fifty grand is a big deal."

"Not to him."

"That was our biggest single donation."

"I feel lucky to count him as a friend," Dane said.

"Is that what you came here to tell me?" she asked, feeling a little confrontational.

His smile faded. "Look, I know you probably didn't want to see me, but everyone was coming, and—"

"No need to lurk back here, join your friends," she said, cutting him off and motioning toward the tables, a little too aggressively.

Win and Tutu were playing "Southern Cross," and they sounded great together. Maybe she could just sneak out over the side railing and slink off like a cat in the night.

"I didn't come here to see my friends," he said, gaze unwavering.

This was not the time or place for any big conversations. Nor could he say anything that would change her mind. All the voices, the music, the wind-rustled trees, they were making it hard to think. Or maybe it was being so close to Dane.

She thought of Winston's words after she had come back from California, heartbroken. *Everything happens for a reason*, he'd told her. She remembered thinking, *fuck that, no reason in the world would make what just happened with Dane all right*. For the next hundred years she would be obsessively reliving the image of him kissing Sunny. Now she bit her lip and drew blood trying to get the memory out of her head.

'Iwa glanced over at Winston; she couldn't help it. Then she looked back at Dane. He was standing there not breathing. When she had said no second chances, she meant it. She could not risk losing him a second time.

Dane eyed Winston. "I saw the picture of you two in the paper. Are you together?"

Her body tensed. Maybe she ought to let him think so, but lying was not her way. "No. The photographer happened to be there when I accidentally kissed him. It was bad timing."

She could not risk eye contact, instead looking at Isla, who had come to sit by his feet.

"Accidentally?"

"I meant to kiss his cheek. He turned. Not that it matters."

She realized how ridiculous it sounded, but stuck to her guns. "Just so you know, it made me want to punch someone. Seeing the photo, I mean," he said.

His words triggered a detonation inside of her. "Yeah? Well now you know how I felt when I walked in on you and your dumb supermodel ex-girlfriend making out. Talk about wanting to punch someone. But I'm over it now," she said, shrugging as if that might bolster her case. "Over *us*."

"Are you sure?" he said, mouth drawing downward. "Because I'm not."

The invisible boundary between them weakened, and 'Iwa felt herself slanting toward him. For one long moment, she wanted more of Dane—the hum of his voice, the way his eyes bored into her as though reading every thought, the indent on his chin that she had kissed more times than she could count. But she knew what she had to do—be polite and send him on his way. And then she could really work on moving on.

Her mouth filled with cotton, but she got out the words. "I guess you should have thought of that before you went and ruined everything. You know, maybe it *would* be better if you left."

Dane leaned against the wall, as if needing its wooden support. She had never seen him so nervous. "Is that what you really want, deep down?" he asked.

There was thunder in her heart. "Yeah, and it's what I need."

"I am sorry for everything I put you through. I was awful. I was hurting. I was a dumbass idiot who made the biggest mistake of his life and is now paying for it." Looking defeated, he handed her a small Patagonia bag with something heavy wrapped inside. "Will you at least take this?"

'Iwa looked up at him. "I can't—"

"Please."

She took it and ran her hands along its hard edges. A book, and she knew exactly which one. *God, please get me out of here, before I do something stupid.*

Dane seemed to sense her growing discomfort. "I'll leave you be, but I had to see you and put this in your hands. Isla wanted to see you, too."

She stood for a moment, taking in his closeness for what would be the last time, then bent down and kissed Isla. When she turned to go, he leaned in and put his hand on her forearm, as though he wanted to say one last thing.

Their eyes locked.

"And just so there's no question—I love you, 'Iwa," he said, voice like running water over rocks.

Trembling, she pulled her arm away and made for the kitchen and the safety of the one man she knew would never hurt her.

Brah

Dane

Dane flew back to the mainland feeling as though someone had poured cement in his stomach for breakfast. Normally, when he left Hawai'i his tanks were full and he couldn't wait to return. He had even gone as far as secretly looking for houses. Not that he could afford much on Maui, but he had found a few old plantation fixer-uppers with potential. New roof, new siding, new red and white paint, and he and 'Iwa could have their own slice of jungle. That dream had just gone out the airplane window.

Even though chances had been slim, he'd still been holding tight to the notion that he might convince 'Iwa to forgive him. What he hadn't counted on was the old guy, Uncle Tutu—the man who spoke to him on the cliff the morning of his Pe'ahi win. When Dane first saw him sitting next to 'Iwa playing music, he had done a double take. The man could play, even upstaging 'Iwa. Then all of a sudden he locked eyes with Dane and made his way over.

"You're the one," he said.

Dane glanced around, making sure the guy was talking to him. There was no one else around, so he reached out his hand. "I'm Dane Parsons, and you are…"

The man shook it, firmly. "Tutu Bertlemann."

He thought the man was going to tell him to beat it, to leave 'Iwa alone, but instead, he said, "I known dis girl since she was in her mama's belly. Nevah you mind what comes out of her mout." He crossed his fingers in front of Dane's face. "You two li' dis."

Each syllable formed its own word. Was he some kind of soothsayer, or just an old man who got off making cryptic predictions about other people's lives?

"No offense, Mr. Bertlemann, but the last thing you told me never came to pass. On the cliff—"

"I remembah. Nothing is ever set in rock, boy. A subtle shift in your wind sends the canoe in a whole new direction. A puff of breath here, a hurricane there."

Dane closed his eyes and imagined the forces working behind the scenes in his life. A swish of a fish tail. Just the right swell direction traveling across the Pacific. A flutter of bird wings high on the mountain. Or the voice of a beautiful woman.

"So if I read you right, you're saying not to give up on her." A nod.

"I'm here. But I won't force anything," Dane said.

"No one said to force. Just trust."

"I tried."

"The work is done. Stop doing."

Isla growled at Tutu, who touched Dane on the shoulder, smacked his lips, then walked off. A weird encounter that left him more confused than anything. Dane had never been good at sitting back and waiting for things to happen. Maybe that was the lesson here.

Back in Santa Cruz, he took on another small carpentry job, sketched out a few table and rocking chair ideas, and kept training. But he felt flat and unenthused. The tides and the waves came and went, and he watched them with a previously unknown detachment. There were two things that consumed him: 'Iwa and returning to Nazaré. 'Iwa was out of the question, despite what old man Tutu had said, but taming Nazaré might be a way out of this melancholy funk. He had glimpsed its possibility, but he wanted to ride it at its full potential. He wanted that XXL that he knew Nazaré could deliver, especially since Pe'ahi had been quiet.

In late January, Dane got a call from Yeti one night. He was still up, in bed reading the waterfall poem for the nine hundredth time. It had become his bedtime story, which was probably not healthy, but there was no one there to stop him.

"It's happening. Get your gear together. I'm booking us flights for Tuesday," Yeti said.

Dane didn't even have to ask where. When they hung up, he checked the forecast. Wave models were showing deep red and purple in the North Atlantic. The seeds of excitement began to stir, accompanied by a heavy pit in his stomach. He knew if he didn't do this now, there was a good chance he never would.

The town of Nazaré had not changed. Unhurried, layered in sea mist and nestled in the calm between the storm. Skies were gray and colder than last time, and Dane, Kama and Yeti huddled together at Cafe O Mar sipping espressos and eating pastries that turned their beards white with powdered sugar. Kama had tried to grow a beard, too, but he didn't have enough hair.

"Don't worry about it, women will like you better without it," Yeti said.

"As if this guy has anything to worry about," Dane said.

They had come to Nazaré early enough to give them more down time, and more time to acclimate and prepare for the swell. They spent mornings running the beach, watching the tides, and getting a sense of currents and wind patterns. Dane was quickly becoming addicted to *meia de leite* and ham and cheese *sandes*, similar to lattes and American sandwiches, but with a European personality. Portuguese bread was double thick, a meal in itself.

In the last month, he had been practicing standing on one leg with his eyes closed, and his balance had returned to baseline. All systems were go. Being here and settling into the rhythm of the place made it seem less daunting than last time. It felt strange not to have Hope with them, but her younger sister was getting married, and this one she couldn't miss.

A few other surfers had flown into Nazaré this time, invited by Garrett, and lured by the promise of mammoth surf and killer photos. It was only a matter of time before winter Nazaré was crawling with surfers and photographers and throngs of spectators. Dane had seen it happen in Hawai'i, in Bali, in California. Crowds, gridlock traffic, everyone trying to make a buck. Sex, drugs, and rock and roll. His mom had been right about that all those years ago. The commercialization of surfing—of everything, really—was taking down the planet.

Yet here he was. In the thick of it.

The cause.

And all for what?

On the night before the big swell, wind whistled down the street. Nearby, a flag or maybe someone's laundry flapped loudly. Dane and Kama lay in twin beds six feet apart in the tiny hotel room, lights out. Dane was second-guessing throwing away the postcard he had almost mailed off to 'Iwa earlier in the day. The photo of a golden plover, just like the ones on Maui, had caught his eye, and he'd felt a strange compulsion to buy it. He wrote the first thing that came to his mind.

Thinking about you.
Miss you.
Love you.
D

Then he scribbled over it and threw it in the trash.

"Are you tired?" Kama asked from across the way.

"No. Are you?"

"Not one bit."

Kama's bed squeaked, like he was rolling over. "I can't stop thinking about paddling in, instead of towing, what about you?" he said.

"It's crossed my mind, but it would take just the right swell. And I don't think this one is it."

Nor am I ready.

"Maybe not, but I can almost taste it—just us and the ocean, no engines, no boats, no riffraff. Seems like it would be the ultimate ride."

Dane stared up at the ceiling, lit from a streetlight outside. "It would be, if we could pull it off."

"I think we could," Kama said.

They had only brought their tow boards. "We'd need different boards," Dane said.

"Our longest, thickest guns."

The thought caused a thump under his rib cage. "Let's do it. Before the end of April, if there's another swell, in time for the XXL. I'm in."

Stating the words aloud felt like making a pact with the universe. A threat and a promise. In the distance, he could hear the sound of ocean on the beach. A light wash that by tomorrow would be shaking houses miles inland.

"What were you thinking about, a little while ago? I could hear the machinery grinding in your head," Kama asked.

"Oh, you know. The usual stuff. Living and dying. Wondering if I can hack it. Wondering if I still have it in me to do this," he said.

"You do."

"How can you be so sure?"

"Because you and I are cut from the same cloth," Kama said.

"I just want that feeling back, you know? The freedom, the energy, the buzz. I want to be hungry for it and one hundred percent in. Right now, the doubt is sitting on my shoulder, whispering in my ear."

"I think if you went through what you did and had no doubt, that would be something to worry about. Doubt was built into us for a reason. Any of the waves we ride out there could easily kill us." He paused. "But...they also keep us alive."

They lay quiet for a while, listening to the flapping flag and the whine of a scooter driving down the narrow street.

"Is it worth the risk?" Dane asked.

"Totally."

He heard the smile in Kama's voice, and he felt so much less alone. "I'm counting on tomorrow to be my initiation back into the club."

"Brah, you never left the club."

Dane felt a swarm of warmth for his buddy. "Love you, brah," he said, quietly.

The words surprised him, but he did love Kama. Like a brother.

"Brah, right back at ya."

"Try to get some sleep. We're gonna need it," Dane said.

"Roger that."

The morning chill cut to the bone. They were wearing five mm wetsuits and still, Dane could feel the cold burrowing in behind his knees, deep in his ears, along his spine. Remarkably, there were no clouds, and ropes of waves pumped in. Bordering on huge, but not huge yet. He and Kama were partnered up, and Yeti was towing with a young local guy named Leandro. Leandro ripped, and he knew the spot. Allegedly, in the past year, he had ridden Nazaré on every rideable day.

"Expect a pulse at nine o'clock," he told them.

Dane looked at his watch. Seven fifty-six. They decided Kama would surf first and then they would switch. They had come without their own photographers this time. Dane didn't want the added pressure, and Yeti and Kama had been fine with that. But there were other skis in the water, and a fishing boat full of telephoto lenses floated in the channel.

Dane had chicken skin the whole way out, and not from the cold. He had dreamed of this for almost a year, and now that he was actually here, a strange pressure was building inside of him.

You are made of salt water.

The ocean runs in your veins.

The ocean is you.

Words from his mother. Words to live by, but easier said than done. A set appeared in the distance and he felt guilty for being relieved that Kama was going first.

"Cheehoo! Outside! You ready?" Dane yelled, putting on a good face, when inside he was scared as hell.

"Now or never."

Yeti and Leandro were deeper, and they watched Leandro pull Yeti into a tall lump of green, leaving a trail of white in his wake. Dane pulled Kama into the second wave of the set, and Kama slid high and then swooped down with a wide arcing turn, barely outrunning the lip. When he kicked out, Dane plucked him out fast as he could. They did the same dance a few times, Kama soldiering on, fluid and effortless. Stoked.

When they were outside again, Kama paddled over to the ski. "Ready to switch?"

Dane felt queasy and unable to get a full breath. "Not yet."

He wanted to explain, but Kama must have read the look in his eyes. "Gotcha. I'll keep going. You tell me when you want to switch."

If, not *when*, he should have said.

"Will do."

Just a little more time to get used to being out here. That's what he told himself. Another wave or two, and his jitters would be gone and he would do what everyone else seemed to be so effortlessly doing.

But at nine on the nose, the pulse showed up in the form of the whole ocean rising up on the horizon. All the skis sped out to meet it. Dane's first thought was *no effing way*, but as the wave moved closer, he could see its perfection.

"This one has my name all over it," Kama said.

"You sure?"

Kama was already in the water. "Hit it! I'm going right."

Without hesitation, Dane pulled Kama along the feathering top, gunning it to gain enough speed. There had been a few rights earlier, but no one had ridden them. He was surprised at Kama's choice, but went with it. The line went slack as Kama let go and dropped in. As the driver, you always hoped to get your guy in the right spot so they had the best chance of making it, while not getting yourself taken down in the process. For a moment, Dane teetered at the crest, then sped off to the shoulder to follow in as best he could.

Because of the sheer size of the wave, Dane swung wide. When he caught sight of Kama again, he was shooting straight down an elevator shaft. Crouched low, legs barely holding on. His position could not be worse. But he stayed planted on that board like a crab. Dane cheered for his friend, while at the same time feeling like a chicken shit. Then the whitewater swallowed Kama, and he disappeared under a mountain of white.

Dane drove alongside the wave, trying to keep an eye on his friend. On the inside, it was mayhem and froth. He spotted Kama bobbing next to his board. He wasn't swimming, but his arms were making awkward splashes. Something looked off. Dane knew the ski could easily lose power in the foam, but he went anyway. Because that's what you did. A cloud passed over the sun, turning the water gray. Or was it red? His mind must be playing tricks on him.

"Kama!" he yelled.

Kama turned slightly. His eyes were out of focus.

Dane shot over to him. "Give me your hand!"

Whitewater slammed against the ski, almost knocking Dane off, but he righted it just in time. Kama's hand flailed around and he yelled something unintelligible at Dane. There was blood on his neck. Then, almost in slow motion, their hands connected and Dane clamped down with everything he had. Kama swung onto the sled behind him and managed to find the handles, just as Dane throttled them out of there.

In calmer water, Dane slowed and turned back. "Are you okay?"

Kama lay face down and groaned. "My eardrum. It must have popped. I have no fucking idea which way is up."

The relief that Dane felt was monumental. A broken eardrum would heal. And it also meant they were done for the day. Dane was officially off the hook.

Standing Ground

'Iwa

February

'Iwa stood under her umbrella outside of Hoapili Hale on Main Street in Wailuku and paused before entering the building. In typical February fashion, a series of cold fronts had swept down the island chain and were focusing the bulk of their moisture on the windward side of Maui. The saturated ground made for squishy walking and her shoes and pant legs were soaked. For a moment, she put her umbrella down and turned her face up, opening her mouth and catching the raindrops on her tongue.

Ola i ka wai. Water is life.

Last night, she'd lain awake for hours as her mind followed all kinds of disastrous scenarios, nervous to finally appear before Judge Atkins. Courts moved slow as mud here, and she was more than ready to end this case on a good note. Though there was always the Supreme Court if it came to that. She hoped it didn't.

She closed her umbrella, walked inside, and after putting her things through the metal detector, took the elevator to the third floor with three other people. The courthouse always seemed so somber and depressing, and the feeling in the elevator was tense. Everyone stared at their feet and by the time the doors opened, a puddle had formed around hers.

Winston and Kawika were already in the courtroom. They'd
met the previous day to discuss their plan and what each one
would say. Fortunately, both sides would be meeting with the
judge separately, so she didn't have to worry about Jones and
his bulldog attorney. She smoothed her hair back and sat.

"Eh, 'Iwa, girl," Kawika said, giving her a thumbs-up.

"Sorry I'm late."

Atkins still wasn't there, though.

"Hey, you doing okay?" Winston asked, concern on his face.

"Just a little wet, why?"

He turned and studied her for a moment, as though expecting a different answer.

'Iwa frowned. "What, Winston? You're making me nervous."

He looked down at the yellow tablet in front of him, shaking his head. "Nothing, nothing. Glad you're here."

"Of course I'm here."

The door to the chambers opened and Atkins came out. A
foot taller than anyone in the room, with wide shoulders and a
thick brow, he was imposing as hell. He sat, looked to be reading something on the podium in front of him, and then slowly
assessed the group before him. When he got to 'Iwa, she smiled,
she couldn't help it. He did not smile back.

As they went through the hearing opening procedures, 'Iwa
was having trouble concentrating, and wondered what Winston was keeping from her.

When instructed by Atkins, Kawika stood up and spoke.
"Your honor, Maui Forest Recovery Project is requesting that
the habitat conservation plan completed for Zen Mountain
Retreat be thrown out, due to skewed comparisons. We also
would like the court to investigate the participation of a land
board member in the creation of said conservation plan, which
we believe to be improper."

Last month, Winston had been the one who called out land
board member Mazie Hart for serving on both boards.

"In addition, the plan does not comply with Hawai'i's endangered species law, with regards to the kiwikiu and many other honeycreepers and native plants on the property. And lastly that all work be halted, since Jones has started clearing without a permit. Habitat, once demolished, cannot be replaced."

And so it began. For each request, Winston and 'Iwa presented reams of evidence.

When it came to showing the footage of the kiwikiu, Judge Atkins looked pointedly at 'Iwa. "And how is it that you came to be on Jones's property, Miss Young?" he asked.

"I was doing field work across the stream and had gone above the waterfall after some birds. At that time I didn't realize where exactly his property started, it's quite wild out there."

"Tell me what happened next," he said.

Though he probably already knew.

'Iwa told him the story. "And that's when I realized how much clearing he'd already done. We see it all the time. Developers getting started without permits, knowing they'll just pay the fine. We need to—"

"Let's stick to the case at hand," Atkins said.

Kawika stepped in and presented aerial photos of Waikula and Jones's property, which now contained an ever-expanding rectangle of scraped earth. 'Iwa knew because they'd flown a drone high above. Judge Atkins yawned several times and kept his face blank as an empty sheet of paper. 'Iwa's confidence waned as the morning went on.

When Kawika let 'Iwa speak again, she put on some heat. "Your honor, we checked the data on the conservation plan that Jones submitted, and there is no question that what's on there is cherry-picked to strengthen their case. Many species that we know to be on this land are not even mentioned, especially the kiwikiu, which is fighting to remain on the planet."

"And your data is based on what? One small video? Anything else?"

The courtroom suddenly felt steamy. "No. But keep in mind that there are at most only a few hundred left in the wild. So even one bird on the property makes it worth shutting down. It's simply not worth the risk."

Atkins glanced over at the photographs, studying them more thoroughly this time. 'Iwa held her breath and crossed her fingers.

"Have you been up there, your honor? To Waikula?" she asked.

At first she thought Judge was going to redirect, but he didn't. "I have not."

"May I humbly suggest you take a ride up there, see for yourself what's going on, and what we stand to lose?"

A long moment of silence passed, everyone glancing around at each other, and 'Iwa worried maybe she had overstepped her boundaries.

But Atkins said, "Noted. Now please continue."

"Do you know what we find even more troubling?"

He leaned back in his chair, now looking almost amused. "Tell us, Miss Young."

"That someone thought it was acceptable for Ms. Hart, a land board member, to serve on the same team who came up with the conservation plan and subsequently made recommendations to the same board she works on. Is this not a blatant conflict of interest?"

She paused, and no one said anything, so she went on.

"It speaks to the many levels of negligence or even wrongdoing that led to ZMR's approval when it never should have been approved. Judge Atkins, I implore you to go through this with a fine-tooth comb."

It was hard to catch a breath and 'Iwa had a feeling that everything hinged on this moment, on Judge Atkins seeing this in three dimensions. She felt a chant boiling up inside, one with a triple dose of *mana*. She tried to hold it in, really she did, but the words came out anyway.

"*I kū mau mau*," she said, softly but fiercely.

Next to her, Winston answered her call, a little louder. *"I kū wā."*

'Iwa would have gone on and done the whole chant, but Judge Atkins was eyeing them sharply. 'Iwa sat; Winston sat. Kawika shot her a look that said, *What the hell was that?* 'Iwa gave a subtle shrug.

"Translate for us, if you will," Atkins said, hands folded neatly in front of him.

"It's a call for the whole community to come high in the mountains and haul the mighty koa log to the sea. But as with many chants and songs, you probably know, it has a deeper meaning—stand together and never give up. Please, Judge Atkins, come with us to the forest and see it for yourself."

'Iwa had done more research on Atkins recently. From the mainland, married to a local girl and been on Maui for eighteen years. He wasn't part of the old boy network per se, even if he moved in their circles. But in poring over his past cases, despite some of his questionable rulings, she found he was more fair than people gave him credit for. And at least he hadn't kicked them out yet.

Atkins stared at 'Iwa for a few beats, then said, "I will ask my assistant to arrange a trip up there."

Kawika dropped his pen, then said, "Great, your honor. Thank you."

'Iwa felt herself sway a little. She stole a glance at Winston, who was looking directly ahead. His Adam's apple did a huge bob and the side of his mouth turned up in a smile.

A half hour later, the three of them stood under a big monkeypod tree outside and rehashed the hearing. The rain was coming down so hard on their umbrellas they had to yell to be heard.

"I can't believe he wants to go up there!" 'Iwa said, buzzing over the new development.

"Nice stunt," Kawika said.

It was a small crumb and who knew where it would lead, but for the first time in a while, 'Iwa dared to hope. They spoke for a bit longer, then Kawika dashed off to his car. Winston turned to leave, but she tugged at his arm.

"What?" he said.

"I need a hug." She stepped into him, and he closed his arms around her. He felt strong and warm. "Have I told you lately how awesome you are, as a friend and a boss and an all-around badass of a human?" she asked.

His palm held the back of her head, lightly. "No."

"None of this would be happening without your vision."

"Not just mine," he said, in typical understated fashion.

She pulled back and looked into his eyes. "You need to own it, Win. You always shy away from the limelight, why?"

He shrugged. "It's not what's important to me."

The air shifted between them, subtly. And for a moment, she thought he might kiss her, or maybe she would kiss him, this time for real. Would it be so bad? He seemed to read her thoughts, though, and a shadow came into his eyes. He let go of her, moved back into his own space.

Winston half smiled. "'Iwa, why are you doing this to your-self? It's not me you want."

A hole had opened in the clouds, and now they were stand-ing in a pool of diffuse sunlight. He knew her so well.

"I don't know?" she whispered.

His hand found hers and squeezed. "You should reach out to him. Give him another chance. Not everyone is deserving, but I think Dane might be."

The passing of time had only made her miss him more, which went against what everyone had told her. *Time heals.* Her legs wobbled. "It terrifies me."

"Sometimes you have to walk through the fear to get to the other side."

'Iwa darted a look up at him, knowing he was right about that. But could she, after everything that had happened?

Consolations

Dane

They pushed back their flight a few days to monitor Kama's perforated eardrum, loss of equilibrium and bouts of nausea. Dane stayed with him for moral support, and because the poor guy could barely move around without falling over. The surf had dropped significantly, returning to a deceptive calm, and Yeti had flown back to California.

Dane roamed the streets and combed the beaches, looking for a peace of mind that wouldn't come. Not only was he a coward when the surf got real, but his mind kept snapping back to seeing 'Iwa at Uncle's, telling her he loved her, and her telling him to leave. It was going to haunt him until he took his last breath.

On the second day, when he reached the end of the beach, he decided he would swim straight out to sea in the frigid water, dive down and grab a handful of sand, then keep going and dive down again. When he could no longer reach the bottom, he would turn around and swim in. If that didn't shake him out of this funk, nothing would.

He and Kama had done this on the north shore of O'ahu one night after drinking a bottle of tequila. It was the middle of winter, and there had been a solid swell. Kama seemed to think it would be fun, and Dane did not disagree. The next morning, they'd both questioned their sanity. But the following winter, they did it again and it became tradition.

Swimming out to sea wasn't as daunting in broad daylight, but the water at Nazaré was in the midfifties at high noon. He only made it out maybe a few hundred yards before it became apparent that his lungs needed work. Practicing breath holds would become top priority when he got home. Every little edge counted.

When he returned to the room, Kama was sitting up in bed watching TV. "You don't have to stay, you know," he told Dane, rubbing below his ear.

Dane sat down and opened a bottle of sparkling water. "And leave you to crawl your way through the airport?"

Yesterday, Kama had been too dizzy to even walk, so he'd gotten down on his knees and crawled to the bathroom.

"I'm feeling better already."

"Still, you don't want to chance it with your eardrum, it could mess you up for life."

Kama looked toward the window, staring out at the blue sky for a few moments. "You should go." Their eyes met and it felt to Dane as though Kama was looking right into his soul. "There are people back home who need you more than I do."

The force was strong, but still, he could not leave his friend. "I'm not leaving you. Just two more days, and we go together."

"To Maui?"

Dane wasn't sure his heart could take another stomping on. "We'll see."

The following morning, after a double espresso at Cafe O Mar, Dane showed up at the beach ready to swim. The ocean was dead calm and reminded him of California. He sat down on the hard-packed sand and stretched for a few minutes, breathing in the sunshine and watching a crab throw sand out of its newly dug hole.

He felt a tickle on his foot, as the crab he had been watching made its way up his leg. Dane shot up and kicked it off, then laughed at himself for being such a wuss. Sun-warmed and stretched, he dove in the water and swam as hard and fast as he could. It was about a half mile out to the trench, where the ocean floor dropped away to twenty-six hundred fathoms. You could tell where the abyss began because the water went from a murky green to a deep, dark blue, almost black.

Today, he swam out and dove down until he could no longer grab sand. But instead of turning around like he usually did, something drove him to keep going. Cold water seared into his skin, but the faster he swam, the less he felt the icy burn. It felt good to push himself, and there was also a freedom in having nothing to lose. The thought crossed his mind that he could keep going, out beyond the trench, to where the wild things swam.

He could sense the trench as he approached, sucking in the light and reflecting back a dark mystery of sea. There was sure to be more than lost submarines down there. Numb and shivering, he stopped and floated, face down as though he might be able to see all the souls the ocean had collected over the years. He wore no goggles, so he only saw shapes. A while later, he had no idea how long, a column of gray torpedoes began rising up beneath him. He took a breath and then looked down again to make sure he wasn't hallucinating.

Something nudged his hip. Another, his arm. He felt a series of clicks and whistles pinging through his body. Dolphins, echolocating him. The pod was a big one, and soon surrounded him. Giant, gunmetal creatures, bullet-like in their speed. Dane was wide-eyed now, every nerve in his body firing. The dolphins began swimming toward shore, herding him along with them. One kept bumping his foot with its snout, another swam alongside him.

As he made for land, he realized his energy was sapped, and

the cold was rapidly draining his strength. He began to shiver. His arms felt like waterlogged branches. The dolphins closed in, swimming only inches away from him. Dane was moved by their presence, almost to the point of tears. The dolphins escorted him into the shallows, until he could stand up. He wanted to somehow show them his gratitude, but how did one thank a pod of dolphins? The big one who had been swimming alongside him the whole way was still close, so Dane reached out and ran his hand along the dolphin's surprisingly smooth back.

"I owe you one."

The dolphin then smacked its tail and shot off, heading for deeper water.

Hana Hou

'Iwa

A week later

Saturday morning, 'Iwa lay with her head under the pillow, trying to shut out the sounds of the morning rooster symphony. Sleep had been eluding her lately, and she moved through her days with glazed eyes, barely hanging on. To make matters worse, Koa had snuck into her bed in the night, leaving her only a foot of mattress space. Every now and then, his tail started thumping and his legs moved, as though chasing crabs on the beach in his dreams. It was too early to get up, and all she wanted was to fall back asleep. Maybe stay in bed all day.

Then her phone buzzed. She groaned. It was unusually early for anyone to call, so she stuck out her arm and felt around for it on the bedside table. It was Winston.

"Hey, Winston, what's up?" she croaked.

"Are you sitting down?" he asked.

'Iwa threw the pillow off her head and sat up. "Now I am, why?"

"Because I heard from Judge Atkins late last night."

There was a smile behind his words. "What did he say?" she asked, breathless.

"No Zen Mountain Retreat in Hana'iwa'iwa. Not now, not ever."

'Iwa almost dropped the phone. "Promise me you're serious."

Winston laughed a deep, throaty laugh. "You heard me. Someone upstairs heard our pleas and the eco resort project is halted, effective now."

"What did he say? Tell me in detail, every word."

Koa rolled over and leaned into her.

"He said the eco resort should have never been approved in the first place on such ecologically important lands. The entire valley is going to be rezoned conservation. Jones won't be able to clear another inch, and he's going to have to tear down that warehouse. Atkins didn't come out and say it, but it sounds like he plans on digging around to see who pushed those permits through."

"Some greedy asshole who needed more money for his next Vegas trip, is who. Listen, I'm having dinner with my dad at Uncle's later. Come in tonight and we'll celebrate?"

"Great minds. I was thinking the same thing," he said.

"Perfect. Invite everyone."

"Everyone?"

"The whole island if you want. My dad will love it."

'Iwa rested her forehead in her hands and began sobbing. *Never stop fighting for what is right and good in this world.* She felt her mother's presence all around her. Rushing water on rocks. The high-pitched call of the kiwikiu. Mist rolling down the mountain. Land was a keeper of memories, and now all the memories of her mother, and those of the forest, the ancestors, would not be erased. Koa sat up and nudged her hands, then tenderly licked her face.

"Thanks, boy, I love you, too," she said.

And thank you, Mom.

Spring on Maui brought rain and sun in equal measure. The *kōlea* were all suited up—their black neck feathers having come in—and ready to fly to Alaska, whales breached in the waters all around Maui, and baby birds proliferated. Even with the waterfall win, she felt off-kilter. Banging into things, misplacing her phone, mind jetting off to California. Santa Cruz. Dane's house.

Before meeting her father for dinner, she took Koa to the beach, where the salty smell of the ocean and the crashing of waves brought her back to earth. She sat down in the powdery sand and watched Koa dig hole after hole down by the water. Winston's words from the other night kept replaying. Maybe Winston was right. Was it fair to let Dane go simply because she was afraid to lose him? She had never thought of herself as a coward, but lately she wondered.

"Loving is the easy part," her father had said. "And oftentimes it's not a choice. But love and loss are inseparable. You can't have one without the other."

Just then, Koa ran up dripping wet and sideswiped her, dropping a coconut on her big toe.

'Iwa winced. "Ouch!"

All riled up, he started barking at the coconut. 'Iwa grabbed it and walked toward the water, letting her feet sink into the deep sand as she threw the coconut a few times. Koa wasn't the best swimmer, but he was definitely the splashiest. Each time he came out of the water, he ran straight for her and she was half soaked. But this last time, he made a beeline off to her right.

"Hey, Koa, I'm right here, buddy," she called, reaching out to try and snag his collar.

'Iwa turned, ready to assure whoever was coming that he didn't bite, when her heart fell all the way to the center of the earth.

"'Iwa," he said, his voice a gust of wind.

"Dane? What are you doing here?"

Koa reached him and offered him the coconut. Dane threw it far into the water. Koa took off at a full gallop. For a moment, 'Iwa thought about doing the same, but no, not this time.

"Your dad said you were here," he said.

Those deep sea eyes held her in place.

"I mean on Maui. Are you here for another contest?" she asked, well aware there were no big swells on their way.

Dane moved closer, until he was a foot away. "No contest. I came to see you."

"You did?" 'Iwa could barely breathe.

"Yes."

"Why?"

He closed the gap, so he was only an inch or two away. "I think you know why," he said.

"I do?" Her voice cracked.

"I needed to come here one more time, where it was just the two of us, and look you in the eye."

He was definitely doing that, and 'Iwa felt his tug like a swiftly moving current. "Have we not been through this?" she asked, trying to buy some time and she knew it, as the familiar fear of loss scraped along her spine.

"I'm here because I couldn't stay away, to be honest. I will do anything you ask, 'Iwa. *Anything.* If you'll just give me another chance." His jaw was clenched and he was all stone-faced and serious. She realized this was just as scary for him.

The truth was: *she* needed to give him another chance. As much as she needed air and water and sunlight. The only way forward, she realized, was through forgiveness.

"What if I said yes?" she said, dipping her head. "Theoretically speaking."

The edges of his mouth flickered. "When I told you I love you, I've never meant anything more. There is nothing theoretical about it. Ever since that first night I saw you at Uncle's, you had me."

A warmth unfurled through her like a tender fern tip. They were now facing each other, and he reached up and touched her cheek. Her body moved from storm to sunshine, and that darkness that had been burrowing into her lately lightened. Dane slid his hand gently behind her neck and drew her in, burying his face in her hair. His familiar smell made her toes tingle.

He exhaled long and hard. "I blew it so badly the night I kissed Sunny, even before that. And I can't blame the alcohol or pain meds. It was me being pissed off and scared and jealous. Seeing you talking to Luke, dumb as it sounds, turned some screw in my head that said, *She's going to leave your sorry ass.* And—"

'Iwa held a finger to his lips. There would be time for understanding, but now was not that time. "I love you, too, Dane. Maybe not from that first night—you were kind of full of yourself," she had to add, "but by the time we made it to Waikula, I was swayed."

Dane pulled back, eyes searching hers. "That long, huh?"

"Better late than never."

A full-bore smile, and he swept her close again. She held on tight, cheek on his shoulder. Having his warm body next to her after all this time uncorked something inside, and tears dampened her face. Rainwater tears. Waterfall tears. Tears of the ocean and friendship and love.

"I'm so glad you came," she said.

"I should have come sooner."

Dane was a living prayer, and now that he was here, she knew that she would never, ever, let him go. The ocean might take him any day, so could a hundred other things, but that was the way of life, wasn't it?

Before the sun had even set, the steady trickle of people coming into Uncle's turned into a river. Eddie had called in backup when she told him the news. Winston must have taken 'Iwa at her word and called in the troops. From Keala, Parker and Laurent—who worked the other side of the mountain—to Kawika, to aunties and uncles who had helped get her petition signed. Kalo farmers. Department of Forestry guys. Paniolos.

Surfers. Cashiers at Mana Foods. Anyone who believed that enough was enough.

Her father came out, banging a skillet with a big ladle, and announced, "Open tab, thanks to Dane Parsons for his generosity."

'Iwa turned to Dane, eyes wide. "You don't have to do this."

"Stop. This is your night. You have so much to celebrate," he said.

He was right. Today was likely to go down in the record books as one of the best days of her life.

The only time she had ever seen so many people crammed into Uncle's was last winter, the night of the Pe'ahi Challenge. Heat from all the bodies caused her to feel lightheaded. Or maybe it was from having Dane there, on the same island, under the same roof, standing by her side.

Out back, Uncle Tutu was softly strumming slack key guitar so that everyone could talk story. Soon after, newspeople showed up, asking for interviews. 'Iwa not prepared for this, was wearing torn jeans and a tank top, and still had damp, salty hair from a quick dip with Dane before leaving the beach.

"Miss Young, this feels like a big win for Maui. How does it feel to have played such a hand in it?"

She did her best to sound intelligent. "It feels right. What I mainly think about are all those birds and trees and the land itself that now has a chance. We are on a small island—if we keep destroying our watersheds and filling them with hotels and condos, we will lose what sustains us. So tonight, I am happy for our win, but also worried for our future battles. Because there will be more, you can count on that."

And so it went.

Then 'Iwa saw a familiar face in the crowd. "Kama, you're here! Dane told me about your eardrum," she said.

He came over and she hugged him tight. "News travels fast."

"The coconut wireless, alive and well."

'Iwa wished she could sit him and Dane down in the far corner of the *lānai* and catch up on life away from all the noise, but
behind them, the microphone crackled to life.

Winston now stood next to Tutu. "Everyone keeps asking
when we're going to sing the Waikula song. How about it, 'Iwa,
you ready to give the people what they want?"

Voices rose around them, hands clapped.

"I have to do this, but let's talk later?" she said to Kama.

She sat next to Winston. Her father had pushed his way to
them with her guitar, and she happily took it. "Here's to chasing waterfalls," she said into the mic, then began to strum.

The words came easily, and for the first time since writing
the song, she felt like light on the water. It was no longer an
urgent call for help, but a song of celebration. Winston accompanied her on vocals and she could tell by the quiet in the air
when they finished that the song had worked its magic. After
the final strum, she looked over at Winston, then to Dane,
who was sitting an arm's length away, looking very touchable.
If only she could bottle this moment.

The Beauty Wave
Dane & ʻIwa

March 2013

Under brooding skies, Dane, Kama, Yeti, Hope and ʻIwa stood outside the door of a small white house in the town of Nazaré. Like every other house in town, it had a red roof, but Dane knew he was in the right place when he saw a gate fashioned out of surfboards.

"I had a feeling some of you might be back," Leandro said when he opened the door.

This was a stealth mission. A giant swell was also battering California, and the whole big wave surfing community would be descending on Mavericks. Not this crew.

Dane cut to the chase. "My board bag was lost on the way over. I need to find the biggest board around, at least ten feet, bigger if possible. Preferably a quad fin. Can you help me?"

Leandro opened the door wide. "Come in, my friends."

The house was sparsely furnished, neat and tidy with a few oversized black-and-white wave photographs on the walls. Leandro led him through a door and into the garage. Boards of all shapes and sizes lined the walls. Longboards, shortboards, guns, squashtails, pintails, swallowtails, twin fins, thrusters, quads. Tow boards and stand-up boards. Even a foil board.

"Tell me what this is for," Leandro said.

"I'm sure you know about the storm tracking this way. We're going to paddle in at Praia do Norte."

Leandro raised his eyebrows and waved a finger. "Not a good idea, man. The weather, it could be ugly, and the direction will make it for closeout. You will need the ski for this one."

Yeti was standing next to him, arms crossed. "No ski."

"You must go with ski."

"Not this time," Kama said.

Dane walked over to the boards, eyeing the guns on a rack in the far corner. He zeroed in on a yellow board, second from the top. A single fin. "How long is this one?"

Leandro sighed. "Eleven."

Dane ran his hand along the rails, liking what he felt. "Mind if I have a look?"

Leandro came and took the board down, laying it gingerly on a strip of old carpet on the floor.

Dane recognized the flower lei logo immediately and his heart kicked up a notch. "How on earth did you end up with a Dick Brewer all the way over here?"

"Garrett, he leave behind boards. This one he say too old-school. Me, I like it."

Dane would take a single fin Brewer over any new quad, and this one looked barely ridden. A collector's item. "I need to borrow it. Please, I'll pay you whatever you ask."

Leandro looked at him with dark, stormy eyes. "You do this for the love, no?"

They all glanced around at each other, nodding in agreement. "We do."

"Then you no pay me."

"You sure?"

"I give you the board to ride on one, how do you say…condition."

"Name it."

"I go with you."

"No ski," Dane said.

"No ski."

"You're on."

The forecast for tomorrow was heavy rain, light wind and a big swell that they were praying swung around so it would hit at just the right angle. No one outside the room, besides Leandro, had any idea what was going down at Nazaré—no sponsors, photographers or friends on the other side of the pond. Dane hardly knew, himself. All he knew was he had to do this. No apologies, no second-guessing.

Having 'Iwa here gave him an extra measure of confidence, and they snuggled in bed as the rain pattered down on the tile roof.

"Thank you for coming with me, I know it was a lot to ask," he said.

She wrapped a finger around a lock of his hair and tugged. "You've already thanked me. Twelve times."

He laughed. "Can you tell it means a lot to me?"

"If it means a lot to you, it means a lot to me."

"What if I chicken out?" he whispered. The thought had begun to haunt him.

"Then you chicken out. You have a long life ahead of you, Dane, and this isn't the kind of thing you rush. If you don't go out, we'll drink coffee and watch the waves. Come back next year."

He kissed her on the temple. "How did you get to be so wise at such a fresh, young age?"

"I'm an old soul."

A beautiful soul.

"I love your soul," he told her.

Soon, they began to drift off, twisted together like marine debris and tangled ropes washed in after years at sea. 'Iwa had a cute little snore, and he felt the rise and fall of her chest as she sank into the mattress. How he could feel so much love for one person confounded him.

In the morning, Dane woke long before the dawn, if he even slept at all. Hope, Kama and Yeti were already up, sitting on the porch. Since their last visit to Nazaré, his little crew had made a pact that they would only go out if all of them felt good about it. No whispering voices in the back of the head, bad tides or shifty conditions. If just one of them said *no*, they would all sit out. "Collective intuition will elevate your game," Belinda had told them when they'd all stayed at her place one weekend for a yoga retreat.

"How's it looking?" he asked.

Yeti shut his computer. "Let's go see for ourselves."

The five of them walked to the cafe, grabbed to-go cups and headed to the beach. Leandro was already there, wearing jeans and a heavy jacket. The Brewer was zipped tight in the board bag next to him, and he stood on a high point, staring out to sea.

"*Bom dia*," Dane said.

Leandro jumped. "Oi, you scare me."

"Sorry, man."

He gave them a once-over. "She looks like she will eat you alive. But I also see many beauty waves, something you may ride."

Dane couldn't help but smile at the phrase, *beauty waves*, and he saw Kama was smiling, too.

"What about you?"

"I talk it over with Maria last night, and we decide I am not going. I never tell you, but we are expecting a child, and I cannot do it. I am sorry, my friends."

Dane burrowed his feet in the sand to keep them warm. "Leandro, it's okay. This is our deal, anyway."

They stood for a while and watched. To the north, thick curtains rained down over the water, and to the south, the skies were a dappled gray. The waves were not as big as last time, but glassy and peeling. From the looks on his friend's faces, Dane already knew they would be going out.

Leandro seemed to sense it, too. "I tell you this—a set will swing wide sometimes, closing out the whole ocean. You watch for that, you paddle out, fast as you can go." He pointed out. "I send a boat if it happens."

"Thank you."

Leandro patted him and Kama on the back, then Yeti and Hope. "*Boa soarte*. I will be up at the fort, keeping an eye. You join me?" he said to 'Iwa.

"Yes, please," 'Iwa said.

Dane had a stomach full of forest birds, but he was ready.

'Iwa hugged him, and whispered into his ear. "You got this, babe."

A bang of thunder caused 'Iwa to jump two feet in the air. Standing at the fort overlooking Praia do Norte, she and Leandro watched as Dane and the rest of the crew entered the water, colorful specks in the vast Atlantic. The weather was dreary and miserably cold, and she pulled the beanie down lower, just above her eyes. For now, thankfully, the rain remained offshore.

The fort and its lighthouse were forged out of the cliffs themselves. Ancient and rugged limestone, they had no doubt seen their fair share of disaster below. Such was the irony of point breaks. In exchange for those perfect, peeling waves, a person faced the real risk of shattering their bones on cold, hard rock.

Leandro leaned up against the wall, peering through his binoculars. Every so often he lowered them, mumbled a few words to himself, then lifted them up again. He also had a telephoto lens draped over his shoulder. From where they were standing, it felt as though they were in an eagle aerie, looking down into the rapacious jaws of the sea. A vertigo-inducing lookout even for someone used to heights.

"It looks like it's getting bigger?" 'Iwa said, half hoping he would say *no, it doesn't*.

"It does."

More and more people began to show up, see what the fuss was about. Other surfers that Leandro knew, a few old women in knitted capes, a fisherman and a dog who seemed to belong to no one. A big set came through, enormous lines of ocean that rolled beneath the surfers as they scratched over the waves, then reared up and hurled toward the shore in nuclear explosions. The people watching began speaking animatedly, all in Portuguese.

"What are they saying?" 'Iwa asked Leandro.

"The woman, she say she would chain her husband to the lighthouse if he mention to go out there."

'Iwa grinned, despite the knot in her stomach. "She might be onto something."

Leandro's eyes lit up, and he let loose a full-throated laugh. "You women are all the same, no?"

"I think you have it backward, you men are."

He thought on that, then said, "Not so much. Some are made from different cloth. No one else is brave enough, or *luoco* enough, to be out there on a day like today."

Dane was passionate and idealistic and threw his whole heart into things, but he was far from crazy. None of them were.

Leandro handed 'Iwa the binoculars. "You take these. When they ride, I capture it on film."

'Iwa had her own camera, but her lens was much smaller, so she gladly took the binocs. None of them stayed in place out there, continuously repositioning. Set after set passed. These waves were nothing like she had ever seen, and over the past year and a half, she had seen a lot. They were hefty and shifty and darkly ominous. The lightning only intensified the feel.

Getting through the shore break had been his first hurdle. On the last trip, Dane had observed the currents and thought he knew where the best entry point would be. But today there had been no gaps, no channels between the sandbars. Even the spot Leandro mentioned looked impassable. He'd touched the water and asked for a blessing. This was the threshold he needed to cross, he knew that.

They'd waited for a lull that never came, finally charging into the water, putting their heads down and paddling. Duck diving an eleven foot, voluminous board in overhead shore break was no joke. Add to that the thick wetsuit and cold water and Dane felt his energy sapping quickly. The other three somehow had made it through, but he noticed himself getting swept toward the rocks with each wall of whitewater he crashed through.

At a point where his arms had been ready to quit and his lungs heaving, he noticed a calm spot ahead. He paddled toward it with a last sweep of energy. Once there, the ocean began sucking him out, fast. This was the conveyor belt Leandro had spoken of. Paddling became easier and he caught his breath again as he moved into deeper water. His three friends were positioned in a big triangle, with Yeti farthest out, all eyes on the horizon. Dane checked his position against the fort, and saw he was right where he wanted to be.

Every place you surfed, the water had its own smell, and this morning at Nazaré, it smelled fishy and briny and electric. Lightning still hovered off in the distance, but if there was thunder, he couldn't hear it above the pounding of the surf.

Now the hard part. Waiting for a wave without losing his nerve. Though there was really no other way in. In surf like this, catching a wave or paddling out to sea were often the options. Sometimes you might have to paddle miles down the coast to an open harbor or bay to wash in, or if you were lucky, get picked up by a boat. Leandro knew this.

Out here, Dane felt almost invisible, and insignificant in the most potent sense of the word. Four surfers alone with the elements. Human, board, ocean, storm. Energy pulsed all around them—in the waves that had traveled thousands of miles to get here, in the charge in the air, and the Coke bottle–green water where their legs dangled. Fear mixed with awe mixed with a singular mindset.

Now and then, sun breached the cloud layer, forming circles of light on the water. Not enough to offer warmth, but enough to remind Dane what was up there. Blue sky behind the clouds.

Eerily, the surf had picked up, surface slick as polished stone. No one had caught anything yet, and they all remained quiet, saving their energy. The waves were violent and spitting and dark. Some were massive closeouts, others not quite big enough. This break owed them nothing. To keep himself calm Dane began talking to himself.

Breathe, motherfucker.

You got this.

You are not alone.

"Brah, you okay?" Kama asked, sitting about twenty feet away.

Dane exhaled. "Never better."

Now, hyperaware of his surroundings, he saw a wave bending his way. Just the right direction, just the right size. He looked toward the fort again to gain his bearings and saw a small crowd had gathered. The wave came in fast, a moving pyramid of water that lifted him up and initially threatened to drag him back out to sea. Dane put his head down and paddled just as a flash of lightning engulfed him. The hair on his arms stood on end. One last time, he turned to look back, then wished he hadn't.

The bathymetry of the abyss had worked its magic, and the wave had tripled in size. Too late for Dane, because he was already hanging at the top, poised to drop, miles to the bottom. When the force field pulled him onto the face, he had no choice but to go with it. The Brewer held tight to the water, slicing through bumps with alarming speed. Rather than riding the wave, it felt as though the wave were riding him, drawing him diagonally across its face in a perilous dance. And that's where he found the beauty and extraordinary bliss.

The *beauty wave*.

Leandro looked through his lens. "Oh *meu deus*."

'Iwa followed with the binocs. A slightly different direction, longer and taller lines. The kind of corduroy you saw in those old photos of the north shore. But this water was not tropical blue.

"*É esse*. This is the one," Leandro said.

When the wave was almost upon Dane, he swung around and paddled back toward shore, flying down the wave at warp speed. Click. Click. Click. Leandro was snapping away, then he stopped. Out of the blue, the wave morphed into a towering steel-colored mountain.

He groaned. 'Iwa covered her eyes. In the distance, a siren wailed. She tried not to think about the worst that could happen, and instead channeled light to Dane, sending him good *mana*.

As in an old film, their time together reeled through her mind. That first night at Uncle's and how he followed her into the kitchen thinking he was going to save her from her own father. Sitting on the beach eating tacos and wondering if he was going to kiss her. And how he'd shown up for an all-day hike wearing brand-new jeans. She thought of his particular brand of humor and the power of his touch. His dark five o'clock shadow, and how it felt rough against her cheek. And most of all, the explosion behind her rib cage when he had shown up on the beach that day, determined not to give up on her.

At the far edge, a ray of sun hit the surface, turning it a bright, shimmering green. Dane headed for the light, unsure he would make it. He was nearly at the bottom now, and could feel the weight of the water slowing him down, trying to lift him back up. He crouched lower, hands out.

"Cheehoo!" he cried, sea spray filling his mouth, clouding his vision.

And then a shadow came behind him. A wall of water thicker than a building, higher than the sky. His board wobbled. He recovered his balance. The lip was chasing him down and there was nothing he could do but surrender. *Hang on*, his mind screamed. But instead of annihilating him, the wave shot him out onto a rolling green shoulder. Shaking and humbled, he dropped to his stomach, his whole body tingling. He took a few long, deep breaths to slow his heart, put his head down, and paddled back out for more.

Yeti caught the next wave, slightly smaller but equally impressive. They all watched from behind as he disappeared over a sloping mountain of water. Kama followed on the third wave in the set.

"How you feeling?" Hope asked.

"Fired up," he said, then added, "Scared shitless. How about you?"

"Stoked." She held up her hand and he could see it trembling. "A little bit shaky."

They both laughed and Dane felt his whole body relax a few degrees.

"Attagirl."

He gave her massive credit for even paddling out. But Hope was tough as nails, and out-trained all of them.

"All I want is one," she said.

"One is all you need."

Wasn't that the truth. One wave. One woman. One life.

A little after noon, 'Iwa went to the cafe to grab sandwiches and sparkling water for Leandro and herself. He had taken it upon himself to be their personal watchman and said he would not leave until each and every one of them was in. When she returned, Leandro was waiting for her at the trailhead down to the beach, hands in pocket, looking anxious.

"What is it?" she asked, breathless.

"They come in. Let's go," he said, turning to follow the sandy path.

"All of them?" she asked.

"All of them."

When they reached the bottom, the four surfers were all lined up facing the water, boards lying in the sand behind them. 'Iwa picked up the pace, as did Leandro.

"A very good day for surfing. Very, very good day," he said.

As they neared the group, Dane must have sensed them, because he turned and smiled. Soaking wet, light socket hair, and now holding a yellow surfboard under his arm. He was sandy and salty with bloodshot eyes, but the electric smile on his face was one of a man who had stared down the unknowable and won. It was a memory she would carry all through her life.

A Hui Hou
'Iwa

Pe'ahi

Even when we know someone is going to die—say, a very old person, or someone long sick and suffering—when they actually do leave this world, we still don't feel ready. It creates indelible fractures in our being. And those who go on living question how life can be so ugly and so beautiful at the same time. There are places we go where we can almost feel their heartbeat, where the veil between here and there is thinner, and where memories live and breathe.

Just after sunrise, 'Iwa and Dane and Eddie hiked down the cliff at Pe'ahi carrying two longboards and a paddleboard. Isla and Koa led the way, running ahead and then circling back as if to say, *hurry up, you slowpokes!* Isla had been so excited to see them when they had returned from Portugal, she would have climbed inside of Dane if she could have, so they brought her to Hawai'i with them. Koa latched onto her like a baby brother, even though he was five times her size.

The ocean had lain down calm as a blue mirror for the occasion. The red dirt path was hard-packed and slick from recent rains, and more than once, 'Iwa almost slid out. But Dane was there to steady her. As she moved downslope, she thought of the passing of time, and how it doesn't erase the pain, but it patches and soothes and glues back what you thought may be broken forever.

She wore nothing but a yellow one-piece swimsuit and a lei around her neck. Made from *Kauna'oa*, a gold-orange thready vine that had once been a gift from the Hawaiian goddess of fire, the lei had been commonly worn by Hawaiians of old on the seashore. Eddie and Dane both wore *maile*. Mountains and ocean both represented.

Under a slack blue and cloudless sky, they reached the boulder-strewn beach at the bottom. Eddie set down the paddleboard carefully on the rocks, with that familiar clunk of fiberglass, and 'Iwa and Dane did the same. Her father took her hand and she took Dane's and together they let out a long, slow exhale. This was going to be hard but also beautiful, and made lighter by all of the blessings that had happened of late.

Not only had Dane survived the acid drop, acres of water and crushing lip at Nazaré, but the wave had allowed him to prove to himself that he still had it in him. That he was stronger than fear. And Leandro had performed some photographic magic, with Forte de São Miguel Arcanjo in the foreground and Dane looking so close, he could have stepped off the wave and onto the cobblestones. The rock walls and red lighthouse gave scale, and the pictures caused a sensation in the surfing world. Measuring from trough to crest, this wave was the largest wave on record anyone had paddled into.

Today, there were no waves, and after a short *oli*, they paddled out over coral heads and followed a sand channel to where the waves broke during a Code Red swell. Isla rode on the front of Dane's board barking whenever she got splashed. Koa hunkered down behind Eddie on the thick and wide stand-up paddleboard, the two of them so heavy it wobbled badly. No matter, they were in no hurry.

"Hard to believe there's ever a wave out here, let alone one of the biggest in the world," Dane said.

'Iwa glanced over at Eddie, who caught her look. "Mom used to say the same thing."

Until last week, 'Iwa had been carrying with her something she had never told Dane. The memory had felt too personal, something private between her and Eddie. But as the second anniversary of her mother's death drew near, and they were planning how to honor Lily, she thought it time.

"There's something I haven't told you," she'd said one night as they watched a burnt ochre sunset from the beach at Ho'okipa. "About my mom."

Dane squeezed her hand. "I don't expect to know everything about your life, 'Iwa, that will come in time. You know that."

"This is kind of important. And special."

He shifted his body so he was facing her. "Then I'm all ears."

"After Mom died, I scattered some of her ashes at Waikula. But we also scattered some at Pe'ahi—those were the two places, *mauka* and *makai*, she wanted us to remember her at," she said softly. "In the summertime, she loved to swim there. Not the easiest place to get to, and I used to whine to no end when I was younger and she would drag me down the hill, but it seems so worth it now. And it feels like this crazy intersection of endings and beginnings."

Dane nodded. "It does."

"I wish you two could have met," she said, wiping her eyes.

Dane put his arm around her and brought her in close. "She knows me, 'Iwa. And I know her. She lives and breathes in you, can you not see that?"

They watched the first star appear in the sky, a tiny pinprick of light, and then another, until the whole sky was a throw net of twinkling stars.

Now, as they paddled through the blue glass water, 'Iwa felt her mother's presence all around. When they neared the break, Eddie triangulated so they knew exactly where to be, where they had released the ashes that stormy morning two years ago.

All 'Iwa could hear was surfboard lapping on water. Dane lay next to her, glowing in the morning sun.

Eddie looked toward shore. "It feels like she just went off after a turtle or something, and should be joining us any minute now."

"It does," 'Iwa said.

His lip quivered. "I miss her."

"Me too."

He took off his lei and held it skyward. "You hear that, Lily? It's not the same without you here. Never will be."

Eddie then threw the lei into the water, at the same time Koa fell off and started dog paddling around. 'Iwa slid hers off and tossed it. Dane flung his, too, then stood up and did a back flip off his board. He swam down to the bottom and came up with a handful of sand. 'Iwa was in the water now, floating with her arms draped over the board. He set some of the sand in front of her on the board.

'Iwa smiled.

"I've seen that same smile in all the photos of your mom. It lights up the world," he said.

'Iwa nodded, unable to answer.

Eddie moved closer. "You have her spirit, too. Her voice, her love of this island. And you've always been a little bit *kolohe*. You got that from her not me," he said with a laugh.

"Yeah right, Dad, that's all you. And don't forget her bony knees and freckles. And need for alone time. How she'd always disappear into the woods on her own."

He sighed. "I could spend all day listing the ways."

Koa circled around him splashing with his giant paws, now joined by Isla. Eddie helped both dogs onto his board then came over and handed off Isla to Dane. 'Iwa dove down and grabbed some sand, brought it up and opened her hand, watching it sink to the bottom. Bones of coral and fish and all manner of creatures—ashes of the ocean.

A lazy current pulled them farther out, to a ledge where

the bottom dropped off. They were sitting on their boards, soaking up the sun in silence, when Dane went stiff and said, "What was that?"

'Iwa looked down in time to see a dark shape far beneath them, moving toward the inky depths. He paddled over, grabbed onto her hand and pulled their boards together. Whatever it was, it had been big.

"Dad, hold on to Koa," 'Iwa said, tucking both her feet under her on the board.

They scanned the water around them. There was no sign of movement, no disturbed surface to show a school of dolphins anywhere nearby. Tiger sharks frequented these waters, so it wouldn't be unusual. Then, just beyond, where the lei still floated, an enormous charcoal-colored dolphin came up for a breath.

"Dolphin!" they all cried in unison.

The dolphin made a few more passes, swimming below them and around them, almost as though circling and rounding up fish.

"I wonder where its pod is?" 'Iwa said.

"Right here," Eddie said, holding his arms wide. "Her pod is right here."

Dane and 'Iwa dove in and swam around, watching as the dolphin darted this way and that, fast as a bullet. That was when she knew without a wave of doubt—there is a power in the universe greater than we are.

A hui hou.

Until we meet again.

★ ★ ★ ★ ★

AUTHOR'S NOTE

A book is like a written piece of memory, and even though this is fiction, it feels like it has come from some alternate corner of my mind.

When I was four years old, my father pushed me into my first wave at Papaʻiloa on Oʻahu's north shore, and that was the beginning of my love affair with the ocean. A few years later, he would take us surfing at Ala Moana "Courts" after school, and on weekends we'd head out to my grandparents' house on the north shore (aka country) or go to Makapuʻu to body surf. Many of his friends were big wave surfing legends like Peter Cole, Fred Van Dyke, Ricky Grigg and a whole host of other wave riding characters. My father arranged his life so he could surf, and lived at Pipeline for a while before building his home at Rocky Point. I moved out to the country from Honolulu in 1999 when I started working as a school counselor at Kahuku High and Intermediate School, partly to be closer to my father and partly because I too wanted that salty air lifestyle full of beach walks and shells and broken boards.

Though I only longboard and ride smaller waves, big surf has always fascinated me. The power and beauty and thunder of giant waves is something one must experience to understand. It's a visceral thing. I've sat on the beach countless hours, watching feathering waves all the way to the horizon, or I've ridden my bike to Waimea and seen the whole bay closing out, surfers all bobbing in a cauldron of white foam. I've sat on the beach at Kammies with my dad watching massive sets march in at Sunset, with Peter Cole in his red shorts and white T-shirt sitting way outside, waiting for a west peak bomb to roll in. This book was born from these memories, and living in a community built around surfing.

I finished writing this novel a few months before the devastating fires on Maui, and my heart goes out to all the people, the culture & history, the animals, and the land itself. Though so much is lost, the memories remain. Maui is such a special island. I have fond recollections of hiking into Haleakalā, paddling in canoe races at Kaʻanapali, camping at Waiʻānapanapa, tromping through the pastures of Kula with my cousins and visiting beautiful Lahaina, among other places. It means a lot to me that I was finally able to set one of my novels on this beautiful island.

As for the mountain and forest parts of the book, they are inspired by my parents, who dragged my sister, my three cousins (Anna, Pam and Denny Cleghorn) and me to the far reaches of Hawaiʻi's valleys, ridgetops and volcano peaks. Later, I used to volunteer at Waimea Valley helping plant native plants up on the ridges overlooking Waimea Bay. This is where I first learned the *oli* in my book, asking for permission to enter the forest, from a dedicated steward of the land named Laurent Pool. We also took students up there, and I remember planting tiny koa saplings and then seeing them two years later, taller than we were. It was hugely inspiring. So, this is my love story to the ocean and to surfing, but also to the native Hawaiian forest. Because as Robin Wall Kimmerer once said, "In some Native languages, the term for plant translates to 'those who take care of us.'"

Also, the poem *Last Gods* by Galway Kinnell inspired the scene at the waterfall (yes, that scene). I picked up the book *Ten Poems to Change Your Life* years ago and it really stuck with me.

To prep for writing this book, I watched countless big wave

surfing videos, spoke to big wave surfers, watched interviews and re-read *Barbarian Days: A Surfing Life* by William Finnegan. It's been the most fun book to research yet! I purposefully set the novel before Nazaré became popular. Also, towing in with jet skis has become less of a thing in many circles, and now most big wave surfers wear inflation vests for safety. Given that the book is set amid these changes in the big wave surfing world, I've taken some creative liberty with the timeline for the sake of story. Also, Waikula and Hanaʻiwaʻiwa are not real places; they are figments of my imagination, based on places I've been. Same goes for the characters, all conjured up by me, but of course inspired by people I know.

I hope you enjoyed the ride!

ACKNOWLEDGMENTS

I am so thankful for the opportunity to grow up in a place like Hawai'i! I'm also ever thankful to my wonderful agent Elaine Spencer, who has been with me every step of the way, supporting, editing, cheerleading, answering copious questions and having my back. And to April Osborn and the team at MIRA, who take what I give them and turn it into magic. It really does take a village to put out a book, and I love my village.

Also, I am thankful for the love and support of Steffany and Tucker Hall, who were there on day one, when the idea for this book came to life. They were all for it, and that gave me the confidence to take the plunge. This book is so different from my others, but I feel like it still retains a certain feel good vibe that I try to maintain in all my novels. And a huge shout out to my early readers—Reeny Seavey, one of my best friends from high school who lives on Maui and helped make sure I had my Maui facts correct, and Maya LeGrande, botanist extraordinaire, for reading and offering insight on the flora and fauna, and Hawaiian language parts of the book. She reminds me of a real live 'Iwa, only cooler. And of course, I would not have been able to do any of it without my love Todd Clark and my family and *hui* of friends who may as well be family. Lucy and Kitty, too, who are usually lying on me or near me as I work. And always, thankful for my parents, my biggest fans. I know they are smiling down on me.

A big warm mahalo!